Judy Nunn's career has been lon[g and multi-] faceted. After combining her in[itial] acting career with scriptwriting f[or ....], Judy decided in the '90s to turn her hand to prose.

Her first three novels, *The Glitter Game*, *Centre Stage* and *Araluen*, set respectively in the worlds of television, theatre and film, became instant bestsellers, and the rest is history, quite literally in fact. She has since developed a love of writing Australian historically based fiction and her fame as a novelist has spread rapidly throughout Europe, where she is published in English, German, French, Dutch, Czech and Spanish.

Her subsequent bestsellers, *Kal*, *Beneath the Southern Cross*, *Territory*, *Pacific*, *Heritage*, *Floodtide*, *Maralinga*, *Tiger Men*, *Elianne* and *Spirits of the Ghan* confirmed Judy's position as one of Australia's leading fiction writers.

In 2015 Judy was made a Member of the Order of Australia for her 'significant service to the performing arts as a scriptwriter and actor of stage and screen, and to literature as an author'.

JUDY NUNN

Sanctuary

WILLIAM HEINEMANN: AUSTRALIA

A William Heinemann book
Published by Penguin Random House Australia Pty Ltd
Level 3, 100 Pacific Highway, North Sydney NSW 2060
www.penguin.com.au

 Penguin
Random House
Australia

First published by William Heinemann in 2017

Addresses for the Penguin Random House group of companies can be found at
global.penguinrandomhouse.com/offices

Cataloguing-in-Publication Entry available from the National Library
of Australia

ISBN 978 0 14378 385 5

Cover photos: island © Karl Monaghan Photography;
birds and jetty © Depositphotos
Cover design: Lisa Brewster/Blacksheep Design
Map: Ice Cold Publishing
Internal design and typesetting by Midland Typesetters, Australia
Printed in Australia by Griffin Press, an accredited ISO AS/NZS 14001:2004
Environmental Management System printer

Penguin Random House Australia uses papers that are natural, renewable
and recyclable products and made from wood grown in sustainable forests.
The logging and manufacturing processes are expected to conform to the
environmental regulations of the country of origin.

To the memory of Niall Lucy

AUTHOR'S NOTE

All the characters in *Sanctuary* are fictional, as is the small fishing port and township of Shoalhaven on the coast of Western Australia. The name is not to be confused with the City of Shoalhaven in New South Wales.

Gevaar Island is also fictional, although loosely based upon one of the many islands that make up the Houtman Abrolhos archipelago.

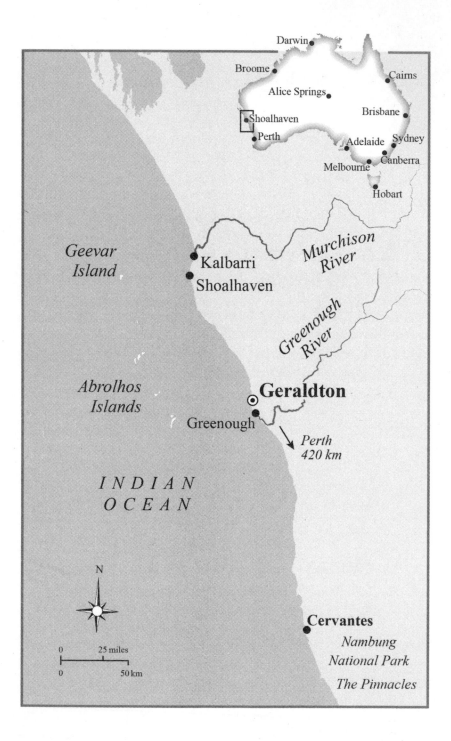

Darwin

Broome

Cairns

Alice Springs

Brisbane

Shoalhaven

Perth

Adelaide

Sydney

Melbourne

Canberra

Hobart

Geevar Island

Kalbarri

Shoalhaven

Murchison River

Greenough River

Geraldton

Greenough

Perth 420 km

Abrolhos Islands

INDIAN OCEAN

N

0   25 miles

0   50 km

Cervantes

Nambung National Park

The Pinnacles

PART ONE
THE ISLAND

CHAPTER ONE

The island appeared out of nowhere. One minute they were relentlessly adrift in a rickety wooden dinghy with nothing in sight but the horrifying blue of the Indian Ocean, then the next they had run aground. On what? Land? A submerged reef? Both it seemed. A rocky barren island with low-lying shrubs, little more than a scrub-covered reef. Why hadn't they seen it earlier? But then they'd seen virtually nothing for days as sky and sea had merged into one all-consuming blur. Even before the storm, which had wrecked their vessel and taken the lives of so many, they'd stopped looking for land. Their minds had been wandering in and out of consciousness for some time now, all nine of them, including the child, who was somehow still miraculously alive.

They couldn't tell how long they'd been adrift in the dinghy. Was it a day? A day and a night? Yes, there'd definitely been a night, a night of unbearable cold that had cut through their drenched clothes and their bones to the very marrow of their being. Was it two days? Perhaps three? They didn't know, and in their state of exhaustion were beyond caring. Even Rassen, the doctor who had taken on the role of leader and in whom the survivors had placed their trust, even Rassen had resigned himself to the inevitability of his death. He, too, had stopped looking out for land. Like the others, he'd stopped trying to even guess in which direction it might lie. And now there it was right before his very eyes.

The dinghy lurched drunkenly to one side and settled itself in the rocky shallows, as if like its occupants in a state of exhaustion and nearing the end of its life, which indeed it was.

No one made a move. Several of the survivors remained in a semi-conscious condition and were unaware of the extraordinary event that had taken place, while others stared dumbly, uncomprehendingly, their minds unable to absorb what they saw.

Rassen squinted through the morning's wintry glare, hardly daring to believe he could be right, for the light of the sun reflecting off the water's surface played tricks with a person's mind. Is this a mirage? he wondered. Surely my eyes deceive me. There are huts on this island. There are huts and there are jetties projecting into the sea. Where there are huts and jetties there are people. We are saved.

'We are saved,' he heard himself croak in a voice that wasn't his, a voice parched and by now so unused as to seem quite foreign. He addressed the words to his wife, Hala, who sat beside him, also unable to believe the vision before her.

'We are saved,' he repeated, but this time to the survivors in general and this time in a voice that, although weakened, held an edge of authority. Someone must lead them. His tone proved effective, bringing the others to their senses, rousing them from the lethargy of their surrender. 'Massoud,' he said to the young Iranian who throughout the ordeal had become his second-in-command, 'help me get everyone ashore. We must find water.'

Both men struggled to their feet, unsteady on limbs unaccustomed to action.

In stepping out of the dinghy, Massoud misjudged the water's depth, which was well above knee-height, and fell clumsily face-first into the sea. His immersion had an instantaneous effect. Suddenly he was revitalised, alert with a giddy form of madness, although he had the distinct feeling his elation was due not so much to a dunking, but rather the knowledge he was not going to die after all. Not yet anyway. As he stood, he let out a strange bark, which in actual fact was a laugh.

'All ashore everyone,' he said, beckoning emphatically for the benefit of those amongst them who did not speak English. He didn't know why he chose to address them in English at all, perhaps simply because the doctor had.

Rassen lowered himself carefully into the water, then assisted Hala, taking her full weight as he lifted her over the side of the dinghy.

'I can manage,' she said firmly when she was standing beside him, although she felt she might fall at any moment. 'Help the others.'

'Give me the child,' Rassen said in Arabic, and held his arms out to the young father.

The father passed the unconscious infant to him before alighting from the dinghy himself and tending to his wife. She, too, was barely conscious and moaned as she was lifted by her husband and cradled in his arms.

The other couple, Egyptians, a man and woman in their early forties, managed to climb out unassisted, albeit shakily. Then the man turned back to offer his hand to the girl. But she appeared not to notice the gesture, making no acknowledgement as she wordlessly slid her body over the dinghy's side, an action that even in her weakened condition was graceful.

The girl, whom they presumed to be around nineteen years of age, was a mystery to them all. She never spoke, but they knew she was not a mute for they had witnessed the occasional whispered response to her companion in the early days of their journey, before the storm and the capsizing of the vessel, when hopes were still high. Perhaps it had been her companion's gruesome death that had rendered her ongoing silence. At least that's what Rassen had first thought, but he'd come to doubt it, recalling how, even as she'd watched the man's blood swirl in the water, even as she'd heard his screams and witnessed the ferocity of the shark's attack, her reaction had been minimal: little more than resignation. The girl remained the same mystery to them all that she had been from the very outset. Her innate grace matched a beauty that was flawless, even now, sun-damaged and exhausted as she was. Eyes constantly downcast, she seemed unaware not only of herself, but of everything around her, as if she had removed herself to another place altogether. The others, who had bonded in the interest of survival, did not even know her name.

When everyone had alighted, they made their way slowly and gingerly across the twenty or so metres of rocky shallows to the shore, the young father carrying his wife, Rassen the child, and Massoud pulling behind him the dinghy, which minus its human cargo was now afloat.

Beneath bare feet, the feel of rough coral sand brought overwhelming relief, and those with footwear pulled off their sandals and shoes, relishing the sensation. Some offered prayers in the form of wordless thoughts giving thanks to their God, while some muttered through parched lips.

Massoud secured the dinghy's anchor in the rocks of the shoreline while Rassen led the way to the nearest hut, which, like its neighbours, was crudely constructed of corrugated iron attached to a timber frame. The hut was incongruously painted bright yellow and its tin roof, supported by roughly hewn wooden pillars, extended over a verandah floored with paving stones, a timber bench beside the front door completing an effect that, although ramshackle, was homely.

The young father, whose name was Karim, settled his wife gently on the bench. She had fully regained consciousness, but once again moaned, putting a hand to her ribs, the movement obviously causing her pain.

'We are safe, Azra,' Karim whispered in Hazaragi, the Persian dialect of his people. He knelt beside her. 'We are safe,' he repeated. Karim did not know if they were safe at all, but for the moment they were free of the relentless ocean and of the sharks and of all the other terrors he knew beset her. Given her intense fear of the sea, Azra had been terrified from the moment they had stepped aboard the vessel. He had deeply admired the strength she had displayed in undertaking such a journey.

Rassen passed the infant to Hala.

'Tend to the child,' he said, although they both knew there was little to be done. The child, a boy of barely three, was now conscious, his eyelids flickering open, his small chest rising with each shallow hard-won breath, but he was close to death. It was really only a matter of time.

Rassen knocked on the front door of the hut. There was no answer. Another knock, with a little more force this time: still no answer. Then he tried the handle and the door swung open to reveal an empty room.

'Hello?' he called. He peered into a roughly furnished living room with shelves and pots and pans to one side, but, through another open door that led to the rear of the hut, he could make out no activity. The place was clearly deserted. He stepped back, closing the door behind him.

'Do what you can for the others,' he instructed Hala, aware that if anyone could help ease their fear and uncertainty it was his wife. Hala was an experienced and highly competent nurse and, like many of her kind, had a way of instilling confidence during times of crisis. 'Massoud and I will make ourselves known to the island's inhabitants,' he said, although gazing about Rassen had the strangest feeling that something was wrong. Where *were* the inhabitants? Why had they not shown themselves?

Surely our arrival cannot have gone unnoticed, he thought. It is mid-morning – surely someone must have seen us. Do they fear our presence? Will they prove friend or foe? Perhaps they are in hiding, or perhaps at this very moment they are preparing to attack.

Then, scanning the line of huts for any sign of life, his eyes hit upon the most welcome of sights. A water tank. In fact more than one water tank. At least they had to be water tanks, his confused and exhausted mind told him, they simply had to be.

Beside several of the huts stood large round tanks with a height at rooftop and guttering level, presumably for drainage. They could be nothing other than a water supply, Rassen thought. He could even make out a tap on the side of the nearest one.

Rassen was not alone in noticing the tanks. Massoud, too, had seen them. And so had Hany, the Egyptian. Glances were exchanged between the three men and they set off with purpose, the renewed will to survive having lent them fresh strength, each praying desperately the tanks were not dry.

Behind them, Hala, obeying her husband's instruction, did the best she could to comfort the others, although without Rassen's medical kit and supplies, which had been lost along with everything else during the storm, there was little practical assistance she could offer.

'Hold little Hamid for me, will you please?' She could have passed the infant to his father, or to Hany's wife, the Egyptian woman, Sanaa, who appeared to have strength enough left to assist, but she deliberately chose the girl. Time to break through the barriers, she thought. 'I need to examine Azra,' she said when the girl hesitated. 'Azra is in pain and needs attention. Please take the child.' Hala spoke Arabic, the language in which they could all communicate, albeit in varying dialects, and in the case of Azra and Karim only to a limited degree. Her general manner and her tone were pleasant enough, but her request was really more a command.

The girl obeyed, taking the little boy in her arms, and

Hala sat on the bench beside Azra. She opened the young woman's rough woollen coat and, pulling back her own shoulder-length hair, now stiff and matted with salt, leant down to press her ear against Azra's chest. Without a stethoscope her ear would have to do, although she was confident she knew what the problem was. Azra had suffered rib damage during the storm and ensuing capsize. To what extent Hala could not be certain, but she was quite sure a broken rib had not punctured the lungs. If it had, by now the woman would no doubt be dead.

'Breathe in,' she said, and Azra obeyed, wincing as she did. 'Yes, I know,' Hala said sympathetically, 'it is painful to breathe deeply, yes?'

Azra nodded.

'And painful to cough also, am I right?' she asked, raising her head. During the past days she'd noticed the young woman holding her ribs and stemming a desire to cough.

Again Azra nodded.

'But if you feel the need to cough, do not stop yourself,' Hala said firmly. 'If you were to do so, it might invite a chest infection. And we would not want that, would we?' She spoke slowly, aware Azra's knowledge of Arabic was limited, but she'd apparently made her meaning quite clear.

'No,' Azra shook her head obediently, 'no, we would not.'

Azra would do whatever was asked of her for Nurse Hala had been sent by the angels, the messengers of God. Before the terrible storm, when the sickness had spread about the boat, they had all benefitted from the ministrations of Nurse Hala. She had saved little Hamid's life. At that time Azra had even thought that perhaps Nurse Hala herself was an angel, sent by Allah to cure their illnesses, as angels were bounden to do. And Nurse Hala's appearance, so different from them all with her fair hair and fair skin and her motherly English-looking face, might well have been that of an angel. Everyone knew that angels came in many guises. Azra recognised now that Nurse Hala was merely a woman, but one of such strength and goodness that it was surely true she had been sent by the angels.

'Do not be alarmed now, Azra, I am going to examine you.'

Hala lifted the young woman's blouse, enough to expose the ribcage, but not the breasts, aware that modesty was of paramount importance to a woman of Azra's devout faith. She examined the midsection with care – some bruising, but all appeared to be in order – then cupping the lower ribs of each side in her hands she gave a slight squeeze.

Azra cried out involuntarily.

'I'm sorry,' Hala said, 'I know I hurt you, but it was necessary.' Good, she thought. Things were just as she'd expected – there was elasticity in the ribs and the damage was fractures only, which would heal in time. 'There is no need for concern, Karim,' she added, having noted the husband's consternation at his wife's cry of pain. 'Azra has a fractured rib, perhaps two, I can't be sure, and they are painful, certainly . . .' she looked back at Azra and smiled '. . . but they will mend. Azra may be small,' she added encouragingly, 'but she is strong.'

Hala spoke as a mother might to a child. The young woman, in her early twenties, petite, pretty, hijab framing a doll-like face, was so disarmingly ingenuous it was difficult not to view her as a child.

They were child-like the pair of them, she thought as she stood and gestured for the bearded young man with the earnest eyes to sit beside his wife. They were a devoutly religious and simple young peasant couple, obviously very much in love, and she wondered what had driven them to take the drastic course of action they had. She wondered also how they would react to the death of their infant son. It was evident they did not realise the seriousness of little Hamid's condition.

While Karim sat on the bench, his arm comfortingly around his wife, Hala turned her attention to the girl, so unfathomable to them all. The Egyptian woman, Sanaa, was seated on the paving stones leaning against one of the wooden pillars, eyes trained on the men in the distance, which gave Hala ample opportunity to study the girl unobserved.

It appeared, for the very first time, that she might be showing something approaching a glimmer of interest as she looked down at the child in her arms. She was displaying no emotion certainly, but Hala noted she had drawn the end of the light shawl, which was draped over her head as it always was, about the child. Such a gesture was surely evidence of compassion.

Hala indicated they should move away from the bench and the child's parents, and the girl allowed herself to be led from the verandah around to the shaded side of the hut, where they stood in silence for a moment or so, the girl's eyes still focused upon the child.

'He is suffering from malnutrition,' Hala said, 'and most importantly dehydration.' Well of course, we all are, she thought, feeling stupid for stating the obvious.

The girl gave the slightest of nods.

'The degree of deprivation we have suffered affects a child far more severely,' Hala explained. 'To be quite honest, I'm surprised he's still alive.' She wondered why she was being so brutally truthful, presumably to shock the girl into some form of reaction.

Once again, the girl gave a slight nod, but her eyes remained on the child.

Hala waited for a moment, then . . . 'What is your name?' she asked.

There was no reply, no reaction whatsoever.

'We must have a name,' Hala insisted. 'In order to survive we must form a bond and work together. This is where our strength lies. What is your name?'

Still no reply, and still the girl did not meet Hala's eyes.

'Give me the child,' Hala said. No point in pushing any further, she told herself, although she felt a flash of annoyance, which she knew was quite irrational. The girl's condition was obviously a result of some trauma that was no fault of her own. But we've all suffered trauma, haven't we? Hala thought. Why else are we here? She was suddenly so very, very weary that she felt she might collapse. But she didn't, straightening her back instead and holding her arms out for the child.

The girl, with her customary grace, drew the end of her shawl aside as if parting a curtain in order to reveal something precious, and in doing so she exposed the little face looking up and the eyes that had been fixed upon her all the while. Then without a word, and with no obvious show of reluctance, she transferred the child into Hala's waiting arms.

Hala steeled herself, determined to remain unmoved; the girl's problems were her own. She took the child and turned away, her intention being to return the boy to his parents – she did not relish their queries about his condition – but she was barely a pace from the girl when . . .

'Jalila.'

She turned back. Silence. Then . . .

'My name is Jalila.' Little more than a whisper.

Their eyes locked and Hala was so startled it was all she could do to suppress an involuntary gasp. The girl's eyes, not unsurprisingly, were beautiful, heavy-lashed, hazel-green and arresting in the olive-skinned perfection of her face. But it was not the beauty of the eyes that so startled Hala – it was the lack of life she saw there. The girl held her gaze unwaveringly, yet appeared to see nothing. The girl was staring through eyes that were dead. Or else she's looking into somewhere else, Hala thought, some other place, some other time, I doubt she's seeing me at all. Hala was mesmerised; the girl's eyes engulfed her.

But whether she sees me or not, the offer of her name means something, Hala told herself, contact has been made. I must engage her. I must further the connection.

'Jalila,' she said gently, to which the girl gave another barely perceptible nod. 'What a pretty name.'

Any hope of more conversation, however, was quickly dashed as the girl broke eye contact and again focused upon the child.

'He needs water,' Hala said, looking down at the infant, once more stating the obvious, but determined to maintain the girl's interest. If the child was the only way to do so, then she would talk about the child. 'He needs water above all else. It is dehydration that is killing little Hamid. If we can get water into him, Jalila, then there is just a chance . . .' She turned her gaze upon the girl and left the sentence hanging.

The girl's nod this time was more positive and, as she raised her eyes, Hala was sure she saw a flicker of something there. A flicker of what, she wondered. Hope?

Then as if on cue the men arrived, Massoud and Hany carrying a bucket of water each, Rassen with a miscellany of tin mugs and cups.

'The tanks are full,' Rassen announced triumphantly, 'and we took these from one of the houses – no one was there. Come, come,' he urged, 'we must drink together.'

As he led the way around to the front of the hut, the others following, Hala glanced at the girl, receiving no reaction, which did not surprise her. Eyes downcast, the girl had once more retreated into her other world. But the girl now had a name. Jalila. And that was a start.

Hala returned the boy to his father, and the group gathered in a circle on the paving stones of the verandah, the buckets in the centre, Rassen handing out the mugs and cups.

'We washed them in sea water, the buckets as well,' he said in an aside to Hala, 'it's the best we could do.'

Hala smiled at the irony of the comment. They had survived typhoid aboard the vessel before the storm broke, they had survived death by drowning following the capsizing of the vessel and they had just now come very close to dying of thirst, so the sanitary requirements of the medical profession seemed somewhat superfluous.

Rassen returned the smile, aware of her thoughts. 'Drink my dear, drink,' he urged, handing her a cup of water. He took the child from Karim. 'I'll look after the boy, Karim,' he said, 'you must drink.'

Rassen, Massoud and Hany had slaked their thirst at the water tank and already looked stronger. The others now followed suit, feeling the dizziness lift, feeling their bodies re-energise.

'Be careful,' Rassen warned, 'do not drink too quickly.'

Then he started, very, very slowly, to feed the child, cup to tiny lips, parched and cracked, pausing carefully between each sip. Aware the boy would likely be unable to swallow, Rassen expected any minute that the water would be coughed back up. But the boy did not cough back the water. The boy was able to swallow. And he did so slowly and steadily, matching Rassen's timing with every single sip. Little Hamid, it seemed, was as intent upon survival as the rest of them.

Rassen and Hala shared a look of understanding: this was a very good sign. Hala's eyes darted to Jalila, hoping to share a look with her also, but none was forthcoming. No matter, she thought, as she watched the girl watching the child. The child is a strong enough link for the moment – given time Jalila will bond with the rest of us. Hala certainly hoped so anyway.

A half an hour later, it was decided to explore the island, or at least the huts, in an effort to find the inhabitants and hopefully food.

Rassen said nothing of his earlier misgivings and, preparing to set off once again with Massoud and Hany, he suggested Karim stay in the shade of the verandah and look after Azra and little Hamid.

'The women too,' he added, 'look after the women for me, Karim.' He did not wish the young man to feel emasculated.

But Hala had something to say about that.

'The women may wish to accompany you, Rassen.' She looked to Sanaa, who returned a vigorous nod. 'And we will no doubt be of great value in negotiating with the locals. We are, as you well know, my dear, far more skilled than you men in matters of diplomacy.'

Rassen acquiesced with a wry smile, considering it an extremely healthy sign that even under their current circumstances his feisty wife, a social activist and confirmed feminist, should behave so true to form.

'Jalila may wish to stay, however,' Hala said, noting the girl's continued lack of interest in anything but the child.

'Ah. Yes, of course.'

Rassen was not the only one taken aback by the comment. So the girl finally has a name, they all thought. But Hala's blatantly casual manner in announcing the fact signalled no response should be forthcoming, so no one uttered a word.

'Well let's be off then, shall we?' Rassen said as heartily as possible, although he continued to have a strange sense of foreboding. 'All those who are coming, join me.'

The others followed as he led the way along the path, Hala by his side.

'I gather you've had a bit of a breakthrough,' he muttered in English.

'Just a bit,' Hala replied. 'Not much, but it's a start.'

There were eight huts in all, each crudely constructed of wood and corrugated iron, but in good condition, brightly painted, homely and each, it was discovered, with a water tank of its own, some at the back and some at the side, dependent on the shape of the hut's roof. The overall effect was that of an attractively colourful miniature village. Freestanding cottages, some with verandahs, some without, yellow and blue, green and red, one even a bizarre shade of magenta, all in a line facing out to sea, a well-worn path of crushed coral running along the front linking them in neighbourly fashion.

Four sturdy wooden jetties projected forty metres or so from the rocky shore, each in excellent condition, ready to receive the vessels they had been built for. But where were the vessels? Apart from the survivors' own shabby dinghy anchored in the shallows there was not a boat in sight.

Equally strange, several hundred metres from the huts were a number of roughly hewn benches; was this a popular gathering place for the inhabitants? Certainly at dawn or dusk there would be no impediment to the view of a fine sunrise or sunset across the ocean. But where were the people who enjoyed this spectacle? A door knock had revealed each hut unlocked, but not one occupant. Apart from themselves, it would appear there was not a soul on the island.

'Well we have water and shelter,' Massoud said optimistically, although like the others he was fully aware that, in this desolate place and without assistance, they now faced the threat of starvation.

'You are right, my friend, it is an excellent start.' Rassen was grateful for his young ally's assistance in buoying their spirits. They had survived so much together; they must not give way to despair. 'We will scour the huts for food and provisions, we're bound to find something.'

Once again they progressed methodically from hut to hut, this time exploring each one in detail and, as they did, marvelling at every new discovery.

Many of the unruly, overgrown gardens at the rear of the houses bore produce. A healthy potato patch here, runner beans gone wild there, carrots, turnips, herbs.

Inside the houses, each kitchen was provided with a basic supply of cooking utensils, crockery and cutlery; and the bedrooms, although devoid of linen, revealed comfortable bedsteads with mattresses and pillows, together with cupboards housing an ample supply of blankets. Each hut even had its own outhouse with septic tank. Here indeed was luxury.

Further exploration of storage sheds revealed tools also, and, most important of all, fishing tackle: rods, hand lines, casting nets, scoop nets, apparently home-made three-pronged spears with broom-like wooden handles . . . The list went on.

A self-sufficient village all of our own, Rassen thought, barely able to believe their good fortune. A tiny ghost town with everything set up for instant tenancy as if we are being invited to move in. He didn't even pause to wonder about who had lived here, or where they were now or why they had left. Here on this seemingly barren island was everything they could possibly need in order to survive.

The group returned to the others to impart their findings and share their elation.

'We are most certainly saved,' Rassen declared.

Some once again gave thanks to God, and in their own way, through unspoken prayer or muttered words, but as they looked at each other one common thought was mirrored in their eyes. We have cheated death.

It was only Jalila who appeared not to care.

CHAPTER TWO

'**D**o you fear what might happen if they return?' Massoud asked. 'Do you think they might try to kill us?'

He posed the questions casually as he studied Rassen, who was squinting into the cracked mirror that hung from a nail above the washbasin. The sound of the blunt razor scraping over the doctor's grey-stubbled chin appeared of far greater concern to Massoud than the possibility of being killed, and he winced as Rassen nicked himself for the third time.

'I have no idea,' Rassen replied, dabbing at the spot of blood with the wet rag that was draped over the basin's edge, then rinsing the razor and doggedly continuing. He'd tried to lather up with the dried remnant of soap they'd found, but it wasn't proving particularly successful. 'Without knowing who "they" are, it's impossible to tell, but I've no doubt "they" would be very angry to discover their homes had been invaded.' He raised a wry eyebrow. 'Wouldn't you?'

The two men spoke English, as they invariably did when conversing with each other, and also with Hala. This gave them the freedom to express opinions that might instil fear or apprehension in the others. Their intention was not to distance themselves in any way, but rather, as the group's natural leaders, to protect their fellow survivors, a fact that the others accepted gratefully and without question.

This was not the first time the identity of the mysterious island inhabitants had come up for discussion, however. The group as a whole had addressed the subject on the very second day, after they had settled themselves into the huts and had a good night's sleep with bellies full of the vegetable stew that Sanaa, a cook by trade, had made on one of the Primus stoves they'd discovered.

Upon Rassen's suggestion, they'd gathered at the benches erected several hundred metres from the huts, all except Azra, who had remained behind with little Hamid, and Jalila, who'd appeared uninterested in joining them, although Hala suspected she, too, wanted to be near the child.

It was mid-morning and the day was fine, but being late August, still winter in the southern hemisphere, there was a bite to the wind that whipped about them. They would discover the island was nearly always windy, but at that moment nobody minded. In fact they enjoyed the wind's vitality. Despite their still fragile states of health, their survival continued to induce in them a sense of euphoria, and the wind made them feel doubly alive.

Their discussion was robust. Who owned the huts, they asked, questions tumbling over one another, why had these people left their homes, what had caused them to flee? But the most important question, the one that had cut through them all, had been voiced by Hala.

'Where do you think we are, Rassen?'

'Impossible to say. Somewhere in the Indian Ocean. Who knows how far the storm blew us off course? We could be in Indonesian waters or Australian,' he said with a shrug that admitted defeat. 'I have no idea.'

'Australian.' Massoud sounded positive and they all looked a query. He pointed to the huts some distance away. 'Those are not the huts of Indonesians,' he said, 'nor are the supplies we found there.'

'Of course,' Rassen agreed, 'of course, good point. And I think given the jetties and the remote location – wherever it might be,' he added dryly, 'we can assume they are the huts of fishermen. But *Australian* fishermen? Why would *Australian* fishermen abandon their homes? Australia is a peaceful country – what threat could possibly have caused them to leave their homes and belongings?'

'Perhaps the island was settled illegally,' Hany suggested, 'perhaps by such as Sanaa and me. A minority people, fleeing from those who would kill them. This would be a very good place to hide out, do you not think?'

There was a pause. Such a theory coming from Hany was not altogether surprising, Rassen thought. Hany and Sanaa were Coptic Christians after all, and certainly fleeing persecution. He exchanged a look with Massoud: here was a theory that had occurred to neither of them, but it was a vague possibility.

Hany, noting the exchange, was proud that his idea had made an impression upon the doctor and the young man who was clearly well educated. 'And perhaps these illegal settlers were forced to leave in a hurry,' he continued eagerly, 'in order to escape the authorities who would arrest them.'

'Or perhaps they were neither fishermen *nor* those seeking sanctuary,' Massoud said, interjecting as a fresh scenario occurred. 'Perhaps this place was set up to house some activity that was more than *illegal*, something that was actually *criminal*.'

The others looked mystified.

'Piracy maybe.' Massoud gestured out to sea with a grand sweep of his arm. 'Just look at those reefs – a perfect spot for luring ships to their doom. Or smuggling?' This time his gesture embraced the island. 'Look at where we are, hidden away in the middle of the ocean, and who knows how far from anywhere. A perfect pick-up or drop-off spot for contraband.'

Things were becoming somewhat fanciful in Rassen's opinion and he wondered whether by any chance Massoud intended to be frivolous. It didn't appear so, but he'd garnered the instant attention of the others, even Karim, who with his limited knowledge of Arabic had not grasped every word. The mention of criminality had introduced in all of them a degree of uneasiness. And little wonder, Rassen thought – the last thing they needed was a link to any form of criminal activity. He decided to give Massoud the benefit of the doubt, as levity did not seem his intention, although it was sometimes hard to tell. Massoud was a highly intelligent and personable young man, but Rassen suspected at times a sense of the theatrical got the better of him.

'Well at this stage the owners of the huts must remain a mystery,' he said, calling a halt to the conversation, which was really going nowhere, 'but whoever they are, we will be eternally in their debt.'

It was a sentiment with which they were all in agreement.

That had been five days ago, Rassen thought, flinching as the blade dug another hole in his face, and this was the first time the likelihood of retaliatory action for their invasion had come up for discussion. But of course they'd been too busy structuring their days and getting their lives in order, hadn't they? Now, alone with Massoud, seemed as good a time as any to contemplate the possibility, which was certainly worthy of conversation.

The painful shaving exercise at an end, he rinsed his face in the bowl of water and inspected the damage in the mirror, dabbing at the spots. No matter, he thought, anything was better than the itchy stubble he'd been suffering. A fastidious man and one given to tidiness in all forms, Rassen was very fussy about remaining clean-shaven. He held out the razor to Massoud.

'Sure you don't want to?'

'No, no, no,' with a shake of his hand Massoud literally backed away, 'no thank you, no.' He was happy to stay with the light stubble he now sported and he was

quite sure Hany, too, would decline the offer despite being
darker and more hirsute than he. What man wants to rake
a blunt razor blade over his face? he thought, looking at
Rassen's bloody spots. The thought sent shivers down
Massoud's spine.

'Let's sit on the verandah,' Rassen suggested.

Massoud nodded and they adjourned outside.

The yellow hut, which had been allotted to Rassen
and Hala, was the group's unacknowledged headquar-
ters, as it was there they gathered on the front verandah
for meetings.

Each couple had been allocated a hut, which also served
a specific purpose according to the talents of its occupants.

Hany and Sanaa's was the kitchen and mess hut, Sanaa
having become the official cook. Their hut, which was
bright blue, boasted a barbecue and gas bottle on its back
porch and the group had set up two of the Primus stoves
inside. The main room of the hut, being larger than that of
its neighbours, could accommodate them all seated on the
various chairs and boxes and milk crates they'd assembled.

The green hut, home to Karim and Azra and little
Hamid, served as the workshop, for Karim, a strong young
man and a builder's labourer by trade, was invaluable in
all things practical. The hut had been specially chosen, its
previous occupant having erected a large workbench at
the rear complete with a vice and an old-fashioned pedal-
operated grinding wheel, which Karim found fascinating.

'Very old,' he said, 'from the fifties or sixties, maybe,
but very practical.' From the storage sheds of other huts
the group had collected all manner of tools that Karim
deemed useful for repairs and maintenance.

Massoud and Jalila each had their own huts, neither
serving any purpose other than accommodation.

'I have no particular talent, I'm afraid,' Massoud had
said when they were structuring their village and deciding
how best to serve the interests of the group as a whole.

'In fact I'm quite useless,' he admitted cheerily, 'but I shall do my best, I promise.'

Rassen knew that Massoud was anything but useless. The two had conversed during the early days aboard the vessel and he was aware of the young man's scholarly background. In Rassen's opinion, Massoud's fluency in Middle Eastern languages could prove invaluable. We are an eclectic group with eclectic beliefs, he thought, and although we can communicate adequately in basic Arabic, should disagreements arise, as they possibly might, Massoud can intervene and mediate in all languages.

Oh no, I beg to differ my friend, he thought, you are not useless at all, you may well serve a purpose. And perhaps also as our jester. Rassen smiled as the young Iranian, in typical fashion, continued to make fun of himself.

'And as I am the most useless among us,' Massoud concluded, 'I shall take the magenta hut, it being the smallest. Besides,' he added, 'I like the colour.'

Rassen and Hala had tried to insist Jalila move in with them for company, but she had declined with the merest shake of her head, making no choice but simply accepting the hut she was allotted.

'It is a good time for us to talk of matters that, if voiced amongst the others, might cause some concern,' Rassen now said as the two men settled themselves on the front verandah's bench. Rassen had discussed the situation in depth with Hala, but he looked forward to hearing Massoud's views. And now was indeed a good time, with Hany and Karim out fishing in the dinghy and the women cooking and tending the garden. 'Do *you* believe there will be retaliation?' he asked, a repetition of Massoud's own question. 'Do *you* believe if they return they might want to kill us?'

Massoud smiled, in turn repeating Rassen's response. 'Difficult to say without knowing who "they" are, isn't it?' His smile faded and he continued in all seriousness.

'If we could only find out what these people did and what purpose this settlement served,' he said, 'we'd be halfway to finding out where we are. Shame our phones didn't survive the storm,' then he added with an air of mock accusation, 'and a damn shame your fancy TAG Heuer doesn't do more than tell the time.' Rassen's watch was the only one of the group's that continued to function.

'I doubt cell phones would receive here anyway,' Rassen replied unperturbed – no point in discussing technology they simply didn't have. 'So what are your views, Massoud? Do you seriously believe in your "criminal activity" theory?'

'I think it's a definite possibility, yes. Like you, I don't see any reason why Australian fishermen would abandon their homes, and as we know this settlement is more sophisticated than it looks. That makes Hany's suggestion of illegal immigrants most unlikely.'

They had discovered that the huts were rigged for electricity; each had light fittings, some small electric stoves and refrigerators, some water pumps, all generator driven, although the generators themselves were gone. The kerosene lamps and torches, the gas bottle and barbecue and the number of Primus stoves appeared, for the most part anyway, to be backup should the generators fail, a provision for which the group was extremely thankful.

'So if our criminal friends have organised a settlement with everything they need in order to live in this wilderness and conduct whatever activity it is they're involved in,' Massoud continued, 'and if they've beaten a hasty retreat fearing discovery, then we have only one of two outcomes to expect.'

'And those outcomes are?'

'Either our criminals are right, the authorities are on to them, in which case we can expect the arrival of the police. Or if, given time, their concerns prove groundless and the police don't show up, they return to resume their activities.'

'We've been here six days so far,' Rassen said, 'and there's been no sign of the police.'

'Exactly, which means we must fear the latter. Perhaps we should prepare ourselves for some form of attack, Rassen. I'm quite sure, as you said yourself, our friends won't be happy to find us here.'

'If we are to follow through with your scenario, there is a third possibility, however,' Rassen suggested. 'Our criminals may have decided to cut all ties and run, never to return. Which could well leave us here, undiscovered, for who knows how long?'

A sobering silence ensued, both men staring out at the boundless ocean.

'The others are happy in the knowledge that they have survived,' Rassen continued after a minute or so, 'and they are embracing the safety of our village after escaping whatever horrors beset them. We are still physically weak and this is a good thing as we regain our strength, but surely we *do* want to be discovered, Massoud, even if it is by your dastardly criminals. Would you wish to spend the rest of your life here? Here in this time warp in the middle of the ocean?'

Massoud did not reply. There was no need anyway, as the question had been rhetorical.

'What I wouldn't give for a cup of truly good coffee,' Rassen said, the conversation over.

Hala, Jalila, Azra and little Hamid were in the backyard of the blue hut where, inside, Sanaa was preparing the fish stock for the evening meal, which would be a seafood soup made from the previous day's catch. The soups and stews Sanaa concocted from a variety of seafood had led to an interesting exchange several days previously.

'After I have cooked this, may I put the flesh in the stew?' Sanaa had asked when Hany had proudly presented to the group the sizeable mud crab he had caught amongst the small clump of mangroves that grew on the northeastern lee side of the island. Sanaa had directed her query to Karim and Azra, whom she knew to be devout Muslims. 'I believe you are not permitted some types of seafood. Perhaps you would rather I did not use this in the stew?'

Karim and Azra, both shy at the best of times, had been so taken aback by the respect afforded them that they'd been momentarily speechless, so Rassen had answered in their stead.

'If there is no halal food available, a Muslim may eat haram food in order to survive,' he said with authority. A liberal Sunni Muslim himself with decidedly secular views, Rassen wasn't even sure if crabs were on the forbidden list to Karim and Azra, who were Afghan Shia Twelvers, but the reply was the only sensible one. 'We thank you for your courtesy, Sanaa,' he added with an encouraging smile to the young couple.

'Yes,' Karim agreed, his wife nodding also, 'thank you, Sanaa. Your offer is most kind, but we shall eat the same meal as our friends.'

The exchange had greatly pleased Rassen. Perhaps there will be no need to call upon Massoud's linguistic skills after all, he thought. Perhaps there will be no disagreement among us. How very refreshing.

Sanaa flavoured the meals she cooked with the herbs that thrived under the island's harsh conditions, and the vegetables, which did not fare as well being near an end, the wild beans depleted and the tubers at a minimum. She had given strict instructions that several runner beans were to be kept to dry out so that the seeds could be sown when the fine weather came. Several potatoes also, she said, must be put aside to sprout in order to be replanted for a fresh crop. Her advice was heeded unquestioningly, although the reaction shared between Rassen, Hala and Massoud had been telling, each wondering how long their stay on this island would be. They had not voiced their misgivings to the group, however.

The others, in continuing to bless their good fortune, had been buoyed up with each new discovery over the passing days. Several pantries had revealed supplies of tinned and dried food, packets of pasta and rice, which could supplement their diet. A canister of tea was found, some powdered milk, even half a jar of instant coffee, although it was virtually dried out. And when these luxuries were gone no matter, they had nothing to fear, they would still be self-sufficient. The coral reefs surrounding the island abounded with marine life; fish of every variety, crustaceans, molluscs, shellfish, just there for the taking. All this was theirs, and with no threat looming, they had surely found paradise.

Hala and Jalila knelt in the dirt digging up the last of the potatoes, the blue hut's garden being the final one to be denuded of its crop. Azra, seated on an upturned milk crate, was watching her son as, several metres from the others, he dug away with a small trowel enjoying the appearance of being helpful while achieving nothing.

Hala was keeping her own watchful eye on Azra, checking that the young woman's breathing had returned to normal. Azra had been picking herbs when she'd been overtaken by a coughing fit that, while causing her much pain, had also exhausted her.

'You must return to your cottage and go to bed,' Hala had instructed, trying to take the herbs that Azra still clutched in her hand, but Azra had retained her grip and shaken her head vehemently.

'No, no I am all right, I promise,' she insisted. Being alone frightened Azra.

'Then you must go to bed here,' Hala insisted, 'Sanaa will not mind if you sleep in her bed until Karim returns.'

'No. Please, Nurse Hala,' Azra had said her voice husky as she fought back another bout of coughing, 'please let me stay with you.' The knowledge of others nearby was not enough for Azra; even being alone in a room frightened her.

Recognising the young woman's fear, Hala had relented and fetched a blanket, wrapping it around her shoulders and seating her out of the wind. She worried about Azra's bronchial condition, which could so easily become pneumonia.

Hala, in her capacity as mother figure to them all, continued to keep a close eye on every member of the group. They were growing stronger, it was true, but the hardship they had suffered had taken its toll. They still tired easily and their bodies were still susceptible, particularly Azra's, her fractured rib continuing to cause her a great deal of pain. And it will for some time to come yet, Hala thought, but the biggest worry now is the possibility of pneumonia.

Surprisingly enough, the one to have made the greatest progress of all was little Hamid. The boy's recovery rate had been remarkable. Since rescued from the brink of death, he had noticeably improved every day. Hamid's survival had brought joy to every single one of them. Perhaps even to Jalila, Hala thought, although it was difficult to tell, as the girl remained unreadable.

Hala's hope that Jalila would form a bond with the others was slow in coming to fruition. The girl helped with whatever menial tasks she was allotted, washing dishes, gardening, simply doing the chores that were asked of her, but the only true interest she displayed was in the child. This had, however, built an unspoken connection between her and the boy's mother. Hala had noticed how Azra and Jalila would occasionally share a glance when Hamid did something appealing, like trying to stalk a seagull, which was a preoccupation of his. Little Hamid was determined the time would come when he would catch one of these birds and he would totter around on his still wobbly legs, lacking the power of a normal three-year-old, it was true, but nonetheless resolute in his pursuit.

Hala considered the connection between the two young women, slight though it was, of immense value, not only for Jalila, but also for Azra, who was painfully insecure.

'Azra keeps her fears to herself, Nurse Hala,' Karim had said just the previous day when he'd sought her out. 'She does not wish to be the weak one among us.' The young couple treated Hala with the utmost reverence, she was Nurse Hala to them at all times, a fact that she found both touching and amusing. 'My Azra has terrible dreams,' Karim continued, 'she will toss and turn in her sleep and sometimes she will wake and cry out. But she does not wish me to tell others this,' he admitted. 'You will say nothing?'

As always, Hala could not help but respond to the child-like quality this strong young man exuded. Karim, bearded and sturdy of build, was without doubt the physically strongest of the men, yet she saw in him such vulnerability. And all for the love of his wife, Hala thought. He worries so for Azra.

'I will say nothing,' she promised.

'Azra feels guilty that she cannot work as hard as she would wish,' Karim went on. 'She wants to carry her share of the burden, but she is weak, she must take care.'

'You are right, Karim, she must take care. And I shall look after her during the times when you are gone. I promise I shall, you have my word upon that.'

'Thank you. Thank you, Nurse Hala.' It was all he'd wanted, Nurse Hala's personal assurance. Karim felt deeply relieved.

Now, keeping careful watch on Azra, Hala could see more than the young woman's weakened state, more than the shadows under the pretty eyes in the pretty hijab-framed face. She could see, in the eyes themselves, the fear of which Karim had spoken. She felt sorry for Azra, but there was little she could do about fears and nightmares. Her own husband suffered similarly. Rassen, for all the

strength of his leadership, also suffered nightmares. There
was little she could do for him too. They were all haunted
by images from the past.

Azra was indeed haunted by images, but her fears did
not lie only in the past. Her fears lay in the future.

Every morning, after she and Karim had completed the
first of the daily prayer rituals each observed, she would
accompany him to the shoreline. She would watch as he
set off with Hany, the two men taking an oar apiece, and
she would continue to watch as they rowed the dinghy
out to sea. Despite their lack of experience, the two had
become skilled fishermen, Hany generously giving most of
the credit to Karim.

'He has the true touch,' Hany had declared. 'Do not
ask me where this talent comes from, but he will catch
three fish for every one of mine. Our friend Karim has
discovered a natural skill,' he'd said, 'while sadly I remain
a humble plumber. These hands,' he'd added jokingly,
flexing his fingers, 'are made for solid piping, not the
elusive nylon of a fishing line.'

For all the shared good humour, Azra hated seeing
Karim row out to sea. The sight aroused such fear in her,
setting off the cycle of nightmares, and conjuring up images
that remained with her throughout the morning until his
return. The sea would devour Karim as it had devoured all
the others. In fearing for her husband's safety, Azra was
haunted by the memory of that hideous night. Of bodies
threshing about in the black, black water; deathly screams
that might have come from those taken by sharks, who
could tell; Karim hauling her onto some floating wreckage,
thrusting Hamid into her arms, keeping himself afloat
without a life jacket, remaining there a protective presence
by her side as all the while she waited for that awful
moment when he would fall prey to the sharks that must
surely be circling. Then the miracle of the morning when
he was still there; and the serenity of the ocean, the sight of

the dinghy broken free from its davits and the several survivors aboard rowing towards them, calling out for others
who may have survived. Then the combined puzzlement
at the sight that confronted them, the sight that remained
the most haunting image of all. They had expected to be
surrounded by carnage, but they were not. Instead, they
were bobbing about on the surface of an innocent sea.
Where had all the people gone? Despite the sickness that
had taken some during the journey, there must have been
close to forty remaining on the vessel before it foundered.
Where were they? The sharks could not have taken every
one of them. But there had been so few life jackets, and
so many unable to swim. It was the sea that had claimed
them. The awful sea.

Azra had offered thanks for the survival of her family.
She had praised Allah many times. But the sea would not
preserve her husband indefinitely. The sea was her enemy,
and every morning when Karim rowed out in the dinghy,
she feared it would be the last time she would see him.

Even now, sitting in the garden, her eyes upon her son,
the images had found their way into her mind and Azra
was not really seeing little Hamid at all.

Then she became aware that other eyes were upon her,
and she glanced over to Hala, whose expression was one
of deep concern.

Azra chastised herself. She was worrying Nurse Hala
and that was wrong of her. She did not want to be a
nuisance. She looked down at the herbs she still held in her
hand and stood. 'I will take these in to Sanaa.'

Hala, realising in turn that she had been caught out,
kept her reply casual. 'Of course, Azra, we will look after
Hamid,' she said, and was pleased to note that Jalila's nod
of agreement was directed to Azra rather than her.

They had dug up the last of the potatoes, a half-dozen or
so, and as Jalila started gathering them Hala rose, easing
the stiffness in her back.

'We must select some for Sanaa to put aside,' she said as she crossed to the bucket that sat in the corner, 'the smaller ones though. We'll save the big ones for eating.'

She expected no reply of course, but as she returned with the bucket she realised the girl had not even heard her. The girl was not gathering the potatoes; she was playing a game with the child.

Jalila had chosen a particularly round potato and had bowled it along the rough ground where it bounced its way to land beside Hamid.

Hala watched as the boy, delighted, picked it up and tried to repeat the action, which didn't work, the potato travelling barely a metre, trapped by a tuft of grass. He tried again with the same unsuccessful result.

Jalila, crawling forwards on hands and knees, picked up the potato, returned to her original position, and lobbed it to him, a gentle toss high in the air. Hamid tried to catch it and missed altogether, but no matter, this was a much better game. He scampered to pick it up where it had rolled a short distance away. It was his turn to throw now.

Hala continued watching as she collected the potatoes in the bucket, Jalila and the boy paying her no attention at all, concentrating instead on their game of catch. Azra should see this, she thought and quietly she left for the kitchen.

'Here are the potatoes,' she announced upon arrival.

Sanaa barely looked up from the bench where she was meticulously sifting through the fish stock, lifting out the backbones that would be discarded, setting aside the shreds of meat that would be added to the other seafood; nothing must be wasted. She was a tall woman, nearly as tall as her husband and equally fine-boned, with black hair pulled back in a bun at the nape of her neck. A capable woman too. Hard-working, never stopping to draw breath, it seemed at times that unlike the others Sanaa was indefatigable.

'Thank you, Hala,' she said. 'Would you mind peeling one of them for me?'

'I'll do that,' Azra offered, eager to help. She'd washed the herbs and placed them in a tumbler and had been standing by feeling useless.

'No, no,' Hala insisted, 'I'll help Sanaa now, you go outside.'

Azra hesitated, feeling more useless than ever.

Hala crossed to her where she stood at the kitchen sink. 'You will be of far more help outside,' she whispered meaningfully.

Azra's spirits lifted. Nurse Hala wanted her to serve some purpose. What it was she had no idea, but she would willingly do whatever Nurse Hala wished. She set off towards the garden.

'Stay out of the wind,' Hala called after her.

Azra stood at the door observing them, her son and the beautiful girl at play, and she knew instantly what it was Nurse Hala wanted of her. Nurse Hala wanted her to communicate with the mysterious Jalila, who never spoke and who was obviously damaged in some way.

She sat on the milk crate, out of the wind as instructed, and patiently waited.

'Mama,' little Hamid called eventually as the game started to pall and he noticed his mother there. He ran to her side.

'Why don't you go in and see Sanaa,' Azra said, ruffling his hair, 'it is time for your cup of milk.' They kept the powdered milk for the boy, rationing it out two cups a day.

As Hamid obediently ran off, Jalila rose to her feet, watching him go.

Azra rose also and crossed to her, both gazing after the child as he disappeared through the back door.

'He is very fond of you, Jalila,' Azra said quietly.

The girl turned and their eyes met, not for the first time it was true, but on this occasion they held the gaze, each recognising a need in the other.

'He is a good boy,' Jalila said quietly.

Azra beamed with pride, barely able to believe that of all the people in the group, it was she to whom Jalila had spoken.

'He is a handsome boy too,' Jalila said, 'so like his father.'

Azra made no reply, but stood motionless.

'Karim must be very proud,' Jalila said.

'He is.' The response was breathless, tears involuntarily welling. 'Oh yes he is,' Azra whispered. 'Thank you, Jalila.' She turned away in order to hide her emotion. The mysterious girl could have no idea how important her words were. No idea at all.

CHAPTER THREE

Azra Sarabi had fallen in love with Karim Samar when she was sixteen years old. The feeling had been mutual, eighteen-year-old Karim equally besotted, but their families, Hazara people from Afghanistan's Daykundi Province, had refused to approve the match. The stance taken by the elders on both sides was unreasonable. They were peasant farmers of equal status, and there should have been no obstacle to a marriage within their ranks. But the families had been feuding for years, possibly two generations. Over exactly what could no longer be remembered – a few livestock, a small plot of land, who could say? But the personal grudge was long-standing. A Sarabi and a Samar did not marry.

So, in defiance, Azra and Karim had run away together. Leaving their village in early 2010, they'd run as far as they could from the families who would undoubtedly seek retribution for such blatant disobedience. With the war raging, travel through Afghanistan had been fraught with danger, but undeterred they'd continued to make their way south-east, crossing the border into Pakistan's Balochistan Province, where they'd finally settled in the city of Quetta. It was there they'd married, and there they'd consummated their relationship, for throughout the ordeals of their journey they had remained chaste, Azra keeping herself pure for her husband and Karim respecting the virginity of his future wife.

The two were blissfully happy as they settled into their new life and their new community. There were many Hazara people in Quetta and they made good friends through whom Karim found regular work, saving all the while for the family they intended to have. But it wasn't long before the problem that had for some time confronted the community reared its head, and with renewed force. The Hazara had long been targets of militia groups in Pakistan, and the assassination of Osama bin Laden by American Navy SEALs in Abbottabad on 2 May 2011 could mean only one thing. Political tensions would escalate and this border region would become a hotbed of violence, leading to ever-fiercer persecution of the Hazara.

Many of the community decided to flee, Karim included. The time had come, he told Azra, for them to leave Pakistan altogether.

'It is as well after all,' he said, 'that we do not have a newborn and that you are not with child, Azra – either situation would impede our journey.' He'd said this in order to comfort her. She had been trying to conceive for the past year and he knew she felt personally at fault in failing to do so. 'We will start our family when we are settled,' he assured her.

They had their hearts set on Australia. The destination had initially been Azra's idea, which had surprised Karim. Until its involvement in the war Australia had been a country unknown to them; they would not even have been able to place its whereabouts on the world map. Now, given their knowledge, it was the country's very location that made Azra's suggestion surprising to Karim.

'But Australia is so very far away,' he said.

'Yes,' she conceded, 'the travel will be arduous, but Australia is such a safe country, Karim, the perfect place for us to bring up our children. And the Australians are our friends. They are allies to Afghanistan. We will be welcome there.'

'It is true,' Karim agreed. 'The Australians have been fighting for us for years, we are brothers.' He was proud of his wife – her argument was most certainly sound. 'Yes, Azra, you are right; they will welcome us there. We will go to Australia.'

On the advice of well-informed friends, some of whose family members had successfully undertaken the journey to Australia, the young couple had travelled north to the capital. There in the bustling, modern city of Islamabad they had made enquiries at a particular 'agency' to which they had been directed. The 'agency' was really no more than a room above a shop just off the Luqman Hakim Road, but it served a very active purpose. One of several such seemingly humble offices situated in a number of major Middle Eastern cities, it was here desperate people sought help to escape the conflict or persecution that threatened their lives and those of their families. In truth, these 'agencies' functioned as recruitment centres for a highly profitable enterprise headed by a man called Benny Hitono.

'Oh yes,' they were told by Nadia, an extremely efficient young woman who spoke any number of languages, including Dari, a dialect mutually intelligible with their own Hazaragi. 'Over the years Benny Hitono has helped many, many people get to Australia, including his own family. He is a good man, Benny, famous for saving the lives of others.' They were warned however . . . 'But you must understand the journey is expensive,' Nadia continued, 'it is a costly exercise getting people all the way to Australia.'

Far too costly for the likes of Karim and Azra as it turned out. But as it further turned out, Nadia proved sympathetic to their cause.

Seated opposite her at her desk, they had told her their story in full, and upon discovering the prohibitive cost entailed, they had then pleaded with her. They would be only too happy to work for their passage to Australia they said. Any form of manual employment would do.

'And we are good workers,' Karim insisted, Azra beside him nodding vigorously, 'we are strong. We are not afraid of hard work, I swear to you.'

Nadia, touched by the young Hazara couple's earnestness and naiveté, felt oddly maternal. How peculiar, she thought, I'm no older than they are. Then she surprised herself. 'You must go to this address,' she said, scribbling in her notepad. 'I shall telephone the housekeeper and explain your circumstances and background. I'm quite sure you'll find employment there.' She had no idea why she was doing what she was doing – she dealt regularly with people fleeing for their lives, and always distanced herself, never became involved. But there was something about this pair . . .

She ripped the page from her notebook and pushed it across the desktop to Karim. 'It's a wealthy Arab home,' she said briskly, 'complete with servants' quarters and always in need of workers. In fact when it comes to workers, there's a rather quick turnover,' she added drily, recalling the time she had served in a secretarial capacity at the household. She didn't bother telling them of her employment there, deeming the fact overly personal and inappropriate under the circumstances, but she couldn't resist adding a little inside information. 'They're typical Saudis,' she said with disdain, 'arrogant snobs who'll treat you like dirt, but this is only one of their many houses dotted all over the place, so half the time they're not even here in Islamabad and you won't see them at all.'

Realising she may have given herself away a little, Nadia picked up her cell phone and got back to business. 'I'll ring the housekeeper right now,' she said in a tone that signalled the interview was over.

Karim pocketed the slip of paper and he and Azra rose

from the table. 'Thank you,' he said, 'thank you so much,' Azra echoing him as they backed towards the door.

But the young woman was paying them scant attention as she keyed in the phone number. 'Good luck,' she called over her shoulder.

Nadia's intervention on their behalf proved a godsend. Karim and Azra were not only hired that very day, they remained in the employ of the Arab household for close to a year, he as a gardener and handyman, she as a kitchen maid and cleaner.

When the Saudi family, together with their large entourage, was in residence the work was hard. The patriarch, an extremely wealthy middle-aged businessman, was mostly absent during the day, together with his adult son and four-man team of chauffeur, bodyguard, interpreter and male secretary. The two wives, three daughters, and various other female members of the extended family, however, were demanding of attention every minute of the day.

The home being the centre for family socialising, the wives and older daughter were particularly fussy about the running of the household and the tidiness of the garden, despite the fact that all had been kept immaculate during their absence and remained that way throughout their stay. The women were also insistent that every household staff member, and every single servant in the family's employ, however lowly, communicate in Arabic. Those heard conversing in any language other than Arabic were to be instantly dismissed. This was the house rule and always had been.

'I'm not sure why,' the housekeeper, a pleasant Pakistani woman in her fifties, had told Karim and Azra, 'perhaps for security purposes. Perhaps they believe others may be plotting against them,' she'd said with a shrug, not believing this to be the case herself. 'But it's rather inconvenient at times,' she'd admitted. 'I've employed many different language speakers over the years, and they've all had to learn in a hurry or risk losing their jobs.'

Forewarned, Karim and Azra had quickly set about broadening their knowledge of Arabic, which had previously been only as much as was required for religious purposes, prayers always being conducted in Arabic. The other servants had been only too happy to help with their tuition, just as they themselves had been helped in the past.

Given their humble status in the household's hierarchy, Karim and Azra had no fear of being caught out should the occasional order be given directly to them, for this would simply require a 'yes sir, no sir' response. But they were nonetheless uncomfortable during the family's visits. They did not in the least mind the extra hard work, but the fact that they dared not communicate in their own language for fear of being overheard added a strain to their lives.

Grateful though they were for the employment, their year spent in the Saudi household was not particularly happy. And no matter how hard they saved, the meagre salary they received was never likely to amount to the exorbitant sum required to get them all the way to Australia.

But they remained resolute in their choice of destination, poring over maps and discussing possible routes. Then one day they came to a decision. The savings they'd accumulated would afford them airfares to Bangkok and enough to set themselves up in cheap accommodation. Bangkok was in Thailand, well on the way to Australia. This was an excellent start, they agreed. Bangkok, furthermore, was a huge city with many tourists, and there was money to be made in such cities. They would settle in Bangkok, illegally if necessary, and they would work hard for however long it took, a year, possibly two years. Then they would travel to Indonesia where, in Jakarta, they would make direct contact with their saviour, the famous Benny Hitono.

Having made their decision, they gave notice to the housekeeper and shortly after left the Saudi household.

Their plans went as smoothly as they could possibly have hoped. Arriving in Bangkok on visitors' visas proved no obstacle at all in gaining employment. The colourfully chaotic city abounded with building sites and there was a healthy demand for labourers. When a strong young man like Karim applied for work no one asked for his passport or made enquiries. No one seemed to care in the least about his residency status so long as he accepted the wage on offer. He and Azra agreed that the figure was probably well below what it should have been, but Karim was hardly going to argue the point.

Azra encountered a similar response upon applying for a job at one of the big city hotels, which in catering exclusively for tourists employed hundreds of staff.

'I was accepted without question, Karim,' she said excitedly upon her return to the cheap boarding house where they'd rented a second-floor room. 'The hotel employs many nationalities from many different countries and I was not asked for my passport. I am to be a chambermaid,' she added with pride, 'and I am to undergo a week of training. I am even to learn some English words so that I can greet the guests as they pass by.'

'I am not surprised they hired you without question,' Karim replied, 'and particularly as a chambermaid. They employ only the pretty girls as chambermaids,' he'd laughed, kissing her lightly. 'The ugly ones they put to work in the kitchen and laundry.' He'd said it jokingly, he knew nothing of grand hotels, but upon reflection he decided he was probably right.

Azra had been employed at the hotel for close to six months when it happened. During that time, she'd proved herself a hard worker and, although shy by nature, was popular with the other chambermaids. Probably because she knew her place: there was a distinct pecking order within the ranks of the housekeeping staff. She'd proved an apt pupil too, happily greeting the guests in her newfound English, always with a smile and a curtsy-like bob.

'Good morning, sir,' she would say to the businessman striding down the hall, 'good afternoon, madam,' to the woman in the towelling robe on her way to the pool, even 'good day, miss,' to the woman's daughter. She knew also how to say 'thank you' when a guest was courteous, and how to say 'it is a pleasure' when she herself was thanked. This was the extent of her English and all that had been taught her by the hotel management, yet it proved perfectly adequate under the circumstances. She had learned from a fellow non-English-speaking worker one other phrase, however, which she found useful on the odd occasion when a guest halted in the corridor and made some incomprehensible remark that appeared to require an answer. Or when, while making up a guest's room in their presence, something was asked of her.

'I am sorry, I not understand,' she would say. She had taken great care to perfect the phrase as it prevented unnecessary confusion, and she would say it with a smile and an apologetic shake of her head. She would add a deferential bob as a further sign of apology, for she did not like having to admit to her ignorance and hoped the guest would not think poorly of her, or find her inability to converse irritating. But on each occasion the guest appeared neither critical nor irritated. Quickly gathering she did not speak English, the guest would pass on down the corridor or turn away, allowing her to continue her work.

Which made the man's reaction that morning all the more confusing.

She had seen him in the corridor on several occasions over the past day or so and had presumed, correctly, that he was attending the international conference that the hotel was hosting. Many Western businessmen were staying there for that purpose. She did not know whether the man was English, American or Australian, they all looked and sounded the same to her, but she'd offered her customary greeting.

'Good morning, sir,' she had said with a bob and a smile, and each time he'd returned the smile, slowing his pace a little. 'Good morning,' he'd said before continuing on his way.

Then on the third day, he'd stepped from his room and appeared deliberately to seek her out. She was a little further down the corridor with her trolley and was working alone that morning, as the maids occasionally did when the hotel was particularly busy. Having finished making up one room, she had moved on to the door of the next.

'Good morning,' he said, crossing to her.

'Good morning, sir.' A bob and a smile and, presuming he would continue on his way, she turned to check whether the light beside the door of the room was showing green. It was not. The light was red so she turned back to her trolley intending to move on, only to discover the man still there beside her. She gave another smile, another bob, and was about to set off, when . . .

'Excuse me,' the man said.

Azra had a vague understanding of 'excuse me', or rather an understanding of where it would lead. 'Excuse me' meant the guest was seeking her attention and it always prefaced something quite unintelligible, which she could only presume was a request of some sort. This instance proved no exception and she waited politely for the man to finish whatever it was he was saying before shaking her head.

'I am sorry,' she said with her customary smile of apology, 'I not understand.' Another bob for good measure.

The man nodded, obviously accepting the fact that she did not speak English, and then pointed down the corridor to his room. 'Come, come,' he said beckoning her to follow.

He strode off and she did as she was bade, following him with her trolley; it was clear that he wanted his room made up.

She took a set of fresh towels from the trolley and he stood to one side holding the door open for her.

'Thank you, sir,' she said as she entered.

'Thank *you*,' he replied.

'It is my pleasure, sir.'

She didn't notice him close the door behind them, and even if she had she would probably have given it no thought.

'The pleasure is all mine I assure you,' she heard him say as she put the towels on a chair and crossed to the bed.

She did not understand the phrase, but the word 'pleasure' was always a polite response so she turned and gave another smile before starting to strip back the bedding.

She had expected he would leave the room, as this was the customary hour of the morning when he passed her in the corridor. Or if not, she expected at least that he would ignore her as she went about her work. But he did neither. Instead he crossed to where she stood and talked directly to her, a fact she found most confusing. Had he not gathered that she did not speak English?

'I am sorry.' She repeated her catch phrase, again apologetically, 'I not understand.'

'Oh yes, I think you do.'

The man was nodding knowingly, and there was an unpleasantness about his tone and his smile now. Azra's confusion grew. What did he mean? Something is wrong, she thought.

'I not understand, sir,' she said as firmly as she was able, but her voice faltered, fear rising in her throat as the man reached out his hand.

Then everything happened at breakneck speed. She was suddenly on the bed, thrown backwards, the man holding her there, pulling up her skirts, ripping at her underwear.

She tried desperately to fight free of him. Then, feeling the outrage of exposure, she tried with equal desperation to cover herself. This could not be happening, this unspeakable thing. But she was no match for the man's strength. He held her down with ease, dragging her legs apart, fumbling with his trousers, forcing himself into her.

There was not the slightest chance of escape after that. Trapped beneath the full weight of his body, she could do nothing but endure the vilest of invasion.

Her defilement did not last long. The man had anticipated this moment. He'd been fantasising for two days about the exotic little dusky-skinned girl with the teasing smile. His passion was spent within only minutes.

'Well then,' he said, rising and pulling on his trousers, 'we'll keep this our little secret, shall we.'

As he turned to pick up the wallet that sat on the bedside table, Azra scrambled to her feet, adjusting her clothing, not daring to think beyond anything but escape.

The man took money from his wallet and, folding the notes, tucked the wad down the shirtfront of her uniform.

She cringed at his touch.

'I think you'll find I've been more than generous,' he said affably, leading the way to the door, which he opened for her.

She dived outside, dazed, breathless, still in a state of shock.

Behind her the door closed.

Azra stood in the corridor, her mind struggling to encompass the enormity of what had happened. Her world had changed in such a short space of time. She could not yet grasp fully the consequences, but of one thing she was certain. From this moment on her life would never be the same.

She went directly to a female staff washroom, which was fortunately empty, and washed herself as forcefully as she could, digging her fingers deep inside, trying to cleanse away the Westerner's filth. But she knew she would never rid herself of the shame.

When she returned home she said nothing of what had happened to her husband, but her shame was multiplied tenfold that night as Karim made love to her. They had intercourse regularly these days, a mutually pleasurable expression of their love, but also in their efforts to conceive a child. Tonight, however, Azra took no pleasure in their lovemaking.

I am not worthy of him, she told herself, I am unclean. If others were to find out they would judge me guilty. My own father and brothers would accuse me of infidelity. They would say I had done something to arouse the Westerner's lust, they might well kill me for dishonouring our family. But what did I do, she agonised, what did I do that caused this to happen? And if Karim were to find out, he would have every right to divorce me, he too would have the right even to kill me.

Azra knew in her heart Karim would not harm her, nor would he divorce her, their love was too strong, but the knowledge that another man had had her would tarnish their marriage forever.

Her mind in turmoil, sleep evaded her that night, but come the dawn she had made her decision, she knew what she must do. Everything must go on as normal. She must live a lie. Not only for her own sake, but for Karim's. If Karim were to know what had happened, he would not kill her. He would kill the Westerner. And where would that lead?

They observed their respective prayer rituals that morning, had their breakfast, and he kissed her goodbye as he left, his work day starting earlier than hers.

'Be safe, God go with you,' she said as she always did.

The thought of returning to the hotel terrified Azra. She was bound to see the man, as she was assigned to the seventh floor and the man's room was on the seventh floor. Perhaps she could ask for a change of assignment, but then that would invite inquiry. No, no, she told herself, she must be strong: life must go on as if nothing had happened. She would make sure, though, that this time she was working in the company of another maid. The man would not dare attack her then.

She steeled herself to face him. She would look him directly in the eyes, she decided, defying him to harm her further, perhaps even arousing fear in him that she might report the incident.

But the man was not there. She did not see him in the corridor and his room was empty, freshly made up and awaiting the next guest. The three-day international conference was over. The Westerner had carefully chosen the day of his departure to rape her. He had left for the airport that very same morning.

Azra had surprised herself with her show of strength in preparing to confront the man, and over the ensuing weeks she surprised herself further with her newly developed talent to lie.

That night she counted out the money the Westerner had given her, fifty-dollar notes, four of them, two hundred American dollars in all. She refused to dwell upon how she had come by such a sum, forcing herself to be practical instead. Here was a wealth of riches that would add considerably to their hard-earned savings.

The next day she visited a money exchange outlet, changing the fifties to five-dollar notes, and during the weeks that followed she made a habit every now and then of presenting to Karim one or two of the five-dollar notes.

'Tips from Westerners,' she explained the first time she produced the money, 'I am occasionally asked to return their laundry or dry cleaning.' Then she'd added knowledgeably, 'The Americans are the best tippers.' She'd heard this from the girls who delivered room service.

Karim had accepted the explanation without question. 'How generous,' he'd said. 'We must hope the Americans keep choosing to stay at your hotel.'

Living a lie, Azra decided, was not as difficult as she had thought it might be. So long as she could block that horrendous morning from her mind, she would be able to manage. No one need ever know. Her defilement would remain her secret, and hers alone.

She had not counted, however, upon the discovery that should have brought with it such unadulterated joy.

She'd waited until she was absolutely certain. It was not until the doctor she'd visited had confirmed the fact beyond all doubt that she made her announcement.

'I am with child, Karim,' she said.

His ecstasy was such that he failed to notice her reaction did not equal his.

'Our dream has come true, Azra.' He laughed as he took her in his arms. 'Our dream has finally come true.'

Yes, she thought, returning his embrace, *finally*. We have been trying to have a child for three full years, Karim, and only now has it *finally* happened.

One thought was uppermost in Azra's mind. Could this child possibly be the product of her unspeakable union? Could the baby now growing in her womb have been fathered by the Westerner?

It was no longer easy, she discovered, to live a lie. The months that followed were fraught with worry as she watched her belly grow. Each stage of her pregnancy, which should have been joyful, only brought her a step closer to discovery. Was her shame to be revealed for the whole world to see? If it were so, then she would kill herself.

Karim's elation knew no bounds when his wife gave birth to a boy.

'Hamid,' he said, gazing lovingly at his newborn; they had discussed the names they planned for their child,

Hamid for a boy, Atefa for a girl. 'Hamid, my son,' he said with such pride.

Azra studied the baby's face continuously, searching for any giveaway sign. No feature looked particularly Western, but how could one tell? The child's skin was a dusky brown, but then so was hers, so this fact did not mean he was without Western blood. She worried that she could see no specific likeness to Karim, but a newborn was a newborn, so again how could one tell?

As the months passed she continued to agonise, seeking signs of her husband's face in the baby. Are these Karim's eyes, she would ask herself, or are they the eyes of the Westerner? Is this Karim's mouth, or the mouth of the Westerner? She could not recall what the Westerner looked like, she'd had no idea at the time; they all looked the same.

Azra loved her baby with a true mother's passion, but her agony did not let up for one moment. She lived in dread of the day her husband might discover something foreign in the face of his son.

As time passed and the child turned one year old, and then was approaching two, Azra told herself her fears must surely be unfounded. Karim loved his son unquestioningly and with a passion that equalled hers.

Finally, with the child a sturdy three-year-old and their accumulated savings hopefully sufficient, they set off on their journey to Indonesia in search of Benny Hitono and the new life that beckoned.

But doubt still lingered. Without proof, questions remained unanswered. Have I been searching too hard? Azra asked herself. Have I been looking so closely I can no longer see what is there? And is Karim, in his love for Hamid and his pride in his son, blinded to some sign that others might recognise?

'He is a handsome boy, so like his father.'

Jalila's words had come like a blessing from God.

Why should this mysterious girl, a complete stranger, say such a thing unless it were true? Here is the proof, Azra told herself, the proof I have been waiting for. This girl who never speaks has chosen to communicate with no one but me. It is surely a message from Allah. The child is Karim's and I am forgiven.

'Karim must be very proud,' she heard the girl say.

'He is. Oh yes, he is,' she whispered. 'Thank you, Jalila,' and she turned away to hide the magnitude of this moment, which would have seemed to others so inconsequential.

During the days that followed, Hala rejoiced in the connection between the two young women, even noticing on occasion they exchanged the odd word. Always relating to the child, for the little boy remained the only area of interest to Jalila, but at least the girl was finally communicating.

The brief exchanges between the two were of course in Arabic, but for some time now, Hala had had the strangest suspicion the girl may possibly speak English. Or at least that the girl may have an understanding of English. She had mentioned as much to Rassen.

'Have you noticed the way Jalila pays close attention whenever we discuss Hamid's condition?' she asked. This was shortly after they had arrived on the island, when the child was still struggling to survive. 'She never looks at us and she pretends she's not listening, but I know she is. And what's more, I think she understands every word.'

'Really? No, I hadn't noticed. How interesting.'

Then the very next day: 'Do you know, my dear, I believe you may be right,' Rassen said. 'She certainly does appear to be listening. I wonder where she learnt the language.'

'Without knowing where she comes from it's impossible to say, isn't it?' Hala replied. She had the vaguest idea herself, but it being only a theory she chose not to share her thoughts.

'I think we should keep our suspicions to ourselves though,' she said. 'To put Jalila to the test might risk alienating her altogether.'

'Oh yes, most certainly, I agree.'

Alone, however, Hala gave thought to her theory. Was it Jalila's companion, the man who had accompanied her on the boat, who had taught her English?

Hala recalled the man vividly. Middle-aged and Lebanese in appearance, she'd presumed at first, given their age difference, he was the girl's father or uncle or some sort of guardian. But she'd quickly gathered from his body language that he was not. His manner towards the girl was intimate, proprietorial; the girl belonged to him.

Any communication that she'd witnessed between the two had been in Arabic, as had the man's communication with others aboard the vessel. There was no reason to suppose he spoke English. But he did. At least he had to Hala. And most fluently. She remembered his words with fearful clarity.

CHAPTER FOUR

'You filthy fucking bitch whore, who do you think you are!'

The man's vitriol was as shocking as the words he hissed at her, and the fact that the words were English words made his attack all the more alarming. Had he chosen to confront her in Arabic, the language most common on board, she would have presumed he was hysterical and attempted to calm him. Given their predicament, many of the passengers were justifiably panic-stricken and panic often led to unreasonable outbursts. But the man was not in a state of hysteria. His attack was personal, and Hala was left speechless, staring into the angry black eyes barely inches from hers.

'What right do you have,' the man went on, 'fucking English bitch whore!'

Hala continued to meet his gaze, not daring to avert her eyes in search of Rassen, fearing it would be seen as a sign of weakness, but knowing also that Rassen was some distance away at the stern of the vessel. He was examining several who were showing symptoms of the typhoid fever that was affecting so many, and, Hala thought, in all probability doling out more of their precious Ciprofloxacin tablets. She very much hoped that he was not. The administering of the tablets had been her job, and, through necessity, she had been exceedingly sparing.

'Who gives you the right to play God!' the man snarled.

'What power says you are above the rest of us, that it is you who chooses who shall live or die? Who gives you this right? English bitch whore!'

Hala did not flinch, but her mind was racing as she sought the most effective form of response. The man's belief she was English was clearly firing his anger, and his assumption was understandable; courtesy of her English mother she certainly appeared so. It was most likely, also, that he'd overheard her talking with Rassen; they always communicated in English when they wished their conversation to be private.

How do I reply, Hala was frantically asking herself, and in which language? Should I tell him in Arabic that I am Syrian and that way hopefully mollify him? But he obviously believes I consider myself superior, so he may think I am patronising him by not responding in English. Perhaps I should simply explain the cold, hard facts, and in the language in which he has chosen to attack me.

She decided upon the latter option, hoping the man's knowledge of English was as comprehensive as it appeared to be, and that he'd not just developed a talent for foul and abusive assaults on women.

'I do not choose who lives or dies,' she said firmly, 'only God has that power –' She was about to go on, but the man interrupted.

'You dare mention God!' She appeared to have angered him further. 'Infidel!' His eyes contemptuously roamed her uncovered head and her fair hair blowing wildly in the wind. 'You do not follow the true God! You believe *you* are God!' He spat the words at her.

'I believe nothing of the sort.' She ignored the interruption and continued from exactly the point where she'd left off, her manner cool, concise. 'I am a nurse and my husband is a doctor. We have limited medications to hand, which I administer to those whom we consider have a chance of survival. Sadly there have been some showing particularly strong symptoms, whom we have considered beyond help. And of course there are many amongst us displaying no symptoms at all. In my opinion you are one of these,' she said in conclusion. 'I am willing to examine you if you wish, but from my observation you appear symptom-free and therefore are in no need of the valuable medication, which we have in scant supply.'

He continued to glare at her, but made no further interruption. Has he understood? she wondered. Then, in her peripheral vision, she noticed that behind him Rassen was returning. She averted her gaze.

'Ah, here comes my husband,' she said pleasantly as if theirs had been an amiable conversation. 'I am sure he will be quite happy to assure you, as I have just done, that you are not at risk.'

She met his eyes once again, only briefly, before the man turned from her to rejoin his beautiful young companion, who had remained staring out to sea. But in that brief moment of contact Hala knew he had understood every word she'd said. Vile though he was, the man's knowledge of English was most certainly comprehensive.

Thinking now about Jalila, and wondering whether the man might possibly have taught her English, Hala couldn't help but reflect upon the unpleasant episode and all its implications.

The man had been right really, hadn't he? She hadn't given the matter a great deal of consideration at the time: there'd been too much to do in the fight to save lives. She hadn't even told Rassen of the confrontation, simply dismissing the man as the loathsome creature he was. But now, here on this island, with little to do *but* think, Hala's mind roamed freely.

She *had* been playing God, of course she had. She'd been playing God from the very start.

She remembered noticing, for the first time, the young woman and baby at the safe house in Sendang Biru. She hadn't seen the woman aboard the truck that had transported them from Jakarta to Bogor, nor had she seen her at the safe house in Bogor itself, but of course there would have been more than one safe house and more than one transport truck. It was only when they'd reached the small fishing village of Sendang Biru, where they'd awaited the vessel that would take them to Australia, that she'd noticed the woman and child. How could she fail to do otherwise? Much as the woman tried to disguise her weakened and feverish condition, to Hala the symptoms were highly suspicious. To Rassen too. They had discussed the case; even without being able to examine the woman for the giveaway signs – the abdominal skin rash, the bronchial condition and other indications – they suspected it was possible she might be suffering from typhoid fever. They had mentioned the matter in private to the organiser of the exodus, the man called Benny Hitono, who had said he would 'look into it'. But the following day the glib reply had come back . . .

'Oh no,' he had assured them, 'all fine. I ask her. She say she has had bad cold. She is getting better, no need for worry.'

Hala and Rassen had by now gathered that Benny Hitono was a charlatan, in fact an out-and-out rogue, but this too had been discussed and they were in complete agreement. They had come so far and been through so much, they must resign themselves to whatever fate had in store. There could be no turning back.

The questions the woman's condition raised were numerous. If she was in the grip of typhoid fever, how long had she been suffering the disease? With how many of their fellow passengers had she come in close contact? For how long had she been confined with others at safe houses? And given these factors, how many amongst them might already be suffering the disease, and at what stage was their infection?

Along with forty others, they'd embarked upon the vessel, a fifteen-metre wooden fishing boat that had seen better days – further confirming their opinion of Benny Hitono – and as they'd set off all these questions had continued to play on their minds.

When, in only a matter of days, the woman's condition had worsened and a physical examination had confirmed their suspicions, Rassen had wanted to treat her with a course of the Ciprofloxacin tablets he carried in his medical kit. Hala had said no, however. Hala was always the tough one.

'I believe she is too far gone, Rassen,' she had said. 'There is bound to be an outbreak. Leave our supplies for those in the earlier stages, those whom we know we can save.'

The woman's baby had been the first to go. A girl, barely one year old.

Hala could still see the little shrouded body spiralling to the ocean's depths, the weight they'd added carrying it to its watery grave. And she could still hear the mother, moaning, delirious, somehow vaguely aware, attempting to resist as the dead child was wrested from her arms.

The mother herself had followed not long after. They'd had no spare material from which to make a shroud and no sufficient weight to add to the body. They'd been at sea for well over a week by then, and were quite possibly off their intended course, although no one knew for sure, as the skipper and two-man crew spoke only Indonesian and were giving away nothing. The vessel was supposed to have reached its destination in a week and people were becoming frightened. The young mother's death only added to the burgeoning sense of panic.

Hala remembered watching the woman's body, bobbing like a rag doll on the ocean's surface as the boat contin-ued to chug its way to God only knew where, and she remembered thinking as she watched, How many more will there be?

There had been a number, she'd forgotten exactly how many, she'd been too busy playing God, but she recalled only too well those rag dolls bobbing. Perhaps she could have saved one or two, who knows? She'd certainly been ruthless in her choices. But the supply of medication they carried had been limited, and of course there was the dehydration factor. Those in the advanced stages of the disease were desperately in need of water, and the water supply was by now so low they could not afford extra rations for some who might already be on death's list. Which meant there was little point in wasting precious tablets when dehydration would claim them anyway, she'd decided with cold brutality.

It was the water factor, Hala now recalled, that had been the catalyst, firing the man's rage and bringing about his grisly end. Aggressive by nature, his anger had already been at fever pitch. As had the anger of so many, she remembered, particularly so many of the younger ones. Even before the storm hit, the vessel had become a tinderbox of human emotion, fear and anger rising in equal proportion. With food virtually non-existent and water rationing at its peak, people were preparing themselves for the end, some with resignation, others with resentment. The older passengers were reciting the Shahada.

'*There is no god but Allah.*

Muhammad is the messenger of God.'

Their chanting, quiet and personal at first, had grown in unison, over and over, all about the vessel, voices joining in a mutual declaration of faith.

But other voices rose above them, the youthful voices of those who had risked their lives and witnessed the deaths of friends and family in their battle for liberation. Even traditional passive prayer angered the young activists who had fought so hard for freedom.

'Ignore God! God will not save you!' they taunted their devout Muslim elders, for whom they would normally have shown respect. 'Where is God? God is not here!'

In their home countries, the cry of 'Freedom' amongst the activists had meant more than freedom from the oppression of a regime that tortured and enslaved and murdered. It had meant freedom from the Mullahs, freedom from the restrictions of radical Islam, freedom from religion itself.

'God will not save you! God is not here,' they cried out in their own mutual show of rebellion.

In the chaos, the youngest of the crew members had considered it safe to take a swig from his flask, which during the night had been illicitly filled from the precious water supply doled out with great care to the passengers twice a day. The captain and his two-man crew had been stealing water on a regular basis, considering it their right – they were after all responsible for the safety of the vessel and passengers, and it was therefore essential they remain strong. The young crewman, a lad of no more than nineteen, presumed his action would go unnoticed. He was mistaken.

With a howl of anger, the man flung himself at the Indonesian, ripping the flask from his hand, screaming obscenities, his rage uncontrollable. He grasped the boy around the throat: he would have killed him if he could. But the captain was too quick. In a matter of seconds, the fishing knife he carried at all times on his belt was released from its sheath and plunged into the man's stomach.

The wound itself might not have been enough to have killed the man, but the impetus of the captain's charge was. Staggering backwards under the attack, the man was suddenly over the side of the vessel and floundering in the sea, blood gushing from his belly, an open invitation. The shark was upon him in an instant.

Everything had happened so quickly, Hala remembered. The bloodied water, the shark's frenzy, the man's brief screams and then it was over. She recalled how, automatically, her eyes had darted to his companion, and how she'd found the girl's reaction so enigmatic. Nothing was there. The beautiful face had remained impassive, devoid even of shock. The man's death had appeared to have for her no significance at all.

Hala wondered now about the relationship between Jalila and her unpleasant companion. Had the man been her husband? Had he treated her cruelly? Was he responsible for her present condition? And if, as Hala strongly suspected, Jalila spoke English, or at least had an understanding of the language, was it the man who had taught her?

As agreed, she kept her suspicions to herself. She did not query Jalila, nor did she attempt to put her ability to the test. But in the company of Rassen and Massoud, if the girl was present, Hala chose always to speak English, hoping that one day Jalila might reveal herself. It could perhaps be the first step towards healing whatever terrible damage the girl had suffered.

With everyone assigned their special duties – Hany and Karim fishing, the women tending gardens and household chores, and the indefatigable Sanaa preparing endless meals – Rassen and Massoud had taken it upon themselves to explore the island and painstakingly measure out its dimensions. They had walked the length and breadth counting every step, and had eventually concluded the island was approximately three kilometres long from north to south and two kilometres wide from east to west. A small isthmus of fifty metres or so projected from the western shoreline to a sizeable rocky outcrop, but they did not include this in their calculations for at high tide the sand bar was well under water with a fierce current running.

'Best we don't explore there,' Rassen had suggested as they'd gazed across the narrow divide. 'We'd either get stranded or swept away by the tide.'

Massoud agreed. Neither of them were strong swimmers, nor were any of the others. 'We're not exactly the right types to be stranded on a remote island in the middle of nowhere, are we?' he remarked with a touch of whimsy.

The prevailing winds being south to southwesterly, the settlement of huts and jetties had been built on the eastern lee side. The mangroves, which grew in a small cluster a little further to the north, were the only trees on the island; the rest of the vegetation was a variety of low-lying shrubs and bushes.

'Not much to tell us where we are,' Rassen had said finally – he'd been hoping their several days of exploration might have revealed some hints.

'And nobody around to tell us,' Massoud replied looking out to sea. 'Not a ship in sight, and after a full two weeks no sign whatsoever of our "friends". I'm very much hoping now, be it for better or worse, that they *do* turn up.'

Rassen made no reply apart from a nod of affirmation. If he had been a man who believed in the miracle of prayer, he would pray, he thought. But he no longer believed. He decided that, like Massoud, he would hope.

The power of hope appeared to be enough, however, when two days later a boat was sighted.

Karim was the first to see it. He and Hany had just returned from their morning's fishing expedition. They had scaled and gutted their catch at the shore, using the flat rock they'd selected to serve this specific purpose, and Hany had taken the bucket of fish to Sanaa, leaving Karim to clean up. This was their daily routine.

Karim went about his duties methodically, filling a second bucket with sea water and washing the rock down, cleaning away the fish scales with a scrubbing brush. After inspecting the dinghy to make sure all was in order for the following morning, he checked the anchor's security and was about to join the others in the blue hut where lunch would soon be served. He was hungry.

But as he looked up, his eyes automatically swept the horizon and that was when he saw it. A vessel, far in the distance. He couldn't tell how far, nor could he tell the size of the vessel, but it was there. He could see it. A boat.

He ran towards the blue hut where he presumed the others were already gathering for the meal.

'A boat,' he yelled as he ran. 'A boat! A boat!'

Rassen and Hala were the first to appear from the yellow hut nearby, as they had not as yet joined the others, but within only moments the whole group had congregated.

They rushed to the shoreline, little Hamid following, wondering what the fuss was about, infected by the excitement. His father picked him up, hoisting him onto his hip and locking him there with one arm.

'Look, Hamid,' Karim shouted, pointing out to sea, 'a boat! A boat, my son, wave to it! Wave!'

Karim was waving wildly himself and beside him Azra was waving, so the little boy waved along with them, enjoying his parents' game.

'Ahoy!' Massoud screamed at the top of his voice, he too waving frantically, 'ahoy there!'

'I don't think they can hear you,' Rassen remarked drily: an understatement, the far-off vessel was nowhere within earshot.

'I know.' Massoud smiled. 'But it feels like the right thing to do, don't you think?'

Hala laughed. The young Iranian's flippancy amused her and his smile, as always, was infectious. Besides, she was in wholehearted agreement. 'Ahoy there,' she yelled, jumping up and down and waving madly. 'Over here! Over here!'

Rassen couldn't help himself. Abandoning his normally dour demeanour, he joined in, and all eyes fixed on the distant vessel they jumped about screaming and waving like over-exuberant children.

In their excitement, they failed to notice those amongst them whose reaction differed from theirs. Jalila's disinterest would hardly have come as a surprise, but the lack of enthusiasm displayed by the Egyptian couple would most certainly have mystified them.

Hany's eyes were not focused upon the vessel at all, but rather upon his wife. He had put a protective arm around Sanaa, drawing her close, shielding her from something. But from what? Sanaa herself was staring out at the vessel, her expression inscrutable, but there might perhaps have been something in her eyes approximating dread.

Despite all their frantic activity, those onboard the vessel appeared not to have seen them, and its image was growing dishearteningly smaller.

'A fire,' Rassen said urgently, 'gather some kindling, we'll start a fire. Hala, fetch a box of matches from the hut.'

As Hala sped off, the others set about gathering bracken and twigs, Jalila joining in, obeying instructions as she always did, fulfilling her duties when required. But again no one noticed the reluctance displayed by the Egyptians, who stood to one side watching in silence, Hany's arm still protectively about his wife.

Hala returned with the matches and Rassen lit the small fire they'd built, Massoud holding out his coat, forming a windshield, then both of them vigorously fanning the flames, the smoke starting to rise.

But they were too late. By now the boat was no more than a speck on the horizon. Then even as they watched, it disappeared altogether and there remained nothing in sight but the endless ocean.

Rassen was not overly dismayed, however. He found the fact they had seen the vessel most promising. Where there is one boat, there will be another, he thought. The next day or the next week, what matter? A boat will pass by at some stage. And when it does, we must simply ensure a way of making our presence known.

'We must keep a fire burning at all times,' he announced.

Massoud had been thinking along very much the same lines, although he saw one major flaw in Rassen's suggestion.

'There's not timber enough on the island to maintain a fire constantly; we'd soon run out of fuel,' he said. 'I think we should build a fire and have it standing by to be lit only when a vessel comes in sight.' His look to Rassen was apologetic; he did not intend to take over the doctor's natural role as leader. 'I mean it could be some time before another boat turns up.'

But Rassen was in no need of apology. 'Of course, Massoud, how silly of me. You're absolutely right, and that's exactly what we'll do. We'll have kerosene standing by to ignite the fire quickly. We'll also keep a strict lookout at all times,' he announced to the group in general. 'If not for Karim, we might have been happily eating lunch today oblivious to the fact there was a boat in sight. Goodness knows how often this may already have happened. I suggest we assign regular watches throughout the day. It's foolish to just sit around waiting to be discovered. We must *do* something.'

'Why?' The question, barked by Hany, was patently belligerent. 'Why must we *do* something?' he demanded.

They all turned to the Egyptian, surprised more by the hostility of his tone than the actual words he'd said.

'Why tempt fate?' With all eyes now upon him, Hany's manner was more desperate than hostile. 'We are living in peace here, and we want for nothing,' he implored. 'Who can tell what might lie ahead if we make our presence known? I do not believe we should call attention to ourselves.'

'Come now, Hany, you're not being realistic.' Rassen's response was calm, his tone reasonable, but he hardly dared look at the others, particularly Hala and Massoud, whom he knew shared his incredulity. 'We cannot settle here. We cannot live out our lives on this island.'

'Why? What would be so very wrong in doing just that?' Hany countered, once again on the offensive. 'We are at peace here. We have no enemies on this island.'

Rassen was about to reason further, prepared to choose his words with care, for the man seemed a little unhinged, but strangely enough it was Karim who got in first.

'We have a son,' Karim said, glancing at his wife. Although not having understood every word that had been said, he and Azra had gathered the gist of the conversation. Hany wishes to stay on the island forever, Karim thought, but this would not be right. 'We cannot raise our boy here,' he said quietly, meaning no disrespect, but intending to state his case, which was important. 'Hamid must go to school. He must learn to read and write, he must meet others . . .'

Karim's voice faltered. The sudden hatred he could see in Hany's eyes bewildered him. What had he done to so anger this man who had been his friend?

'Our son must have a life, Hany,' he said by way of summation.

It was all that was needed to tip the Egyptian over the edge.

'Your son must have a *life*,' he snarled as if in accusation. 'Why must our world revolve around *your son*? We have lost all we had and yet we are to serve your interests? *Why*? We are Copts! We are Christians! It is your people who robbed us of all that we loved. It is your people who murdered our family!'

Sanaa turned from her husband, her hands covering her ears trying to block out the sound, but Hany's attack continued relentlessly.

'You believe your son deserves a life, Karim? So did *our* sons! So did *both* our sons! They deserved a life too!'

As he screamed out the words that so vividly brought back the past, Sanaa crumpled to her knees where she remained, silent, defeated, head bowed to the ground.

'Two fine young men, not even twenty.' Hany's voice was cold now as he spelled out the facts; his rage spent, he'd exhausted himself. 'And your people tortured them, murdered them, cut off their heads. So you tell me, Karim, you tell me if you can . . . Why should we care for *your* son?'

He'd finished, and in the silence that followed he looked at his wife, who was now rocking back and forth, softly keening to herself. Beside her knelt the doctor's wife, trying to offer comfort, which Hany knew would be useless. What comfort could be offered a woman who had witnessed her sons' decapitation? What solace was there for a woman who had seen her boys' heads held aloft and paraded down the street? Hany deeply regretted having let his anger get the better of him. For Sanaa's sake.

The others remained silent, taken aback first by Hany's maddened outburst and now even more so by Sanaa's naked anguish.

Hala knelt beside the woman, gently stroking her, aware the action was useless, but needing to offer something. Who could have guessed Sanaa carried such pain? Indefatigable Sanaa, the strongest of us all, she thought. Sanaa who works tirelessly feeding us, looking after us. But perhaps that's why, Hala thought, perhaps she needs the distraction.

Those most affected by the outburst were Karim and Azra, who were in a state of shock. They had not fully understood what Hany had said, the words had been spat out with such speed and venom, but they had registered his hatred and also his accusation.

Karim was the first to break the silence, but he did not address the Egyptian, speaking instead to his wife, and in their Hazaragi tongue.

'Hany says he has lost his two sons, is this so?'

'Yes,' Azra replied, 'this is so.' Her eyes, filled with sorrow, remained fixed upon Sanaa.

'And he accuses us of their deaths, is this also so?'

'Yes. I believe that is what he said.'

'Why? Why does he blame us?'

'I do not know, Karim.' She turned to face him. 'I do not know.'

Massoud, who had understood every word of their exchange, chose this moment to intervene, and while the others quietly watched, he addressed the young Afghani couple in Dari, a Persian dialect that encompassed their own.

'Hany does not accuse you personally,' he explained. 'Hany's anger is directed at the Islamic State militants who murdered his sons.'

Karim and Azra exchanged a look of sheer bewilderment.

'But we are simple Muslims,' Karim said, 'we are not Islamic militants.'

'I know this, Karim, and I know that deep down Hany does also. But he is a Christian whose people have suffered at the hands of the extremists. His outburst of anger was an expression of this, no more.'

'Ah.' Karim and Azra exchanged another glance, which this time said *of course*. They understood now.

Karim turned and addressed Hany in the limited Arabic he had at his command.

'I am sorry for your sons, Hany,' he said. 'I am very, very sorry for your sons.'

Hany nodded, gazing distractedly down at the ground, already regretting his wild accusations. He liked Karim and he knew the Afghani couple were innocent peasants. He'd had no right to turn on them with such ferocity.

'Yes, yes,' he muttered.

But Karim, desperate to make his feelings known, struggled on as best he could.

'We are Hazara,' he beseeched. 'Our people, too, have suffered. The soldiers have hunted and murdered Hazara for many years. It makes no difference that we follow Islam and wish to live in peace, still they kill us.'

'I know.' Hany looked at the younger man, so anxious and imploring, and felt ashamed of his outburst. 'Forgive me, Karim. The jihadists and the militant regimes do not discriminate, this much I do know.' He held out his hand. 'Will you forgive me?'

'Of course. Of course.' Karim eagerly clasped the hand on offer, shaking it vigorously in both of his. 'Yes, yes, of course, Hany, we are friends.'

Hany turned then to his wife, who remained on her knees, no longer keening, but staring dully at nothing, and leaning down he gently raised her to her feet.

'I am sorry, Sanaa,' he said. 'I am sorry, please forgive me.'

Sanaa nodded: of course she forgave him. After all, what was there to forgive? The past would always be there whether they spoke of it or not. But she knew nonetheless that Hany had been wrong. His anger, which always seethed below the surface, should never have been directed at Karim and Azra.

She looked at the young couple, their little boy beside them, and as her eyes met Azra's she saw the sorrow there. Azra too was a mother with a son. Sanaa's eyes signalled an apology.

Azra stepped forwards and embraced the older woman, a bold move for one so shy, but she felt compelled to do so.

Sanaa returned the embrace without hesitation.

Watching, the rest of the group recognised not only the bond between the two women, but the bond shared by them all. There on the island they belonged together. They were each other's salvation.

The moment registered most particularly with Hany. This was why he wanted to stay. Here, being needed by and looking after her new 'family' had given Sanaa a reason to exist. For a long time now he had feared for her sanity, worrying even that she might take her own life. And he blamed himself.

Forty-five-year-old Hany Awad lived with regrets that would remain with him until the day he died. He regretted his decision to take his family from their hometown of al-Awar in southern Egypt to Libya in order to work. It had seemed a good idea at the time. As a plumber he'd earned six times more than he could have made in al-Awar, a whole thirty dollars a day in American money. He regretted also that he'd fobbed off initial warnings from friends that Libya was dangerous. 'We can look after ourselves,' he'd scoffed. 'My sons will join me in the business, we will become rich.' And they had: richer than they could ever have become in al-Awar. He regretted too that, because of this he hadn't left when danger had indeed threatened. But most of all, he regretted that day. That day when he hadn't been there and she'd seen it all. Coptic men and youths rounded up and slaughtered in front of their homes and families. Islamists ridding their land of the infidel! He should have been amongst those slaughtered of course, he should have been beheaded alongside his sons, and at first that too he'd regretted. But if he had been murdered what then would have become of his wife? Hany's ongoing challenge was the preservation of Sanaa's sanity, and in doing so he had preserved his own. They'd fled Libya and he'd made immediate plans to take her to Australia by whatever means possible. His brother and his brother's wife lived in Australia, and his brother and his brother's wife had four children. A ready-made family for Sanaa to look after. Deprived of all she had lived for, Sanaa needed to be needed.

This is what the island has provided, Hany thought watching the women embrace and feeling the empathy surrounding them. The doctor had said it was unrealistic to suppose they could stay there forever, and Hany recognised this fact. But having observed his wife's gradual return to normality, he wished with all his heart that they could.

'We will build the fire,' Rassen announced. The women's embrace over and the moment broken it was time to get back to practicalities, he decided, although he was glad the altercation had ended peaceably. 'And this afternoon I will draw up a roster for the daily watch.'

Aware that they'd all been moved by the exchange and that possibly he sounded a little brusque under the circumstances, he added a further word of advice. 'Given today's sighting, I have no doubt another boat will appear at some stage. We don't know how long it will be before this happens of course, but in the meantime during our stay on this island we will help each other become well and strong.'

He looked about at the group, everyone attentive, everyone respectful of his leadership, and he met all eyes directly singling out no one, although his gaze did linger briefly on his wife.

'We need to heal,' he said, 'all of us.' Then he turned abruptly. 'Come along now, let's get back to lunch. The fire can wait until after we've eaten.'

They followed in his wake as he led the way back to the blue hut.

Hala, dawdling behind the group, was overcome by a powerful mix of admiration and tenderness. 'We need to heal,' he'd said, 'all of us.' As she'd heard those words and as her husband had looked at her, they'd both known it was a confession. For all the strength of his leadership, Rassen too was amongst the damaged, although until this moment he had never acknowledged it. His admission was now there to be read by the others if they wished, but most of all it was an offer of thanks to his wife. And she loved him all the more for it.

CHAPTER FIVE

Hala had decided she was in love with Rassen Khurdaji the very day they'd first met in 1988. Being the honest young woman she was, she'd initially told herself that it may perhaps be infatuation as the doctor's reputation preceded him and she was automatically predisposed to admire such men, but she hadn't expected to find him so physically attractive. It was odd because he wasn't really attractive at all by conventional standards. A little below average height, not muscular in build, mid-thirties and with hair prematurely greying, most girls might have found his appearance rather ordinary. But Hala was not 'most girls' and to her the doctor was anything but ordinary. She was drawn immediately by the fierce intelligence she perceived in eyes, mid-brown, that to others might appear placid, and the fine bones of the clean-shaven face seemed to her stronger in character than the overt masculinity she associated with the majority of men in her home city of Damascus. What most impressed her though was the quiet air of command Dr Khurdaji exuded with no apparent effort. This did not altogether surprise her for he was highly respected by all at Great Ormond Street Hospital for Children, where she'd recently accepted a nursing position. In fact Dr Khurdaji was one of the most respected paediatricians in London, which was the principal reason she had wanted to meet him, and also hopefully to work with him.

Having achieved her aim, young Hala had very quickly concluded that her feelings towards the doctor had nothing whatsoever to do with infatuation, that at the age of twenty-five, and for the first time in her life, she was genuinely in love. It was unfortunate, therefore, that over the ensuing weeks the recipient of her love appeared not to notice her. Something would have to be done about that.

'Do you mind if I join you, Dr Khurdaji?'

It was a fine autumn day and she'd cornered him during his lunch break in nearby Russell Square where, having completed his constitutional round of the gardens, he'd bought himself a sandwich from the café and was sitting on his favourite park bench. A creature of habit, this was his daily routine when the weather allowed; she'd been spying on him for some time now. Occasionally he'd read a book, but for the most part he seemed to enjoy just soaking up the atmosphere. She was glad there was no book in evidence today.

He made no reply, but chewing away at his mouthful of chicken sandwich stared up at her dumbfounded.

'I hope I'm not intruding,' she said, 'but it's such a lovely day I thought I'd have lunch in the park.' She gave a wave of her own café-wrapped sandwich and her can of Diet Coke. 'I quite understand if you prefer to be left alone,' she added with a smile, 'there are plenty of other benches.'

'No, no,' he hastily swallowed and shuffled along to make room for her, 'please do join me,' he said, his face still registering amazement. She had spoken to him in Arabic. This attractive young English girl whom he'd noticed from time to time as he'd done his rounds of the hospital wards had actually spoken to him in Arabic, and like a native. How could this be?

'Thank you.' Hala sat, pleased she'd made an impression, as had been her intention. She was fully aware that he'd presumed she was English.

'How is it that you speak my language?' he asked, continuing the exchange in Arabic.

'Because, like you, I am Syrian,' she said with a nonchalant shrug. 'I was born in Damascus.'

'Really?'

'Yes. My name is *Hala*,' she added with telling emphasis and perhaps just a hint of accusation, 'Hala Faruk.' She'd been introduced to him, along with several other nurses, well over a month earlier and although he'd been pleasant she'd known at the time he was paying little attention so she hardly expected him to recall her surname. But since then she'd been referred to by her first name in his company on numerous occasions. *Hala* is surely a bit of a giveaway, she thought. It's hardly Elizabeth, Mary or Jane.

'Ah.' He nodded as if it was somehow coming back to him, but in truth he couldn't remember ever having heard her name. 'You don't look Syrian,' he said bluntly, taking in the fair hair and grey-blue eyes, although on closer examination he noted her skin was more olive-toned than the creamy complexion of most English girls.

'My mother was from Derbyshire and my father from Damascus,' she said, unwrapping her sandwich, 'has a nice ring to it, don't you think?'

She took a healthy bite and they shared a smile. He liked her directness. The other young nurses and hospital staff were always deferential in his presence, as was to be expected given his seniority, but this girl was bold. Bold without being disrespectful, which was as disarming as it was unusual. But then the situation itself was unusual, wasn't it? Being joined on a park bench in the middle of Bloomsbury by a decidedly English-looking girl who spoke fluent Arabic rather lent itself to boldness, he supposed.

'They met here,' Hala continued after downing a swig of Diet Coke. 'Dad was in London on business and Mum had moved to the city to pursue a career in nursing. It's why I became a nurse myself,' she said, 'and why I came to

London after I qualified.' She took another large bite of her sandwich and chewed away vigorously for a moment or so. He liked, too, the robust way she ate, unlike most English women he'd met who favoured a daintier approach to food.

'Funny, isn't it,' she continued, 'my mother was working at Great Ormond Street when she met my father. Well, they didn't actually meet at the hospital itself,' she said, 'but at a hospital fundraising function. Dad's company has always been involved with philanthropic concerns, particularly those dealing with children's health, so their meeting seemed sort of destined.' She gave a self-deprecating shrug, knowing she was talking too much, but not really caring. 'I grew up with hugely romantic notions about Great Ormond Street, courtesy of my mother. She told me its wonderful history, the fact that J.M. Barrie had gifted the rights of *Peter Pan* to the hospital and all that, but mostly she talked of the part it had played in changing her life. I always knew I was going to come and work here one day myself.' She turned to him with a smile. 'Following in my mother's footsteps, I suppose.'

Rassen was nonplussed. She had not made the statement meaningfully, a passing comment no more, but she'd looked directly at him and in the most personal manner as if the thought amused her. She can't be flirting with me, surely, he thought. Young women never flirt with me – I'm not their type. And besides, I must be a good decade or so older.

'Where did you do your training?' he asked, reverting to English and changing the topic. He felt a little flustered, which was most unlike him.

'The Nursing Institute at the University of Damascus,' she replied, also in English. 'After qualifying I worked for two years at Al Assad University Hospital before coming over here to London.'

'Goodness me, what a coincidence. I graduated from the University of Damascus and served my internship at Al Assad.' His tone was avuncular as he added, 'Many

years before you would have been there of course.' He
took a bite of his forgotten sandwich, no longer flustered
now they were on home ground.

'Did you?' She pretended surprise although she knew his
background; she'd made enquiries. 'Coincidental indeed.
Extraordinarily so, wouldn't you say?'

'Well not really when you think about it,' he replied.
'All six main government-owned hospitals are affiliated
with the university and close to the campus. Most medical
graduates do their training at one or another.'

'Yes, but still coincidental that we both did ours at Al
Assad,' she persisted. This fact, which was true for Hala
never lied, was only one of many coincidences she considered portentous, proving their respective fates were inter-
twined. For a highly practical young woman she could at
times, when it suited her, be surprisingly superstitious.

'And here we are,' she continued, 'working together at
Great Ormond Street Hospital where my mother worked
all those years ago. Another extraordinary coincidence,
wouldn't you agree?'

Rassen wasn't quite sure how to answer. She'd given him
another of those looks that was a mixture of amusement
and secrecy, as if they shared something special. Which,
in a way, he supposed they did. He didn't know why –
perhaps simply because of their mutual background and
language – but he felt somehow that he'd gained an ally.

'Yes, yes, I believe you may be right.'

They exchanged a comradely smile and sat in comfortable silence eating their sandwiches and looking out at
the park. Then, draining the last of her Diet Coke, Hala
looked at her watch.

'Oh dear, I'd better be getting back to work.' She stood.
'It's been so nice talking to you, Dr Khurdaji.'

'It has indeed, Hala.' He stood also, offering his hand.
'And to those who know me, my name is Rassen.'

Their handshake was firm, friendly.

'Good to meet you, Rassen.' She grinned broadly, doing little to disguise her elation. Breakthrough, she thought.

Walking back to the hospital, Hala was visited by a strange sense of déjà vu, as if she had lived this part of her life before. She hadn't of course. This part of her life was simply echoing a part of the life her mother had led. But she fervently hoped hers would continue along a similar path.

It did. She and Rassen were married one year later, exactly the same length of courtship as had been observed between her mother and father. And two years after their marriage she gave birth to a child, just as her mother had.

Hala always remembered that day in the park.

To others, Hala and Rassen Khurdaji appeared as unalike as was humanly possible: he the quiet, scholarly, serious-minded doctor; and she the outspoken, non-conformist nurse, committed to all manner of social activism. But as a pair, they were one, their ideals and beliefs identical. The parents of both being intellectuals, they had been brought up in liberal households with secular beliefs, a fact that in the past had at times caused problems for Hala. Even in a secular city like Damascus, home to a range of faiths and sects, she had met with confrontation from conservative Muslims. And London was no different.

'Why do you not cover your face?' she would be asked. 'Why do you not at least wear a headscarf?'

'Because I will not be labelled,' she would reply. 'I believe it is a woman's choice to wear whatever she wishes.'

'But you profess to be a Muslim, do you not?'

'I profess to be a secular Muslim,' she would insist. 'This is the way I wish to be identified. My religion is not who I am, it is simply my faith.'

Rassen, whose own beliefs had never been challenged, was surprised to find that, following his marriage, he too was occasionally criticised.

'Surely you should insist your wife cover her head,' he would hear now and then.

'She does when in a mosque,' he would mildly reply, 'otherwise neither of us sees any need. Hala is free to wear what she wishes.'

The man who had confronted him – for it was always a man who made such comments – would either shake his head in profound disgust or raise an eyebrow and tut-tut his disapproval. But whatever the reaction and however strongly delivered, it was clear Rassen Khurdaji was considered weak for allowing his wife to commit such outrage.

And here in London of all places, Rassen would think. But of course there are many Muslims living in London, and many of them are conservative. Ah well, he decided, no matter.

Following the completion of his agreed five-year tenure at Great Ormond Street, Rassen and Hala returned to Damascus. They were eager to do so, having missed their homeland and, besides, their son Elias was by now three years old, and it was high time he came to know his family. Both sets of parents had flown over to London for the wedding, but neither had yet met their new grandson.

Upon his return Rassen accepted a position as paediatrician at Children's University Hospital, Hala working there also on a part-time basis while bringing up their son. The reunion not only with family but also old friends, mainly those of Hala's acquaintance, resulted in a far more active social life than Rassen had anticipated. Both maternal and paternal grandparents were only too eager to babysit little Elias, in fact they begged for the privilege, so a pool party at the popular Le Meridien Hotel or a boisterous dinner at one of the colourful restaurants in the Old City was easily encompassed. And then there were the weekends when they, and other couples with young children, would head out of the city for group picnics or visits to amusement parks. The social whirl of their lives seemed to Rassen endless.

'I'm quite aware Damascus has long been a party city,' he remarked drily, 'but my activity of choice was always an occasional visit to the Opera House. Unlike you and your young friends I've never been a particularly social creature. I must say I find it all rather tiring.' In case she thought he was being overly critical, he added with a good-natured and world-weary sigh, 'Ah well, it's probably just the age difference.'

She laughed. 'Don't worry, my darling, this is a flurry of "welcome home" invitations, that's all. Things will die down before long, you wait and see.'

Things took longer to die down than Hala had predicted for she was enjoying her social life. As soon as Elias reached school age, however, she embraced the extra shifts she was able to accept at the hospital and work once again became her priority. Just as her husband was devoted to his vocation, so too was Hala. The medical profession remained, along with the abiding love they shared for their son, a true mutual passion.

Not unsurprisingly, the example set by his parents had a profound influence on young Elias's choice of career. From his earliest teenage years there was just one path the boy was set upon. Elias would become a doctor like his father, and like his father he would specialise in paediatrics.

Their son's career choice proved most fortuitous for Rassen and Hala in the long term. By the time the unrest was at its peak and Syria was on the brink of civil war, twenty-year-old Elias was in England, studying medicine at Oxford University. For this, Rassen and Hala would be forever grateful, particularly suspecting as they did the horrors the future might hold.

Civil unrest had been brewing for a decade, but it was in the early spring of 2011 that the nationwide protests against President Bashar al-Assad's government came to a head. Over the years, the conflict had grown exponentially from mass protests organised by activists in the hope of bringing about democratic reform to an all-out armed rebellion, and upon orders the government's military forces responded violently. It would not be long before the burgeoning fray would include international intervention on a grand scale, creating an ongoing, multi-sided, armed conflict of massive proportion.

Damascus was becoming centre stage in a theatre of war, yet as 2011 rolled into 2012 and the months kept passing the city's hedonists continued their revels as if oblivious to the fact. The pool parties at the ever-popular Le Meridien Hotel were more frenetic than ever, except Le Meridien had undergone two full refurbishments, becoming the Dedeman Hotel and more recently the elegant Dama Rose. The elite still flocked to the popular restaurants in the Old City, most particularly to the Naranj, which took up virtually a half a block and was known to be Assad's personal favourite. Women still rushed to hairdressers in preparation for whatever social event was in store; luxury cars still headed out of the city – along the roads that remained open anyway – to country villas for weekend parties; and wealthy homes still served guests lavish dinners, their tables laden extravagantly with the richest of foods.

All this while not far away those in Hom were dying of starvation; a massacre was taking place in Houla; and refugees were crossing the borders into Lebanon, Turkey and Jordan in frantic search of food for their starving families.

Are the party people of Damascus as oblivious as they appear, Rassen wondered, or are they turning a desperately blind eye? Any enquiry he made resulted in the same answer. 'We don't want our world to change.' But their world had already changed.

Towards the end of 2012, Rassen and Hala answered the urgent call for doctors and medical personnel needed in Aleppo, the most populous city in Syria, where the civil war was reaping the worst of its carnage. Determined to commit to the long term, they sold up their house and belongings in Damascus, deposited the funds in their son's London bank account and left with only the barest of essentials.

The ancient metropolis of Aleppo, roughly three hundred kilometres to the north of Damascus and forty-five kilometres east of the Syrian–Turkish border, had become the scene of house-to-house fighting between rebels and government forces, often in residential areas and therefore causing huge civilian casualties.

When the armed opposition had initiated a series of car bomb attacks on government buildings and had openly executed prominent supporters of Bashar al-Assad, the government forces had retaliated with relentless jet, mortar and artillery bombardment, including the dropping from helicopters or planes of 'barrel bombs'. These improvised explosive devices, consisting of a large metal container filled with high explosives, shrapnel, oil and chemicals, were dropped at random, inflicting shocking wounds. Flesh was shredded from bones, limbs were shattered and massive head-to-toe injuries were suffered by those unfortunate enough to be caught within the bomb's considerable blast radius. All too often these victims were civilians, and all too many of these civilians were children. Already, there were not enough doctors, nurses and medical staff to handle the workload in Aleppo's hospitals. Volunteers were desperately needed.

Upon their arrival in the city, Rassen and Hala took up positions at a hospital in East Aleppo on the southern edge of the Old Quarter, and from that moment on their work did not let up. They'd rented a small tenement in an apartment block not far from the hospital, but as the months passed they found they were rarely there. It was simpler to stay in the hospital's medical facilities, eating and sleeping when they could, remaining close by their work stations ready for each new attack and each new influx of patients, be they government forces, rebel fighters or civilians.

By now, the Syrian army had entrenched itself in the western part of Aleppo, with a military base further to the south, while the rebels had established their stronghold in the eastern part of the city. Between the two was no-man's-land where people lived in a state of siege, fearing every day for their lives as all about them chaos reigned and buildings were razed. The once noble metropolis of Aleppo, including the Old City World Heritage Site with its precious antiquities and its magnificent architecture, ancient and medieval, was being systematically reduced to rubble.

By early 2014 a further complication had come into play, as if the war were not messy enough already. In the rebel-dominated areas of Aleppo, splinter groups had formed and many fighters were changing sides in order to join the forces of ISIS. Those who believed in the Islamic State of Iraq and Syria claimed the purpose of their battle was the enforcement of Sharia. The focus of their attack, therefore, was now upon their fellow rebels rather than the government. The war's madness was spiralling. And more was to follow.

In September of that year, with ISIS in control to the west of Deir Ezzor Province and the border region of Raqa Province, the United States led coalition air strikes inside Syria as part of its military intervention against ISIS and its bid to rid the world of terrorism.

It would be exactly one year later that Russia, a long-time supporter of the Assad government, would mount an air campaign, stating its purpose was also the direct targeting of ISIS and other terrorist groups. The escalating conflict in Syria had gone far beyond civil war.

Over the two years they had been in Aleppo, Rassen and Hala had steeled themselves to the daily horrors that confronted them, but it was difficult, particularly when children were involved. They never spoke of it; there was no point. Their eyes did not even meet when a child's freshly mutilated body was delivered – they simply got on with the task at hand. But Hala knew the helplessness of the situation was taking its toll on her husband. Rassen's entire adult existence had been devoted to the healing of children, making them whole and healthy, not cutting off small limbs or confronting, with such hideous regularity, the deaths of those who had barely known life. She worried for him, and she kept herself as strong as possible for his sake. We will have to leave soon, she decided; he cannot keep going at this physical pace and under this emotional strain.

Having served for as long as he had, Rassen was by now the most senior doctor at the hospital. He had, like so many before him and like so many others working in hospitals throughout Aleppo, adapted to performing operations for which he'd had no formal training. He was now an expert. There was little he couldn't do, simply because there was so much that *had* to be done. They'd all discovered this – doctors, nurses, medical aides, humanitarian volunteers with no specific qualifications – all laboured day and night and were often called upon to improvise under the most appalling conditions. There was a constant shortage of equipment and medication, and at times, in order to avoid another bombing raid, the hospital's lights were turned out and they operated in the beam of a torch. Adding even more to the pressure was the awful knowledge that staff numbers were steadily dwindling as many amongst them were killed or detained or forced to flee. Yet still those remaining worked on.

It was an afternoon in late September 2014 when the rebel leader strode into the hospital, flanked either side by two of his henchmen. A strongly built man in his early forties, neatly bearded, he wore the style of quasi-military uniform that had become the badge of many revolutionary groups: peaked cap, black T-shirt, Kevlar bulletproof vest, khaki trousers and boots. His comrades were similarly attired, although they favoured check shirts beneath their vests, headbands rather than peaked cap and their beards were ill-kempt. All three had AK-47s slung over their shoulder.

'Dr Rassen Khurdaji,' the leader barked, his voice distinctly audible even above the general mayhem of the reception area, where a nurse and a number of orderlies were busily tending to the wounded and dying who lay groaning, some on stretchers and gurneys, others sprawled or curled up in agony on the floor, while the less severely injured squatted against the walls.

'Bring me Dr Rassen Khurdaji.' The man, clearly accustomed to others jumping to his command, appeared not to notice the bedlam surrounding him as he barked his order to the nurse, who was kneeling beside one of the stretchers.

Hala took her time before standing to confront him. She had been checking the vital signs of a young woman, one of the many newly delivered victims of the latest air strike. The woman was dead. With the pen she carried Hala made the requisite mark on the hand of the corpse and stood, signalling two of the orderlies to collect the stretcher.

She turned and faced the rebel leader, meeting his eyes enquiringly, indicating she was not a lackey and wanted more information, but her mind was ticking over at an alarming rate. She'd been unnerved by the man's demand for Rassen. Others had been summoned on occasions, for no apparent reason, and had never returned. But she noted now that the two henchmen either side of the man each carried an unconscious child in his arms. Boys, from what she could see of their dress, and from their size probably around eight and ten years old respectively, although it was difficult to tell, as both children were completely grey, their clothes, their skin all covered in dust. They'd obviously been dragged from the rubble of the recent blast. Hala felt her initial panic subside. It would appear the rebel leader was not on a headhunting mission after all, but seeking medical attention.

'I am told Rassen Khurdaji is a great doctor,' the man said, 'the best in all Aleppo.'

'Dr Khurdaji is the senior physician at this particular hospital,' Hala answered with care, 'there are many fine doctors working throughout Aleppo.' As she continued to meet his gaze, her unease grew. The man, with his strong-boned face and trimmed beard, would have been handsome, but for the unsettling light of madness in his eyes.

'You will tell Dr Khurdaji that Captain Yusuf Khalil, Commander of the East Aleppo Free Syria Contingent, demands to see him.'

For the first time the man's gaze shifted briefly to indicate the children his comrades held in their arms.

Hala turned to the two orderlies who were standing, stretcher in hands, awaiting her command. She nodded and they left with the woman's body and the unspoken but clear instruction to fetch Dr Khurdaji.

So this is Khalil, she thought as she stood silently awaiting the arrival of her husband. She'd heard of Yusuf Khalil from any number of patients she'd treated in the past. Everyone in the region knew of him; his reputation was fearsome. A psychopath, he was known to turn on his own men, shooting them at will should they happen to displease him. No one was safe in Khalil's presence. The two henchmen, now standing eyes front, not daring to move, their sad burdens hanging limply in their arms, attested to this.

Amidst the moaning and groaning and the writhing of bodies, the four stood motionless waiting for the doctor to appear. So did the other three orderlies in attendance. They were volunteer workers, but they too had heard of Yusuf Khalil.

The tension was palpable and as the seconds ticked by Hala's fear for Rassen's safety returned tenfold. But there was little she could do. She could not request the men leave the children in her care – Khalil had demanded to see the doctor and any denial would infuriate him. Besides, the children must be tended to as soon as possible.

She ran her professional eye over the dusty grey forms of the two little boys. She could see no sign of mutilation, but from where she stood she could also see no apparent sign of life. She had witnessed many such bodies, deceptively whole, but with internal organs crushed under the weight of the rubble. She hoped that in this case she was wrong, but she very much doubted it.

'Captain Khalil.' Rassen appeared and crossed directly to the rebel leader, ignoring his wife, making no eye contact at all with Hala. If there was to be trouble he dared not signal any personal link between them. 'I am Dr Khurdaji.'

Khalil gave a curt nod and indicated the children carried by his henchmen. 'These are my sons,' he said. 'They were injured in the bombing: you will heal them.'

Rassen knew at first glance that the boys were dead. His eyes flickered to the men who held them in their arms. Surely these men were aware they bore the bodies of dead children. But the men's eyes did not meet his; instead they continued to stare directly ahead.

Following normal procedure, Rassen checked the children's vital signs, holding the small wrists, waiting in vain to feel their pulses. Then . . .

'I regret to inform you, Captain,' he said quietly, stepping a respectful pace or two back from the rebel leader, 'there is nothing I can do for your sons.'

But Khalil appeared not to hear. 'You will treat these boys and you will make them well.'

'This I cannot do,' Rassen said, again quietly, but with authority. 'These boys are dead.'

'These boys are not dead,' Khalil snapped contemptuously, 'these boys are unconscious. Look,' he indicated each of his sons, 'not a mark upon them, as you can see.'

The man's mad, Rassen thought. 'Their injuries are internal, I'm afraid.'

'You will do your duty, doctor.' Khalil gestured to his henchman, who knelt and, with great care, laid the boys' bodies on the floor, then stood, eyes still front awaiting further orders. 'I will return in one week and my sons will be here to greet me. This is my command.'

'I cannot restore life where there is none, Captain.' Rassen remained respectful, but adamant. 'I cannot bring back the dead.'

It was then the full force of Khalil's insanity was unleashed.

'You dare disobey me!' he screamed. 'You who owe me so much! I fight for you! I fight for your freedom from the accursed Assad and this is my thanks? You would let my sons die?'

With one swift motion, the AK-47 slung over Khalil's shoulder was suddenly in his hands, his eyes focused down its sights, the barrel pointing directly at Rassen's head. 'Do you know what happens to those who disobey me?'

Rassen stood his ground, resisting the urge to close his eyes as he awaited the madman's bullet.

Hala remained frozen, unable to look away as she awaited her husband's execution.

Then the shot rang out. But it was not Rassen who fell. Khalil had infinitesimally shifted his aim, and fifteen metres away, directly behind Rassen by the door to the hospital's main corridor, one of the orderlies, a young United Nations volunteer from France, dropped to the ground dead. A perfect head shot. Within easy range perhaps, but proof nonetheless of Khalil's excellent marksmanship.

'That is what happens to those who disobey me,' he said calmly, slinging the rifle once again over his shoulder. 'That is what will happen to you, my friend.'

The murder of the orderly seemed to have acted as a salve to Khalil's irrational outburst of rage. But the icy threat that followed was equally frightening in its madness.

'If my sons are not here to greet me upon my return in one week, doctor, I will kill you. If my sons die, you will die, and your family too will die. If you attempt to flee I will hunt you down wherever you go: you cannot escape me. I have spies everywhere. My men will find you, and they will find those of your bloodline, and you will all die, be assured of this.'

He signalled his men and spun about on his heels.

'I will see you in one week, doctor,' he called over his shoulder, 'and I shall see my sons standing by your side.'

Khalil strode out of the hospital followed by his two fellow soldiers.

But one of them hung back for a rebellious moment. Stepping towards Rassen, he muttered just one word.

'Run,' he said. The man was not issuing an order, but offering advice. 'Run,' he repeated, before turning and following his comrades at a brisk march.

Rassen and Hala took the rebel soldier's advice. They fled Aleppo, but not before ringing their parents, with whom they had kept in regular touch. Rassen's father had died many years previously, but his mother was still alive, as were Hala's parents.

'You must leave Damascus, all three of you,' Rassen instructed. 'You must go to England. Do not attempt to find us or make contact in any way, it is possible this might put you at risk. We will get in touch through Elias when we believe it is safe.'

They rang their son with the same instructions. There was to be no contact between them and he was to help his grandparents settle upon their arrival.

'Thank God Elias is safely in England,' Rassen said upon completing the call, echoing his wife's sentiments entirely.

Hala's reaction to their predicament was peculiarly ambivalent, however. She feared Yusuf Khalil's threat of retribution as any sane person would, but Rassen's renewed strength she found heartening. For so long now, as he'd struggled on in a state of exhaustion, demoralised by the continuing mutilation and death of Aleppo's children, she had worried for his physical and mental well-being. A fresh purpose was now driving him, and that purpose was the preservation of her life. Initially he had suggested she flee on her own, believing his death would satisfy the madman, but she had refused.

'You heard him, Rassen,' she'd argued. '"If my sons die, you will die, and your family too will die" – that's what he said. I don't doubt for a minute he has contacts throughout Syria and he would find me and kill me. If we are to die, my darling, then we die together.'

Rassen had been galvanised into action from that moment on, just as she had hoped. *Perhaps this is what we needed*, Hala thought. *Perhaps in driving us from Aleppo, Khalil has done us a favour.*

It was only a short distance northwest from Aleppo to the Turkish border, but Rassen decided they would not take that route. Khalil would expect them to do exactly that, he said, and the man was crazy enough to follow them over the border. Hala agreed.

Instead, they made their way south through war-torn Syria, crossing the border into Lebanon, where they settled in Beirut, Rassen having made contact with a long-time colleague who was Chair of the Medical Faculty at the university there.

Professor Abdul Bukhari was quite happy to arrange positions for them both, Rassen as a lecturer and Hala in a secretarial capacity. Furthermore, upon hearing their story of the dead children and of Yusuf Khalil's deranged threat, he organised their employment under false names. Abdul Bukhari himself knew only too well the mayhem and insanity that abounded in Aleppo.

'I'm surprised you both lasted as long as you did, Rassen,' he said. 'Many who volunteered have not returned. If they don't fall victim to the bombs they're killed by these madmen like your Khalil, or so I hear.' The professor, a tall, lean man with a leathery face and laconic manner, gave a shrug that seemed to say it all. 'I don't personally know of him,' he said, 'but the soldiers of the regime, and the rebels, and now ISIS, they're as bad as each other, murderous thugs the lot of them. People have a habit of disappearing in Aleppo.'

'Yes,' Rassen agreed, 'they certainly do.'

'Well you mustn't worry. We'll keep your identity a secret – better to err on the side of caution under such circumstances, I feel – but you're well away from Aleppo and Khalil's lunacy here.'

The professor proved right, or so it seemed, and after one year Rassen and Hala felt it safe to contact Elias. They were relieved to discover their parents had settled happily in England and that their son was delighted to have his grandparents nearby. They were free now, all of them, to keep in regular touch, which they did. Indeed, everything appeared so blissfully resolved that Rassen and Hala planned their return to London. They would reunite with their family and work once again in their true vocation.

'And who knows,' Hala suggested teasingly, 'perhaps even at Great Ormond Street Hospital? How romantic.'

Then, one night, a month before their departure . . .

'You must leave Beirut,' Abdul said. 'You must leave as soon as possible and you must travel as far away as possible.'

It was after dark when Abdul Bukhari called around to the apartment they rented not far from the university campus. They were surprised to see him at such an hour and during a weeknight. Socialising with the professor and his wife was usually an occasional weekend get-together. They were surprised too by his urgency.

'There have been enquiries made at the university for a Dr Rassen Khurdaji,' Abdul explained, 'and I am told also by my staff that there are enquiries being made at hospitals and medical centres throughout Beirut. Rumours abound,' he added ominously.

'What sort of rumours?' Rassen asked.

'Dr Rassen Khurdaji is wanted for the murder of two children who were placed in his care.'

Rassen and Hala stared incredulously at one another. Then after a moment's silence Hala turned back to Abdul.

'But the children were dead,' she said.

'I know. You told me. Nonetheless this Khalil character is spreading the word far and wide that Rassen is wanted for murder.'

'Good God,' Rassen shook his head in disbelief, 'close to eighteen months now, and still he's obsessed. Hasn't anyone been able to convince him his sons were dead when they were pulled from the rubble?'

'If they'd tried they probably didn't live to tell the tale,' Hala said drily. 'You saw how terrified those soldiers were. They were carrying dead children, they must have known that, and yet they didn't dare tell him. Khalil is insane, Rassen. He has sworn an oath to kill you and your family, and he's not going to give up.'

'Hala is right,' Abdul agreed. 'You are not safe, Rassen, you must leave the Middle East. You must travel as far from here as you can and you must sever all links.'

They discussed amongst the three of them the best course of action, Rassen and Hala deciding for their family's sake not to return to London. Irksome as it was, they must once again distance themselves and avoid all contact. They could not afford the risk of a reunion.

'We must somehow *disappear*,' Rassen said, 'but to where?'

Abdul, who had already given the matter some thought, told them about an agency he'd heard of in the city centre, an agency that specialised in helping refugees get to Australia.

'Australia!' Once again Rassen and Hala exchanged an incredulous glance.

'Why not?' A shrug and a laconic smile so typical of the professor. 'It's about as far away as you'll find, and a very nice place I believe.'

Deliberating further on Australia as an option, Abdul advised them it would be useless to apply through official channels. 'It would take forever,' he said, 'and speed is of the essence in your case. Well, it is in most cases,' he added wryly, 'but the Australian government is renowned for acting slowly when it comes to matters of urgency, like life and death.'

Rassen, who knew very little of Australia, did some research on his computer that night, and the following day they visited the agency, where they were told by an extremely knowledgeable young man called Isaac about the great humanitarian Benny Hitono.

'Oh yes,' Isaac assured them, after mapping out the route that would finally take them to the shores of Australia, 'Mr Hitono is a man who really *cares*. He saved his own family in getting them to Australia by boat from Jakarta and ever since then he has dedicated himself to the cause of saving others. Others from all over the world,' he added expansively, 'there are well established routes from many major cities.'

'But I read on the net that "people smugglers" is a term much demonised in Australia,' Rassen argued, 'and that is what we are talking about, is it not, smuggling people into the country?' The young man was well spoken and his manner confident, but there was an element of contradiction, Rassen thought.

'No, no, no.' Isaac airily brushed aside the notion. *People smuggler* was a term he was instructed never to use, and he had his patter down perfectly should it come up in conversation, as it had on occasion. 'That is propaganda from Australian far-right groups, nothing more. Those who wish to keep refugees out of the country defame the reputations of true humanitarians like Mr Hitono. They deliberately vilify these so-called "people smugglers" for their own political purposes.' Isaac's smile was self-assured. 'After all, historically people smugglers have been heroes, haven't they? The term would never have been derogatorily applied to those who helped Jews escape Nazi Germany. Nor would it be applied in any war where resistance fighters smuggle their allies across borders to freedom, would it?'

The young man appeared extremely erudite on the subject so Rassen accepted the argument, which seemed sound enough, but he had a further query prompted by the news report he'd read just the previous night.

'The final and main leg of the journey,' he said, 'the journey by sea from Jakarta, does that not present a problem? I believe the Australian government refuses to accept refugees who arrive by sea. In fact I read a news report stating there is even a policy known as "turn back the boats", and that refugees who attempt to arrive by sea are summarily rejected. How does Mr Hitono propose to overcome such an obstacle?'

Isaac had never been queried quite so precisely in the past, having dealt mostly with desperate people, many of whom were semi-literate, but he was undeterred. There was an answer for everything.

'Ah, the "turn back the boats" policy,' he replied as if it was something that had momentarily skipped his mind. 'Yes that, too, is propaganda. Admittedly from the government, this is true, but merely put out as a deterrent. The Australian government does not wish to appear overly encouraging so they publish such warnings in order to limit the numbers. But of course their coastline is vast, and it is impossible to police all arrivals. Mr Hitono always makes a personal guarantee that his excellent captains and crew will safely land their passengers on Australian soil. Once this has been achieved, the local authorities of course take in the refugees, who are then processed and permitted to stay. Particularly those such as your good self, Dr Khurdaji, and *you also*,' Isaac added with a smile to Hala, who had remained silent throughout. 'Given your excellent qualifications, you would both be welcomed into Australia, I can assure you.'

Did they believe him? It was easier to do so. Easier all round to have a solid plan of action. They believed they'd made the right choice.

They continued to believe this throughout their flight to Indonesia and also during the waiting period when they were settled in a dirty little hotel room in Jakarta. Despite the huge sum of money they'd paid up front, close to twenty thousand American dollars, easily accessible from the sale of their Damascus property, they had no expectations of luxury. 'Beggars can't be choosers,' they'd agreed.

They'd continued to believe in the wisdom of their choice even after their first meeting with Benny Hitono, although they'd recognised immediately the man's cunning.

'You will call me Benny,' the Indonesian had said in his broken but clearly understandable English. 'I get you to Australia safe and sound, no worry,' he'd assured them with a broad grin, pumping their hands effusively. 'My boats they are strong, safe and sound, my captains and crew good seamen, the best.' *Safe and sound* was a phrase Benny liked and had adopted as a mantra.

'More opportunistic than humanitarian,' had been Hala's comment once they were alone.

'Granted,' Rassen replied, 'but we should probably have expected that. Just so long as he can deliver, that's all that matters.'

They worked hard to keep each other's hopes high over the ensuing weeks, during the trip with others by truck to the safe house in Bogor two hours out of Jakarta. And then later, when they were moved, again by trucks, on to the next safe house at Sendang Biru in Malang Province, where they were to await the vessel Benny was arranging. But by then it had become difficult. By then they knew in their hearts they were deluding themselves.

Their fears were justified. Even as they waited at the safe house for news of their departure, Benny was out lining up a local fisherman and boat. The skipper would be paid one thousand American dollars, equivalent to a year's earnings for himself and his two-man crew, a goldmine for any peasant. And the way Benny painted it, the job was simple. The skipper was to transport his passengers to the northwest coast of Australia and land them where they could wade ashore and make their presence known to the local authorities. Then he was to turn around and come home. Easy.

Benny was drumming up as much trade as he could these days, his once lucrative people-smuggling business having taken a dive. For years he'd been recruiting Middle Eastern refugees from his links in Kabul, Damascus, Islamabad and Beirut, but recently people were heading for Europe instead. And not only the 'desperates', as he was wont to call them, but those seeking to improve their economic state, which seemed to him grossly unfair. It was, wasn't it? A principle applied here: the 'desperates' shouldn't have to compete with those whose lives were not at risk. And then of course there was the 'deaths at sea' argument the Australian government put out in order to back up its 'stop the boats' policy. That was a sure killer for business. Of course accidents did happen, which was only to be expected. People accepted that sort of risk when they were fleeing for their lives. Either way, Benny didn't actually care, he'd received all his money by the time the boat set out to sea. What happened after that was hardly his concern.

Benny Hitono was one of those commonly referred to as 'the scum of the earth'.

Rassen and Hala recognised this fact the moment they laid eyes on the old wooden vessel they were being herded towards like sheep. But by then it was too late. Australia had become their destiny. Australia, or death.

CHAPTER SIX

They didn't build their fire that afternoon. Ominous clouds were gathering, and given the threat of rain Rassen decided it safer to collect whatever wood they could find while conditions remained dry.

The women set about gathering kindling, dead bushes for the most part, while Hany and Karim, carrying an axe and a saw respectively, travelled north to hack off several of the drier branches from the mangroves. With the knowledge that timber was in short supply on the island, Rassen and Massoud remained at the settlement scavenging whatever extraneous material they could from the huts; a damaged chair here, some broken fence palings there, odd planks and cuts of wood presumably leftovers from building repairs.

Eventually, between them, they'd amassed a healthy supply, which they stored under cover on the verandah of one of the unoccupied huts, safe from the downpour that threatened. Beneath a canopy of grey cloud, the island landscape was now bleak, drained of all colour and surrounded by a black sea.

The weather did break that night, while they were having dinner. Not an electrical storm, as they might have expected, but rather a deluge of rain that bucketed down upon the hut's tin roof so loudly it drowned out their voices. Amazingly, little Hamid, asleep in the corner of the room, was oblivious to the cacophony, which had he been awake he might have found frightening. The sound was not at all fearsome to the others, however. On the contrary they welcomed it, knowing their water tanks were being filled to the brim. They had been very protective of their fresh water supply and sparing in its use.

No one bothered to speak, there was no point, but minds were running rampant.

Perhaps I'll be able to wash my hair in fresh water, Hala thought longingly. Just the once. It mustn't become a habit.

Sanaa's and Azra's thoughts were along similar lines. Perhaps we'll be able to wash our clothes in fresh water, they were thinking. Not on a regular basis, but perhaps just this once.

Since they'd been on the island, all washing and bathing had been done in sea water, the men carting bucket loads up from the shore to the laundry tubs where the women scrubbed away at the clothes as best they could, despite the fact the last of the soap was gone – not that soap worked particularly well in sea water, they'd discovered. From the healthy yield of blankets and bedspreads and tablecloths at their disposal, they had fashioned rough, kaftan-style garments, tied at the waist with twine or rope, and these they wore, the men also, while their own clothes quickly dried on the lines in the backyards, flapping about in the ever-constant wind. Separate male and female bathing areas had been established too, in small protected bays with white coral sand. Here they washed their bodies in the sea, allowing the women in particular the privacy they needed.

Now, listening to the downpour and feeling the prickliness of their salt-stiffened clothes and the dry itch of salt in their hair and upon their skin, the women could think of nothing more welcome than a thorough cleansing in fresh water.

The men did not ponder such domestic issues. The men merely shared grateful smiles that nature, or fate, or God, or whichever particular power they saw fit to recognise, was so favouring them.

It was Hala who had the bright idea, wondering even as she did why the notion hadn't occurred earlier. Why on earth, she thought, have I been sitting here for the past hour simply listening to the rain? What a terrible waste.

She stood. 'I'm going to have a shower,' she said, 'anyone else interested?'

Massoud was the first to jump to his feet. 'What an excellent idea,' he said.

Rassen laughed as he, too, rose from his chair. How very like my wife, he thought with pride; unconventional, outrageous even, yet eminently sensible.

With the exception of Azra, they all trooped outside, even Jalila who, while fulfilling her duties, continued to remain uninterested in any activity that didn't include the child.

Azra had wanted to join them, but Hala would not allow it.

'No, no, it would be foolish,' she said. Azra's ribs remained painful as they would for some time, but her strength had grown immeasurably over the past week and Hala no longer believed pneumonia to be a danger. There was still her bronchial condition, however, which must be kept under observation. Standing in the rain was hardly a good idea. 'Stay here and keep warm and look after Hamid,' she instructed. 'If he wakes he might be frightened on his own.'

'Yes, yes, of course.' Azra was quick to obey. Nurse Hala was always right.

Out in the blackness of the night, silhouetted by the kerosene lamp light that shone through the hut's windows, they stood in silence, fully clothed, eyes closed, faces upturned to the downpour, relishing the experience, despite the fact that the evening was quite chill. To an outsider they would have looked for all the world as if they were practising a bizarre form of worship, which in a way they were, even the non-believers amongst them. Little more than two weeks earlier they'd been dying from dehydration.

The next day they awoke to find the weather had cleared. The rainstorm had come and gone, the sky was newly washed, and within only an hour or so, as they continued to wander around rugged up in their home-made garments, the sun was steadily drying their clothes, saturated from the previous night.

While the others tended to their customary chores, Rassen spent an hour or so of the morning huddled over the supply of paper and the miscellany of pencils and pens he'd gathered, drawing up a roster for the daily watch.

Then in the afternoon they built their fire.

They chose the location with care, clearing the site, ensuring it was nestled as much out of the wind as was possible, and when they had completed erecting the fire itself, they covered it with a tarpaulin in case of more rain and placed beside it a can of kerosene. All that was needed now was the sight of a ship. Their fire, one of impressive proportion, was ready to be instantly ignited, a beacon that would be seen for miles and could not be ignored.

As they stood back admiring their work, the symbolism was not lost on them. To some, the towering bonfire represented escape; to others, fear and uncertainty, possibly even terror, but there was no denying that, to every single one of them, it signified an end to their life on the island. Be it sooner or later, the fire was bound to lead to their discovery.

Are we ready? Rassen wondered, Hala beside him feeling exactly the same way. Both were aware of the authority they had over the others and it aroused in them a distinctly parental concern. They could sense the vulnerability surrounding them. Even Azra and Karim, for all their desire to lead a normal existence with their son, appeared insecure at the thought of breaking the ties that bonded them to the family they had come to know and trust.

What lies ahead? Rassen asked himself, gazing at the fire they had so painstakingly erected. Are we ready?

He glanced over at Massoud who, upon meeting his eye, responded in a way that was typical. The slightest raise of his eyebrows, the smallest shrug of his shoulders simply said, 'Who knows?'

Were they ready to be discovered? Only one thing was certain. They would not know until they had lit the fire.

But as fate would have it, they did not light the fire. They had no need to announce their presence, nor to seek discovery at all. It was they who were discovered, and surprisingly enough, just the very next day.

Seventy-two-year-old Luigi Panuzza, retired fisherman, still held an amateur fisher's licence. With the two pots he was allowed, he enjoyed supplying fresh rock lobsters for his family and friends. He enjoyed keeping them supplied also with fine table fish: baldchin groper and snapper, the highly sought-after dhufish and even the occasional red emperor. Lou, as he was known by all, was not only an expert fisherman, but very generous with his catch. The truth of the matter was Luigi Panuzza loved the sea. He loved the sea and he loved his boat and he loved everything about the life he'd lived from the age of sixteen, when he started serving as a deckhand aboard his father's professional fishing vessel. And during the past two years, since he'd handed his own business on to his adored young grandson, Paolo, in a deal that was mutually beneficial, he enjoyed even more the freedom of his existence as a recreational fisher. Lou was not only a man of the sea; he was a man with a true zest for life.

Today, he'd been out on the water since dawn, as was often the case when the weather was inviting, and a fine catch sat in the boat's freezer. He could have continued to fish on a lot longer, he knew all the best patches for prize table fish, but he never took more than he needed, so it was time to head home.

Following the previous night's rainstorm, however, the sea was particularly tranquil and he was enjoying cruising around on *Principessa*, taking in the beauty of the day. 'The old Princess', as he referred to her, was getting on in years, but remained a comfortable vessel nonetheless. A thirty-foot hard-chine bondwood boat with a single marine diesel motor, he'd bought her several years previously from another Italian fisher who was upgrading, and she reminded him very much of the vessel he'd started out with himself all those years ago. She was a far cry, certainly, from the fifty-foot *Palermo Miss* he'd handed down to Paolo, complete with twin three-fifty-horsepower Cat diesel motors and a licence for sixty lobster pots. But since his retirement, the old Princess, modest as she was, suited Lou to perfection.

Now, cruising along at a comfortable eleven knots, he decided he'd visit the island. He'd tie up at the jetty and pop ashore, he thought, perhaps even make himself a cup of tea there.

Inside the blue hut, with the exception of Azra, the group was just finishing lunch. Azra had dined earlier than the others as she was allotted the midday watch. Intent upon sharing in all duties, she had insisted she be included in the roster, and Hala had insisted with equal force that she only take part when the weather was fine, only at the warmest time of day, and even then she was to rug herself up against the wind. So having eaten the bowl of rice Sanaa had served up for her, and with a blanket-kaftan obediently over her clothes, Azra had set off for the communal benches several hundred metres from the huts. The site where the benches were situated offered the best views of the surrounding waters and had been elected the official lookout.

Little Hamid gobbled up his final spoonful of rice with relish. Tadig was a favourite of his, particularly with sultanas the way Sanaa cooked it. She'd announced to them that this was the last of the sultanas from the packet they'd discovered, and that they were nearing the end of their rice supply also. All of which was a pity, but with his belly now full Hamid wasn't about to dwell on the fact. He wanted to go outside and play.

He snuck away quietly, convinced that as everyone was still eating no one would notice him go, but of course someone did. Jalila was watching, as she knew Azra would expect her to; the two women had an ongoing understanding. She would venture outside herself shortly and check on Hamid, perhaps play a game with the boy if he wished. She had become very much an aunty figure to him.

Hamid walked down toward the shore, intent upon exploring for more shells and strangely shaped pieces of coral. He had an excellent collection, which he added to daily.

But when he saw the man he came to an abrupt halt, his little jaw dropping, his eyes, large and expressive at the best of times, growing wide in bulbous amazement.

Barely ten metres away, the man was inspecting their dinghy anchored at the shore. He was an old man with a big round stomach and a shock of white hair. Hamid couldn't see his face as he bent over the dinghy.

The boy remained frozen, a tiny comical figure gobsmacked at the sight. Then, unable to contain his curiosity any further . . .

'Hello,' he said loudly, 'who are you?' He spoke instinctively in Arabic rather than his Hazaragi mother tongue. Everyone on the island spoke Arabic, as they had on the boat also and at the halfway houses in Indonesia. Little Hamid, quick to learn, had become even more fluent than his parents in his newly adopted language.

Lou looked up. He, too, was amazed at the sight that met his eyes. A small boy was standing only metres away; he couldn't have been more than three years old. A small *foreign* boy. Where had he come from? Who was with him? Lou was suddenly wary. The child's presence explained the shabby, wooden dinghy, which was certainly not Australian-made. There must be other foreigners here on the island, he thought. Will they be hostile?

'Hello there.' He offered a smile, careful not to scare the child, although the child appeared more curious than frightened. 'Who are you, young fella?' he asked. He'd not understood a word the boy had said, nor even recognised the language he'd spoken.

Hamid didn't understand what the old man was saying either, although he suspected it was English, for he knew the English greeting 'hello'. But he liked the look of the old man's face. It was a jolly face, crinkly and leather-brown with button-black eyes beneath bushy grey eyebrows, and a bushy grey moustache beneath a generous nose.

'How did you get here?' Hamid asked, closely studying the old man's every feature.

'Where did you come from?' It was Lou's turn to enquire.

Neither had any idea that each time they'd communicated they'd asked each other virtually the same question. Then Lou's gaze shifted slightly as he looked beyond the boy's shoulder.

'Hello there,' he called to the figure that had appeared.

Hamid turned. Jalila was standing there.

'Are you the child's mother?' the man queried.

Jalila paused for a moment. Then she shook her head.

Hamid was most impressed. Jalila had understood what the man was saying. The man had asked her a question and she had replied.

'What is your name?' the man asked. No answer. He pushed a little further, very gently, without demand, an enquiry no more. 'What is the boy's name?'

Again she hesitated. Then . . . 'My name is Jalila,' she replied haltingly in English. 'The boy, his name is Hamid.'

'Ah, good, good. Nice to meet you, Jalila; nice to meet you, Hamid.' Lou gave another smile to both, hoping to appear as affable as possible. The girl did not seem frightened in any way, but she was extraordinarily solemn for one so young and beautiful. 'My name is Lou.'

Jalila passed the news on to Hamid. 'His name is Lou,' she said in Arabic.

Hamid gave an enthusiastic nod and grinned back at the friendly old man. Things were becoming very exciting.

'Are there other people here on the island?' Lou asked. What language are they speaking? he wondered. Where have they come from?

'Yes,' Jalila replied.

'Where are they?'

'Come.' She gestured for him to follow, and Lou tentatively obeyed, still wary of what might lie ahead, but determined nonetheless to unravel the mystery. Surely a group travelling with young women and kids would be safe?

As Jalila led the way up to the blue hut, Hamid sped eagerly on ahead. This was now a great adventure and he wanted to be the one to make the announcement.

He did. Most dramatically. Racing through the open door of the hut, where inside Sanaa and Hala were collecting the dishes from the men who remained seated, he came to an immediate halt drawing the instant attention of all.

'There is a man outside,' he proclaimed at the top of his voice. 'He is an old man and his name is Lou, and Jalila has been speaking with him.'

All eyes turned to the door, where Jalila appeared, the man beside her.

Jalila stepped inside first, and then the man followed.

The silence in the room was palpable, everyone, not least of all Lou, in a state of shock, the scene being so unexpected.

Lou wasn't at all sure what he'd anticipated, but it certainly wasn't this. A group was comfortably settled in the hut. Several were dressed in odd kaftan-style garments made from old grey army blankets, the sort left year-round in many of the huts on the island, but apart from that they were gathered about peacefully sharing a meal as if this were their very own home. Thoughts tumbled through his mind. They're refugees, he told himself, they must be, but from where? They look Middle Eastern. The language the girl and the child had been speaking might have been Arabic.

In the unbearable stillness, all eyes upon him awaiting his reaction, no doubt fearing what it might be, Lou couldn't help thinking how vulnerable they looked.

In Rassen's mind was one thought only: We have been discovered.

Then Karim sprang to his feet. 'Azra,' he said, panic in his voice. 'This man must have arrived by boat. She is on the watch – how is it that she did not see him?'

The question rhetorical and fearing for his wife's safety, Karim fled the hut without waiting for an answer, in his haste brushing rudely past the stranger standing by the door, nearly knocking the man over.

Rassen stood, prepared to act as spokesperson for the group, as the group expected of him. He briefly appraised the man, who was older certainly, as the child had said, probably in his seventies, but burly of build, a strong man for his years. To Rassen's eyes, he did not appear of Middle Eastern appearance, rather more Mediterranean. But little Hamid had said Jalila had communicated with him, in which case the man must speak Arabic.

'Welcome to our midst, sir,' he said with respect; stepping forwards he formally offered his hand. 'I am Dr Rassen Khurdaji.'

The man accepted the handshake and returned it firmly, recognising the introduction but clearly not understanding the language.

'My name is Luigi Panuzza,' Lou said, signalling hopefully to Jalila that perhaps she might translate for him. With the exception of one woman, all of the group appeared Middle Eastern, so it may well be the girl was the only one who spoke English. 'But I am not called Luigi,' he said, speaking very slowly in order, hopefully, to be understood. 'Everyone who knows me calls me Lou.'

'Ah.' Rassen cast a brief look to Hala; so their suspicion about Jalila's knowledge of English had been correct. Surprising that it had taken the arrival of the stranger to reveal the truth, he thought; surprising and fortuitous both, for it was surely a healthy sign.

'And I am Rassen,' he said, discarding the formal approach and reverting to English. 'Please do join us, Lou. Take my seat, I insist.' He indicated his own chair, pulled up a spare milk crate for himself, and motioned for Jalila to sit also. Then he began the introductions, giving a little background for each person as he did so, although in Jalila's case it was impossible. They didn't even know her full name, let alone where she came from.

Lou was flabbergasted. Good God, he thought, as he nodded acknowledgement to everyone and shook the men's hands, this bloke speaks better English than I do. He sounds like a Pom, and an upper class one what's more. Lou was aware of his own mangled accent. Beneath the broad Australian twang there remained heavy elements of his Sicilian origins, despite the fact he'd been in the country since the age of ten.

'Would you like some rice?' Hala offered when the introductions were over. 'We have ample left,' she added, gesturing to the serving bowl that still sat on the small table around which their miscellany of chairs and milk crates were circled.

Lou was further taken aback. She sounds like an upper class Pom too, he thought. Well she looks like a Pom and she's married to the doctor, so I suppose it's only fair that she should.

'The dish is very tasty, I can assure you,' Hala said invitingly. Lou seemed a little lost for words.

'Oh yes, that's very kind of you, um . . .'

'Hala,' she reminded him.

'Yes, Hala, thanks, very kind.'

She fetched a fresh bowl and spoon and when she'd served him some rice, they all watched intently as he ate.

Lou scooped up a large mouthful, despite the fact it looked rather dry and unappetising. He was aware that even if he hated the stuff, this was a welcoming gesture of hospitality and that he would have to lie.

He didn't need to.

'Delicious,' he said. The rice wasn't dry at all: it was crunchy on top and moist underneath, with the sweetness of sultanas, a taste and a texture unlike anything he'd eaten. 'This is really, really good. What is it?'

'A Persian dish,' Massoud replied, 'burnt rice, we call it tadig. It is very popular in my home country of Iran.'

As they continued with the niceties, Lou quickly realised that the doctor, his wife and the young man they called Massoud were the only true English speakers in the group. The girl, Jalila, had lapsed into silence and did not even react when the doctor translated for the others. Her knowledge of English was obviously very limited.

Several minutes later, Karim arrived with Azra, who was distraught.

'I am sorry, I am sorry,' she begged, 'please, please forgive me.' She was so distressed that Karim explained the situation on her behalf.

'Azra fell asleep in the sun,' he said apologetically. 'She feels very guilty for failing in her duty.'

'Oh, I do, I do, please forgive me.' She could have attempted to explain the circumstances. She had slept very little the previous night, the awful images of the sea continuing to taunt her, and there on the bench, with the warmth of the sun on her back and the comfortable meal of tadig in her stomach, sleep had stolen over her with such ease. She had no idea how long she'd slept, but Karim had had to shake her in order to awaken her.

Azra made no attempt to explain or to seek excuses, however. She was too riddled with guilt – her dereliction of duty was shameful. 'Please, please forgive me,' she begged.

'There there,' Rassen said briskly, 'calm yourself and sit down, Azra, no harm has been done. See?' He indicated Lou. 'We did not need to light the fire. We have been discovered.'

Rassen introduced Karim and Azra as the parents of little Hamid, and when Lou had finished his rice and they were all drinking cups of black tea, he decided it time to pose the many questions that begged answers. First and foremost, the question that had plagued them above all else.

'Where are we, Lou?' he asked. 'Where is this island?'

'You're forty kilometres off the coast of Western Australia,' Lou said, aware of the instant reaction that followed. Even those who did not speak English had registered the word 'Australia'.

'This island is called Gevaar Island,' he continued, after Rassen had translated the information to the others. 'It's roughly fifty kilometres north of the Wallabi Group of the Houtman Abrolhos Islands.' He could tell this was confusing even for the doctor, who had plainly never heard of the Abrolhos. 'Hang on,' he rose from his seat, 'I'll get my navigation chart from the boat and show you.'

The non-English speakers looked confused as Lou abruptly walked out of the hut, but Rassen explained he was fetching a map from his boat.

'May I go with him and look at his boat?' Hamid asked eagerly.

'Not now,' Rassen replied, 'a little later, perhaps, we'll see.'

But they all ventured from the hut to look out at the vessel where it was tied up at one of the two larger jetties. They couldn't resist. Here, finally, was their contact with the outside world, the new world that would hopefully become theirs. The sight aroused in them a multitude of conflicting emotions as yet impossible to analyse; things were suddenly moving very fast.

When Lou returned with the navigation chart, he spread it out on the small table. After clearing aside the various seats, they all stood around watching as he pointed to their location.

'You're here,' he said.

Everyone peered down at the tiny island barely visible on the chart.

'The closest township is Shoalhaven, here,' he said. 'It's just a small coastal village really, that's where I live. And the closest major city is Geraldton, about a hundred kilometres to the south.' He pointed to another name in larger print a little further down the coastline.

Rassen and Hala were surprised. They had studied a map of Australia prior to embarking on their journey.

'So far south,' Rassen remarked. 'We were told the boat had been headed for somewhere around Broome. I had presumed we were much further north.'

'The storm could have taken us anywhere,' Massoud said.

'True,' Rassen agreed.

'These are the Houtman Abrolhos that I mentioned,' Lou said, tracing the chain of island groups with a broad forefinger, 'and up here,' he stabbed once again at the small island further to the north, 'up here is where we are right now. See the name? Gevaar Island. Funny actually,' he went on, 'everyone who isn't from around these parts pronounces it "Jeevar", but they're wrong. It's a Dutch word meaning danger, and it should be pronounced "hoofire".

We all reckon it's hilarious the way everyone mucks it up. But they do,' he said with a shrug, 'and we don't bother correcting them – it's the way you can tell strangers from locals.'

He gave a brief laugh before continuing in a more serious vein. 'Actually, all of these reef islands are a danger,' he said, sweeping his hand over the general area of the Abrolhos, 'big shipping hazard to the early explorers. Gevaar's not the only name that spells out a warning. The word "Abrolhos" comes from an old Portuguese seafaring term that means "keep your eyes open", or at least that's what they say. Heck of a lot of shipwrecks around these parts,' he said with an ominous shake of his head.

'You see, Rassen, I was right,' Massoud declared triumphantly, 'the perfect spot to lure ships to their doom. What did I tell you? We've been holed up in a pirates' den.'

Rassen flashed him a warning look. Lou was a local and could well find Massoud's attempt at humour insulting. Although did Massoud intend to be funny? As usual it was difficult to tell.

But Lou just laughed. 'Hardly,' he said. 'I don't reckon you'll find many pirates around here.'

Which led Rassen to the next question that had plagued them.

'Who owns these houses,' he asked, 'and why are they deserted? The people who lived in this village, where did they all go?'

'This is a fishers' camp,' Lou explained. 'The fishers themselves own the huts, they pay an annual lease to the Department of Fisheries. I own the green hut just down the path. Well I used to,' he corrected himself, 'my grandson has it now. I retired a few years ago, but I still think of it as mine and use it now and then. We're a pretty close community, all of us fishers.'

'Oh.' Rassen was struck uncharacteristically silent, as were Hala and Massoud, all three exchanging incredulous glances. So this genial man, this man so willing to offer information and be of assistance to them, was actually one of those whose homes they had invaded, whose personal belongings they had ransacked, whose supplies they had stolen. 'I see,' he said finally, as if things now made sense. But he didn't see at all, he was thoroughly mystified.

The others had noted the reaction and their focus was now trained on Rassen, awaiting his translation.

Not unsurprisingly, the general response to the news he imparted was one of great surprise to all, and they were quick to give voice.

'He owns the green house?'

'Why is he not angry?'

'We have looted his home and the homes of his people.'

'We have robbed him and we have robbed his friends.'

'Why does he not hate us?'

Everyone started speaking at once, but when Rassen finally called for silence and the babble died down, Karim demanded to be heard.

'I wish to make an apology,' he said. 'I may do so, Rassen? You will translate the words for me?'

'I will, Karim.'

'Sir . . .' Karim faced Lou squarely, addressing him with the utmost respect. Already he felt guilty for having so rudely pushed past the man in his haste to get to Azra. As a rule he was most respectful toward his elders. 'I have been living in the green house; my wife, and my son also,' he said, speaking very slowly and choosing his words with care, uncertain of his Arabic, hoping he was getting each word right. 'We have been living in the house that is your house.' He looked to Rassen and waited while the doctor translated the sentence faithfully word for word. Then . . . 'We wish for no harm to your house,' he continued, 'but what we do is not right. From my heart, I apologise that we invade your home.'

When Rassen had completed the translation, which the

others, including Rassen himself, recognised really spoke
for them all, they waited in silence for Lou's reply.

'There is no need for apology, Karim,' Lou assured the
young man. 'I hope you have been comfortable in my
house, and I know that my grandson would wish the same.
You and your family are welcome guests in our home.'

Lou knew he was correct in speaking for his grandson.
Paolo will understand, he thought and even if at first he
doesn't, he will listen to me.

As Rassen translated his reply to Karim, however, Lou
pondered the reaction of the other fishers to the invasion
of their huts. Would they be equally embracing of these
poor desperate people? Some will, he thought, those with
an immigrant past anyway. There are others like me. They
will remember.

Lou recalled all too vividly the prejudice he and his
family had encountered as postwar immigrants in the mid-
1950s. Unable to speak English, considered second-class
citizens, his Sicilian parents had been constantly humiliated, and as a ten-year-old he had been mercilessly bullied
at school. Australia was not ready for those perceived as
different back then, he thought.

Now, watching young Karim, who appeared only several
years older than his grandson, hanging on to every word
of the doctor's translation, Lou was touched by the sight.
He was touched by the sight of them all, clinging so dearly
to a word of welcome. How easy it is to be kind, he thought.
Yet there are still many not ready for those they perceive
as different. Australia hasn't really changed all that much.

Karim, nodding and beaming like a happy ten-year-old,
his arm around his wife, was now gabbling some response
in his own language, whatever it was, so Lou offered his
hand and they shook.

When the general reaction had died down, Rassen
continued with his line of questioning.

'Why have the fishermen deserted their homes?' he asked.

'Because of the season,' Lou answered. 'They're lobster fishers, western rock lobster fishers to be precise – a very profitable industry around these parts and a big Australian export trade, particularly to the American market.'

Rassen nodded, the business part made sense, but it didn't explain the deserted huts.

Registering the doctor's need for more information, Lou went on to explain. 'The whole of the Abrolhos, as well as Gevaar, this little island to the north, is a breeding ground for the western rock lobster,' he said, 'so the species needs to be protected. Fishing was once forbidden altogether during the breeding season, but these days fishers are allowed to work on a year-round quota system in order to keep catches under control . . .'

Lou realised things were sounding altogether too complicated and that, even if the doctor understood, it would be impossible to translate to the others in a simple form, so he cut to the chase.

'There are four or five months in the year when the weather conditions aren't the best,' he explained, 'and half the catch has to be thrown back anyway, because it's the breeding season and there are too many spawners, so the fishers return to their homes in Shoalhaven, leaving their huts vacant.'

Rassen was thankful: this was certainly a lot easier. His translation to the others was brief, a mention of poor weather and off-season fishing, no more.

Everyone nodded, content with the explanation.

Given the brevity of the doctor's translation, Lou was left wondering how he might possibly simplify his answers, but the next question requiring an answer of him was easy.

'So I take it we will be discovered when the new lobster season starts and the fishermen return to their huts?'

'Yes.' The direct answer may have been simple, but in actuality the situation was far more complex. You might well be discovered a whole lot earlier, Lou thought, but he didn't go into the details at this point. It would be easier if he could talk to the doctor on a one-to-one basis, he decided. He didn't want to frighten the others.

The following question sealed his decision.

'And what will happen when we are discovered?' Rassen asked. 'I recognise of course that the other fishermen might not be as generous in their welcome as you have been, Lou, which is quite understandable given the fact we have ransacked their homes. But I would like it known that I will make personal reparation to all for the costs incurred. I have the means to do so,' he added when the Australian appeared hesitant. 'I have funds that can be forwarded from my bank account in London, I can assure you of this.'

'Yes, yes, I believe you,' Lou replied, and he did, there was no reason to think otherwise – the doctor was eminently believable.

'So what will happen when we are discovered?' Noting once again the man's hesitation, Rassen repeated his question. 'Will there be trouble from the fishermen?'

'Things are a bit more complicated than just the reaction of the fisher community,' Lou said with care, including Hala and Massoud in his response, flickering a look also to the girl who spoke English, although she did not appear to be following the conversation. 'Maybe we should talk in private,' he suggested, 'it would be easier for you to translate, Rassen.' Lou was painfully aware of the breathless anticipation surrounding them, everyone eager to know what was unfolding.

'Yes, of course, you're right,' Rassen agreed, alerted to the fact the Australian was sending a distinct signal there was news that might alarm the others.

'I'd be happy to deliver any supplies you need between now and when the fishers return to their huts,' Lou prompted. 'Why don't we draw up a list?'

'An excellent idea.' Rassen returned a grateful smile and translated the suggestion to the others, who accepted it unquestioningly. 'We have paper and pencils to hand in the yellow hut,' he said. 'Massoud, perhaps you'd care to join us?'

Massoud nodded, Lou collected his navigational chart and the three of them prepared to leave, Rassen signalling a request to Hala, which she instantly understood. She was to apparently observe the customary female role and allow the men full control, but in actuality she was to remain as a pacifying influence to the others, keeping them unaware of the fact there might be reason for concern. Rassen was thankful when her eyes replied she was prepared to obey. He never quite knew which way his wilful wife might jump.

'We will report back to you all shortly,' he said.

Once settled around the table in the yellow hut, paper and pencils before them, Lou spelt out the facts to Rassen and Massoud. He told them of the regular Coast-watch surveillance flights conducted across the islands on lookout for border protection breaches. The Department of Fisheries vessels, too, he said, made regular trips around the islands, mainly checking on the fishers' properties, it was true, but any sign of illegal immigrants was bound to be immediately reported.

'The Australian government has strict rules about people smugglers and refugees who arrive by boat,' Lou warned. 'It's amazing you lot got this far. They even have a policy called "turn back the boats", so very few make it to the coastline, let alone this far south. Although I do remember some years back, 2013 it was, a boatload of Sri Lankan refugees actually came ashore at Geraldton. It was unheard of, made headline news at the time. Put Gero on the map, even over in the East, and this part of the world doesn't usually get much of a look – in there . . .'

By now Rassen had all but stopped listening. From the outset, everything Lou had said echoed an all-too-frightening familiarity. *People smugglers . . . Turn back the boats . . .* He recalled the questions he'd asked of the

young man at the agency in Beirut and the easy assurance
he'd been offered in return . . . 'Propaganda, no more,
merely put out as a deterrent,' the young man had said.
'Mr Hitono assures us of this.'

'And what is the outcome for those who *do* manage
to arrive by boat,' he asked, 'those like us?' There was
resignation in his voice, already certain of the answer and
anticipating the worst.

'I'm not really sure,' Lou said, 'I mean, I can't be certain.'
He could see the defeat in the doctor's eyes, and he loathed
being the bearer of bad tidings. 'But I don't reckon it's too
good,' he admitted in all honesty. 'The boat people get
sent to camps for processing, I know that much,' he said,
'but what happens from there on . . .' He gave a shrug that
spoke multitudes, at least it did to Rassen. Massoud, for
some reason, was remaining oddly silent.

Rassen didn't push the Australian any further on the
issue, there seemed little point; besides which it would be
demeaning to do so. He could still hear the young man's
sales pitch. '*The local authorities take in the refugees, who
are then processed and permitted to stay.*' He recalled now
that the young man's name had been Isaac. '*Particularly
those such as your good self, Dr Khurdaji. Given your
excellent qualifications, you would be welcomed into
Australia . . .*'

How could we have believed such lies? Rassen wondered.
Because we wanted to, that's why, Hala and I, we both
wanted so much to believe. At least I did. Hala is the more
sensible of us; perhaps in humouring me she was deliberately blinding herself to my stupidity.

He chastised himself for being indulgent and snapped
his mind back to the present and the problems at hand. He
must look after the others.

'There are those among us not yet strong enough to
survive the rigours of a refugee camp,' he said briskly,
'some who need further time to heal.' As he said it, Rassen

was thinking more of Sanaa's emotional vulnerability than
of Azra's broken ribs. 'How long do you think it will be
before we are discovered?'

'By the lobster fishers themselves, several months,
possibly more,' Lou said. 'The fishers here on Gevaar
don't tend to return to their huts during the off-season the
way they do at the Abrolhos. As far as the Coastwatch and
the Fisheries go, that's a different matter altogether: you'd
have to stay in hiding to avoid detection by them.'

Rassen looked to Massoud for a response, surprised that
throughout the exchange he had asked no questions and
offered no input. It was unlike him.

'I'm willing to help you if you wish to remain in hiding,'
Lou said during the brief pause that followed.

'Massoud?' Rassen prompted the young Iranian, who
now proffered a typically nonchalant shrug.

'Whatever you think, Rassen. You always have our best
interests at heart.'

Again Rassen was surprised. The nonchalance may have
been typical, but given Massoud's intellect and enquiring
nature he would have expected more discussion or at least
an opinion of some sort.

'Very well,' he agreed. 'We will accept your offer with
thanks, Lou. What is it we must do to remain hidden?'

'Well for starters we'll have to get rid of that dinghy of
yours. It's a dead giveaway sitting there in the shallows. No
one from around these parts would own a boat like that.'

'But we use it for catching fish,' Rassen said. 'Our daily
catch is our main source of protein.'

'You'll catch plenty of fish from the end of the jetties,'
Lou assured him, 'and I'll deliver you fresh supplies
anyway. Besides which,' he warned, 'when the authorities
do eventually find out you're here, that boat of yours will
make for a whole heap of complications. They won't like
it one bit.'

'Complications? In what way?'

'Big quarantine concerns. They worry about the introduction of diseases, you see. It'd have to be inspected,
fumigated, then it'd probably be towed back to town for
storage over a quarantine period. They did all that to the
vessel that landed at Gero, or so I heard. Best bet is we take
the thing a little way off-shore and sink it.' Lou grinned
in an attempt to lighten the mood. 'There's a graveyard
of wrecks out there, trust me. You can tell them you hit a
reef and swam ashore; nobody's going to disbelieve you.'

'Very well,' Rassen agreed, albeit reluctantly. He did not
relish the prospect of lying, but everything the Australian
was saying appeared to make sense.

'As for the rest,' Lou continued, 'just keep your eyes
open and make yourselves scarce when a boat or a plane
comes anywhere near. You're lucky you landed here
where it's pretty remote and not further south – there's a
lot more activity around the Abrolhos.'

There certainly is, Lou thought, and not only the lobster
fishers. With the aquaculture industry there're operators
coming and going all the time to the pearl farms and
coral farms. This mob'd most likely have been discovered
already if they'd been down there.

'That's about it, I reckon,' he concluded, grabbing
a pencil and getting down to business. 'Now let's start
drawing up a list of the supplies you need.' He remained,
pencil poised over a sheet of paper in readiness.

'Very well, but first we must come to an arrangement
regarding payment,' Rassen said. 'I have cash and can
reimburse you in full. Massoud, you have cash also?'
The two had discussed the fact that their wallets had
survived the storm, tucked securely in the inner pockets of
their coats.

Massoud nodded. 'American dollars,' he said. It was
just the second time he'd spoken during the entire meeting.

'We were advised to bring American money,' Rassen
explained. 'Every country takes US dollars, that's what

they told us. I doubt whether the others in our group will have much cash between them, but I'm quite willing to pay their share. And I'm sure Massoud is willing also to contribute.'

Again Massoud nodded, though he still appeared distracted.

'No, no.' Lou shook his head. 'I can't take your money.'

'But I insist. It is imperative you accept, I will have it no other way –'

The Australian held up a hand. 'No, doctor,' he said firmly, 'you don't understand. Things are not quite that simple. It's not that I can't accept *payment*, I can't accept your *money*.'

Rassen stared blankly back, confused.

'Shoalhaven is a tiny place where everyone knows everyone,' Lou explained patiently. 'They'd all start talking if I went around flashing American dollars, and we can't afford to arouse suspicion.'

'But you could change the notes at the bank, surely, or at a currency exchange.'

Lou laughed outright. 'You obviously don't know small towns, mate. We don't have a bank, we don't have a currency exchange either, and even if we did they'd be the first to spread the news. We have to keep this strictly secret, just between us.'

Lou's argument was valid and offered in absolute earnest, but he would not have accepted payment anyway. The idea of taking money from people in such dire straits was, to Luigi Panuzza, utterly unconscionable. He did, however, recognise the doctor's dilemma. Rassen Khurdaji was a man not accustomed to being indebted to others. 'Don't worry,' he said reassuringly, 'we'll figure out something further down the track,' then he waved the pencil aloft, 'now let's get on with things, shall we.'

Rassen was left with no option but to obey, and they embarked upon their list, starting with the staples of rice

and tinned beans and biscuits and other items that would
keep without the need of refrigeration. He'd buy the bulk
of the supplies in Geraldton, Lou decided, in order to
avoid unnecessary suspicion.

Then, quite unexpectedly, Massoud spoke. 'After the
refugees have been processed at the camp, wherever that
might be, what happens to them?'

The other two looked up, momentarily taken aback;
they'd all but forgotten he was there.

'As I said earlier, I don't really know for sure,' Lou
replied apologetically, hedging a little, loath to be the
harbinger of doom. 'But I believe if genuine refugee status
can't be proved they're returned to their country of origin.
Or at least that's what I've read in the papers.'

Rassen was not at all surprised by the answer. He
acknowledged Lou's response with a polite nod, but
made no reply. We'll face that hurdle when we come to it,
he thought.

Massoud, too, made no reply, lapsing once again into
silence, and the other two returned to their list-making.

After covering tea and coffee and powdered milk,
together with fresh milk for the child, Rassen asked
whether they might include some basic hygiene materials
for medical purposes.

'Nothing that would require a prescription, naturally,'
he said, 'just items like antiseptics, disinfectants, soap?'

'Of course,' Lou replied, scribbling away.

'And I don't suppose,' he added hopefully, 'there would
be any chance of shaving foam and a razor?'

Lou didn't even answer, just smiled and added the items
to the list.

Massoud watched them, but he wasn't listening. His
mind elsewhere, he wasn't even seeing them really. He was
thinking what a fool he'd been for not doing his homework
and following a whim as he had. Just idle chat in a bar had
led him to this. He should have stayed safely in Bangkok.

How do I prove my refugee status? he asked himself. It would be impossible. But I can't go back to Iran. If I do, they will kill me.

Those had been his mother's very words, he recalled.

'You must leave Tehran, Massoud,' his mother had said. 'If you do not, they will kill you.'

He'd thought at the time she was referring to his ongoing activism, which did indeed place him in grave danger. He'd been a pro-democracy activist from way back in his early student days, when he'd devoted himself to the Iranian Green Movement.

His mother had always voiced her concern about his activism, but this time she was referring to something of even greater concern, something she had sensed for a number of years.

'If they do not kill you for the stand you take, my son,' she had said, 'they will kill you for who you are.'

He'd been dumbstruck in his amazement. He'd had no idea she knew.

'You must leave Iran, Massoud, and you must not come back.' She'd wept as she'd embraced him, holding him close. 'I would rather never see you again and know you are alive, my son, than never see you again and know you are dead.'

The moment had moved Massoud himself to tears. It even threatened to do so now in the recalling of it. He had been so sure that, if his mother ever found out, she would disown him.

CHAPTER SEVEN

Massoud Ahmadi had become aware of his homosexuality at the onset of puberty. Around the age of thirteen, when other boys' eyes were turning towards girls, and young male teenage minds were fantasising about the bodies that lay hidden beneath the modest garments of the opposite sex, his thoughts had not strayed along similar paths. Even the covert passing around of illicit Western magazines depicting scantily clad women had failed to interest Massoud. The fact hadn't worried him at the time – he'd simply presumed he was a late developer – until he found himself attracted to a boy. Deeply attracted. A boy newly arrived at his school. He wanted to kiss Rashid. He wanted to run his hands over Rashid's skin and touch Rashid in the area where he wasn't even supposed to touch himself, although he did. He'd like to arouse Rashid, the way he aroused himself, to share the thrilling discovery of their sexuality.

Massoud kept his shameful lust to himself, even avoiding Rashid for fear his feelings might in some way be readable. But it was Rashid he thought about when he masturbated.

Rashid was not the only boyhood crush Massoud would experience. As time passed there were others who aroused such feelings in him. He made no advances, he did not dare, but he refused to be ridden with guilt, accepting rather that this was not some sexual aberration: this was who he was. He was homosexual.

Self-recognition did not stop him from closely guarding his secret, however. To admit to his sexuality would be to court danger on all sides, both from the government and from society in general. Homosexuality was illegal under the religious dictatorship of Iran, those found guilty risking torture and death at the hands of the regime's secret police. The citizens, too, were not tolerant of homosexuals. Young men suspected of 'sexual deviancy' were persecuted, publicly humiliated, and even cast aside by the families to whom they were told they brought shame. Young Massoud kept his secret not only through fear, but also through love. He had no wish to hurt his family.

Massoud Ahmadi grew up in the city of Qom, roughly one hundred and twenty-five kilometres south of Tehran, where his father was a senior shipping clerk at the state-owned Islamic Republic of Iran Railways. Hassan Ahmadi's work involved cargo handling and transition to other destinations, and he, his wife, son and daughter, lived in a modest house in one of the old districts near the old city centre.

Massoud's childhood was a happy one. Qom was a peaceful city, for the most part devoted to religious studies, its seminaries and institutes making it the largest centre for Shia scholarship in the world. As a boy, Massoud never questioned his devout Shia Muslim upbringing, and upon accepting the fact he was homosexual, he still followed the dictates of his faith, convinced that so long as he kept his secret to himself God would understand. As a form of distraction, he eschewed a social life, focusing his full concentration upon his schoolwork instead, which was not a difficult exercise for an intelligent youth with a hunger to learn.

Consumed as he was by his studies, it was no surprise at all to his teachers when he gained a scholarship to the University of Tehran.

'I never doubted for one minute you would succeed, Massoud,' his form master said boastfully. The man was as proud of himself as he was of the boy, for it was he who had insisted Massoud sit for the scholarship. 'You're a fine student and you will go far.'

Hassan Ahmadi was overcome with amazement.

'Just think, Maryam,' he said to his wife, 'our shy little boy is to become a scholar. Who would ever have thought it possible?'

Maryam had simply smiled. She would have thought it quite possible herself. Hadn't Hassad noticed the boy's devotion to his studies? Wasn't he aware of his son's intelligence? She blessed the teacher who had insisted Massoud sit for the test.

'We are so proud of you, my son,' she said. 'But we will miss you. You must promise to come home every single holiday.'

He promised, and in the years that followed he fulfilled his promise, returning faithfully at the end of each term.

It had not been very long before Maryam had started to notice a change in her son.

From the outset, eighteen-year-old Massoud embraced his new life with fervour. He settled into a student boarding house some distance from the university and thoroughly enjoyed the brisk half-hour walk to and from his studies. He loved the anonymity afforded him in the huge, bustling city of Tehran, the feeling that here among the hordes he was unknown, invisible. Despite the fear of the times, and they were most certainly fearful times, he was imbued with a sense of freedom. That he could now raise questions, seek answers, disagree with convention if he wished, dangerous though disagreement might at times be. Massoud's beliefs were becoming decidedly secular, like those of his rebellious fellow students.

The year of his arrival in the capital, 2009, saw the Iranian presidential election, which was held on 12 June,

and the furore that followed was of unbelievable proportion. Official election results declared the dictator,
Mahmoud Ahmadinejad, had won by a landslide, but
followers of Mir Hossein Mousavi, the reformist, pro-
democratic leader, claimed otherwise. The results were
rigged by the Mullahs, they maintained, the whole election
was a sham in order to keep Ahmadinejad in power.
Massive crowds of demonstrators gathered in Tehran,
supporting Mousavi, rejecting religious dictatorship and
calling for freedom. Mass uprisings erupted across the
whole of Iran, growing larger and more heated by the day,
'the biggest unrest since the 1979 revolution,' the global
television network Al Jazeera English claimed.

'Death to the dictator!'

'Give us our votes back!'

'We will not surrender to humiliation!'

'Death to this deceitful government!'

In Tehran City's Azadi Square, the hundreds of thousands of protestors continued to chant their rebellious
slogans, on and on, defiant, insistent. And among them
was Massoud Ahmadi.

Students were among the loudest and strongest of the
regime's dissidents. Young people with strong democratic
beliefs, eager to embrace a new secular society, free of the
dictates of radical Islam.

Massoud joined the Iranian Green Movement, the legion
of Mousavi supporters who, at the behest of their leader,
staged non-violent rallies in public places, sit-ins and demonstrations outside government buildings, all in the hope
that change might be brought about peacefully by the
power of the people. But over time, the 'green revolution'
became far from peaceful as angry throngs of Ahmadinejad supporters attacked the opposition, breaking into the
shops of sympathisers, tearing down signs, starting fires.
Civil unrest grew rife.

The government's response was to send in baton-
wielding riot police on motorbikes to break up the Green

Movement demonstrations. Then followed armed security forces. Shots were fired into mass groups of protesters, many of whom suffered bullet wounds, but who knew how many were dead? *The Huffington Post* reported 'thirty-two deaths to date', but the true number was not determined and never would be. The government censored any form of media supporting the opposition, so how could anyone possibly know?

One death that *was* recorded, and which became news internationally, was that of Mousavi's nephew, Seyed Ali. At a demonstration in late December, Ali Mousavi was shot in the back by security forces. Following his death, protestors gathered outside Ebn-e Sina Hospital, where his body had been taken. They were quickly dispersed with the use of tear gas, after which the government transported the body to an undisclosed location in order to avoid further protests.

In a BBC interview, the official spokesman of Mousavi's campaign abroad revealed that Iranian secret police had called Seyed Ali Mousavi a number of times, saying, 'We will kill you,' and that these calls had taken place only days before he was shot.

The death of Mousavi's activist nephew understandably angered the many hundreds of thousands of campaign supporters, but despite their outrage the green revolution appeared doomed.

Until the Arab Spring.

Following the revolutions in Tunisia, Libya and Egypt, Mousavi and his fellow opposition leaders called for demonstrations to take place on 14 February 2011. Their followers eagerly turned up, and the mass outbreak of Green Movement rallies that day was the largest to take place in Iran for over a year. It seemed to the faithful that perhaps their dream of reformation was still attainable, but their hopes were short-lived. The demonstrations were declared illegal, and pro-government MPs called for the death of Mousavi. However, perhaps fearing the world-wide condemnation that would follow the execution of one so prominent, it was decided instead that Mousavi and his wife were to be placed under house arrest for an indeterminate period.

The dream was over.

The Mullahs' medieval regime was once again in full power, its murderous practices unquestioned by the populace. Or so it would appear. But there remained those brave souls who continued to choose martyrdom over submission. Those who openly maintained their support for the principal opposition group, the People's Mojahedin Organisation of Iran. Those who spoke out against the abuse of human rights – the stoning of women, the public floggings, the gouging of eyes, the amputation of body parts, the mass public hangings – all punishments wrought upon citizens who, either deliberately or inadvertently, disobeyed Islamic rule. The PMOI activists who dared defy the government and openly decry such atrocities con-tinued to suffer unspeakable torture at the hands of the regime. Locked away in Tehran's notorious Evin Prison, declared *mohareb* – 'enemy of God' – the acts perpetrated upon them, sometimes over a period of many months and sometimes over a period of many years, were inde-scribable. Escape was attained only through the final and inevitable event of their hanging, an act for which they had no doubt prayed daily. The hangings took place privately, behind prison walls, in order to avoid any public advertise-ment of their martyrdom, and even in death these heroic men and women were not returned to their loved ones for burial unless the required 'blood money' was paid. If rela-tives did not have the necessary funds, the body was not released to the family, but ignominiously disposed of by the prison authorities.

Massoud and his fellow students were aware of these barbaric practices, just as they were aware of the methodology adopted by the Ministry of Intelligence. Secret police abounded undercover, plain-clothes spies mingling throughout the community, ready to pounce on any suspected of political leanings. The students knew also that they were particularly targeted. Youth and intellectualism formed a dangerous combination for the regime, as it had historically to any dictatorship.

None of this prevented the young activists from developing their own form of rebellion, the ever-present threat of discovery simply driving them underground. Recognising the need for stealth, they exercised caution at all times. Through the use of Facebook, YouTube and Twitter, the bold ones launched a digital campaign, careful always to stay one step ahead, changing identities, protecting their anonymity. Others held secret meetings with those whom they knew they could trust, passing the word on, keeping the hope for change alive.

The less bold, too, had their way of rebelling. Their statements were made a little more safely, it was true, but even so they were definite statements. Given the fact that the wearing of black in mourning for a relative who had been killed by the regime, or even to be seen crying in public over the death of such a relative, was viewed as insubordination and proof of revolutionary leanings, it was imperative everything, even human sentiment, remain hidden. No one dared display any sign that could be interpreted as disobedience. But many youthful Iranians, and most particularly students, while appearing to observe convention, made silent protests. A young man might have a hidden tattoo on his body; a young woman might colour her hair or wear jewellery and makeup beneath her veil. Such actions were rebellious and, shared between like-minded youth, created a bond of defiance.

Of the committed university activists, and there were many, a medical student called Ali Hashimi was without doubt the most reckless. Ali was not only involved on all fronts – the digital campaign, the movement's secret meetings and the recruitment of new members – Ali brazenly wore an earring. Through his pierced left earlobe was a hoop of silver. Modest in size and dull of colour, it was not particularly ostentatious, but it was a declaration nonetheless, a very distinct declaration of who he was. Ali, although discreet enough in the conducting of his private life, was homosexual, and the earring signalled his right to be so.

Ali Hashimi was charismatic. A handsome young man, tall and well built, with an aura of authority and passionate beliefs, he was a born leader. He'd been in the third year of his medical course when Massoud had joined the university and from their first meeting, at a protest rally following the presidential election, Massoud had been lost in admiration. Ali himself had quickly registered a kindred spirit in the young student from Qom, and by the time Massoud had moved on to the second year of his arts course, by then majoring in linguistics, the two had become lovers.

For nineteen-year-old Massoud, the long-awaited recognition and expression of his sexuality had been an overwhelming relief, not only physically, but also psychologically, which was perhaps of even greater importance. At last he could share the truth with another. No longer must he bear alone the secret that would shame his family and alienate him from society. Not unsurprisingly, his newfound liberation had a profound effect on him. The hero worship he'd instinctively felt for Ali upon their first meeting and which had further developed over the months of their friendship suddenly became something much greater. Aware that his feelings were now quite different from the boyhood crushes and sexual fantasies of the past, Massoud was forced to admit he was in love, a fact that he kept very much to himself.

Ali Hashimi's defiance, or bravery, or, as some might have maintained, his downright foolhardiness appeared to know no bounds. His commitment to human justice did not stop with the Green Movement's pro-democratic campaign: he was also a gay rights activist. In a country where the slightest hint of homosexuality could mean torture or death, or most likely both, the gay rights group he led operated in a highly clandestine manner. Their campaign was conducted mainly via the internet, with discussions and articles about discrimination and persecution, the contributors always using false identities, but Ali believed also in human contact. He believed very much in assisting others to abandon the burden of guilt they'd been shouldering for years and 'come out'. Homosexuality was not a sin, he would tell them at the group's secret meetings. They must be true to themselves, and accept their sexual orientation.

'Fuck the government,' he'd declare, 'whatever they say it's no crime to be gay.' Then he'd add with that devilish grin of his, 'But always take care not to flaunt yourself, and stay well clear of the police.'

Sadly, for Massoud anyway, there was just one problem with Ali's charisma. *Everyone* fell in love with him. And Ali was not always able to resist temptation. It was less than a year before Massoud was forced to accept the fact that Ali was not cut out to be a faithful partner – though of course he had never pretended he was. This inescapable reality did little to quell Massoud's love, and nor did it lessen his admiration for the man. He merely accepted, albeit with reluctance, that their relationship had changed. He and Ali Hashimi were no longer lovers; they were good friends with mutual humanitarian and social ideals, and that would have to be enough.

It was. The two continued to work well together on their many causes, including gay rights, and Massoud concentrated upon his studies, which had been sorely neglected while he'd been so besotted.

Over the passing of time, he was careful to hide his feelings whenever Ali embarked upon a fresh affair with a new adoring acolyte, although by now he recognised the fact that Ali basked in adoration and that he had simply been one in a long line of admirers. So what, he chastised himself, that's Ali, he can't help being who he is. But Massoud worried nonetheless – Ali was becoming careless. Heed your own advice, my friend, he thought. '*Always take care not to flaunt yourself*,' remember? You're flirting with danger, Ali. Please, please do take care.

Massoud was right to worry about Ali Hashimi. The inevitable happened one early afternoon in June 2013, and when the news was relayed to the members of the gay rights group, the reaction following their initial dismay was not surprise. In fact, many wondered how he'd got away with all he had for so long. They had always admired his audacity and they would revere his memory, but Ali's death had been a tragedy destined to happen. It was even, they agreed, as if he'd been seeking martyrdom.

Perhaps he had, Massoud thought, leaving the others who were in deep discussion about the fact. He had no desire to dissect Ali's death with them, but was unable to control his own views on the subject. Perhaps Ali *had* wished his death to be a symbol of all he had fought, of the barbaric treatment suffered by those of his kind in Iran. But would he have wished such an end for Reza, his young lover? No, Massoud thought, he would never have wished this hideous death upon Reza, he would have faced his tormentors on his own. It was Ali's carelessness that had led to the death of his lover.

Massoud's assessment was close to the truth, careless-ness had certainly played a part, but it was actually Ali's earring that had led to the death of his lover.

Ali Hashimi and his young companion, Reza Baghar, a second-year university student, had been set upon by four thugs in a busy city street in the middle of the day. The 'thugs' were in fact plain-clothes policemen who had been ordered to make an example of 'the one with the earring'. Ali, now Dr Ali Hashimi and serving his internship at Tehran Hospital, had been under recent surveillance by the secret police. They had no concrete proof, it was true, but he was suspected of being a political agitator, and also a homosexual. The earring, an obvious badge of his depravity, made him easily identifiable to those obeying orders from the Ministry of Intelligence.

The two young men had been bludgeoned with clubs and then dragged to the rooftop of a nearby four-storey building block from where, nooses around necks, they had been flung over the side and crudely hanged. The police had decided to include the younger man simply because, as he was in the company of the homosexual with the earring, it was only to be presumed that he, too, was a homosexual. An example could therefore be made of the two. They would be left dangling from the building, where their bodies would serve as a warning to other sexual deviants, and to any sympathisers or family members who might harbour such degenerates.

Things went according to plan with Reza Baghar's execution, although his end was not quick. Barely nineteen years of age and a slightly built young man, Reza suffocated to death, his body kicking and jerking on the end of the rope. When it was finally over, he was left successfully dangling there to serve the intended warning.

Ali's death was much quicker, though not as successful in its purpose. Ali Hashimi was a bigger man than his companion, taller, more muscular and heavier of build. Thrown from the roof as he was with such vigour, having put up a fight until the bitter end, the snap of the rope broke his neck certainly, but with such force he was decapitated. Body and head fell separately to the pavement below, and only the rope was left dangling.

Following Ali's death, the gay rights group he'd led quickly disintegrated, perhaps through fear, perhaps through lack of leadership, but only Massoud and two other loyal stalwarts remained to carry on the fight.

Massoud himself assumed the mantle of leader, determined that his friend's death must serve a purpose. If Ali had chosen the path of martyrdom then the world should know the gruesome facts. The rest of humanity must be informed that this was the level of persecution suffered by Iran's homosexual population.

Pictures had been taken of the bodies, pictures naturally for publication only within Iran; like all public tortures and hangings and mutilations, such images were intended as a lesson to those who disobeyed the regime.

Flaunting the government's strict censorship laws, Massoud wrote a detailed account of the event and he and his two colleagues posted it with the pictures on the internet, ensuring they reached a far wider audience.

The article and its accompanying images created a furore. True, the pictures themselves were quickly removed, considered too gruesome for general viewing, but the story about the hideous murders of the two young Iranians, purely upon the grounds of their homosexuality, was widely read on the net and appeared in newspapers throughout the Western world. People were appalled. Average people in the street. Americans, English, Australians – they'd had no idea this was going on.

Massoud was gratified. It won't change things of course, he thought with resignation, the atrocities will continue. But perhaps Ali's and poor young Reza's deaths have served a purpose after all. They've certainly set the world talking.

With the international publishing of the story, the gay rights group disbanded altogether, quickly destroying any evidence that might lead to them. The Ministry of Intelligence was after blood and there were undercover spies everywhere. Ali Hashimi was known to have been a recent graduate of Tehran University, so they would all be under investigation.

Massoud completed his Master's degree later that same year and left university, returning to the comparative safety of Qom and his family. But he still feared the police would come after him. There were many at the university who would recall his friendship with Ali. If hard-pressed enough, there would be fingers pointed in his direction. And who could blame them? Everyone had their breaking point.

He'd admitted his concerns to his mother, who knew of his activism, and that's when she had told him in no uncertain terms that he must leave Iran, and that he must never return.

'If they do not kill you for the stand you take, my son,' she had said, 'they will kill you for who you are.'

Massoud took his mother's advice, but he did not cross the border into Iraq as many Iranian dissidents had done in the past. The situation there had become too dangerous. ISIS was increasingly targeting those known activists housed in the Iraqi refugee camps; the regime and ISIS had a great deal in common. Iraq was no longer safe for the likes of Massoud Ahmadi.

He headed south instead, to another world altogether. He'd been informed by fellow activists that visitors' visas from Iran into Thailand were relatively easy to acquire. A flaw in the system, perhaps? Thankful to discover they were right, he flew to Bangkok.

Shortly after his arrival, he settled into a small apartment not far from Sukhumvit Road, the city's main commercial street. He advertised in a local Arabic paper and steadily gained employment teaching English from home.

Work was slow to start with, but word soon spread and he found himself becoming quite selective in his choice of pupils. The children and wives of wealthy Middle Eastern businessmen who'd settled in Bangkok; overseas students who wanted to get ahead with extra tuition and whose parents were willing to pay the price: within a year or so

Massoud was doing very well for himself. But he wasn't particularly happy. A stranger in this city, he didn't feel he belonged.

He made several new friends, particularly amongst his students, and even had a casual affair with a local young man. Sirawit worked as an assistant concierge at the Sheraton Grande Hotel and was keen to improve his English in order to move up in the ranks of the hospitality industry. It was Sirawit who introduced Massoud to the city's gay bars, which he initially found most confronting.

How can people expose themselves publicly in such a way? he'd wondered as he'd sat at the Balcony Bar in Soi 4, Silom, watching two men standing affectionately together, their arms around each other. Sirawit had been quick to assure him there was no public condemnation of such behaviour.

'Thai people is good people, Massoud,' he had said in his broken English. 'Gay, straight, here no matter. Thai people is . . .' He struggled for the word.

'Tolerant?' Massoud suggested.

'Yes, yes,' Sirawit smiled happily, 'tolerant. Is good word, tolerant. In Thailand you be who you want. People no care.'

Massoud welcomed the news, but the gay nightclubs and dance venues Sirawit favoured in Soi 2, the more salacious area of Silom, remained altogether too confronting for him. He had no wish to pick up strangers for sex, nor to be approached himself.

However, when his affair with Sirawit ended, as it was destined to, Massoud found himself still visiting the occasional gay bar. Why? He wasn't sure. He wasn't seeking an affair. But it was there he met the Australian. And it was the Australian who, within just two short weeks, changed the course of his life.

Stanley Pearce was thirty years old and a typical Aussie. At least he appeared to Massoud everything one would expect a typical Aussie to be. Not that Massoud had been aware of the term itself – 'Aussie' was an expression he learnt from Stan during their brief time together. But had he given the matter any thought, he would probably have expected all Australian men to look like this – tall, lean, sun-bleached sandy hair, piercing blue eyes, rather like the surfie images one saw on the internet.

'Mind if I join you?' Stan had asked, which had rather surprised Massoud, as the man didn't appear in the least gay, and there were several empty tables. But of course the bar was in Silom, so he presumed the man would have to be gay and that this was an attempt at a pick up.

'Of course, please do,' he replied politely, but also a little circumspectly, careful not to appear too inviting.

Plonking his beer on the table, Stan sat. They introduced themselves, shook hands and then the Australian launched into a one-sided conversation, possibly because he sensed Massoud's reservation and wanted to relax him. In any event he proved very pleasant.

'I'm from Sydney, just arrived,' he said, 'off on the first leg of my big trip abroad. Thailand for two weeks, then Vietnam, Cambodia, Myanmar, a fortnight in each place, a whole two months, flights all booked, but just travelling around, seeing the sights . . .' A quick swig of his beer. 'Looking forward to it, I must say, never been further afield than New Zealand. Too busy working. Too many responsibilities.' A likeable grin that seemed somehow meaningful. 'Free of all that now. Time to play.'

The Australian spoke in a form of shorthand, in energetic bursts, but now as he paused to take a more leisurely sip of his beer, Massoud felt some sort of reply might be required of him.

'Free of all what?' he asked.

'Marriage,' came the surprising answer, 'busted up with my wife.'

'Oh.' Massoud didn't know what to say.

Again the disarming smile. 'Should have happened years ago. When I finally admitted to myself that I batted for the other side.' Then, in all seriousness, 'Bit unfair on my wife, I know, but I was in denial. Becoming a partner in my dad's building business, wanting to be like him and like all my straight mates . . . You know how it is.'

Massoud managed a nod.

'Oh well. At least we didn't have any kids, and Jan's only twenty-six, plenty of time for her to find the right bloke. That's how I see it anyway.' Stan skolled the rest of his beer and stood. 'Knock that back and I'll get you another one,' he said, gesturing at Massoud's half-empty glass.

The offer was made with such bonhomie that Massoud nodded once again, said 'thank you' and obediently drained his glass.

When Stan returned from the bar, he settled himself, they clinked glasses, and then . . . 'So tell me about yourself, Massoud,' he said. 'You're obviously not a local, and I heard you ordering your beer at the bar in English, so I'm curious. Where you from? What you doing in Bangkok?'

Given the Australian's frank account of his own background, Massoud did not find the questions intrusive, recognising they sprang from a genuine interest. He didn't go into great detail in his response, but he did tell his story, succinctly, just the bare bones, and he enjoyed the freedom he found in the telling. He was from Iran, he said, where being gay was a crime. He'd belonged to an underground group of gay activists when he was at university in Tehran.

'The group's leader was a good friend of mine,' he said. 'He and his partner were murdered a couple of years ago. Bashed and hanged from the rooftop of a building.' Then he added cynically, 'It's not easy being gay in Iran.'

'Hey, hang on,' Stan said, 'I read about that. Bloody terrible. It was in all the papers back home. Sydney's the gay capital of Australia, and there was a hell of a reaction in the gay community, at least so I read. I was still married then,' he admitted a little shamefacedly, 'so I wasn't a part of it, but they're a very politically minded mob in Sydney, and they put on a right song and dance. There were posters all around the place and demonstrations of support outside parliament for gay rights in Iran, the works.'

'I'm very glad to hear it.'

That was how Massoud's two-week affair with the Australian started.

Stan had intended to travel around Thailand for the fortnight of his stay before flying on to Saigon, but he didn't. He remained in Bangkok instead. It was an affair and nothing more, they both knew that, and there was no suggestion from either that he consider changing his plans. But they very much enjoyed each other's company and were reluctant to part.

'You ought to come and live in Australia, mate,' Stan said, 'you'd love it. Particularly Sydney. It's a great city. Like I said, the gay capital of the country. You should just see it at Mardi Gras,' he rolled his eyes comically, 'I wonder what your regime back home'd have to say about that!'

Massoud laughed. The thought of Mardi Gras didn't particularly attract him, a little too ostentatious for his liking, but Stan had painted beautiful pictures of his home-land and the freedom of lifestyle that prevailed there.

'Perhaps I'll pay a visit,' he said. 'Some day,' he added with a shrug that suggested the prospect was highly unlikely.

By now Stan knew the full story of Massoud's back-ground, they'd talked a great deal about their respective lives over the past fortnight, and an idea suddenly struck him.

'You'd probably qualify for refugee status, you know.' The thought hadn't occurred before, but right now it appeared an excellent suggestion.

'I very much doubt it.' Massoud's reply was dismissive. 'I'm safe here in Bangkok, I'm not exactly on the run.'

'Bullshit. Of course you are,' Stan vehemently disagreed. 'You're here in order to escape, aren't you? I mean you're just marking time. You're not settled! You can't go home! If you go back to Iran they'll kill you, Massoud. You're a man without a home! Hell, I don't know about you, mate, but that sounds pretty much like refugee status to me.'

'We'll see,' Massoud replied amicably enough, but he was calling a definite halt to the conversation, which he felt was becoming altogether too fanciful. 'I'll give the matter some thought,' he said. He wouldn't.

'I hope you will.' Stan returned a good-natured smile, aware he was being told to back off. But he had the last word nonetheless. 'I'd like to see you again, Massoud. I really mean that. You'd do well in Australia, too. I know you would.'

They'd already exchanged their contact details. They now said their goodbyes, and that was that.

But in the weeks that followed, the words of the Australian kept returning to Massoud and he did give the matter some thought. Everything Stan had said was slowly starting to make an impact. I *am* marking time here, he thought. I'm *not* settled . . . I *can't* go back to my homeland . . .

He chastised himself. Wishful thinking: that's all it was. You're lonely in Bangkok, he told himself. You've just had a brief affair with a very nice man and you're lonely, that's all it is. Stop romanticising.

But it was actually Stan's parting words that continued to impact most of all. '*I'd like to see you again, Massoud. I really mean that. You'd do well in Australia, too. I know you would.*' Simple words, very simple, but had they been said with a special meaning? It had certainly sounded that way. Massoud couldn't fool himself any longer. He was more than lonely. He longed for a partner in his life, and brief though his affair with the Australian had been, he hadn't felt that way about anyone since Ali. Of course it's a case of wishful thinking, he told himself, but what's wrong with checking things out? There's nothing here for me in Bangkok.

His enquiries led to exactly the dead end he'd expected. Any application he were to make to the Australian government for refugee status would take possibly years to process, even if it was accepted in the first place, and particularly as he was under no immediate threat.

Ah well, he told himself, end of story.

Then a month or so later another chat in another bar. A passing conversation, no more. About Australia. Hearing of a man's cousin, a refugee, who'd made the trip from Indonesia by boat. The name Benny Hitono had cropped up.

Why does every life-changing prospect seem to start in a bar? Massoud wondered. I never even drank in the old days. But on a whim, he decided to seek further information. A move from Bangkok would do him good anyway. He was unhappy stagnating there, and a trip to Indonesia would be an adventure, even if nothing eventuated.

During his meeting at the agency in Jakarta, when he'd been told that, along with other refugees, he would be safely delivered by boat to the shores of Australia, he did think to ask one sensible question.

'And upon arrival,' he enquired, 'after we've landed? What happens to the refugees then?'

'Community detention,' came the airy reply. 'While applications are being processed those seeking asylum live within the community. It's all very civilised. Refugees are allowed to move about freely, and the application process doesn't take long. Mr Hitono assures us of this.'

How easy it had all sounded.

'Massoud, do you want to add anything to the list at this stage?'

Rassen and Lou were both looking questioningly at him, Rassen obviously puzzled by his lack of input.

'No,' he replied, 'not at this stage, no thanks.'

'Right.' Rassen stood. 'Let's join the others and tell them our plans.'

Massoud rose automatically to his feet, his mind still preoccupied. And now here I am in this mess, he thought, probably to be sent back to Iran. All my own fault. What a fool I was, following a whim and a tissue of lies. No, not lies. What would Stan call it? Bullshit. That's right. Bullshit. How dumb am I!

He followed the men from the hut.

CHAPTER EIGHT

There was a degree of relief for the others when, once again seated together in the blue hut, Rassen explained they would remain on the island for at least several more months until the fishermen returned.

'We will use this time to grow strong,' he said, 'and to prepare ourselves for whatever may lie ahead.' He made no hint as to what that might be. How could he? He didn't really know himself. We'll find out in good time, he thought. All of us. There's nothing to be gained by instilling fear at this stage.

'Lou says the first thing we must do is destroy the boat.'

Some consternation followed this announcement, particularly from Hany and Karim, but Rassen ignored the interruption and went on to explain that they were now in hiding. The boat was a telltale sign of their presence, he told them, and furthermore upon their eventual discovery would cause delays and quarantine complications for the authorities.

The group accepted the reasoning behind the decision, with the exception of the young Afghani couple, Karim and Azra, who appeared a little confused. The doctor had spoken more briskly than usual and they'd had trouble understanding some of the words he'd said.

Recognising the problem, Massoud intervened and spoke to them in Dari, explaining the situation.

Rassen waited until he'd finished. Then 'I think we'd all agree it is wise we cause as little trouble as possible,' he said, this time speaking slowly and simply. 'Although I must warn you that in destroying the boat we will unfortunately need to lie.' He explained Lou's plan and the concocted story about their hitting a reef and swimming ashore. 'We will practise this story together so there are no conflicting views when the time comes.'

'But what about our fishing?' Hany demanded with a look to Karim, who nodded vigorously. 'We need the boat to catch fish.'

'Lou says the boat is not necessary, that we can catch fish from the jetties, and there is no reason to doubt him. As you know, we are already in his debt for all the helpful advice he has offered. But I must tell you, my friends, he now offers a great deal more than advice. Lou has become our most valuable ally.'

Rassen turned to the Australian, who had not seated himself, but remained standing near the door, patiently waiting for the translation to come to an end.

'Lou has agreed to keep our secret for as long as is possible. He has also very kindly offered to supply us regularly with fresh provisions.'

All heads had turned to the figure at the door, all eyes now focused on the burly Australian. Everyone was mystified. Why, they were thinking, why would this man be so good to us? What have we done to earn such kindness?

Lou had no idea why the refugees were all staring at him in such a puzzled fashion, but he gave a nod and a smile and a wave. Perhaps they just needed a bit of reassurance.

Returning to practicalities, Rassen took the sheet of paper and pencil from his shirt pocket. 'To this end,' he continued, 'we have drawn up a list of items. I shall read them out to you and if you have any further ideas, within reason of course, I shall add them to those noted.'

At the appearance of the paper and pencil, Lou gathered the basics had now been covered and that they were going to discuss the list.

'Why don't we scuttle the boat first, Rassen?' he suggested. 'It's high tide right now, which'll make things
easier, and the sooner she goes the better.'

'Ah. Yes, of course, an excellent idea.' Rassen rose
dutifully to his feet, then paused. 'How exactly do we go
about it?'

'We tow her out and pull the bung,' Lou said in a tone
that implied *of course*. 'We'll do her a bit of damage as well
though, so she goes down quickly before wind and tide
take her. Perhaps one of your strong young men could row
the dinghy out to my boat.' He looked at Hany and Karim.
He could remember Karim's name, but what was the name
of the Egyptian bloke? 'And we'll need to fetch an axe.'
These foreign names are so damn hard to remember, he
thought, I must get Rassen to write me a list of who's who.

When Rassen had translated the instructions, Hany and
Karim jumped up, eager to obey.

'Tell them they'll find an axe in my hut,' Lou said.

'Yes, we know,' Rassen smiled apologetically, 'we've
already had a great deal of use out of it.'

'Oh good, good, that's good.'

Karim fetched the axe while Hany set off to row the
dinghy out to the boat.

As the others all walked down to meet up with him at
the end of the jetty, Karim with the axe slung over his
shoulder, little Hamid jumped about excitedly. His father
was going out on the old man's boat. It was a pretty boat,
white with red trim and a cabin in the middle. Much
prettier than the boat they had boarded in Indonesia.

'Can I come too?' he begged. 'Please, please, can I come
too?' Unlike his mother, the sea held no fear for Hamid.
His near-death, semi-conscious state had proved merciful,
for he had no memory of the storm and the shipwreck and
all that had followed.

On a signal from Karim, Rassen made the request. 'The
boy would like to join us, Lou, would that be all right?'

'Of course, of course, Hamid,' Lou said with a nod and the broadest of smiles to the child; he well remembered Hamid's name. 'You're more than welcome to join us, mate, more than welcome.'

Hamid's elation knew no bounds.

Rassen, Hany and Karim, together with the child, boarded the vessel and the others stood watching from the end of the jetty as the dinghy was towed out to sea.

'What is this boat called?' Hamid asked the old man.

'She is called *Principessa*,' Lou replied.

Rassen translated their exchanges word for word, and as he did he was amused by the way the child and the Australian spoke directly to one another, not referring to him at all. Even while they paused to absorb the meaning of what had been said they remained focused upon each other. Their conversation seemed unimpeded by language differences, just a little boy and an old man making contact.

'*Principessa* means "princess" in Italian,' Lou explained, 'but I call her "the old Princess", because she is no longer young.'

'She is not young,' Hamid said solemnly, 'but she is beautiful.'

'Oh yes, she's beautiful all right,' Lou agreed. 'A grand old girl of the sea.'

'I like her very much.'

'Then I shall take you out for a ride in her again, Hamid. Would you enjoy that?'

'Oh yes,' face beaming, eyes eager, 'I would enjoy that very much.'

Rassen and Karim, who had been closely following his son's conversation, shared a smile.

They circled the area for a further ten minutes or so, Lou searching for an ideal shallow reef a swimmable distance from the shore.

'About here'll do,' he announced, putting the engine into neutral. 'Your dinghy could have struck that reef there,' he gestured to the breakers barely twenty metres away, 'and she'd have gone down around this spot. She'll stay out of sight: it's a good four fathoms or so here even at low tide.'

Watching from the jetty, the others saw Karim climb into the dinghy and hack about with the axe. Then as the boat started to founder, he clambered back aboard the larger vessel and the tow rope was released.

Lou didn't steer *Principessa* clear, but kept her engine idling in neutral as he observed the sinking of the dinghy, checking it was going straight down and not being swept away by the current. But the process was proving speedy, efficient, all according to plan.

'Good job,' he said with a nod to Karim, 'well done.'

Azra, watching along with the others from the end of the jetty, had found the image acutely symbolic. Seeing her husband wield the axe, personally bringing about the destruction of the dinghy. In destroying the dinghy Karim was destroying the very threat to his life. And after he'd climbed back aboard the larger vessel, she'd continued to watch the dinghy, transfixed as it entered its death throes. *He is saved*, she thought, *we are both saved. No longer will Karim be at the mercy of the sea.* She gave thanks to Allah as the waves claimed their victim and the fearful dinghy was gone forever.

'We'd never have been able to make that distance,' Massoud muttered to Hala in English. 'That's at least four hundred metres, more likely five, and most of us can barely swim.'

She raised a whimsical eyebrow in reply. 'Do you think when they find us they'll put us to the test?'

'No.' He returned a wry smile. 'No, I think they'll have far more on their minds than the credibility of our story.'

Massoud wondered whether Rassen would share with his wife the bleak expectations they'd gleaned from their meeting with Lou. Yes, the good doctor is bound to tell her, he thought, they share everything those two. How very lucky they are.

When *Principessa* had been returned to her berth at the end of the jetty, Lou gave the group the whole of his day's catch of fish, together with several lobsters.

'Have to save a few of those for mates,' he said apologetically as he doled out only half of the lobsters. 'I'm on a promise.'

'The whole of your catch!' Rassen declared in amazement as the Australian methodically lifted the fish from the boat's freezer and placed them one by one into a large polystyrene container. 'You can't do that!'

'Why not? I'll be out at dawn tomorrow, and I'll catch the same amount all over again. It's what I do, Rassen. What I love to do,' he said, his weathered face wreathed in a happy grin. 'You can retire an old fisher, mate, but you can't stop him fishing.'

Back ashore, while Hany and Karim set about scaling and gutting the catch, the others returned to the hut, where Rassen read out the list and, upon invitation, several further requests were put to Lou.

'We have very little cooking oil left,' Sanaa said to Rassen, 'and virtually no sugar.'

Rassen translated, Lou nodded, and oil and sugar were added to the list.

'Could we perhaps find some cough medicine for Azra?' Hala spoke directly to Lou. 'Nothing requiring a prescription of course, just an expectorant mixture or a eucalyptus-oil inhalant – something to help break up her chest cough?'

'Of course.' Lou gave another nod and Rassen added it to the list.

'And . . .' She hesitated, reluctant to make a further request that would surely sound not only trivial but selfish. 'I don't suppose . . .' Her voice tailed off.

'Come on, Hala, what is it?' Rassen urged.

'It sounds terrible of me, I know, but would there be any possible chance of shampoo? Just a small bottle,' she added hastily, 'that we could share, and use very sparingly?' She glanced at the other women as if hoping for backup, but of course they hadn't understood what she'd said.

Rassen laughed out loud at his wife's timidity, something rarely witnessed. 'You can but ask, my dear,' he said. 'I've already put in a bid for shaving foam and a razor myself.'

'Shampoo it is,' Lou agreed, 'and what about young Hamid here, does he have any special request?'

Upon being asked by Rassen, Hamid's response was immediate.

'Sultanas,' he said, 'sultanas to go in the tadig.'

When shampoo and sultanas had been added to the list, no other requests were forthcoming, so Lou made a couple of additions of his own.

'I'll bring you a fresh gas bottle for the barbecue,' he said, 'and some more meths for the stoves – you don't want to run out and have to rely on wood fires for cooking. The smoke might attract attention.'

And clothes, he resolved, looking about at the motley collection of blanket kaftans most were wearing, I'll bring them some extra clothes too. There are so many things they could have requested and haven't, he thought. I don't think they've seen much goodwill in the past.

Lou then addressed Jalila directly. For some odd reason he felt compelled to hear her speak English in front of the others. Why does she choose not to do so? he wondered.

'And you, Jalila? Is there anything you would like me to bring you?'

Jalila looked to Rassen, waiting for the question to be repeated in Arabic.

But Rassen did not translate for her, recognising Lou's desire to converse with the girl in English as he obviously had upon their first meeting.

Jalila looked back to the Australian. She was hesitant. She did have a request and she did want to reply, but she did not relish being the centre of attention.

The others exchanged glances, wondering what was going on, bewildered by the pause in proceedings.

'A ball,' she said finally. 'I would like a ball that I may play catch with Hamid.'

The reaction all round was instantaneous: delight from Rassen and Hala, who saw the exchange as a break-through; astonishment from the others, who rarely heard the girl speak at all, let alone in English; and from Hamid an immediate response to the sound of his name.

'What did Jalila ask for?' he demanded of Rassen.

'A secret,' Jalila said in English. Ignoring the child alto-gether, her comment was made to Lou.

'Ah,' Lou nodded, 'I see. It's a gift, is that right?'

'Yes,' Jalila said, 'a gift.'

Rassen added the ball to the list, and upon a quick whispered request from Lou, he added also the names of everyone in the group.

'Just the first names will do,' Lou hurriedly added under his breath.

And then the meeting was over.

Half an hour later, they stood on the end of the jetty, waving goodbye to *Principessa*. Lou had promised he would return in five days with their supplies and as they watched the old Princess steadily chug out of sight, there was much conversation, the general consensus being one of puzzlement. Why does this good man care so for us?

It was a question none could answer, but it was one that was of no concern at all to Hamid.

'What did you ask for, Jalila?' he insisted.

'A handkerchief,' she said. 'I asked for a handkerchief, because your nose is always running.'

Hamid lost interest immediately.

*

True to his word, Lou returned five days later, and he brought with him an abundance of supplies that were quite beyond their wildest expectations. Along with the list that had been drawn up and the requests they'd made were eggs and fresh fruit and vegetables, there were packets of sweet biscuits, a large jar of honey and, much to Rassen's delight, ground coffee and a plunger. There were also clothes. An odd selection to be sure – 'Cast-offs,' Lou said, 'from the back of our wardrobes. Paolo and I had a good clean-out' – but the old cardigans and shirts and tracksuit pants were eagerly embraced. There was a set of binoculars too. 'In order to keep a sharp lookout for planes and boats, Rassen,' Lou said, 'but you'll find some pleasure in them I'm sure. The birdlife out here is quite spectacular.'

Every new item produced was joyously greeted, but the greatest thrill of all belonged to Hamid, upon the presentation of a tennis ball and a soccer ball.

'I didn't know what sort of ball you wanted, Jalila,' Lou said, 'so I brought both. A game of "catch" you said, but every boy wants to kick a footie around, doesn't he?'

There was a further recreational surprise in store – two board games – a set of draughts and a chess set, both well-worn, having seen years of use, for which Lou apologised.

'Pretty old, nothing fancy, but they'll serve to while away the time,' he said. 'I don't know why, Rassen, but you're the sort of bloke who strikes me as a chess player, am I right?'

He was indeed right. Hala was a keen chess player too, as was Massoud.

'Expected as much,' Lou said a touch of nonchalance, although secretly he was thrilled by the pleasure he could see on their faces as each fresh gift was revealed. They're like kids at Christmas, he thought, all of them, even the posh-voiced doctor and his wife, just like kids at Christmas. Although, he corrected himself, they don't have Christmas where they come from, do they?

'But this is your personal chess set, Lou, is it not?' Rassen queried.

'Yep.'

'We can't deprive you of chess for months on end, man. What on earth will you do with yourself?'

'I'll watch TV.' Lou gave an impish grin, suspecting the good doctor thought he was joking, before admitting to the truth. 'I don't play much these days actually, haven't for ten years, not since my wife, Barbara, died. It was Barb who taught me and I was never much chop anyway.' He cast a fond glance at his young grandson. 'He was the champ in the family,' he said, 'even as a lad he could outplay his grandmother. He's got his own chess set now, so he certainly doesn't need this old thing.'

Of all the surprises that day, Paul had been the greatest.

In the mid-morning, when they'd seen the boat approaching from afar, they'd expected it to be *Principessa*, but they'd remained out of sight just in case. Then, when the old Princess was clearly recognisable, they'd gone down to the jetty to welcome Lou.

But as the boat had drawn closer, despite the assuring wave they'd received from Lou at the helm, the young man standing, mooring rope in hand, up the bow had come as a shock to them all.

'This is my grandson,' Lou said when, after securing the vessel, the two had stepped on to the jetty. 'I call him Paolo, but he's Paul to everyone else. Paul Miller – he's my daughter's son, and his dad likes to downplay the Italian connection.' There was no rancour in the comment, just a statement of long-accepted fact.

They took in the image of the young man. Unlike his grandfather, there appeared very little of the Mediterranean about him. Tall, lanky but fit, straight, mid-brown hair in need of a cut, a face unbearded but in need of a shave, and youthful skin, as yet unweathered, unlike most

Australians who lived a life outdoors. Twenty-two-year-old Paul was ill-kempt but pleasant-looking. The one hint of Italian heritage was perhaps the dark brown of his eyes where one might have expected blue.

As they warily assessed Lou's grandson, it was quite obvious Lou's grandson was assessing them with equal wariness. The moment was awkward. Then, just as Rassen was about to commence the introductions, Lou took over.

He proceeded to introduce, one by one, every member of the group, starting with the doctor and his wife, whose surname he included. The others he introduced by first name only, but he'd memorised the list and, with methodical precision, got every single person's name right and correctly pronounced. Rassen was most impressed.

'How do you do,' Paul said formally, shaking each hand in turn, friendly enough, but the wariness still evident.

'And this is Hamid,' Lou concluded.

The little boy held his hand up to the tall stranger. 'Hello there,' he said loudly and clearly in English. That was what the old man had said to him upon their first meeting, he remembered.

Hamid was determined to learn English and, having privately nagged Jalila, he had made some progress over the past several days. Not only could he say 'hello', but also 'goodbye', 'please', 'thank you' and a number of other words. He now committed to memory 'how do you do' and intended to ask Jalila its meaning when they were alone.

Paul squatted on the worn, warm planks of the jetty, accepting the child's firm little handshake. 'G'day, mate,' he said, and something in the boyishness of his smile and the way he said it broke the awkwardness.

G'day, mate, Hamid thought solemnly; he would ask Jalila about those words too.

The cardboard boxes and polystyrene container and sacks of supplies were all lifted from the boat and, shouldering the loads they could handle, the women insistent upon carrying their share, they set off for the blue hut where the kitchen and pantry were housed.

The heaviest burden appeared to be Paul's, although at first they were mystified as to what it could be. Hoisted over one shoulder was a hessian sack that obviously contained something very large and very hefty. He was quick to explain.

'Crushed ice,' he said to Rassen. 'Four bags straight from the boat's freezer; we need to get it to my hut as soon as possible.'

When the general supplies had been deposited in the blue hut, Lou instructed Karim to take the polystyrene container of fresh fish to the green hut where it could be kept on ice.

'Rassen and I will come with you,' he said. The offer was made in the spirit of camaraderie, but Lou was aware it might be a good idea to have an interpreter present, particularly as Karim and his family were the ones currently occupying Paul's hut. Lou remained unsure about his grandson's acceptance of the refugees. Paulo's initial reaction to the news had been anything but receptive.

Rassen picked up on the message immediately. 'Wait here,' he instructed the others. 'We'll be back shortly.'

By the time the three of them reached the green hut, Paul had already placed the bags of ice in a huge old icebox that sat gathering dust in the corner of the workshop out the back. The icebox seemed both oddly old-fashioned and quite unnecessary as inside the hut was a refrigerator, which would surely be used during the fishing season when there was generator-powered electricity on the island.

Lou, however, crowed his triumph. Vindicated at long last, he was inordinately proud of himself.

'See,' he declared to his grandson, 'I told you it'd come in handy.'

'Bullshit,' Paul scoffed, 'you just couldn't bear to get rid of the damn thing. A useless piece of rubbish from the fifties, that's all it is, a waste of space.'

'Hardly useless, I'd say,' his grandfather countered argumentatively. 'We couldn't have supplied them with a generator. It would have been a dead giveaway that someone was helping them.' He added in a quick aside to Rassen, 'No one leaves generators on the island,' before continuing his tirade to Paul. 'This way at least they've got refrigeration. All they need to do when they're discovered is chuck the ice out.' He concluded his argument in a gloatingly superior tone, 'I think under the circumstances, Paolo, you'd have to agree I was right all along. The old icebox has proved highly useful.'

'These aren't exactly normal circumstances, Lou,' Paul said, this time tetchily. 'In fact I'd say this is a totally one-off situation.'

Rassen was starting to feel uncomfortable, and even Karim, although not understanding a word that was being said, appeared ill at ease with the tension between the two.

Aware of their discomfort Lou apologised. 'I'm sorry,' he said. 'Paolo and I argue all the time. He's been trying to make me get rid of the old icebox for years, and I always dig my heels in.'

'I have, and you do.' Paul gave an easy smile and the tension dissolved immediately. Arguments between grandfather and grandson rarely lasted long.

Relieved the confrontation was over, Rassen briefly translated the exchange to Karim.

'Good that they did not get rid of the icebox,' Karim replied, 'very useful for us.'

Rassen did not bother translating his response to the Australians.

They packed the various parcels of fresh fish into the icebox. The fish had been thoroughly cleaned and gutted, Lou explained, but not scaled.

'They'll keep better that way,' he said. 'Scale them just before you cook them.' Then, as he closed the door, he determined to have the last word. 'It'll work a treat, you'll see,' he said to Rassen, but mainly for Paul's benefit. 'That old icebox is as good as any fridge.'

Paul took no notice. Much as he loved his grandfather, the old man could be dogmatic when he chose, and there were times when it was best to ignore him.

Looking around the shed, Lou noticed that the old pedal-operated grinding wheel had been freshly cleaned and oiled. Beside it on the workbench sat several well-honed tools, including the axe. No wonder Karim chopped through the dinghy as efficiently as he did, he thought with a sense of satisfaction. The old wheel is obviously back in action.

'He's been trying to make me get rid of that too,' he said smugly. 'But I won't let him.'

'True,' Paul said to the others. 'I have. And he won't.'

The young man's smile once again defused the situation, so Rassen considered it safe to translate the exchange for Karim.

'I like the wheel,' Karim said, 'the wheel is good.'

Rassen, as before, did not bother with the English translation.

'Lou always hangs on to the past,' Paul continued pleasantly, but nonetheless having a mild dig at his grandfather, 'even when the rubbish he hangs on to is useless.'

'This is most certainly true,' Lou acceded, 'I do. Why would I not wish to hang on to the past? The past has been good to me.' Then he couldn't resist adding under his breath to Paul, taking care Rassen didn't hear, 'Unlike these poor bastards.'

Upon their return to the blue hut they discovered the others waiting patiently, even Hamid. Or rather Hamid was making a pretence of patience. He was desperate to discover what was inside the boxes and sacks, but he'd been told he must wait, that they must all share in the moment.

And then the unveiling began, producing 'oohs' and 'ahs' of wonder at the most basic of items. Eggs, honey, fresh fruit, ground coffee: everything was greeted with excitement. It seemed Hamid was not the only child present. And when they got to the sack of clothes, there was laughter as they pulled cardigans on over their shirts or held garments up against their bodies, humour mingling with the deepest of gratitude.

Kids at Christmas, Lou thought, listening to the chatter of a language he did not understand, but which communicated itself as clearly as if he did. Just like kids at Christmas. He offered the odd comment now and then for Rassen to translate to the others. 'Cast-offs,' he said, 'from the back of our wardrobes, Paolo and I had a good clean-out . . .' but for the most part he just stood and looked on.

So did Paul. And as he looked on, he recalled the night, only several days previously, when Lou had told him all about the refugees.

'You're not going to report them?' He'd been outraged by the idea. 'What do you *mean* you're not going to report them?'

'Just that. I mean I'm not going to report them, and you'll know why when you see them. Stop being so quick to make judgements, Paolo.'

'But they're illegal immigrants, for Christ's sake. They've invaded our camp – they've taken over our huts! Why the hell would you *not* report them?'

'They're welcome to stay in my hut,' Lou replied with icy dignity. 'I'm only too glad I can be of some help to these poor souls who find themselves in such dire circumstances.'

Paul could have hit the old man. It always infuriated him when Lou got on his high horse, which he regularly did, and solely in order to infuriate.

'You do realise,' he responded with equal iciness, 'that the hut is *my* hut, not yours.'

'Yes, you are the fisher in the family now, Paolo, I know this.' Lou was instantly contrite, aware he'd been wrong to adopt their usual combative routine. He needed his young grandson on side; in fact, it was essential Paul become an ally. 'But we did agree some time back that we'd call it *our* hut, didn't we?'

'Fair enough.' Paul recognised a truce was being called. 'But you can't help these people the way you intend to, Lou. You simply can't do that.'

'Why not?'

'Why not?!' Even communicating reasonably, as he obviously believed he was, the old man was maddening. 'Why not, for Christ's sake! You don't know them, that's why not! They're Middle Eastern you say. That means they're Muslims. Jesus Christ, Lou, they could be terrorists for all you know.'

'They're not. I know they're not. Two of them are even Christians. And stop blaspheming.'

Despite his outrage, Paul couldn't help but be vaguely amused by the comment, which was made purely out of habit. His grandfather was a severely lapsed Catholic who didn't give a damn about Jesus Christ or the Pope or anything to do with the Church. For years now, ever since the scandalous cover-up of paedophilia in the priesthood had been exposed, Luigi Panuzza had been scathing in his condemnation of the Church of Rome.

'You should see these people, Paolo,' Lou continued in earnest. 'No, no,' he held his hand up as his grandson threatened to interrupt, 'no, no, you *must* see them, and then you'll know what I mean. They're walking around in clothes made of blankets and they have tragedy in their eyes. All of them. You can see it; you can feel it. Several are educated and the others are peasants from what I can gather, but they're people who've been through a hell you and I couldn't imagine. There's even a little boy – he wouldn't be more than three.'

Paul didn't interrupt, waiting instead for his grandfather to go on. He couldn't recall ever having seen Lou like this.

The old man, strong and proud, at times even arrogant, was all but begging.

'I remember the animosity my parents suffered when they first came to Australia.' Lou's voice was quieter now he had his grandson's attention. 'These people deserve better than that, Paolo. They deserve some kindness. For as long as we can offer it anyway,' he said with resignation. 'God knows what'll happen to them when they're discovered. In all conscience I couldn't bring myself to report them, I honestly couldn't.' Once again there was a plea in his voice. 'You will help me, won't you? Please promise you will.'

'Yes, I'll help you,' Paul agreed with reluctance. 'We'll probably end up in bloody jail, but I'll help you, I promise.'

'And you'll keep the secret?

'Yeah, I'll do that too. But I'll make my own judgement about these people, Lou. They might not be the innocents you reckon they are. I have a right to my own opinion, you know.'

'Of course you do, Paolo, of course you do.'

'We can't deprive you of chess for months on end, man. What on earth will you do with yourself?'

'I'll watch TV.'

Paul heard the discussion about the chess set, but he didn't really take it in – his mind was too preoccupied, and when it came to the reference to him he made no reaction at all.

'. . . the champ in the family, even as a lad . . . got his own chess set now . . . doesn't need this old thing.'

The words barely reached him. He'd set out to study these people, to make his own judgement, as he'd told Lou he would. But he could make no judgement about them: there was none to be made. Lou was quite right. The very pleasure they were currently displaying was revelatory in itself. These were damaged people. People unaccustomed to kindness. He'd seen in their eyes, too, the tragedy Lou had mentioned. That first meeting on the jetty. Beneath the wariness, he'd seen glimpses of fear, vulnerability, pain. Even the doctor, stylish, confident man that he was, the leader of the group, even the doctor's eyes had held something indiscernible. Sorrow? Regret? Impossible to tell.

But it was the girl who intrigued Paul the most, the girl they called Jalila. Her beauty was mesmeric, certainly – he'd been struck by her appearance the moment he'd first seen her, what man wouldn't be? But Jalila's eyes differed from the eyes of the others in more than their beauty. Jalila's eyes held nothing. He could see no fear there, no vulnerability, no sorrow, no pain: Jalila's eyes were dead. Which perhaps made her the most tragic figure of all.

He'd studied her particularly closely when Lou had produced the gift she'd requested for the boy.

'I didn't know what sort of ball you wanted, Jalila, so I brought both. A game of "catch" you said, but every boy wants to kick a footie around, doesn't he?'

Little Hamid's reaction had been ecstatic upon the appearance of the tennis and soccer balls.

'That's what you asked for, Jalila!' he'd squealed excitedly at the top of his voice. 'That's what you asked for!'

'Yes,' she'd replied calmly, 'that is your handkerchief.'

Paul hadn't understood the exchange between the two, but the boy's delight in the present she'd asked for on his behalf was so obvious that he'd expected some pleasure in Jalila's reaction. There had appeared to be none, at least none that he could see, which he'd found most odd. And he'd realised in that moment how much he'd longed to see her smile.

Now, as the unveiling of the supplies and the presents came to a close, he continued to study the girl, and the group in general, pondering the various relationships.

The doctor embarked upon a speech of thanks, particularly to Lou, but as Paul found himself also included, he politely paid attention, even as his eyes flickered about the hut.

'On behalf of us all, I cannot express deeply enough our gratitude to you, Lou,' Rassen said. 'And to you also, Paul . . .'

The others listened in rapt attention. Even though the majority of them did not understand the actual words, they knew what was being said.

Hamid, seated on the floor, wriggled about impatiently. He was itching to be outside playing catch, but he knew better than to leave while the doctor was speaking. That would be rude and he'd get into trouble.

They're all couples, Paul was thinking. The doctor and his very English-looking wife; Karim and his wife and child, who are staying in my hut; and the Egyptian husband and wife, who are Coptic Christians. So what about Jalila and the young man called Massoud? Are Jalila and Massoud a couple? They don't seem to be – there's no body language between them. Could they be brother and sister? But there's no evidence of that either. And Lou would've mentioned it if they were, he gave me a bit of background on everyone. There seems no connection at all. And no interest in forming one, what's more.

That was the part Paul found most odd.

The brief speech at an end, Rassen started a round of applause and everyone joined in, all eyes on Lou and Paul, who acknowledged the thanks with a wave of their hands.

Then the women got to work sorting out the foodstuffs, packing things in the shed that had been converted to a pantry, shooing the men away; the blue hut was their domain.

Karim and Hany were more than happy to go outside. They were both eyeing off the soccer ball, which Hamid was happy to relinquish. For the moment anyway. Right now the tennis ball was more his style.

He looked an enquiry to Jalila. Was it all right for him to play now and would she come with him, his eyes asked. Jalila returned a nod and the two slipped outside.

'Right, we'll be off then,' Lou said.

'No, no,' Hala insisted, thinking how rude they must have appeared. 'I insist you stay for tea and biscuits. Or coffee,' she added with a smile to her husband. 'I know Rassen is aching for a cup.'

'And perhaps you'll join me in a game?' Rassen suggested hopefully, picking up the chess set. A cup of coffee and a game of chess in the quiet of the yellow hut; he could think of nothing better.

'Thank you, Hala, but no, Paolo and I will be on our way – perhaps next time. And as for chess, Rassen,' Lou gave a woeful shake of his head, 'you wouldn't want me as an opponent, I can assure you. Why don't you ask Massoud to join you instead?'

Massoud agreed eagerly. 'More than happy to oblige,' he said.

The men shook hands all round and Lou and Paul made their departure, with the promise they would return again in five days.

'We'll bring more fresh fish and produce and run a check on any other supplies you might need,' Lou said.

They stepped out into the late morning sun and walked down towards the jetty, but when they were halfway there Paul paused to look back at the scene behind them.

Up near the benches, Karim and Hany were kicking the soccer ball around, while on the footpath in front of the huts Jalila and Hamid played catch. Then, as Paul watched, Rassen and Massoud appeared from the blue hut, the chess set tucked firmly under Rassen's arm.

On their way to the yellow hut, the two walked right by the young woman and the child, even detouring a step or so, yet Massoud, chatting away to Rassen, did not once look at Jalila. Not even a glance, as if he failed to notice her altogether.

Massoud has no interest in her at all, Paul thought. How could a young bloke his age fail to notice a woman like that?

PART TWO
THE TOWN

CHAPTER NINE

The small town and fishing port of Shoalhaven on the mid-west coast of Western Australia boasted a population of approximately three hundred, although the head count of residents was rarely consistent as numbers fluctuated according to the lobster fishing season. Since the introduction of a quota system, there was no specific 'season' as such, but little fishing took place between late August and early February and some fishers, particularly those who leased their pots, chose to seek employment on off-shore vessels working the oil and gas fields to the north of the state. Those who owned their pots more often than not remained in town, repairing their boats and gear in preparation for the following year when some would return to their huts on Gevaar Island while others concentrated upon coastal fishing.

But despite the occasional variance in numbers, Shoalhaven was a tightly knit community, more a village than a township, where everyone knew everyone and everyone had their place.

The main street was called Main Street, and the coastal beachfront road that ran parallel to it was called Marine Parade. The town evolved around these two hubs of activity, the several smaller connecting and intersecting streets being lined with the houses of residents, some modest cottages and some a little more grand. The grander ones were situated in the vicinity of North Terrace to the town's north and those a little more modest in the vicinity of South Terrace to the town's south. Outsiders might therefore have presumed that the town's simple grid system reflected its hierarchy and that those from the north might look down on those from the south, but this was not at all so. Shoalhaven was a tidy town, a practical town, where everyone's position within its small society was recognised and respected.

Main Street housed the town's centre. A wide road, lined on either side by a colourful variety of conjoined single-storey shops and businesses, all companionably linked by a common corrugated iron roof stretching over the footpath, there was no denying Main Street had a distinctly 'outback' look. Many of the shops and businesses were multi-purposed: the post office served also as the general store and newsagency; the clothing store (men's and women's) served also as a drapery, haberdashery and bed linen outlet; the bakery (selling excellent home-made pies, pasties and sausage rolls) doubled as a milk bar and café; and Henry Wong's Chinese Restaurant, being particularly versatile, offered steak, eggs and chips alongside chow mein, dim sims and fried rice while also doubling as a takeaway hamburger bar. Next door, and linked to Wong's Chinese Restaurant, was a laundry run by Henry's wife, Florence, who also worked in her husband's kitchen; the Wongs were an enterprising couple.

Some shops and businesses were simply what they were. Hutchings and Son was the butcher's shop, with a residence out the back; the pharmacy was the pharmacy, run by the chemist Alfred Tran and his wife, although the premises did house to one side their daughter Vanessa's small hairdressing salon (male and female clients); and the hardware store was the hardware store, possibly the most successful business in town, catering not only for the needs of fishers, but also those farmers whose nearby properties produced wheat that was shipped all over from Geraldton, one hundred kilometres to the south.

Marine Parade, while picturesque, looking out as it did over a sweep of pristine white beach and aquamarine ocean, did not live up to the grandiosity of its title. Marine Parade wasn't a parade at all really; in fact, as roads go it was quite ordinary, without the impressive width of Main Street. But then North and South Terraces weren't terrace-like either: they were all just country-town roads, nothing more. Marine Parade was, however, the true face of Shoalhaven, reflecting the town's very purpose. For this was a fishers' town.

The north end of the parade looked out over the marina, alongside which sat the small fishing co-operative that served as a sales outlet for the locals. The majority of a fisher's catch was shipped to Geraldton for export.

The marina was not a large marina by normal fishing port standards, but eminently suitable for Shoalhaven's needs. A man-made rocky mole stretched out into the sea, serving as an effective breakwater; there was one sizable jetty with boat pens either side and a smaller jetty and bowser for fuelling; there was a mechanics' shop, permanently staffed, and a repair yard with two slipways; there were several boat launching ramps also, and a large car park able to accommodate the trailers of smaller recreational vessels. All this together with a toilet block – what more could be needed? There'd been talk at one time in the Shoalhaven Residents' Group of possibly building a clubhouse and restaurant, but nothing had eventuated. It had been decided, a little reluctantly by several of the town's merchants it was true, but amicably enough, that the Shoalhaven marina wasn't intended as a social centre, but rather was the domain of fishers. For socialising you went to the pub.

The pub was to the south end of town, a rambling wooden structure on the corner of Marine Parade and South Terrace. One of the few two-storey buildings in the whole of the township, its wide verandahs and broad upstairs balcony looked out over the beauty of the Indian Ocean.

The pub, or rather 'Shoalhaven Hotel', offered accommodation to the occasional tourist or visitor who happened along, but principally it catered to the locals and was highly popular, serving not only as a drinking hole, but provider of the best pub tucker at the best pub prices. From fish and chips to rissoles and gravy, from bangers and mash to things more fancy like spaghetti bolognaise, there was even, for those prepared to pay a lot more, local lobster and salad.

Salted amongst the residences fronting onto the ocean between the marina and the pub were several small businesses.

There was Kellys' Garage, with two petrol bowsers and an adjacent yard where the owner and his wife, both skilled mechanics, repaired every form of engine from road vehicles to tractors and other farm machinery. The Kellys did not, however, undertake the repair of marine engines, which was a different matter altogether requiring a highly specialised skill. Marine engine repair was the realm of Archie Lang, who worked at the marina. Needless to say, Archie was one of the town's most valued citizens.

A little further up from the garage was Mac's, a shop that catered for recreational needs: fishing rods, handlines, bait, masks, snorkels, flippers. Nothing that competed with the professional equipment on offer at the hardware store, though – in Shoalhaven one did not trespass on another's territory.

In the very middle of Marine Parade was Ian Tuckey's tuckshop. The Tuckshop, or 'Tuckey's', as it was more commonly known, sold soft drinks, ice-cream, lollies, potato crisps and simple takeaway fare like sandwiches and meat pies. Tuckey's did surprisingly well, particularly on weekends and during the school holidays, or perhaps unsurprisingly, for it sat right opposite the jetty.

The public jetty, sturdy, reliable, stretching proudly from the sweep of white beach into the vibrant blue of the bay, was iconic to the citizens of Shoalhaven. Broadly T-shaped at the end with pylons at each corner, well maintained at all times, the public jetty, like the town's shops, served a multitude of purposes. The occasional fishing boat might call in briefly, but the jetty's boating use was mainly for recreational vessels, the picking up and dropping off of passengers. Then of course there was the fishing. The fishing was good from the end of the jetty and families would arrive with rods and handlines and even picnic hampers to make a day of it. But above all there was the swimming: kids climbing the jetty's pylons and, knees tucked to chests, chucking 'bombies', vying for who could make the biggest splash. Every Shoalhaven kid for generations had thrown themselves off the end of the jetty in one way or another only to haul themselves up the old barnacle-encrusted ladder, getting a little bloodied on the way, but raring to go again, the boldest climbing the pylons to perform dives or even somersaults in order to come out on top.

A tacit agreement existed between those who fished and swam from the T-shaped end of the jetty. Those fishing had claim to the right-hand side and those swimming had claim to the left. For as long as the oldest residents could remember, it had always been so. Things never changed in Shoalhaven.

'Thanks, Arch, I'll leave you to it.'

As Paul climbed from the bow of *Palermo Miss* onto the jetty, he received no reply from Archie, whose thatch of red hair was barely visible and whose beefy shoulders remained hunched over one of the vessel's diesel motors. But Paul had expected no reply other than the customary salute of acknowledgement, and he would possibly have had cause to worry had he received one. When Archie Lang was servicing a boat's engines the only time he made a comment was if something was wrong. It was a different matter altogether if he was at the pub – Arch just loved a chat over a beer.

It was late afternoon on a day unseasonably warm for mid-September and, walking along the beachfront of Marine Parade, Paul was tempted to have a dip in order to cool off. His lightweight cotton shorts served equally well as bathers and he had no need of a towel; it was a regular habit of his in the height of summer to shed his shirt and wade in, or else throw himself off the end of the jetty along with the kids who were invariably there. Not today though, he decided. He'd head home instead and do the bit of research he'd planned. He and Lou were taking off for the island in the morning with the fresh supplies they'd purchased the preceding day, and before they did, there were a few things he wanted to check out on his computer. He wouldn't leave it until tonight. Being Sunday he was on a promise for the customary roast dinner at his mother's house. As was Lou. During the off-season, Sunday dinners were a regular family custom, a gathering of three generations, more often than not including Paul's older sister, who would drive up from Geraldton. Twenty-four-year-old Beverly had relocated south just two years earlier, having accepted a position at Geraldton Library. A qualified librarian and a feisty young woman, she preferred the faster pace of Gero to the sleepy hollow of Shoalhaven, particularly as there was no library nor even a bookshop in the village, apart from the several shelves of second-hand offerings available for sale at the small charity collection centre run by the pastor's wife. Beverly was always scathingly outspoken about the dearth of literature available in Shoalhaven.

'Doesn't anyone in this town read books?' she'd rant, which would only serve to egg her brother on.

'Sure they read books,' he'd reply with a laconic superiority intended to madden, 'but they download them. This is the twenty-first century, Bev – you've got to move with the times.'

Which would of course only set his sister off on a further rant. But despite their differences – Bev openly rebellious always prepared to take a stance, Paul for the most part reluctant to reveal his inner feelings – the siblings were close. And perhaps *because* of their differences they greatly respected each other.

Paul turned off Marine Parade into Cooper Street, a block up from the pub, where he had one of the old fishers' cottages at the south end of town. He'd moved into the place on a share-rental basis with two other deck-hands a good five years previously when he was seventeen and had left school to work full-time on his grandfather's fishing boat. He could have shifted in with Lou, who had certainly wanted him to once they were a permanent team, but close though he was with his grandfather, indeed more a son than a grandson, Paul had craved independence. Besides, he and Lou were in each other's pockets enough as it was during the fishing season, stranded out there in that hut on the island.

Now a successful fisher and businessman in his own right, and his old share-rental mates having moved on, Paul had recently taken out a bank loan and purchased the cottage, an achievement of which he was inordinately proud having only just turned twenty-two. More than ever these days he relished his independence. The little old cottage was his and his alone and he loved the solitude it afforded him.

During his walk home from the marina, Paul's mind would normally have been on *Palermo Miss* – on the servicing of her engines and the fact that she was due up on the slip for anti-fouling the following week, and a great many other issues worthy of attention at this time of the year. There was much to be done in preparation for the marine engineer's annual survey, which would guarantee the vessel's certification of seaworthiness.

But Paul's mind was not on *Palermo Miss*. He was thinking of the refugees, and most particularly of the girl, aware that he would be seeing her the following morning. It had been five days since his visit to the island, during which time he'd given her little thought, but now the image of her, the mystery of her, played on his mind. He remembered the brief exchange he'd had with Lou aboard the old Princess as they'd chugged their way back to Shoalhaven that day.

'Hey Lou,' he'd said thoughtfully not long after they'd left, 'what do you know about Jalila and Massoud?'

Lou had simply given a shrug. 'Massoud's from Iran, well educated, I told you that. And Jalila,' another shrug, 'no one knows who she is or where she's from, I told you that too. They didn't even know she spoke English until I prompted her into it,' he added with some considerable pride.

'Yeah, yeah. But what about their relationship?'

'What do you mean?' The question obviously mystified Lou. 'Their relationship to what?'

'To each other. I mean they're not brother and sister, are they?'

'Course they're not. Rassen would have told me if they were. Why do you ask?'

'Because there's no . . .' Paul fumbled for the right word '. . . no particular *contact* between them, you know what I mean?'

'Nup. No idea what you're on about. What sort of contact?'

'Oh come on, mate,' Paul replied half-jokingly in an attempt to bluff, hiding his frustration at Lou's obtuseness, but reminding himself that his grandfather was over seventy after all. 'Massoud's a young bloke, and a girl like Jalila . . .' A shake of the head spoke multitudes. 'Well you'd think he'd bloody well *notice* her, wouldn't you?'

A dawning light appeared in Lou's eyes. Of course, he thought. How stupid of me. Have I really become that old?

He looked back towards the island, now quite distant, but Jalila still visible, staring up at some birds wheeling in the sky.

Lou's expression was grave as he turned to his grandson. 'I'd be careful if I were you, Paolo,' he warned. 'You mustn't be attracted to that girl. You can't make advances. You'd frighten her.'

For a moment Paul was struck speechless, his grandfather's words, simple as they were, sending a host of jagged thoughts streaking lightning-like through his mind. Of course I'm attracted to her, what bloke wouldn't be? Of course I don't intend to 'make advances' as you bloody well call it – why the hell would I? Of course she'd be frightened, she'd be bloody terrified. How could you think I'd come on to her, how could you even *suggest* . . .? Paul was angry, very angry, but he did his best to hide it.

'Don't be bloody stupid, Lou,' he said with what he hoped sounded like mere irritation. 'The situation interests me, that's all. Everyone out there on that island is a couple, everyone except Jalila and Massoud. They're all in pairs, haven't you noticed? I'm just wondering where those two stand with each other, that's all.'

'Of course you are,' Lou replied. 'I didn't mean to insult you, Paolo, I only wanted to warn you. For your own sake, as well as hers.'

Lou applied his attention to the wheel and the sea ahead, as if he was on lookout, as if he didn't know every inch of this crossing and couldn't accomplish it blindfolded. I'm not as old as all that, my boy, he thought, not so old that I don't remember what it's like to be obsessed by a beautiful woman.

Paul made no reply. He felt more than insulted – he felt invaded, as if some private part of him, a part of which he hadn't even been aware himself, had been given voice. And it was ugly. Ugly and wrong. He knew he was overreacting, that his grandfather had meant no harm, but he couldn't help himself. Fuck you, Lou, he thought, fuck you!

The remainder of the crossing had been made in a silence that, rather than its customary companionship, was just a touch uncomfortable.

After finishing his intended research on the computer, Paul showered and scrubbed himself up with a little more care than he usually did for the Sunday family roast dinners. He'd had his hair cut the previous morning at Vanessa's, the tiny salon in the pharmacy run by Alfred and Linda Tran. He'd been long overdue for a haircut and young Nessa Tran had done a good job – now it seemed only right he should shave to complete the image.

'My, my, how spruce,' David Miller said as he opened the door to his son. He was quickly joined by his wife, who hugged her son warmly.

'Absolutely,' Maria agreed, standing back to survey him. 'Very, very spruce, my darling – to what do we owe the honour?'

Paul stepped over the threshold and into the lounge room of his family's comfortable single-storey bungalow in North Terrace to be met by a quirky reaction from his grandfather, already seated on the sofa, stubby of beer in hand. It was no more than a mild moue that said, Well, look at you, but Paul felt another irrational flash of anger. You think I've scrubbed myself up for Jalila, don't you? he thought. Well you can get fucked, Lou, you can bloody well go and get fucked!

'I've been known to have a shave and a haircut before,' he said caustically.

'Of course you have, darling.' Maria wondered why her son was in such a prickly mood.

'Get you a beer, son?' David asked, wondering exactly the same thing.

'Thanks, Dad.'

Catching a confused and querying look from his grandfather, Paul felt caught out. Oh shit, he thought, I've overreacted again.

'Bev not here yet?' he asked, seating himself beside Lou on the sofa, keen to make amends for his tetchiness.

'Not coming, apparently,' Lou replied.

'Of course she's not,' Maria said, placing the tray of pickings on the coffee table before them. She was a fleshy woman in her late forties, but comfortable with her body, still sexy, still attractive to men, yet seemingly unaware of the fact, which only made her all the more sexy. She seated herself opposite her father and son; the family always sat and chatted for a while before the serving-up of the ritual roast.

'Bev's preparing for the festival – she's been working day and night,' Maria went on. 'She won't be here next Sunday either of course, the festival will be at its peak over the weekend.'

A blank pause.

'The Big Sky Writers' Festival starts in Geraldton next week,' Maria painstakingly spelled out. 'Surely you remember. She told you. I heard her.'

Paul and Lou looked dutifully guilty. Bev had told them all about the impending festival just the previous Sunday. They'd forgotten.

Bev had more than told them about it, she'd positively boasted. 'Some really big-time writers are coming,' she'd said with pride, 'and not just up from Perth, but several from Sydney and Melbourne – it'll be one of the biggest festivals the library's had.'

'It's a very exciting time for her,' Maria said in mild rebuke. 'Thank you, dear.'

She accepted the glass of wine her husband offered and David joined the circle around the coffee table, handing a stubby of beer to Paul.

'Yes, we're very proud of our Beverly,' he said.

They toasted each other, and also Bev, the three men drinking in comradely fashion from their bottles, which for David was strictly an acknowledgement of family: he never drank from the bottle in public. His job as the town's postmaster demanded a certain image, or at least that was the way he saw it. He wasn't a snob, nor was he pretentious, but rather a man who had always taken his position and the responsibilities that attended it seriously.

When, as a young accountant in a Geraldton bank, David Miller had applied for the position of bank manager at the tiny branch in the tiny town of Shoalhaven to the north (the position vacant due to the death of the previous manager, who had served there for twenty-five years) he'd seen the move as an excellent career opportunity. His application had proved successful mainly because few were interested in a branch housing a staff of only two (including manager), but this fact had not bothered David. He was quite sure the experience and qualification he would gain would eventually lead to a managerial position in a much larger branch of a much larger bank in a much larger town. He may have been right, but one would never know as the bank had closed three years later, along with so many banks in so many small country towns, and he'd never applied for another bank job in another bank in another town. The truth was, David hadn't anticipated falling in love with the beguilingly attractive daughter of a local Italian fisher, and now twenty-eight years on he was still there.

He'd been not only enterprising, but of great value to the town. When, shortly after the bank's closure, the elderly and recently widowed owner of the general store had been forced to retire and sell up, David had bought the property. The store having also served as the post office, he'd applied for the licence of postmaster, thereby ensuring Shoalhaven would not lose one of its principal services. From that day on he'd worked hard, as had the postmaster before him, to maintain the quota of mail necessary for the service to keep functioning efficiently and successfully.

The position of postmaster was one of grave responsibility in David's eyes, and the title, while hardly ranking alongside that of bank manager, remained of great importance to him. He no longer wore a suit and tie to work, admittedly, but he did maintain a degree of smart dress during post-office hours and observed a certain decorum at all other times, which included not drinking from a beer bottle in public. He didn't realise, perhaps sadly for him, that the people of Shoalhaven wouldn't have cared in the least if their postmaster had turned up for work in the traditional garb of shorts, T-shirt and sandals, which was only sensible in the height of summer, and had guzzled beer from a stubby along with the rest of them.

David Miller, fifty, tall, and very good-looking, perhaps more so than ever these days, with the greying-haired dignity that befitted his perceived position, was and always had been a highly conservative man.

The chat around the coffee table continued, Maria producing a program of the festival's events, including biographies of the various authors, poets, artists and illustrators attending.

'We're going down next weekend,' she said with a smile to her husband. 'Saturday afternoon when we've closed the post office, and all day Sunday – I must say I can't wait.'

David returned her smile fondly. 'I'm very much looking forward to it, too. Beverly has booked us in to all the events she thinks will be of most interest to us.'

'You should come along too, Papa,' Maria urged, 'and you, too, Paul. We should make it a family affair. Bev would be thrilled.'

Neither Lou nor Paul could think of anything worse, but they both loved Bev, so they made their own form of commitment.

'Let's go a bit earlier, you and me,' Lou suggested, 'say either Thursday or Friday, what do you reckon?'

'Yep,' Paul agreed, 'good idea – lot of work to do on the boat over the weekend. Sorry, Mum, can't take too much time off. Why don't we make it Friday, Lou?'

'You're on.'

Well that got them off the hook.

It had taken Lou some time to come to grips with the husband his daughter had chosen. What could Maria, black-haired, vibrant, passionate Maria, who had so much of his Sicilian blood in her veins, possibly see in such a stitched-up man? He presumed David's looks had something to do with it: the two certainly made a handsome couple. Perhaps they aroused each other to lustful heights, he thought cynically. Perhaps a boring man could be exciting in bed. But lust was not enough upon which to base the lifetime commitment of marriage. At least it wasn't in Lou's opinion. Lust doesn't last, he thought, and lust can be destructive. He should know. A brief lustful dalliance in the early years of his marriage had nearly cost him Barbara. Funny, tough-Aussie, loyal-to-the-end Barb, the love of his life and the best wife a man could ask for. He only hoped there was more to his daughter's marriage than lust.

Lou's views had been right to a certain extent – lust had been a governing factor, and over time there did appear occasional cracks in the Millers' marriage, resulting principally from David's conservatism. Particularly symbolic was the naming of their children, or rather the aftermath. David, besotted with his wife, had agreed that their secondborn be christened Paolo (thus pleasing Lou no end), this being the customary middle name of the males in her father's family, particularly as Maria had agreed their firstborn be christened Beverly after David's mother, who was of English descent. All of which had seemed quite fair, an equal balance. But the balance had not been equal at all. Paolo had very soon became Paul, his father introducing the little boy to all and sundry by the Anglicised version of his name, to the point where nobody knew him as anything else. Even his mother, albeit reluctantly, had adopted the name, although to start with she had protested the case.

'But he's Australian, darling,' David had argued in his mild, common-sense way; disagreements never involved a shadow of hostility, David was a firm believer in good old-fashioned logic. 'And what's more he's *second generation* Australian; he'll be much more comfortable known as Paul, believe me.'

Maria had to admit that her husband might have a point, but in any event she didn't wish to confuse the child, so she gave in, bludgeoned by good old-fashioned logic.

Only the boy's grandfather refused to conform. Paolo remained Paolo to Lou, which produced some tension between him and his son-in-law, although both assiduously avoided a confrontation on the topic.

David had something of a fetish about names in general it seemed. He didn't like diminutives. Beverly was always Beverly to him, even while to everyone else she was Bev. And if anyone, in a bid to be friendly, inadvertently called him Dave, he or she was quickly corrected. 'David,' he would say, very, very politely. 'I prefer David.'

The one diminutive that appeared acceptable to David Miller was 'Lou', because it was less foreign-sounding than Luigi and therefore less likely to draw attention. Luigi Panuzza claimed sweet victory on that score.

His daughter, too, claimed a victory of sorts. Maria always called her father Papa, knowing how much it pleased him, despite her husband's protestations.

'But it sounds so foreign, darling,' David had said.

'Yes,' she'd replied demurely, but mischievously, 'it's meant to.'

Over the years, the antipathy Lou had initially felt toward his son-in-law had waned, for one reason and one reason only: he had come to recognise the true and enduring love the man had for his daughter. Maria had found a loyal husband who would never look at another woman, one who would stand by her to the bitter end, and for this Lou was grateful. These days he didn't even find David all that irritating – in fact, there were times when he actually felt sorry for him. The poor bloke can't help being stitched up, he thought.

Now, with talk of the writers' festival successfully out of the way, Lou broached another subject, diving in quickly before the beers were finished when they would adjourn to the kitchen and dining room to get on with the setting of the table, the opening of the wine and the dishing-up of the veggies and gravy. The final preparation for the Sunday dinner was a family affair where everyone mucked in, although once they were gathered around the table it was of course always David, standing at the head, who carved the lamb. Which was just as it should be.

'Did you find time to chuck any stuff together for Thelma to send to St Vinnies, Maria?' Lou asked casually, drawing querying looks from both David and Paul. 'I called your mother the other day, Paolo,' he explained to his grandson. 'I told her about the big clean-out of old clothes we had and said Thelma could do with some women's stuff too if she felt like having a clean-out herself. Said I'd take them around to the church for her, good idea, don't you reckon?'

Paul's look was one of alarm. Certainly getting some clothes, apart from men's tracksuit pants and shirts for the women on the island was a good idea, but what about the risk? The subject was bound to come up in passing with Thelma, the pastor's wife, who ran the small charity collection centre at the church only several blocks away on the corner of Marine Parade. Thelma was devoted to what she called her 'good works'. The donated clothes and blankets she sent to St Vincent de Paul's in Geraldton, and the books she put on display in the shelves of the church vestibule, the money raised from their sale going directly into the church funds. But even more than her 'good works', Thelma was devoted to gossip. She loved nothing more than a good old 'chinwag', as she called it. In fact it was often difficult to get away from Thelma.

'Yeah,' he agreed, 'why not? If Mum's got some old gear I'm sure Thelma'd be grateful.' But his eyes signalled a warning. He could just hear Thelma's parrot-like voice echoing what had been said to her, and echoing even her own reply. *Clothes from your father, you say, clothes from your father? No, no, I didn't receive any . . . didn't receive any clothes from your father.*

Lou was quick to put his grandson's fears to rest. 'Yes, I know she would,' he replied coolly. 'She was most grateful when I dropped our supplies in. And when I asked her, she said she'd welcome some women's gear.'

You canny old bastard, Paul thought admiringly, you set this up right from the start. You gave Thelma some of our stuff last week and promised her some women's stuff this week; half for the refugees and half for Thelma. You canny, canny old bastard.

'Yes, Papa,' Maria said, blissfully unaware of the collusion between her father and son, 'I've looked out two large plastic bags' worth; a clothes clean-out was way overdue. There's some of Bev's old stuff there too. I phoned her to check, but she told me to chuck the whole lot out. Don't bother taking them around to the church, though, I'll drop them in myself – it's only down the street.'

'Rubbish, you're far too busy.' It was true, Maria was certainly a busy woman. On weekdays she taught at the small junior school (which also housed the kindergarten) and during the weekends she helped her husband and his young assistant in the general store. 'I have all the time in the world,' Lou insisted. 'I'll take the bags with me tonight and drop them off tomorrow arvo when I get back from fishing. Besides,' he added, 'you don't want to get stuck with Thelma.'

'Yes,' Maria added in hearty agreement, 'there is always that. Thanks, Papa, I'll take you up on the offer.' She drained her wine glass and stood. 'Now let's eat.'

Later that night back at Paul's cottage they sifted through the bags of dresses and skirts and blouses and slacks, leaving aside the shorts and the tops with shoe-string straps and other revealing items that obviously would not suit the modesty of dress required. They were selective in their choices, practicality being their principal objective, but there were a number of items they felt might bring some pleasure to the women on the island. There was even a mustardy, golden-hued shawl, lightweight, with brown thread running through it and fringes at each end, a little faded and worn, but still attractive. Paul remembered his mother wearing it on her evenings out many years back. Jalila, he thought as he folded it and put it to one side. Jalila would like that.

The following morning at the break of dawn, Lou picked Paul up in the old Holden ute he'd been driving since the eighties. 'Never given me a day's trouble,' was his proud boast. 'Why should I swap the old girl when she's been so loyal to me?' The back of the vehicle was packed with all the supplies they'd gathered over the past days, some bought locally and some purchased from a quick trip Lou had made to Geraldton.

They drove to the marina, where they loaded *Principessa*. The few other people around who were embarking upon a dawn fish themselves took no notice apart from an acknowledging wave; they were too busy preparing their own vessels. Even the large hessian sack packed with four fresh bags of crushed ice was no cause for comment – it could have contained gear for the boat, anything. Who cared? Other fishers certainly didn't. The smuggling of goods to Gevaar Island was no problem at all.

They chugged their way over at a pleasant twelve knots upon the calmest of seas, and arrived two hours later when the sun was high.

As before, the group, having safely established the approaching vessel was the old Princess, had come out of hiding and was gathered on the jetty waving a welcome. But as Lou and Paul stepped from the boat they were met with a further welcome, one that took them by surprise.

'Hello, Lou!'

'Hello, Paul!'

'Good morning, Lou.'

'Good morning, Paul.'

A chorus of voices greeted them as hands were shaken all round, a chorus of voices all speaking in English.

'Well what do you know,' Lou said with an approving nod, 'that's pretty impressive, that is.'

But Hamid, having patiently waited for the fuss to die down, had an even more impressive greeting. He offered his hand up to Paul.

'G'day, mate,' he said as loudly and clearly as he could, and with a distinctly Australian accent.

Paul didn't laugh, although he was tempted to do so, as was Lou, who also kept a straight face. Instead he accepted the greeting in all seriousness. 'G'day, mate,' he said as they shook. 'Good on you, Hamid, well done.'

Hamid beamed triumphantly about at the others, particularly Rassen. He'd been practising for days and he knew he'd got it right.

'We haven't been able to translate the "gudeye" part,' Rassen explained in his polished rounded vowels. A glance at Hala and Massoud revealed them to be equally mystified. 'We know "mate" means "friend", but "gudeye" has us somewhat stumped. Obviously it's some form of "hello", but literally . . .?'

'Literally it's "good day",' Paul replied.

'Ah. Yes. Of course. How silly of me.'

It had been little Hamid's determination to learn English that had inspired Rassen to conduct classes with the group in general. Upon discovering the boy had learnt several words from Jalila (who had been unable to translate 'g'day', hence the query being directed to him), Rassen had realised this was why Hamid hovered about eavesdropping whenever he and Hala and Massoud were conversing. He'd then decided what an excellent idea it would be if everyone were taught a little English, just a word or two, a phrase here and there. It could only stand them in good stead when they were discovered. He didn't know why the idea hadn't occurred before. Perhaps he hadn't wished to appear too dictatorial.

Together, they unloaded the gear from the boat, Karim this time insistent upon carrying the heavy hessian sack of ice to the green hut, Paul accompanying him with the polystyrene container of seafood. After replacing the bags of ice and packing the fish, all neatly parcelled, into the old icebox, the two men rejoined the others, who had carted the rest of the supplies to the blue hut.

It was only then, when they were all together, that the unpacking commenced, accompanied once again by 'oohs' and 'ahs' of delight. This time, along with the fresh fruit and vegetables, the milk and the eggs, there was meat, in the form of lamb and chicken.

Paul addressed Rassen for the translation to be made, but his words were directed in principal to Karim and Azra, whom he knew to be orthodox Muslims.

'I'm afraid the meat may not be permissible for some,' he said. 'It hasn't been certified as halal.'

Rassen quickly made the translation, Karim and Azra nodding their thanks to Paul for his concern.

But Paul had more to say. 'I'm sorry,' he went on, 'but we don't have a Muslim butcher in Shoalhaven. I realise that for the correct form of slaughter it's necessary –'

'Enough, my friend,' Rassen interrupted with the

broadest of smiles, 'there is no need for apology. The supply of foods you have brought us,' he said, gesturing at the bounty before them, 'is more than ample for the needs of all, I assure you.'

Karim and Azra, understanding the gist of the exchange, were once again vigorously nodding their gratitude.

'Oh. Right then,' Paul said, 'that's good, I'm glad.' He was just a little disappointed – he'd wanted to impress them with his knowledge of zabihah – but it now appeared his research had been for nought.

Realising the Australian had gone to some pains to discover the traditional treatment of halal meat, Rassen pointed the fact out to the young Shia couple before turning back to Paul. 'We are very touched you should go to such trouble on our behalf,' he said formally, 'and we thank you, Paul.'

The young couple echoed his words. 'Thank you, Paul,' Karim said in English, Azra quickly following suit and patting her heart in a gesture that said far more than words.

Their appreciation was so evident that Paul was relieved his research had not been for nought. He flashed a triumphant smile at Lou and refused to be disheartened by the look he received in return that simply said 'show-off'.

The unpacking continued: nuts, cheeses and biscuits, a large bag of mixed sweets, much to Hamid's delight, and a brand-new pack of playing cards. 'I may not be a worthy chess opponent,' Lou commented to Rassen, 'but I play a damn good hand of poker, I can promise you that. Oh, and Paul had an old mobile we were going to offer you, but reception on the island's lousy,' Lou said, 'at times non-existent, so . . .'

'Mobile?' Rassen was thoroughly confused. 'Mobile what?'

'Phone.'

'Ah. A cell phone, yes of course.'

'Yeah,' Paul chimed in, 'but even if you'd managed to get some form of reception, you'd have needed a charger, so no point really.'

Finally it was time to dole out the women's clothing.

'Some gifts for the ladies,' Lou said rather grandly, upending the plastic bag and spilling the dozen or so items out onto the table, to the pleasant surprise of the women.

He stood back allowing them to make their own choices, but it was his grandson who unexpectedly got in first.

Paul picked up the light, golden-hued shawl. 'I thought you might like this, Jalila,' he said, holding it out to the girl. He sensed Lou's gaze fixed firmly, and no doubt critically, upon him, but he refused to look at the old man. This was his gift to Jalila, something that he desperately hoped might arouse a smile, or at least some infinitesimal sign of pleasure.

She took the shawl from him, stroking the fabric with her fingers. 'Pretty.'

She made the remark in English, which Paul found most promising. Smile, his mind begged. Please smile, Jalila, please! But there was not a vestige of personal interest; the remark had been only a remark, nothing more. Then he watched as she offered the shawl to Azra.

'This will make an excellent hijab for you, Azra,' Jalila said in Arabic.

'No, no,' Azra demurred, 'I am quite happy with the one I have.' She had made herself a new hijab a good week or so earlier from an attractive green cotton tablecloth they had discovered. 'You must keep it for yourself, Jalila, it will suit you well.'

But Jalila simply placed the shawl back on the table to be selected by any who might wish to take it. No one did. Aware that the young Australian had presented it to Jalila as a personal gift, they were a little embarrassed.

'Well, well, it's been a long time since I've worn something as smart as this,' Hala said, donning a pinstripe jacket and twirling about to relieve the slight awkwardness that followed.

'There's a skirt that goes with it,' Paul said, equally eager to move on, feeling self-conscious. 'It's a suit that belonged to my mother.' He ferreted about and produced the slim-line, knee-length skirt.

'How wonderful,' Hala said, holding the skirt up against herself. 'I do believe your mother and I are around the same size. I claim these as mine,' she announced to the other women, knowing full well none of them would be interested in the items. 'Do thank your mother for me, Paul; I feel very modern and at home in a pinstripe I must say.' She didn't feel particularly modern, rather more retrospective than anything, remembering the pinstripe business suit she'd acquired in London thirty years earlier when, after marrying Rassen, she'd been required to attend official functions. She found both the memory and the suit most comforting.

'Mum's not altogether in the know,' Paul admitted sheepishly. 'Lou and I are keeping you lot a secret, strictly between ourselves. She thinks her old clothes are going to charity.'

'Which of course they are,' Hala said with her bold, infectious laugh. 'One day, perhaps though, we may be able to thank her in person.'

The sorting out of the clothes continued, everyone finding an item or two of personal interest – a blouse here, a pair of slacks or a dress there – but the shawl sat conspicuously unclaimed.

Hala felt sorry for Paul, recognising his disappointment at the rejection of his gift. She did not find anything suspect about his interest in Jalila. Naturally, as a young man, he would be attracted by the girl's beauty, but there was nothing to fear from the Australian, she thought – he had no ulterior motive. Hala sensed that, like all of them, Paul wished simply to kindle some spark of life in Jalila.

While the supplies were being packed away, Sanaa brewed a pot of tea, made coffee for those who preferred it and set out plates of biscuits. Everyone was insistent Lou and Paul stay for morning tea, and as they all settled themselves, Hala deliberately placed herself beside the young Australian, engaging him in conversation. She had a certain tack she intended to take, but started out on safely conventional and deeply sincere ground.

'You could have no idea I'm sure, Paul,' she said, 'how immensely grateful we are for all you and your grand-father are doing for us. We realise that if you were to be discovered aiding illegal immigrants you would be in trouble with the law.' It was a subject she and Rassen, and Massoud also, had discussed at some length.

'No worries,' Paul replied casually, 'it's a risk we're willing to take. Rassen told Lou you need to buy time while you build your strength, and the huts are here so . . .' he gave a nonchalant shrug '. . . no skin off our noses. Why not give you a hand?'

'Perhaps,' Hala said, 'but many would not see it that way. You are very generous, both of you. And not just in the material sense,' she added. 'You're very generous in spirit, you and Lou.'

She gazed about at the group. 'We *are* building our strength, you know. This time on the island is doing us all a great deal of good.' Her eyes came to rest upon her husband, who was chatting with Lou. The pack of cards in his hand and Lou nodding eager affirmation, the two were obviously keen to embark upon a poker game. 'Being here is strengthening every single one of us,' she said with a quiet gratitude this young man would never understand and which she had no intention of explaining; Rassen's nightmares were far fewer these days. Then she took a slight conversational detour, moving on to the tack she'd intended. 'In fact, even those of us who appear broken beyond mending are beginning to make some progress. Jalila, for instance . . .'

Paul was immediately on guard. Lou's warning, which he'd taken as the grossest of insults . . . His gift of the shawl to Jalila, the shawl she'd declined . . . Did Hala also think he was on the make? The mere thought appalled him. But Hala calmly continued.

'Jalila has been using the binoculars you brought us,' she said, a remark he found rather incongruous. Then, in response to his obvious bewilderment, she asked, only furthering the incongruity of the conversation, 'Do you know much about the birdlife on this island?'

'Yes,' he replied, trying to mask his confusion, 'I know a great deal.'

'Excellent, I had presumed you might.' She smiled her lovely, motherly smile. 'I think you should go for a walk with Jalila. Take the binoculars and teach her something about the birds she has been so admiring.' Hala's smile faded; she was very much in earnest. 'Apart from little Hamid, the birds are the only thing to have aroused in Jalila the slightest flicker of interest.'

Paul didn't know what to say. He looked across to where Jalila was sitting sipping at her mug of tea like an automaton, no enjoyment, no animation, the same nothingness in her eyes.

'Will you do this for me, Paul?' Hala asked, aware of his uncertainty, aware that perhaps he again feared the embarrassment of an offer that might be rejected. 'I believe you will be helping the girl immensely,' she urged. 'Will you do this?'

'If Jalila wants me to,' Paul replied with caution, 'yes of course.'

Hala stood. 'Jalila,' she called, interrupting the general flow of conversation around the hut, 'Paul has very kindly offered to teach you about the birdlife on the island.' She spoke loudly and in English. 'Would you like to take the binoculars and go for a walk with him?'

Lou and Rassen had been on the verge of leaving the gathering themselves, intending to adjourn to the yellow hut for a game of poker. Now the two older men sat, jaws agape, particularly Lou. What the hell is the woman up to? he wondered.

Then to everyone's surprise, Jalila rose to her feet. 'Yes,' she said, 'I would like this.'

'Good.' Hala's voice was brisk, business-like, masking the sheer thrill she felt at the successful outcome of her plan, an outcome that incidentally had taken her as much by surprise as it had the others. 'Off you go then and fetch the binoculars.'

As the girl disappeared briefly to the adjoining room where the binoculars were kept high on a shelf and out of harm's way, Rassen attempted to allay Lou's concern, which was palpable. Hala's suggestion had amazed him too, but like his wife, Rassen considered Jalila's acquiescence a major breakthrough.

'Don't worry, Lou,' he muttered, wondering even as he did what exactly it was the Australian found so worrying. Was he concerned for the girl, or was he concerned for his young grandson? Did he think the boy might become enamoured?

'I'm sorry, my friend,' he said comfortingly, stopping just short of patting Lou's hand, 'my wife is bossy, she always has been. But Hala knows what she's doing. Hala always knows, believe me.'

Lou could only watch helplessly as the girl returned with the binoculars and she and Paul set off for their walk. He tried to catch his grandson's eye as they passed by, to signal some sort of warning, he didn't know what, but Paul's gaze was resolutely fixed on the door. And then they were gone.

'Have a nice walk,' Hala called after them cheerily.

CHAPTER TEN

Paul started talking the moment they were clear of the hut, perhaps due to self-consciousness, he wasn't sure, but there happened, very conveniently, to be a bird feeding frenzy a hundred metres or so off-shore. The sight was a common one, particularly at this time of the year, and he happily launched into his lecture, thankful to be rescued from a silence that might have proved awkward.

'They're wedge-tailed shearwaters,' he said, pointing to the masses of dark, grey-brown birds with large wedge-shaped tails that were fiercely dive-bombing their bodies into the sea. 'They're feeding on bait-sized fish or maybe squid, something close to the surface, but they can dive really deep if need be, up to fourteen metres or so. It's coming up to their breeding season and there'll be thousands of colonies all over the place soon, particularly the islands of the Abrolhos a bit further south.'

He had no idea how much of what he was saying she was able to understand, but he was gratified to note that, as she gazed at the birds through the binoculars, she appeared to be listening.

'They nest mainly in burrows,' he went on, 'and pairs often form a long-term bond, which might last for several years. They dig their burrow together and come back to repair it the next year. If the breeding season doesn't turn out a success, they call it quits and get divorced.' He smiled as if making a joke, although in essence what he said was fact. There was no reaction, which was hardly surprising, but he told himself it was because she didn't understand the word 'divorce'.

They walked on further north, heading for the mangrove trees, Paul still talking all the while.

'There's an osprey nest up this way,' he said, 'a magnificent bird of prey, beautiful to watch. Some people call them sea eagles, but they're not actually eagles at all, they're sea hawks or fish hawks. We do get eagles from time to time though,' he added, 'white-bellied sea eagles, quite spectacular.'

Again, no reaction, she hadn't uttered a word since they'd left the hut, but something urged him to keep talking. He suspected it was probably nerves, although strangely enough he didn't feel uncomfortable in her presence.

As they walked he pointed out the difference between the gulls and the terns, Jalila focusing her binoculars on the birds circling overhead and out on the island's coastal water.

'They're Pacific gulls,' he said, 'and those ones with the crests, they're crested terns. There are lots of different sorts of terns on the islands in these waters. I'll show you where the fairy terns are nesting later.'

Then as they neared the mangroves, he reverted again to the ospreys. 'Like the shearwaters, the osprey breeding season's coming up soon,' he said, 'but the ospreys don't just bond for a couple of years like the shearwaters, they mate for life –' He was about to go on, but stopped, coming to a sudden halt. 'Oh, that's a shame.'

Up ahead, he could see the mangroves, the sturdy dead trunk of the largest tree towering above the greenery of the others, locked firmly in place by the grove's surrounding root system, and in the tree's bare, uppermost fork the huge, untidy osprey nest. But the nest was unoccupied.

Beside him Jalila too halted, his disappointment bewildering her.

He pointed. 'There's the nest,' he said, 'nothing in it, no osprey. Pity, I was hoping you'd get to see one.'

Jalila focused her binoculars on the nest, and as she did so the slight intake of her breath produced a frisson of pleasure in Paul. Surely that was something close to a gasp, he thought. At last, a reaction.

'Yes, it's pretty amazing, isn't it?' he said. 'They're not neat builders, but they're impressive ones all right.'

The nest was enormous. Close to two metres wide, it was a great clutter of driftwood and seaweed, sticks and vegetation, layer by layer all solidly nestled in the treetop like a fortress: messy, but strong.

'It's been there for ages,' he said, 'year after year. The pair build several nests, but they keep coming back to this one, repairing it each season. This is their favourite.'

Paul watched the girl as she gazed through the telescopic lenses at the giant nest. She was motionless, lips parted in amazement, fascinated, and he felt as if he had just received the greatest reward possible. Perhaps this was even better than the smile he'd hoped for. Jalila had, for this brief moment anyway, been brought to life.

He was so taken by the sight that he didn't notice the slight change in the angle of the binoculars. She had lifted her gaze just above the nest now to the sky beyond, and her words came as more than a surprise. They came as the most wonderful shock.

'Look,' she said, pointing into the distance. 'Look, Paul. Bird come.'

He looked in the direction she was pointing and sure enough there it was. The osprey. He could see the creature quite clearly without binoculars. Its massive wingspan close to three times the width of its sixty-centimetre body length, the osprey was homing in on its nest from afar – a magnificent sight.

Jalila thrust the binoculars at him. 'You look, Paul, you look.'

'No, no,' he pushed them back to her, 'I don't need the binoculars. I've seen it before. Keep looking, Jalila, keep looking.'

She needed no further bidding, firmly fixing her focus upon the osprey as it made its approach. Closer it came, and closer.

Then the bird was above them, wheeling overhead, no flapping of wings, the creature just arcing a graceful path through the sky. It circled twice, checking out the land, checking out its nest, checking out the two of them where they stood watching.

Paul laughed. 'He's putting on a show just for you.'

Finally the bird came to rest, hovering momentarily, then settling into its nest, giant wings neatly folding, stern raptor face looking out over the island, like a king surveying its realm.

'Or of course it might be a "she",' Paul said. 'I can never tell.' He considered giving a further lecture on the nesting and breeding habits of the osprey, but for the first time since they'd left the hut, he felt unthreatened by silence.

Instead, they crept a little closer to the nest, where they sat on the ground watching the osprey.

'Such beauty,' Jalila murmured. She had put aside the binoculars now and was gazing at the creature, lost in admiration. 'We have no bird like this where I come from,' she said. 'We have no bird like any bird on this island.'

'These are sea birds,' he replied.

'Yes.' She nodded. 'We have no sea where I come from.'

It seemed the perfect opening, so he took it. 'Where do you come from, Jalila?'

She didn't answer, continuing to stare up at the osprey. But she didn't seem offended by the question so he pushed a little further.

'What land do you come from?'

'I am Yazidi. I come from a mountain in nowhere land.'

Her voice was a monotone, and still she stared up at the

bird. He knew he should stop now. But he didn't. 'And your family? Your family still live there on the mountain?'

'No. Family dead. All dead.'

The fact seemed to mean nothing to her. Her attention remained on the bird, although Paul doubted she was seeing it. She herself had once again become dead. He cursed himself, sure his questions must have brought back fearful memories. What's she thinking? he wondered. What could possibly be going through her mind? But she displayed no sign of trauma, no evidence of turmoil. She was simply lifeless, as she had been before.

'Do you want to see the fairy terns?' he asked, feeling utterly useless, the question sounding moronic.

She turned to him, and he saw, to his complete surprise, that the light of interest was back in her eyes.

'Yes,' she said, 'I would like this.'

The images, when they returned, did not torment Jalila. There were often moments that brought jagged reminders of the past, as Paul's questions just had, but she made no attempt to block these distant memories. They meant nothing to her. The past belonged to a person who had ceased to exist. The past could do her no further harm. There was one image only she fought always to keep locked away in the darkest recesses of her mind, one unbearable image. She managed for the most part to prevent it resurfacing, but sometimes in the depths of the night it would return to remind her of the day she had died.

She stood. 'I would like very much to see the fairy terns.'

They cut across to the western side of the island, to where the small isthmus projected into the sea, culminating in a sandy beach and a rocky outcrop. It was here the terns would be nesting.

They walked in silence, Paul still cursing himself, riddled with guilt, wondering what he could possibly say by way of reparation.

'I'm sorry.' Finally he blurted the words out.

'Sorry?' She seemed puzzled.

'I'm sorry for prying.'

She appeared to find his apology confusing, but walked on, not breaking her stride, a mixture of indifference and incomprehension.

'I should never have asked you those questions,' he said. 'I had no right. I'm sorry, Jalila, I'm really sorry.'

'No need for sorry. You ask what you wish. You are friend.' She strode on, unconcerned. His questions, like her past, were of no consequence.

Paul was relieved to discover he'd caused no irreparable damage, but again he was mystified.

Arriving at the seaward side of the island, they stood on the shoreline and looked across the swirling water to the beach and the rocky outcrop fifty metres or so away. With the high tide and a fast running current covering the sandbar, it appeared for all the world like a tiny island.

'At low tide, you can walk out there,' Paul explained. 'Well,' he corrected himself, 'you could walk out there now, really, the water would only be around waist-high, but the current's pretty strong and you'd risk being swept off the sandbar. There's no problem if you're a strong swimmer of course, but . . .' He looked a query.

She shook her head. 'I can no swim.'

'Yeah, I didn't think so. Lou reckons most of you can't swim, is that right?'

'Yes.'

'Must have made things scary on the boat.'

She offered no reply; this was another subject that was meaningless. She'd not been in the least scared on the boat. Paul's words brought back fragmented images certainly – Hassan's blood swirling in the water, his screams, the black, black eye of the shark as it had torn at his flesh – but the sight had aroused no fear at the time, no regret. Nor did its memory. She recalled a mild resignation to the fact that she had lost her protector, but Hassan had meant nothing to her, and death held no fear for one who was already dead. Even when she'd clung to the boat's wreckage throughout the night, hearing the screams of others, she would have quite welcomed being taken by a shark. At least her body would be serving some purpose.

Looking across at the little rocky island, Jalila could see bird activity on the beach. She raised the binoculars to her eyes. 'I see them, Paul,' she said. 'I see fairy terns.'

Paul couldn't help but thrill to the fresh element of vitality he heard in her voice, and once again the sight of her staring at the birds in rapt attention moved him immensely. Was it really this simple to break through Jalila's shroud of unhappiness and bring her back to life? Were the birds the answer? He was unable to take his eyes from the girl as she studied the terns. I've made some sort of connection, he told himself, I must have – Jalila called me 'friend', that has to be a sign I've won her trust. Can it really be this easy to bring her back to life?

She turned, offering him the binoculars. 'You look, Paul. You look.'

'No, I can see well enough, they're building their nests. You keep watching, Jalila, and I'll tell you a bit about them.'

He looked away, edging closer to the shoreline, feeling caught out, hoping she hadn't read his thoughts, and, gazing across to the sandy beach where the tidy little birds with their pretty yellow-brown bills, their neat black caps and white forked tails were busily at work, he embarked upon his lecture.

'Fairy terns build their nests on open, sandy beaches, just bits of shells and vegetation mainly,' he said, 'which means that when the eggs are laid they're pretty much at the mercy of predators. Along the mainland coastline the threats are usually from foxes, dogs, cats, that sort of thing. We don't have those animals out here so it makes the island colonies particularly valuable.' He turned back to her. 'The fairy terns are a protected species, you see –'

His voice dropped away and he stopped mid-sentence, horrified. She was no longer looking at the birds, but standing before him half-naked. The blouse she had been wearing lay on the ground at her feet beside the binoculars, her breasts were bared and she was in the process of unfastening the waistband of her skirt.

'What are you doing?' Panic overwhelmed him. 'Good God, what are you doing? Stop it, stop it.'

She took her hands from her skirt, but made no effort to clothe herself, facing him unashamedly in her half-nakedness.

He dived for the blouse, picked it up and handed it to her, averting his eyes.

She took the blouse from him, but did not put it on, and he was forced to meet the directness of her gaze.

'Why, Jalila? Why are you doing this?'

'You wish to take me.' No accusation, a simple statement of fact. 'So I give myself.'

'No, no, I do not wish to take you.' Paul found himself stammering in his confusion. 'Why would you think that I –?' Her eyes continued to stare unflinchingly into his. 'Get dressed, Jalila,' he pleaded, 'get dressed, please!'

Still she did not move.

'Why are you doing this?' He demanded once again. 'Why?'

'You are good to me. You are friend. I offer payment.'

The words came out by rote. In Jalila's mind the words were Hassan's. He always spoke English to her and always insisted she respond in kind. 'This man is good to us, Jalila. He is our friend. We must offer payment.' That was when she must give herself to the man with whom Hassan was conducting business. Which she did not mind. The men with whom Hassan did business were not as brutal as the soldiers, and after her years of rape she no longer felt pain. Easy to close the mind off.

Paul backed away. The sound of her words and the look

in her eyes filled him with dismay. Everything about her was soulless, soulless and terrifying.

'I do not want payment,' he said, trying to keep the tremor from his voice. 'I want to be your friend, yes, but I do not want payment.' He turned his back on her. 'Get dressed.' He made the order sound strong, authoritative. 'Get dressed immediately. I will not look at you until you're dressed.'

The sheer subjugation of her action appalled him. She'd obviously done this many, many times before. What was her past? Had she been a prostitute? Had she been forced to offer herself?

Jalila understood a command and obediently donned her blouse. 'I am dress.'

'Good.' He briefly acknowledged the fact, then returned his gaze to the sandy beach, wondering what on earth he should do next.

Jalila had picked up the binoculars and was once again gazing through them, entranced. 'Fairy terns pretty.'

'Yes, yes, they are,' he agreed. 'They're very pretty birds.'

She joined him and they stood together, looking across the stretch of water.

'When the eggs are laid the terns get very protective,' he said, talking just for the sake of talking, avoiding once more the threat of silence. 'If you walk around on the sand you can see the eggs just sitting there, and the terns attack you from above. They dive-bomb you, scores of them. They don't hurt you, but they put on quite a show – really something to see.'

Binoculars dangling by her side, she was watching him now, he could see her in his peripheral vision, intent upon every word he was saying.

'Next time we'll come here at low tide,' he said, eyes still on the terns, 'and we'll walk across the sandbar, would you like that?'

'Yes,' he heard her say, 'I would like that very much.'

He turned on his heel, she followed, and they walked back to the settlement as if nothing had happened.

They arrived to discover Karim and Hany kicking the soccer ball around near the benches. The men were including little Hamid in the game just enough to keep the child engaged without spoiling their own fun, while Azra sat nearby watching and enjoying the sun.

In the blue hut, Hala was helping Sanaa prepare lunch.

'Hello, you two, did you enjoy your walk?' she asked as they appeared in the doorway, her query obviously directed to Jalila.

'Yes,' Jalila replied. 'I see very big bird. Osprey . . .' She glanced at Paul to make sure she'd got the word right. He gave a nod. 'And next time Paul take me to see fairy terns.'

'How exciting.' Hala kept her response casual while trying to contain both her surprise and delight. Then as Jalila disappeared briefly, returning the binoculars to the storeroom, she congratulated Paul. 'My goodness, you've wrought miracles. That's talkative for Jalila, and all in English, what's more. I've never seen her so animated – how did you manage it?'

'I didn't,' he replied, 'the birds did. You were right, she's really interested in the birds.' He looked about, desperate for some form of distraction. 'Where's Lou?'

'He's with Rassen in the yellow hut; they're playing poker I believe.'

'Right. I'll collect him and we'll be off then.'

'But you'll stay for lunch, won't you? It's nearly ready and there's more than enough.'

'Thanks, but I don't think so. Lou and I've got a fair bit of work to do at home. Next trip maybe.'

'Oh, the others will be so disappointed. We'd all love to spend some time with you. Perhaps Lou could change your mind?' she asked hopefully.

'Sure. I'll check with him.' Paul couldn't wait to get out of the blue hut and away from Hala's scrutiny. Did she suspect something? He wanted not only to get out of the hut, but off the island altogether. Jalila had reappeared from the store room and even the sight of her jangled his nerves; he didn't want to spend any more time in her company, not just yet anyway.

'Let me know if you decide not to stay for lunch,' Hala called after him as he started out the door. 'We must come and wave goodbye from the jetty.'

He paused to look back, wondering if there was some hidden meaning in the remark, but she returned a motherly smile.

'We can't break with tradition, Paul,' she said, 'not right now. Not when you and Lou are so special to us.'

He returned a brief salute and left. She suspects something, he told himself, or she senses something at least, she's so damn intelligent.

Paul set off for the yellow hut, his paranoia mounting by the second, intent upon breaking up the poker game and getting away from the island.

The poker game had never really eventuated, not in any serious form. During the first couple of hands, Rassen had asked Lou if by any chance he'd heard further news of the situation in Aleppo, or Syria in general. He'd made his enquiry in as offhand a manner as possible. Why should this Western Australian fisherman be interested in matters a world away? And why should Lou, his very saviour, be expected to act also as a reporter upon happenings in his homeland? Rassen's approach was infinitely tasteful, offering the Australian an easy reply. 'Sorry, mate, no idea,' was all Lou needed to say, after which they'd get on with their poker game. It was his turn to deal after all. He had the cards in hand, already shuffled.

But Lou had most certainly been following events in the Middle East. Since his discovery of the refugees he'd been glued to the television screen more keenly than he ever had been in the past, wanting to learn as much as he could about the world of his new friends. Now, however, upon being questioned, he wasn't sure how much Rassen might enjoy hearing; it all seemed very gloomy.

'The rebels in Aleppo have surrendered to the government,' he said, 'but the peace settlement process has come to a halt, or so I saw on the news. The city's reduced to rubble and the civilians are stranded with nowhere to go.'

Rassen nodded. Hardly surprising, he thought, the Assad regime and the terrorists are as bad as each other, both cut from the same cloth. And the rebels, too, even those who may have once fought for a purpose, are now as ruthless as the government they wish to overthrow. No one cares about those caught in the middle.

'The UN's saying the government's military campaign has displaced tens of thousands of civilians and may have violated the laws of war,' Lou went on.

'Something of an understatement,' Rassen replied, unable to disguise his contempt. *Displaced*, what about those *murdered*? he thought, images of children's mangled bodies coming all too vividly into his mind. And the *United Nations*? That toothless tiger? The regime 'may have violated the laws of war'. What sort of condemnation is that? And what a farcical term anyway. *The laws of war*. What laws? Are people really naive enough to believe laws are observed in a battle zone? Any battle zone, let alone the conflict raging in my homeland!

Rassen was tempted to vent his disgust, but in deference to Lou he curbed his tongue and remained silent while the Australian continued.

'There's big trouble brewing in Turkey too,' Lou said, aware that Rassen would want whatever information he might have to impart. 'A whole string of terrorist attacks in Istanbul, one after the other, right out of the blue, totally unexpected, civilians and tourists deliberately targeted by ISIS.'

'ISIS?' This news was clearly a surprise to Rassen. 'Islamic terrorists gaining a foothold in Istanbul? Oh dear, that *is* sad. I know there's been trouble for some time with the Kurdish separatists to the north, and there have been riots amongst those from Northern Iraq seeking refuge, but these are political and humanitarian issues. *ISIS?*' His expression was one of utter dismay. 'Oh dear me, that's a different matter altogether.'

It was around then Rassen had appeared to lose all interest in poker.

'Istanbul,' he mused, 'once the leading secular city of the world. A place where East meets West and where men are free to worship as they will.' He quietly muttered a quote to himself, a quote from one of his greatest heroes. '*Every man can follow his own conscience, provided it does not interfere with sane reason or bid him act against the liberty of his fellow men.*' Then he heaved a heartfelt sigh. 'How disappointed Mustafa Atatürk would be,' he said.

Lou, having imparted the news he'd gleaned from television, was starting to feel a little out of his depth, but at the mention of Mustafa Atatürk his mind was instantly activated. He knew that name. The Turkish military leader and president who had made the profoundly moving speech about Gallipoli. How often had he heard it quoted and seen it in print? Certainly every year on Anzac Day. He'd even memorised the last part of the speech.

He put the pack of cards to one side, like Rassen he'd lost all interest in poker, and without hesitation he proudly recited, '*You, the mothers who sent their sons from far-away countries, wipe away your tears; your sons are now lying in our bosom and are in peace. After having lost their lives on this land they have become our sons as well.*'

Rassen stared at the Australian, astounded; a recitation like this was the last thing he'd expected. In lamenting the loss of Atatürk's Istanbul, he'd been talking to himself, not Lou. Selfishly, he now realised, or at least indulgently. He clapped his hands in a brief round of applause.

'Brings a tear to the eye, doesn't it?' Lou said, pleased to have impressed the doctor as he obviously had. 'Does to me anyway. Every time I hear it or read it,' he said with a shake of his head, 'I swear it brings a tear to the eye. That's a really great quote that is.'

'I agree wholeheartedly,' Rassen said, 'a really great quote from a really great man. And only one of many great quotes from Kemal Atatürk, Lou. I tell you, if the countries of the Middle East had followed his example back in the 1920s, today's conflict wouldn't be happening. That man could have changed the world. Had the world been willing to listen,' he added regretfully.

Lou paid avid attention as Rassen went on to wax passionate about Mustafa Kemal Atatürk, founder of the Turkish Republic and its first president.

'The removal of the caliphate ... The separation of governmental and religious affairs ... The unification of education ... Freedom for women ... Compulsive primary education for both girls and boys ...'

It was a lot of information for Lou to take on board in one go and he was sure he was missing out on quite a bit, but strangely enough he felt he could have listened to Rassen all day. There's such a lot to learn, he thought. Luigi Panuzza was one who very much liked to learn.

'Mustafa Atatürk was a man way ahead of his time,' Rassen said, 'a modern man who believed in the principles of democracy. Under Atatürk's rule, for the first time in history Islamic law was separated from secular law and restricted purely to matters of religion. Imagine if such a policy was adopted by all nations today – what do you think would happen?'

'No more religious wars?' Lou suggested.

'Well, that's my theory,' Rassen said, 'perhaps even my true belief. Of course I may be oversimplifying matters just a little,' he added self-deprecatingly, 'or even being naively idealistic, but in my opinion secularism would be a damn good place to start.' Then he came to a sudden halt, realising how long he'd been holding court. 'I'm sorry, I haven't let up for a second. I must be boring you terribly.'

'Nope. To the contrary, I could listen to you all day.'

Which only set Rassen off again. He hadn't enjoyed himself this much for a very long time.

Mustafa Kemal Atatürk was still the major topic of conversation when Paul interrupted them, although by this time Rassen was on to the reason the man was Hala's hero as much as his.

'Equal rights for women,' he'd announced. '*Human-kind is made up of two sexes, women and men.*' He leapt directly into Hala's favourite quote of all time. '*Is it possible for humankind to grow by the improvement of only one part while the other part is ignored? Is it possible that if half of a mass is tied to earth with chains that the other half can soar into skies?*'

It was Lou's turn now to give a round of applause.

Rassen acknowledged the appreciation with a gracious, albeit self-mocking, bow and was about to go on, but was halted by the voice that called from the open door.

'Hey Lou, you ready to go?'

'Oh.' Lou turned towards his grandson. 'Time to leave already, is it?' he called back.

'Well, Hala asked if we'd like to stay for lunch,' Paul admitted, 'but we should probably be heading off.'

'No, no, you must stay for lunch,' Rassen insisted, 'what an excellent idea.'

Lou thought so too. 'What do you reckon, Paolo?'

Paul reluctantly entered the room and crossed to the table. 'I dunno,' he said with a shrug as if he didn't care. 'It's getting on, and there's a lot to be done at home.' He couldn't think exactly what. 'You promised you'd drop that gear around to Thelma at the church, remember? I'm easy though,' another shrug, 'up to you, Lou.'

Lou read the message loud and clear. 'Yep, I reckon you're right. We'll be on our way.' He rose to his feet, Rassen joining him, and the two men shook hands. 'Next time we'll stay for lunch. I promise.'

'And next time we'll play poker,' Rassen replied, 'I promise. No more pontificating.'

'Pity,' Lou said with a broad grin, 'I liked the pontificating.'

Lou and Paul returned to the blue hut to collect the hessian sack into which they'd packed all the rubbish – the containers, the plastic ice bags – anything that, upon the refugees' discovery, might suggest they'd received assistance. After which the group accompanied the two of them down to the jetty.

Lou told them all not to bother, but they refused to listen, and Rassen, like Hala, was adamant.

'Mustn't break with tradition,' he said, unaware he was parroting his wife. 'That would be to court bad luck. Besides, we like waving you off from the jetty.'

Paul swung the hessian sack of rubbish into the cockpit, climbed aboard and, as Lou started up the engine, released the stern and bowlines and they were on their way.

He looked back at the group standing there waving, all of them, with the exception of Jalila, who had remained on the shore and was watching the birds. As his gaze shifted briefly to her, he wondered if she was going over the names she'd learned – Pacific gull, crested tern, wedge-tailed shearwater – and whether she remembered them all.

He dragged his eyes from the girl back to the group on the jetty, to the women in particular, who were dressed in various items of donated clothes: Hala in the smart pin-striped jacket, Sanaa in a light cotton shift of his mother's over warm and modest layers, Azra in a long-sleeved blouse that had belonged to Bev. He gave a derisive snort.

'So much for being meticulous about the rubbish,' he said, glancing at the hessian sack. 'When that mob's brought ashore those clothes'll be a dead giveaway. What do you reckon Mum's going to say when she sees her gear? Or Bev, if she's in town? Or Dad for that matter? He's bound to recognise the stuff too.'

'I agree,' Lou said calmly, wondering if his grandson's edginess had something to do with the girl. Was Jalila the reason Paolo had wanted to get away? Had something happened between them? 'There will come a time when we must let the family in on the secret, Paolo. We may need their help, or at least their support.'

Paul appeared distinctly dubious. 'Do you really think they'll understand why we're doing this?'

'Yes I do. I most certainly do. Maria and Bev particularly.'

'Oh yeah, Mum and Bev perhaps, but *Dad*?' he queried, now openly scornful.

'Yes,' Lou said after a moment's hesitation, 'yes, I believe even your father. David is a good man.'

Paul didn't altogether agree, but couldn't be bothered arguing, and they lapsed into silence. Lou wondered again why his grandson was so tense. It has to have something to do with the girl, he thought, it has to, surely.

Ten minutes or so later, he brought up the topic, his manner casual as if it had only just occurred to him to make any comment.

'Well you were obviously a great hit with Jalila,' he said jovially. 'Hala was very happy indeed.'

'Yes,' Paul replied, his voice tight, 'she was.'

You've been dying to ask what happened from the moment we left the jetty, haven't you, he thought, you nosy old bastard. He could still hear Hala's voice; he could still see the meaningful look she gave Lou when they collected the rubbish and promised they'd return in one week. 'Jalila said Paul is taking her to see the fairy terns on your next trip to the island.' And Lou's response, accompanied by his own meaningful look. 'What a good idea. Very pretty birds, and they'll be nesting of course.' What are you both playing at? Paul thought. It's a bloody conspiracy. Leave me alone, for Christ's sake. And leave Jalila alone too, she doesn't need you two interfering in her life.

Paul was so confused that he didn't think to question why he felt protective of Jalila. She needed no protection. She was not the one who had been frightened. He was.

'It's apparently quite something to have made contact with the girl,' Lou went on, 'and to have her communicate with you so openly. What did you talk about?'

'Birds,' Paul answered curtly. 'We talked about birds.'

'Ah. Yes, of course.' There couldn't be a clearer order for him to shut up, Lou realised, so he tailed off as graciously as possible. 'Good for you anyway, Paolo. Rassen says Hala always knows best, so if Hala's pleased with the outcome you must have done well.'

Perhaps, Paul thought, this is one time Hala doesn't know best.

They chugged along once more in silence, Paul trying to put the girl from his mind. He was still in shock. He needed time to think, but not now – later when he was alone. He needed to analyse what had happened.

After they'd penned *Principessa*, they walked together to Paul's cottage, where Lou collected the bag of women's clothes to be delivered to the church.

'Sure you don't want me to take them?' Paul asked, making amends, aware he'd been brusque, even rude, to Lou out on the boat. Hell, it was hardly his grandfather's fault the girl had so rattled him. 'I don't mind, honest.'

'Bullshit,' Lou replied good-naturedly. 'You can't stand Thelma for more than five minutes.'

'True.' Paul smiled, aware he'd been forgiven.

'See you at the pub around six?' Lou asked, slinging the plastic bag over his shoulder. 'We'll have dinner there, eh?'

'Sure. If you can get away from Thelma by then.'

Alone, now with time to think, Paul relived that moment on the island. The shock as he'd turned to find her half-naked, prepared to offer herself to him. Her response when he'd asked her why. 'You wish to take me,' she'd said. 'So I give myself.' But he *hadn't* wished to take her. He hadn't wished to take her then and he didn't wish to take her now, much as he admired her beauty. But the words kept repeating themselves over and over. *You wish to take me . . . You wish to take me . . . You wish to . . .* Had she read in him some desire of which he'd been unaware?

He was torturing himself, this was ridiculous, he must think logically. Perhaps if he could find out something of her past? Where did she say she came from?

He heard his own voice. 'What land do you come from, Jalila?'

And he recalled the exact words of her response. 'I am Yazidi. I come from a mountain in nowhere land.'

It was the start he needed. He turned on his computer, and the search began.

An hour later, he sat back, convinced he had discovered the answer. If he was right, it explained everything about the mystery that was Jalila.

CHAPTER ELEVEN

When Paul arrived at the pub Lou was already there, seated and in deep conversation with several of the regulars at a table on the verandah. Or rather, the others were in deep conversation; Lou appeared for the most part to be listening while the three of them rattled on in typical fashion.

Archie Lang, marine mechanic, Ian Tuckey of Tuckey's Tuckshop, and Hamish McDonald of Mac's Recreational Fishing Store were always to be found at this same table at this same time every day of the week. There'd often be others with them – townspeople or fishers; how many and who varied – but these three stalwarts were as regular as clockwork.

'G'day, Paul,' they chorused.

'G'day, Arch, Ian, Mac, how're you going?'

'Good, good,' another chorus.

'Pull up a pew,' Mac said. He was a squat, burly Glaswegian in his late sixties with a gruffly strong accent despite the fact he'd lived in Australia for well over fifty years, thirty of those in Shoalhaven.

'Sure. I'll just a grab a beer. You fellas all right?' Even if one could see that the men's glasses were full, as Paul could, and as they were, it was always essential that one make the offer.

'Yeah, we're right thanks, mate,' Ian said. 'Lou just shouted the first round.' Ian Tuckey's voice, perceived by some to be 'typically Aussie', was nasal and tinny, a 'thin' voice as scrawny as his sixty-year-old Ichabod Crane frame. He and Mac, firm friends that they were, made a very odd couple.

'Rightio, back in a tick.'

Paul disappeared to the bar. Good on you, Lou, he thought, knowing exactly why his grandfather had insisted upon buying the first round. You could always leave the company with a shout owed, but never with one owing, and given there were now five of them at the table it could be some time before dinner. Paul was grateful. Having skipped lunch he was ravenous.

He returned to discover the men had resumed their intense conversation, which happened to be about the American presidential campaign that was currently headline news worldwide. Could a flash-in-the-pan billionaire reality television star really become president of the United States?

'Bloody oath he could,' Arch declared vehemently. 'The Americans want change. Obama's a good enough bloke, but they're sick of the Establishment looking after its own, and they sure as hell don't want Hillary Clinton.'

'Yeah,' Ian Tuckey agreed, his reedy tone cutting through the surrounding chatter at nearby tables as fresh customers gathered, 'and Trump's got some damn good ideas what's more.'

'Like what?' Lou asked. In closely following the Middle East crisis, he hadn't paid much attention to the US campaign, apart from gathering that Donald Trump was considered by most to be a rank outsider and little more than a bad joke. But then it was quite likely Ian and Arch hadn't been studying the situation in great detail either, he decided, they were probably just mouthing off about what they'd read and seen in the media. Nothing wrong with that, he thought. All the blokes did that, himself included. Everyone loved a good chat at the pub.

Paul sat sipping his beer and listening, realising as the conversation progressed why Lou, normally one to join in, chose on this occasion to keep quiet. He did so himself, for the very same reason.

'Well for starters, Trump's spot on when it comes to illegals,' Ian said with an air of belligerence, as if defying others to disagree; there was nothing Ian Tuckey liked more than a good verbal stoush. 'Build a wall, keep those Mexicans out, that's what I'd want if I was a Yank. And then there's the refugees. You can't afford to let them in, can you? Look what's happening in Germany.' He turned to Mac for confirmation, and Mac gave a benign nod. The Scot was rarely ruffled.

'True, true,' he said.

Archie Lang, half the age of the other two men, but equally keen to voice his opinion, re-entered the fray. 'And then there's the Muslims,' he said. 'Trump wants to get rid of them, doesn't he? Well good luck to him I say. We could take a leaf out of his book there.'

'Too right we could,' Ian replied, altogether fired up now. 'Donald Trump and Pauline Hanson have both got a point, you know . . .' He was going to go on but Archie jumped in.

'Yeah. Don't let in any more Muslims and chuck out the ones who are here.'

That hadn't been exactly what Ian meant and he was about to correct Arch, but Mac surprised them.

'Well, you can't really do that, can you?' he suggested mildly.

A brief hiatus as Arch and Ian both looked at him.

'I mean a lot of Muslims have been here a long time – they're legal immigrants. Heck, a whole lot of us are, aren't we? I'm an immigrant myself.'

'That's hardly the same thing.' Ian's response was scathing.

'Aye, it is,' the Scot replied unperturbed, sounding

exactly like his father, who'd died twenty years previously. 'My parents came to Australia in the late fifties on the Bring out a Briton scheme. That makes me an immigrant. And you could hardly throw *me* out now, could you?' he said as if he'd clinched the argument.

'That's got bugger all to do with it, Mac,' Ian exploded, 'you dunno what the fuck you're talking about.'

'I do. Oh yes I do indeed.' As always, Mac refused to be ruffled by his argumentative friend. 'I'm talking about immigrants,' he said. 'Immigrants who arrive in a country and contribute to that country as my parents did and as I do. I'm talking about multiculturalism.'

'No, you're not.' Ian heaved an immense sigh as if he was Einstein attempting to communicate the theory of relativity to a five-year-old. 'The Bring out a Briton Campaign was designed to keep Australia *British*, Mac! Jesus bloody Christ, the whole country was shitting itself about the European migrants who were pouring in. You'd hardly call a scheme like Bring out a bloody Briton *multicultural* now, would you?' he said scornfully.

Mac downed the rest of his beer in one go, a dismissive gesture indicating he didn't wish to discuss the matter further. When Ian went out of his way to make him feel inferior, Mac always closed off, which at no time indicated any form of submission, and most certainly not in this case. Mac was a firm believer in multiculturalism, regardless of whatever his smartarse friend Ian Tuckey might have to say on the matter.

Ian, however, was insistent the last word be his; the argument did not stop here. 'And now everyone's scared about the Muslims, aren't they? The Muslims and the refugees,' he said. 'And so they bloody well should be. Trump and Hanson might be a bit extreme, I grant you, but as I was saying, they do have a point.' He sat back smugly. There, he'd had the last word.

'Hear, hear,' Arch echoed.

Lou and Paul followed Mac's example and hastily gulped down their beers, both keen to get away.

Crikey, Paul was thinking, what the hell are they going to do when they discover who's out there on that island?

Lou's thoughts were a little more convoluted. He rather wished some of the other fishers had been present. Some of the townspeople too, whose opinions might have been more along Mac's lines. No point in joining in a conversation like this though, he thought, no point at all.

'My round.' Mac stood, gathering up the several empty glasses.

'Not for us, thanks, Mac,' Lou said with a glance to Paul. 'The place is filling up and we want to grab some dinner, don't we, Paolo?'

'Too right we do – I'm bloody starving.'

They rose to their feet.

'Right you are then,' the Scot said. 'Owe you one next time, Lou.'

The three of them headed inside together, Mac for the bar and lounge just off the verandah, Lou and Paul turning left through the doors into the large dining area, where another bar sat against the rear wall and where huge plate glass windows looked out over the spectacular coastal view.

After ordering steak and chips and collecting the buzzer that would announce when their food was ready, they bought another beer and settled themselves at a window table in the far corner.

They said nothing as they gazed out at the Indian Ocean, where the last rays of what had been a splendid sunset fanned the horizon, but each knew the other was thinking about the island out there. The island and the purpose it was now serving.

Paul was the one who finally broke the silence. 'When they're found the shit's really going to hit the fan, isn't it,' he said, a statement rather than a question.

'Yep,' Lou agreed, 'but not everyone feels the same way as Ian and Arch, you know. There are many in Shoalhaven who'd sympathise with our friends rather than judge them as the enemy.' He thought of the fishers, some of Italian descent like himself, and there were Greeks, and a Finnish man and his sons. He thought of the towns-people: of Henry and Florence Wong and their Chinese restaurant, of Alfred Tran, the Vietnamese pharmacist and his family, of Nina Adrejic, the hard-working Serbian woman who, with her daughter, ran Nina's Bakery. All of these people, not to mention any number of Irish, Scots and English residents, were immigrants, or at least their parents had been. 'Let's face it,' he said, 'we're a pretty multicultural bunch ourselves.'

Paul, however, did not appear convinced. 'And you honestly reckon that'll make a difference?'

'To the outcome?' Lou shook his head sadly. 'Nope, not one bit. I'm afraid the die is cast for our mob on the island. But I'd like to think the people of Shoalhaven would show them some kindness. We're a close-knit com-munity, one that doesn't pass judgement. Even blokes like Ian and Arch, they don't mean to stir up hate, Paolo, they're only spouting what they've read in the paper, trying to show off like blokes do. Particularly Ian, he loves being the town know-all, but he's not a bad bloke. We're good people in Shoalhaven. At least that's the way I like to see us.'

'You're a bloody romantic, mate,' Paul said fondly, 'that's your problem.'

'Yes, yes,' Lou agreed, 'you're quite right of course.' Unperturbed, he was about to go on but was startled by the sound of the buzzer.

'Perfect timing.' Paul picked up the remote and pressed the off button. 'Maybe food'll shut you up,' he said with a good-natured grin.

They both stood.

'I'll grab the tucker, you get the knives and forks,' Lou ordered, 'and don't forget the tomato sauce,' he called over his shoulder as he headed for the servery.

During the days that followed, Paul didn't accompany Lou on his fishing trips as he often did during the off-season. Instead he worked hard on the necessary repairs of *Palermo Miss* and his gear, all the while doing the best he could to put the girl from his mind. But it wasn't easy. Having discovered what might possibly be Jalila's background, he wondered how he could find out whether or not he was right. Did he dare ask her? He recalled how, when he'd apologised for prying into her past, she'd seemed quite unconcerned. 'You ask what you wish,' she'd said, 'you are friend.' But did he dare ask her outright about the horrors he'd learnt of, the horrors that she might have lived through? How was he to broach such a subject? And did he have the right?

Paul was becoming driven by the belief that if he could discover the truth about the girl, he just might be able to help her. How he could do so he had no idea, but young Paul Miller was desperate to help Jalila.

Friday dawned and with it the promise Lou and Paul had made to attend the writers' festival in Geraldton. They'd get there early and shop up for further supplies to take to the island, they'd decided.

Reluctant as they were, they'd resigned themselves to their commitment for Bev's sake, and were actually looking forward very much to seeing her. The Big Sky Writers' Festival, however, they agreed they could do without, such occasions demanding a form of socialising that was not at all their style. Even Geraldton itself, a highly attractive city with a great deal to offer, held little appeal for Lou and Paul who, like most long-term Shoalhaven residents, ventured from their small coastal realm only when necessary.

Shoalhaven was indeed its own tiny oasis, taking great pride in its solidarity and self-sufficiency. As a township it had no desire to compete with all Geraldton had to offer. Why should it bother? It didn't even compete amongst its own. The town's merchants were supportive of each other, rather than competitive, and the same attitude existed between the fishers who shared the island and coastal waters amicably, without the hindrance of sophisticated aquaculture or the irritation of tourists. The busyness of Geraldton and the Abrolhos Islands, where fishers worked alongside pearl farms and coral farms and where tourism was rife, was not for those from Shoalhaven, who lived at a far slower pace and in a world of their own.

'You were very well behaved, both of you,' Bev said. 'I had my eye on you the whole time and you barely fidgeted at all.' Bev was a younger, slimmer version of her mother, vibrant and unselfconsciously sexy. She gave one of her delicious throaty laughs, so reminiscent of Maria's. 'You do realise, don't you, that you were under no obligation to come to the feminist writers' panel discussion?'

'Course we were,' Lou insisted. 'You were running the show and introducing the guests – we couldn't miss out on all that. I found bits of it quite interesting actually.' He wouldn't have under normal circumstances. Under normal circumstances his mind would have drifted off and he wouldn't have heard a word. But he'd thought of Rassen and of Hala. He'd remembered how Rassen had boasted of his wife's feminism and the bold stance she'd taken on equal rights for women, particularly within her own Muslim community. He'd remembered, too, how Rassen had recited Hala's favourite quote of Mustafa Kemal Atatürk's. Thinking along such lines had proved a perfect distraction to Lou and had even helped make sense – just now and then anyway – of some of the women writers' comments. At least it had stopped him nodding off.

'I liked the interview with the two crime blokes best,' Paul said. 'They were really good.' Having had no such memory to distract him during the feminist event, Paul presumed Lou was lying for Bev's benefit, and thought he'd better show a bit of enthusiasm himself.

'That's great,' Bev said, grinning heartily as if she believed every word. They're lying through their teeth, the two of them, she thought. She was surprised, and also touched, they'd attended both her events that day when just the crime writers' interview would have sufficed. Poor darlings, she thought, they must have hated every single second. 'And you even took part in the Q and A, Paul,' she said. 'That has to be a first. Well done.'

'Yeah,' Paul said, glad she was pleased. He'd had his question all prepared before the event just in order to please her. 'That's how interested I was, you see.'

'Yep,' Lou added his congratulations, 'good question too, mate – really got things going.'

Bev did her best not to laugh, they were trying so hard, and she loved them for it. 'It certainly was and it certainly did,' she agreed. She didn't have the heart to tell them 'Where do you get your ideas from?' was the question every single fiction writer was asked during question time after every single event.

It was late afternoon and they were seated, beers in hand, around a large bowl of potato wedges at a table in the Freemasons' downstairs bar. A grand two-storey hotel in Marine Terrace not far from the library, the Freemasons was one of Gero's most popular watering holes.

'So how's everyone back home?' Bev asked, a deliberate change of subject, knowing any further talk about the festival would bore them witless. She leant forwards and helped herself to another potato wedge, systematically dunking it into the dishes of sour cream and sweet chilli sauce. 'Any goss to give me?'

'Thelma said thank you very much for the clothes you donated,' Lou replied.

'Come again?' Bev queried through a mouthful of potato.

'We had a big clothes clean-out for Thelma to send off to St Vinnies and your mum donated a bag full of your old stuff.'

'Oh, that's good.'

'Yes, yes, it is, isn't it?' Lou's eyes signalled mischief as he slowly added, 'Thelma was very –'

'Very grateful,' Bev parroted, instantly getting the hint. Her words were not quite in unison with his, but just the slightest beat later. 'Yes, yes, very grateful,' she repeated in the sycophantic, head-nodding way Thelma always did, 'very grateful indeed.'

'She said to say –'

'Say thank you,' Bev once again followed a fractional beat after him, then added another repetition, 'yes, yes, said to say thank you very much.'

'And she sends –'

'Sends her best, yes, yes of course. Sends her very best.'

Paul was by now laughing out loud, threatening to choke on his fourth potato wedge. Bev's mimicry of Thelma was wickedly accurate and always had been. It was Bev herself who, as a teenager, had nicknamed the woman 'the Echo', a term that was extraordinarily apt. Thelma Lyttleton, the pastor's spidery wife, had the most irritating habit: she was a compulsive lip reader. She had no need to be, she was not hearing impaired, but her eyes trained upon the lips of a speaker, she had become exceedingly adept at anticipating the imminent end of a sentence. She would echo a person's words just a beat behind them, then repeat herself, often several times as if in agreement or self-congratulation. Paul had always avoided the woman whenever possible, but Bev had invented her 'Thelma game' instead. During a conversation, she would stop as if distracted just before the end of a sentence, leaving poor Thelma dangling. Or else, at the very last minute, she would nonsensically change context altogether, totally confounding the woman. Bev enjoyed the game hugely herself, but Thelma didn't. Thelma Lyttleton found Bev Miller, for some reason she couldn't quite fathom, a most confused young woman, one who might perhaps have mental issues.

Quite simply, Bev was fun. Her send-up of Thelma was neither hurtful nor cruel. There was not a shred of malice in Bev; she just saw the funny side of things. Paul often envied his older sister her lack of inhibition and ability to laugh at the world and herself. She was so like their mother, vivacious and outgoing – 'It's the Sicilian blood in her,' Lou was wont to say proudly – while Paul had a sinking feeling he was more like his father, a conservative man who took himself too seriously. Loath to admit that the Miller blood might run more strongly in his veins than the Panuzza, Paul had always gravitated to his grandfather, preferring the spontaneity of the old man's company, perhaps hoping some of it might rub off on him.

Given the siblings' two-year age difference, Bev had been very much the bossy big sister during their childhood, but as they'd grown older, the relationship had become more complex. Bev no longer bossed her younger brother around, but she could sense when something was troubling him, and on the occasions when Paul, frustrated, expressed a wish he could tackle things the way she did, she would show her support by sending him up.

'Bullshit,' she'd say in typical fashion, 'I'm a show-off and you're not, I'm the extrovert, you're the introvert, it's that simple.'

But Bev knew things were not really 'that simple', and that Paul was a private young man who kept his feelings tucked away deep inside. She respected him for it, never intruding. The very differences between the two siblings, and the fact they both recognised and valued their differences, made the bond between them particularly strong.

Over the bowl of dwindling potato wedges, the conversation led inevitably to the American presidential campaign. Well, as Bev said, how could it not? Donald Trump was the name on everyone's lips all over the world.

'Insanity,' she said. 'There are people who are actually taking him seriously. Americans can't be that mad, surely!'

'You should hear Ian Tuckey on the subject,' Paul said. 'Ian adores Trump, reckons he has all the right answers.'

'Ian Tuckey!' Another throaty laugh from Bev and a dismissive toss of the head that set her black curls bouncing. 'Ian Tuckey just adores the sound of his own voice.'

'That's a fact,' Paul agreed.

'Oh he's not a bad bloke,' Lou said in defence; he didn't like to hear one of his mates maligned, and Ian was a mate of sorts – they all were in Shoalhaven. 'He's good with kids, you've got to admit. The kids just love him.'

Bev gave a derisive hoot. 'Of course the kids love him – he sells ice-creams and lollies and chucks them a few freebies to keep them on side.' There was no winning against Bev.

The conversation continued for a further half-hour or so, Bev railing against Trump's inane views, particularly regarding Muslims and refugees in general, Lou and Paul agreeing with her entirely, both longing all the while to tell her about their friends on the island.

Then it came time for reluctant goodbyes. She'd asked them to stay in town for the night at her flat in Fitzgerald Street, little more than a ten-minute stroll from the library. 'Only one spare bedroom,' she'd said, 'but a very comfy couch, and then we could have dinner together with *heaps* of wine, and you wouldn't have to worry about the drive home.'

Much as she'd tried to make the offer sound attractive, they'd refused of course, as she'd known they would.

'No, no,' they'd said, 'you've got a busy weekend ahead, and we wouldn't want to hang around and get in your way.'

So she stood in Marine Terrace, waving goodbye to Paul's Land Rover as it took off on the hundred-kilometre drive that would take no more than an hour.

Crazy, she thought, as she watched them go. They can't wait to get back to their cosy little town, so close and yet a whole world away. That's Shoalhaven for you.

Bev had loved her childhood in Shoalhaven, but the very things she'd loved most had turned out to be the reasons she'd had to leave. The insularity, the familiarity, the cosiness would eventually have driven her insane. Perhaps it's different for Lou and Paul, she thought. As fishers they spend half their lives on a remote island – but to be locked in the township? No, no. She cringed at the thought. Even Gero, much as she loved the place, was becoming too small for her. After completing her degree at Curtin University in Perth, she'd applied for the position at Geraldton Regional Library in order to be near her family, but now, after three years, she couldn't wait to return to Perth. And after that, who could tell? Perhaps Sydney. Then she'd like to travel abroad. London, Europe, America . . . The world was an adventure crying out to be experienced.

But that's the difference between those who are born to be Shoalhaven people, and those who are not, Bev thought. You're either one or the other; there are no in-betweens.

It was true. When youngsters from Shoalhaven reached high-school age, they commuted to Geraldton – a Shoalhaven shuttle service had long ago been established for that very purpose – and after completing their schooling, one of two things happened. They either departed Shoalhaven altogether to pursue a tertiary education and follow a chosen career, or they settled down and became true Shoalhaven citizens. Old residents rarely left; they died in the saddle, passing their businesses on to the next generation. And if there were no family takers the business was sold up, more often than not to a fellow Shoalhaven citizen. Over the years the town's population had swollen a little, to be sure, but young people seemed to leave in roughly equal proportion to those who stayed and carried on the tradition.

A self-perpetuating society, Bev thought as she walked back to the library to meet up for dinner with the gang, that's what Shoalhaven is. But a society that looks after its own, and even if you don't want to be part of it, you've got to respect that.

'You were dying to tell her, weren't you?' Lou said during the drive home.

'Yep,' Paul replied, eyes fixed on the darkening road ahead.

'Yeah, me too. We will, Paolo. We'll tell Bev when the time's right.'

'Good.'

Several days later, as the old Princess, once more loaded with fresh supplies, approached the island, Paul was pleased to see Jalila in the group at the end of the jetty. She was not waving like the others, but she was there, just standing, watching and waiting, which he took to be a good sign. And as the boat drew nearer, he felt more than pleased, he felt positively elated. Draped over her head was the shawl he'd given her.

He made no comment upon the fact as he and Lou alighted at the jetty to the chorus of *hellos* and *good mornings* in English, the *g'day, mate* from little Hamid, and the customary shaking of hands all round. He didn't even look at Jalila, who took no part in the greetings, but stood to one side. It was only when everyone had shouldered their share of supplies and the group as a whole was making its way to the blue hut that he addressed her, for she had deliberately chosen to walk beside him.

'Good morning, Jalila,' he said, as if noticing her for the first time.

'Good morning, Paul,' she replied.

And again, after the supplies were unpacked, the men dismissed, and the women were storing the items, it was Jalila who made the approach.

'We go fairy terns, Paul?' she asked as he was about to leave.

'Sure, if you like,' he said, trying to sound offhand. 'It's low tide and we'd need to go now if you want to cross the sandbar.'

'I like,' she replied, then turning to Hala. 'Is all right I go fairy terns, Hala?'

'I think that's an excellent idea, Jalila.' Hala's reply was as offhand as Paul's, but having heard their exchange she was secretly delighted. 'Don't forget the binoculars,' she said, and as Jalila disappeared briefly she raised an eyebrow to Paul that said, 'What have you done to the girl?'

Paul quelled his instinctive reaction, which was one of wariness, and as the two of them walked out the door he told himself he must stop being paranoid, that far from harbouring suspicions, Hala had been congratulating him.

They set off for the windward side of the island, Jalila with the binoculars looped around her neck, and as they walked she lifted them to her eyes every now and then.

'Pacific gulls,' she said, pointing up at the sky. Then, moments later, 'Crested terns.' Then, further on, pointing out over the sea, 'Wedge shearwaters.'

'Wedge-*tailed* shearwaters,' he corrected her. 'But you've remembered them all. Well done, Jalila.'

He received no smile in return, but she did react, nodding seriously; she had been rehearsing to herself the names of the birds.

'Wedge-*tailed* shearwaters,' she repeated.

They walked on in silence for a while, then . . .

'I like the shawl,' he said. 'It looks good on you.'

'Is pretty,' she replied, fingering the cloth briefly, then returning her attention to the binoculars and the birds.

Upon their arrival at the isthmus, where the ever-present wind was stronger than ever, Jalila appeared surprised to discover the rocks were linked to the shoreline by a narrow stretch of sand.

'No island,' she said.

'That's right. I told you, at low tide you can walk out across the sandbar, remember?'

'Oh.' She did remember he'd said something like that, but she hadn't really understood what he'd meant.

'Come on, follow me,' he instructed, 'and stay in the middle of the bar – it gets quite deep either side.'

Jalila tied the shawl around her waist, the wind threatening to rip it from her, and they crossed the fifty metres to the beach and rocky outcrop. As they went, Paul issued a warning.

'Don't be frightened when the terns dive-bomb you,' he said, 'they won't hurt you, I promise, they're just trying to scare you off.'

Again she wasn't quite sure what he meant and didn't know what to expect, but as they arrived at the edge of the sandy beach, she very quickly understood. Upon their intrusion, the neat little birds with their black caps and yellow-brown bills went berserk, wheeling about overhead, catching the wind and swooping down at them.

'See? What did I tell you,' Paul laughed, 'they're trying their best to be as scary as they can, but it doesn't really work, it's just show.' He indicated the surrounding sand. 'Look at all the nests, Jalila. Be careful you don't tread on any eggs.'

Jalila ignored the birds and looked down at the nests, which weren't really nests at all, just shallow hollows dotted about on the sand and coral fragments that made up the beach. Some were lined with bits of shell and vegetation, others were no more than indentations, and in each were eggs. Mottled silvery-grey eggs, some darker than others, some heavily patterned like marble, others delicately translucent, but all very beautiful. She bent over to examine them more closely, not touching them, moving warily about the beach, taking care with each step. One egg only here, two eggs there, three there, and in one little hollow four eggs nestling neatly together: each nest housed eggs that were slightly different, but equally beautiful.

'Oh,' she breathed quietly. 'So pretty.'

He loved to see her entranced like this. 'Yes, they are pretty, aren't they? And very vulnerable too, just lying about on the sand like this. No wonder the parents are so mad at us for being here.' He gazed up at the terns that hovered overhead. 'Look at the way they use the wind, Jalila.'

She looked up.

'See? They seem to be flying backwards, don't they?'

'Yes,' she said in amazement. The little birds with their outstretched wings seemed most definitely to be moving backwards, not forwards.

'It's their method of attack,' Paul explained, 'their way of fooling you. They hover for a moment and let the wind take them so it seems they're no threat and then they swoop down from behind you and take you by surprise.'

Even as she watched, the birds behaved exactly as he described, and to Jalila it did appear a very conscious battle tactic.

'Fairy terns clever,' she said.

'Maybe,' Paul agreed, 'but not very effective I'm afraid. Which is probably why they're an endangered species.'

They stayed for another hour, Jalila examining every single nest on the beach, assuring the angry birds she meant no harm. 'I no hurt,' she promised them over and over, but they didn't take any notice. So she and Paul left the beach and explored the rocky outcrop in order to give them a rest, Jalila studying the terns from some distance through the binoculars. After which it was time to leave.

'The tide's on the way in,' he said. 'If we leave it much longer we'll have to take our shoes off and wade across.' She was wearing sandals and he the rubber-soled runners he always favoured. 'Come on, we don't want to get wet. Follow me, and stay in the middle.'

Jalila tightened the shawl at her waist – the wind was well and truly whipping about them now – and looped the binoculars around her neck. Then they set off across the sandbar.

They were halfway towards the shore when Jalila, distracted by bird activity out over the water, forgot to watch her footing. Her eyes weren't even on Paul and without being aware she'd wandered a little off course to one side of the sandbar.

Her foot slipped. The ground seemed to fall away from beneath her and all of a sudden she was in the sea, being swept away by the current. Everything happened so quickly, she did not cry out. But she would not have cried out in any event. Even had she had sufficient warning, she would not have screamed for help. Her brain had signalled in an instant that this was the way she was intended to die, and just as instantly her will had surrendered. Jalila had no wish to fight for survival.

Several steps ahead, with no idea of the drama unfolding behind him, it was sheer chance that Paul happened to turn and check on her. By then, she was twenty metres away, the current sweeping her out to sea.

He ripped the runners from his feet. Jesus Christ, he thought as he dived in and swam strongly towards her, why the hell didn't she call out?

He reached her, supporting her in the choppy, wind-churned water, surprised to see that although she was coughing and spluttering a little she was not panic-stricken as most people on the verge of drowning were. He had saved others in the past and panic was always a major concern for both victim and rescuer.

'I've got you,' he barked. 'Now turn on your back! You need to float on your back!'

She obeyed, putting her trust in him completely, and grasping her over one shoulder, his arm across her chest, his hand under her other armpit, he swam for the shore. The current was strong, but he had no trouble, her body travelling passively beside him: this was an easy rescue.

Upon reaching the shoreline, he picked her up and carried her over the rocky shallows. Then when they were seated together on the foreshore, he made her lean forward, her head between her knees, and smacked her firmly several times on the back.

'You all right?' he asked after she'd coughed up some of the water she'd swallowed.

'Yes,' she replied, her voice husky.

'Why the hell didn't you yell out?' he said accusatively, angrily even. Now the danger was over, he allowed his fear to show. 'Christ alive, you could have bloody well drowned! Why the hell didn't you call out to me?'

'Sorry.' He was angry with her, she realised. She didn't quite understand the reason for his anger. Why should she have called out to him? The thought hadn't once occurred to her, she'd accepted her fate. However, she didn't like him being angry with her and wanted to make amends 'I sorry, Paul,' she said.

'All right. Forget it.' His anger faded, but he refused to feel guilty for having snapped at her. Jesus, what if she'd drowned? What would he have told the others? *I took her to see the fairy terns and now she's dead.* 'Well at least you didn't lose the binoculars,' he said, taking them from around her neck and trying to sound calm. *She should have got rid of the binoculars,* he thought, *they would have helped drag her down.* 'Let me get some of the water out of that for you,' he said, pointing to the shawl still tied around her waist.

She untangled it and handed it to him. He squeezed the shawl free of as much water as he could and gave it back to her. Then he stood, ringing the moisture from his shirt and from the legs of his shorts. 'The wind should dry us off on the walk home. Are you cold?'

'No,' she replied, wringing out the hem of her skirt.

'I'll go and get my shoes,' he said, 'back in a tick.' He walked off to the sandbar to collect his runners.

Jalila was glad he was not angry with her any more. She was confused though. Paul confused her. She confused herself. She had been so prepared to die. More than prepared: she would have welcomed death. For years now she would have welcomed death at any time: nothing in life was of consequence. But when he had come to her out there in the water, when he had taken a hold of her and she'd realised she was about to be spared, she had been surprised to discover that she wanted to live. And when he'd swum her ashore, so strongly, so surely, so inevitably to safety, she'd looked up at the sky and the gulls soaring there, *Pacific* gulls, she'd told herself, and she was glad she hadn't drowned. Why?

He was back several minutes later. He picked up the binoculars, looping them around his neck, and she draped the shawl, damp as it was, over her head.

'Let's go,' he said.

She took the hand he offered and stood, but once on her feet, instead of releasing his hand, she maintained her hold and took a step closer.

They were very near one another now, her face turned up to him, her eyes looking into his, as if deciphering something, Paul had no idea what, but it made him feel uncomfortable. He did not back away, nor did he avoid her scrutiny, but he did release his hand.

'What is it, Jalila?' he asked.

'You save my life.'

'I did what anyone'd do,' he replied, then trying to make light of the moment, he added, 'anyone who can swim anyway.'

But she had edged closer still, her breasts, so alarmingly evident beneath the wetness of her blouse, about to make contact with his body, and he realised that once again she was offering herself.

He backed away, shocked, but did not break eye contact, wanting desperately to get through to the girl. 'Stop this, Jalila. Stop this right now,' he said. 'You're offering payment for my saving your life, is that it?'

'Yes.'

'I don't want payment: you must understand that. Do you understand me?' he insisted, 'I don't want payment!' He repeated each word emphatically.

She seemed puzzled. 'You no want me?'

'That's right.' He felt an irrational flash of guilt. Is that what she had been deciphering in him, the male lust to which she was obviously accustomed? Did it show? Was it readable? He'd not been aware of any such feeling himself, but he might well be denying the truth. 'That's right,' he repeated firmly, 'I do not want you. I want to be your *friend*.'

And then the moment he'd been waiting for. Finally and unbelievably it happened.

'Is good,' she said, and the perfect lips shaped into a fleeting smile, an infinitesimal smile, just for one brief second. If he hadn't been watching closely he would have missed it. But it was there. 'Friend is good.'

'Yes,' he said gently, 'friend is very good. Now let's get out of this wind and find somewhere warm.'

They left the windward side of the island and started back towards the settlement, walking comfortably side by side, their clothes wetly flapping. And as they walked Paul decided it was now safe to broach the subject.

'May I ask you some questions, Jalila?'

Her nod was unequivocal.

'You told me you're Yazidi, that you come from a mountain and that your family are all . . . dead.' It sounded shockingly brutal, but he knew the time was right, that he must ask her now. And unflinchingly she answered.

'Yes.'

'I've done some research on the Yazidi people and their recent history,' he said. He could tell she didn't understand, but made no attempt to explain, getting straight to the point instead. 'You come from Northern Iraq and the mountain is Mount Sinjar, am I right?'

'Yes,' she replied.

'How old are you, Jalila?'

The slightest shrug, she really couldn't be sure. She hadn't counted over these past several years. 'Nineteen.'

Nineteen . . . That would fit the time frame, Paul thought.

'Are you uncomfortable?' he asked. 'Do you feel cold? Do you want to get back to the huts and change your clothes?'

She answered all of his questions with one simple shake of the head.

'Good.' They were well away from the windward side of the island now. 'Then let's find a nice sunny spot and talk,' he said. 'I want to know about you, Jalila.'

CHAPTER TWELVE

Not wanting to bump into the others, they stopped just north of the settlement and sat in a sunny clearing, the surrounding saltbush and chenopod shrubs forming a windbreak.

She looked at him expectantly, awaiting whatever questions he might wish to ask her, but Paul didn't know where or how to begin. The only way, he decided, was to tell her what he'd found on the internet and see if it related to her.

'In August 2014,' he said, taking care to speak slowly, 'Islamic State militants overran villages in Northern Iraq and massacred thousands of Yazidi people, the idea being to exterminate the entire minority group because they weren't – you weren't – Muslims.'

He paused, expecting some comment, but none was forthcoming. Perhaps she doesn't understand, he thought, perhaps her grasp of English isn't good enough. He continued regardless.

'ISIS also took hundreds of Yazidi women and children prisoner,' he said, wondering briefly how he should voice the next part, which was confronting to say the least, but there was no way he could soften the facts so he blurted it out anyway. 'These women and children were held by the extremists as sex slaves. Some were given as gifts to the fighters.'

He awaited her reaction. Had she understood him? If his reasoning was correct and she was one of those taken captive it would certainly explain her subjugation to men, but his reminder of the fact was bound also to arouse some terrible memories.

'Is right,' she said in the most matter-of-fact manner. She may not have understood every single word, but Jalila had followed with absolute clarity the gist of all he'd said. 'We is *malik yamiin*. Slaves. Hassan teach me that mean also in English "spoils of war".'

He didn't dare ask who Hassan was, not wanting to break the flow.

'They take us to Syria. My sister too. My family they kill in Sinjar town. Is where I grow up,' she added. 'Many of our people run away, hide on mountain, but my family no. They is all kill. Only my sister and me. They take us to Syria, many other girls too. We is property of soldiers. I never see my sister again. I no look for her. She be dead now –'

'That's enough, Jalila – you don't need to go on any further.'

She looked him squarely in the eye. 'You are friend. You ask, I tell you.'

She did not appear upset, so he decided it was safe to continue. 'How long were you held captive?'

Jalila was uncertain. The first soldier to own her had kept her for some while. He'd been proud that she was a virgin: virgins were greatly prized. But then things had changed and she'd been passed on to other soldiers who had wanted to buy her.

'Soldier who own me sell me to other soldier who want me,' she said, trying to piece together a sense of time. 'Then that soldier he sell me to other soldier . . .'

Paul interrupted once again. He got the picture, and this really didn't seem right. Reliving her experiences in such detail must be harrowing. 'How did you get away?'

'I am captive one year, more maybe,' she said thoughtfully, her mind still on the previous question. 'Last soldier, he sell me in market.'

Piecing together the past in clinical fashion had been no trouble for Jalila, at least it hadn't so far. She had long since closed her mind off to the soldiers. But at this point she issued a warning to herself. She must not tell Paul why the last soldier had sent her to the marketplace for sale. She dared not say the words out loud. To do so would bring back the image she fought always to obliterate. She moved on to the next stage of her story.

'At marketplace, Hassan see me,' she continued, pictures suddenly and unexpectedly flashing through her mind, vivid pictures, sounds coming back to her too, and smells even. The slave market in Raqqa. Standing there with so many others, naked, a price tag around her neck. Men touching her, prodding her, opening her mouth with their fingers. Several in a bidding war, raising the price for her, Hassan one of them, determined to be the victor.

Memory of the slave market had never once returned to Jalila and she wondered now how she had been able to bear such humiliation. But of course she'd been a dead person by then.

'Hassan, he buy me,' she said. 'He tell me he is my pro-tector. This word he teach me. Yazidi speak Kurmanji, but Hassan he teach me Arabic, and he teach me English too. No more soldier, is good.'

'So Hassan was kind to you then?'

Paul's promptings caused the return of other memories, vague memories of months spent in a haze. A medical centre, Hassan insisting upon treatment to ensure she was clean; she had been diseased they said. Hassan acquiring the medicines that cured her and the contraceptive pills that ensured she would not become pregnant; Hassan buying her clothes and pretty things. She supposed all of this meant he'd been kind, he'd certainly been obsessed with her – he'd even told her he loved her. But that hadn't stopped him offering her as part of a deal when it suited.

'Hassan spend much money on me,' she said. Hassan

had quite a lot of money to spend; amongst his many enterprises he'd been a small-time but successful arms dealer. 'I am good for business, he tell me. I am payment to friend for favour.'

'. . . I see.' God!

'Hassan take me to Beirut,' Jalila said. 'He want come to Australia. He need escape from DAESH who say he rob them. He have friend in Sydney say Australia good place to live, can make much money. Hassan like money very much. So we come. But,' she concluded with a shrug that said everything, 'he is eaten by shark.'

Which is no more than the bastard deserved, Paul thought.

'So there my story, Paul. Is done.'

Jalila lay back on the ground and stared up at the sky, her mind empty.

'Thank you for telling me,' he said. He could think of nothing else to say.

He lay back on the ground himself and they both stared silently up at the sky.

After a while he turned his head to look at her, but she was still gazing vacantly skywards as if seeing nothing. He wondered guiltily if his questioning had returned her to a dark place. With a past like that, he thought, it's a wonder she's still sane.

He propped himself up on one elbow, watching her. She seemed oblivious to his gaze, her mind somewhere else altogether, but he was relieved to note she didn't appear disturbed. After a moment or two he broke the silence.

'What is it you want, Jalila?' he asked. 'What is it you would wish for more than anything in the world?'

She pointed at the birds overhead. She hadn't been gazing mindlessly at the sky at all; she'd been gazing at the birds.

'The birds?' he queried, looking up at the gulls. 'What do you mean? You mean you wish you could fly?'

She made no reply, her eyes following the easy flight of the gulls as they glided, then gave a brief flap of their wings, then glided again, playing effortlessly with the wind.

He waited so long for her reply he presumed she'd forgotten the question, or that she was ignoring him. Then . . .

'Free,' she said, 'the birds, they is free.'

Of course. 'You want freedom?'

She just nodded.

Paul lay back on the ground, hands behind his head, thinking of the future that lay in store for her upon the group's inevitable discovery. Detention centre briefly, Darwin in all likelihood, then directly to Nauru for God knew how long, after which she might even be returned to her homeland, where she had no one and where her people continued to be persecuted. There was no freedom in sight for Jalila. Where's the justice in that? he thought.

Having heard her story, Paul wished now more than ever that he could do something for Jalila, but he knew he was helpless. If only he could give her just a *taste* of freedom, he thought, something that might remain as a happy memory amongst the horrors of the past and the hopelessness of the future . . .

But maybe I can, he told himself. An idea was starting to form, an audacious idea, but it was feasible. *A taste of freedom.* Yes, he thought, yes, it's possible. I could give her that.

Five minutes later he sat bolt upright, a plan clear in his mind. But he needed to check whether Jalila herself was interested. She might possibly find the prospect too daunting.

'Would you like to come out with me for a ride on a boat, Jalila?' he asked.

She sat up, instantly alert. 'Yes,' she said, 'I would like very much.' She would go anywhere with Paul; he was the only friend she had ever had in the whole of her life. 'We go now?' she asked eagerly.

'No, no, not now,' he said, 'in a week or so. And not in Lou's boat: a much faster boat, would you like that?'

'Yes, yes.' There was a light in her eyes, and once again that hint of a smile, perhaps even more than a hint this time.

'I have an idea,' he said. 'It's pretty bold, but it could work. Are you up for an adventure?'

'Yes, yes.' Jalila didn't know what the word 'adventure' meant, but she was up for any idea Paul had.

He looked at his watch and stood. 'We'd better be heading back,' he said, 'they'll come looking for us soon.' He and Lou had promised this time they'd stay for lunch. 'I'll tell you on the way, and not a word to anyone.'

By the time they got back the others were all gathered in the blue hut.

'Sorry,' Paul said, 'hope we haven't kept you waiting.'

'Not at all,' Hala assured him, 'we're just about to serve.' She looked them up and down. 'What on earth happened to you two?'

Their clothes were no longer sodden, they'd dried off to quite a degree, but they were still damply bedraggled.

'We went for a swim,' Paul said, with a look to Jalila, who nodded.

'Oh I see, yes of course.' Hala didn't pursue the matter, but had her eyes deceived her? she wondered. Had she just witnessed an exchange intended to be *humorous*? Whatever it was, something extraordinary had happened. 'Do you want to change your clothes, Jalila?' she asked. 'We'll wait for you if you wish.'

'No thank you, Hala. Is good.'

Throughout lunch everyone noticed the difference in Jalila. She was not talkative, remaining her usual quiet self, but she was no longer withdrawn from all about her. It was obvious she was taking an interest in things, paying attention, listening to conversations, even reacting a little now and then. No one commented on the fact, but they were all thinking the same thing. Jalila has been brought back to life.

What the bloody hell did you do, Paolo? Lou wondered, sitting on his milk crate beside Rassen and gazing at his grandson.

'Who won the poker game?' Paul asked.

'Your grandfather,' Rassen replied. 'To my shame I must admit defeat on all fronts. Massoud remains the current chess champion and now Lou has claimed the poker title. It's really most humiliating.'

Hala laughed as she handed around the bowls and the spoons. 'Well you'll just have to lift your game on both scores, won't you, my darling.'

Hala was happy Rassen had found peace within himself; this sojourn on the island was doing him the world of good. They both knew the road ahead would be hard, they'd discussed the matter often enough, but they'd agreed they would be eager to offer their services wherever they might be sent. Personally, Hala couldn't wait to serve a purpose. She knew Massoud felt the same way; they too had talked a great deal. An activist like herself, Massoud longed to rejoin the fight for human rights. Besides which, she thought, he's a young man, an intellectual who needs to socialise and exchange ideas. Unlike the others, she and Massoud were beginning to stagnate just a little there on the island.

No matter, she thought as Sanaa and Azra brought the steaming bowls of food to the small table in the centre, right now the friendship that bonds us is all that counts.

Along with the lamb stew and vegetables, Sanaa had cooked tadig. She had cooked it especially for little Hamid, not only because it was his favourite, but in order for him to practise his English. He wanted very much to impress Paul, who, they were all quite sure, had never tasted tadig.

'This dish is named tadig,' Hamid announced, standing

beside Paul and enunciating each word very slowly and with great care, exactly the way Massoud had taught him. The little boy's English was more advanced than that of the other non-English speakers, and in order that he shouldn't be held back Massoud had taken over his personal tuition while Rassen taught the rest of the group.

'It is a ta–' Hamid paused. This was the tricky bit. 'It is a ta–' His eyes darted to Massoud.

Massoud broadly mouthed the word, separating each syllable, his hand conducting along with the beat as if the child were a symphony orchestra.

'Trad-i-tion-al,' his comically exaggerated mime spelt out.

'. . . A tad-i-tion-al Persian dish.' Hamid completed the phrase, nearly getting the word right and Massoud, bursting with pride, led them all in a round of applause.

'Good on you, mate, well done,' Paul said, joining in the applause.

He stared dubiously, however, at the large bowl of crusted, brown rice that Sanaa was starting to dish out to them all and wondered how he could ask for a small portion without appearing rude; it looked most unappetising.

Lou gave him an encouraging nod but didn't say anything, remembering how he'd been served the same dish as a welcome on the very first day, and how he'd been equally dubious.

Everyone watched as Paul took his first mouthful. Then as he chomped away . . .

'You like, yes?' from Karim.

'This food good, yes?' from Hany, determined to outdo his friend, both men eager to show off the English they'd acquired.

'Yes,' Paul replied to both. 'I like it very much. This food is very good.'

Another round of applause, whether for the success of the tadig or the English, no one knew or cared.

Lunch continued like a family affair, which indeed they seemed to have become, the two fishers and the disparate group of refugees. And why shouldn't we be family? Lou wondered. We're all the same really, aren't we? Just people.

The usual farewell followed an hour or so later, everyone waving from the end of the jetty as the old Princess chugged away. This time Jalila was there too, and this time she was waving along with the others.

'So what bloody miracle took place?' Lou demanded when they were well under way. 'What the hell did you do to the girl?' He made no attempt to couch the question delicately – what was the point? The whole bloody group had noticed the difference in Jalila, and they'd all bloody welcomed it what's more. The boy should feel proud. But remembering how defensive Paul had become during their previous discussion, Lou awaited the backlash anyway.

There was none.

'We've become friends,' Paul said. 'She trusts me.'

Then he proceeded to tell his grandfather Jalila's story; she wouldn't mind, he was sure. Besides, he intended to tell Lou also of his plan, as he would need Lou's support in carrying it out.

'Holy Mother of God,' Lou breathed when he came to a halt, 'how is she still sane?'

'Maybe she isn't, entirely,' Paul said, remembering his initial reaction had been exactly the same.

Looking out over the ocean, which was relatively calm, Paul was not really seeing the white-tipped waves. Instead, he was seeing the soullessness in Jalila's eyes, the way she'd offered herself to him like a piece of goods, not once, but twice now. He had naturally omitted any mention of these occasions to Lou. 'I think Jalila's mind is so damaged it might never mend,' he said. 'She'll never relate normally to other people, not to men anyway, that's for sure.'

'Hardly surprising.'

Lou was touched by the depth of Paul's concern for Jalila.

The boy's obviously attracted to her, he thought. Hell, he'd hardly be human if he wasn't, but he's a kind man, Paolo, a sensitive man. 'Well she's lucky to have found a friend in you, mate,' he said. 'You're doing the girl a world of good.'

Paul saw the perfect opening to share his plan, so he dived straight in. 'Jalila wants freedom more than anything in the world, and as we can't give her that I've come up with an idea.'

Lou proceeded to listen without interruption, which rather surprised Paul; he'd expected disagreement.

'So what do you reckon?' he asked finally. 'Do you reckon it'll work?'

'I reckon it'll land you in a whole heap of trouble, that's what I reckon.' Lou kept his eyes on the course ahead. They were in sight of land now, and far in the distance he could see the marina. 'You know what you're planning is against the law, don't you?'

'And aiding and abetting illegal immigrants isn't?' Paul countered happily, aware that his grandfather was already won over. 'We've been on the wrong side of the law for quite some time now, Lou. So you'll help me? You'll field things with the others?'

'Yep. I'll help you.' Giving Jalila a taste of the freedom she yearned for didn't seem a bad idea at all to Lou. And he was quite sure Bev would be onside too; she had to be as she was an essential part of the plan. In fact, he was pleased his granddaughter was about to become involved. Keeping her in the dark hadn't seemed right somehow, particularly as she and Paolo were so close. He knew Paolo felt the same way.

Paul rang his sister that night. They talked for well over an hour, during which he explained everything to her, the refugees on the island, Jalila's story, everything.

'All of this was going on a week ago when you were down for the festival,' she asked in amazement, 'and you didn't tell me?'

'It's been going on for closer to six weeks,' he said. 'Well, from the day Lou first discovered them anyway. We decided we'd tell you when the time was right, Bev. And the time's right now. I need your help.'

'Sure, in what way? What way can I help?'

He dropped the bombshell. 'I'm going to bring Jalila to Gero.'

They talked for another half-hour after that.

Late Saturday afternoon saw Paul hanging around at the pub, ostensibly having a few beers with the gang, but this time he was there for a specific purpose. The Laaksonen brothers were regulars on a late Saturday arvo. They'd meet up with their fisher mates and then, being single men, stay on for a pub dinner. Paul would more often than not join them along with the other single fishers of the group, who were all good friends. Indeed, the whole of the fisher community was close, but most particularly those who, during the season, lived on Gevaar Island as the Laaksonens did. On this particular occasion, however, Paul wanted to corner the brothers alone.

His timing was perfect. He'd arrived early and was seated at a table at the far end of the verandah with four other Gevaar Island fishers, two single men and the tough couple Kath and Bill 'Buck' Buckley. Kath was actually the tough one – Buck danced to whatever tune Kath played and at whatever tempo she set. They were the oldest fishers on the island, working side by side, well into their sixties, gnarled like old mangrove trees, but with no intention of retiring. Kath had just risen to her feet. 'My round,' she'd announced in the voice some said could cut glass. She was about to set off for the bar, but that was when Paul had seen the Laaksonen brothers in the street heading for the pub: he'd been keeping a sharp lookout.

'No, no, Kath.' He stood. 'I'll get this one, you stay where you are.'

'Why?' she demanded with her customary belligerence. 'We're goin' clockwise and it's my round.'

He flashed her a smile. 'Because you're a lady, that's why.' Such a remark was bound to get a colourful response.

It did. Her face cracked into a leathery smile. 'Fuckin' oath I'm a lady,' she said, giving the others a good belly laugh, as had been the intention.

'Jukka and Hekki are here,' Paul said, 'they can help me carry the beers. OK with you?' he asked as if begging permission. 'Or do you reckon we need you to come and lend a hand?'

'Bugger off.' Kath gave a dismissive wave and sat.

Paul met the brothers just as they mounted the several steps to the verandah.

'G'day, Jukka, Hekki.'

'G'day, Paul – how're you going?' from Jukka.

'G'day, Paul. How's things?' from younger brother, Hekki.

'Good, good.'

Brief slaps on the back from the brothers, who were tall, well-built young men in their twenties, square-jawed and fair-haired like their Finnish father, but, born in Shoalhaven, Aussie to the core.

'I'm just getting a round,' Paul said, 'want to come and give us a hand?'

'No worries.'

'Actually I was hoping to get you on your own for a tick,' he went on as they weaved their way through the crowd to the queue at the bar. He was hardly 'getting them on their own', but men in crowded bars paid no heed to the conversations of others. Those gathered over beers around a table most certainly did. 'Got a favour to ask.'

'Oh yeah?' Jukka said as they joined the queue. 'Fire away.'

'I was wondering if I could borrow *Anni* next week, just for the day, take her out for a run. What do you reckon?'

Anni was the brothers' modern, high-powered, half-cabin speedboat. She was a semi-professional fishing boat in design, but they'd acquired her strictly for leisure purposes. A seven-metre aluminium vessel with twin two-fifty horsepower Honda outboards, she could go like the wind. The brothers had a mutual love of speed.

'Don't see why not,' Jukka said, he and Hekki exchanging a look as all three shuffled a little further forwards in the queue. 'Next week'd be fine. We're out of commission next week anyway, we wouldn't be able to use her.'

'Yeah,' Hekki agreed, '*Annikki* goes up on the slip next week.'

Annikki was the brothers' professional lobster fishing boat, a magnificent eighteen-metre vessel. Both *Annikki* and her smaller cousin *Anni* had been named after the mother Jukka and Hekki adored.

'Oh well, that makes things handy, doesn't it?' Paul said. 'Thanks a lot.'

And that's how easy it was. He'd expected it would be. He'd known *Annikki* was due up on the slip; he'd checked at the marina. Like his own *Palermo Miss*, which had been up on the slip and anti-fouled just a week or so previously, she'd been booked in well ahead. When a boat was up on the slip, the owner was busy. You didn't waste a minute of the marina's time with others waiting in line.

They made arrangements between them for Paul to pick up the keys to *Anni* and then as they once again shuffled forward in the queue . . .

'Going out for a bit of a fish, eh?' Hekki asked.

Paul was prepared for this part too, covering himself just in case he and Jalila were seen.

'Nah,' he said, 'at least I don't think so. I don't reckon she'd be interested.'

'She? Who's she?' Jukka queried.

'The girl I'm trying to impress,' Paul said with a grin.

'She's in Gero, just up from Perth. She's a friend of my sister's and she's a real looker.'

'Ah,' knowing nods from the brothers and a wink from Jukka, 'well *Anni* should do the trick. I don't know a bird who isn't turned on by *Anni*.'

'What'll it be, boys?' Mawsie the publican's wife asked.

The weather turned nasty over the next few days, blustery winds followed by a storm that was unusually heavy for October, and Lou and Paul found themselves grounded. Lou was not in the least worried about the group on the island.

'They've got plenty of supplies to see them through a few extra days,' he said, 'and they'll know why we haven't turned up – they're not stupid.'

But Paul's concern was about his plans for Jalila.

'Jukka and Hekki are lending me *Anni* while their boat's up on the slip,' he said, agitated, 'they'll have her back by next week.'

'And they'll still lend you the speedboat,' Lou remarked in a voice that clearly said *calm down*, 'they're good mates. Stop being so impatient, Paolo.'

Aware of the rebuke, Paul's reaction was a little sullen. Am I being impatient? Is that all it is? Yes, he thought, maybe I am, maybe Lou's right.

His plan now set in motion, Paul was certainly raring to go, but there was a genuine concern at the back of his mind. He must continue the momentum while Jalila was still communicative. What if, when he next saw her, she had retreated once again behind that impenetrable shell?

Then finally, as the weather forecast had predicted, Saturday dawned bright and clear; there was a post-storm ocean swell, but nothing that warranted deferring their course of action.

Bev had been pleased when Paul had rung her on the Friday night to say all was going ahead. She'd been on

standby ever since their previous phone conversation, and
Saturday was far more convenient than a weekday, when
she'd have to have taken time off work.

'How very kind of the weather,' she said, ignoring the
impatience in his tone as she always did when he allowed
his irritation to show.

'I'll call you when we're half an hour out,' he replied
brusquely. 'If all goes according to plan we should be there
around lunchtime.'

They set out for the island early that morning, Lou
aboard the old Princess and Paul aboard *Anni*, having
fuelled up both vessels the previous day. They kept pace
with each other during the crossing, their intention being
to arrive together at around nine o'clock, although *Anni*
could have roared on ahead at four times the speed.

The group awaiting them at the end of the jetty was
astonished to see the shiny new, modern speedboat.
They'd been rather wary at first by the sight of two
approaching vessels, but the fact that the strange craft was
accompanying the old Princess surely meant they were
safe. And then, as the boats had come a little closer, they'd
recognised Paul at the helm waving through the open side
window and their own returning waves of welcome had
commenced in earnest.

'My, my,' Rassen said as Paul stepped up onto the jetty,
'what a speedy-looking vessel.'

'Yes, she'll move all right.' Paul's eyes had sought Jalila's,
where she stood silently as the group chorused their 'good
mornings', and he'd been instantly reassured by the complicity he saw there. Jalila had not retreated at all.

They unloaded the provisions and carried them to the
hut, Paul doing his best to curb his impatience, longing to
be on his way. Then, when the women finally set about
storing the food they'd unpacked and the men prepared
to go their separate ways, he made his rehearsed 'casual
remark' to Hala.

'I thought I might take Jalila for a ride in the speed-boat,' he said, 'that is, if she'd like to come – would it be all right?'

'Good heavens,' Hala said, surprised, 'yes of course.' She turned to the girl. 'Would you like that, Jalila?'

'Yes,' Jalila replied. 'I would like that.'

'Me too! I come too!' There was no escaping little Hamid. But they had anticipated this. Paul glanced over at Lou, who had deliberately lingered before departing for the yellow hut and his customary poker game with Rassen.

'I've got a better idea, Hamid,' Lou said. 'Why don't you come out on the old Princess with me?'

Hamid's huge, doe-like eyes glanced from Lou to Paul and then back again. He'd been out on the old Princess twice now, and both times had been thrilling, but he'd never been out on a speedboat.

'I'll let you steer her if you like,' Lou said enticingly, miming the steering wheel to ensure the boy understood. 'No steer speedboat,' he said with a stern shake of his head, 'too fast. But the old Princess . . . What do you say?'

A squeal of joy. The deal was sealed.

The two boats took off on their respective jaunts together, Karim and Hany accompanying Lou and Hamid while Rassen and Massoud, who were not in the least interested in boats, retired for a game of chess.

As *Anni* sprang into action, Karim and Hany couldn't help feeling a touch of envy. They would love to have been invited for a run on the speedboat, but they recognised this was a private arrangement between Paul and Jalila; it was not their place to interfere. Like the rest of the group, they were all too aware of the remarkable effect the young Australian was having on the girl – he might even have set her on the road to recovery.

It didn't stop them watching enviously though as Paul upped the revs of the massive twin outboards and *Anni* spanked across the water, leaving a broad white wake, while the old Princess chugged away from the jetty at her customary, sedate pace. Perhaps Paul might give me a quick ride when he gets back, each thought hopefully.

Being aboard *Anni* was certainly exciting for the uninitiated – flat out she could get up to around thirty-five knots – and Paul kept his eye on Jalila in case she found the experience alarming. Quite obviously she did not.

They stood side by side in the high half-cabin, Paul at the wheel. He preferred to skipper standing rather than sitting, so she'd opted to stand also, ignoring the sturdy bucket seat at her disposal. Jalila kept a firm hold on the metal grip of the dashboard as he'd instructed she must, for the boat was at times practically airborne, skipping across the ocean's swell. The side windows of the cabin were open and the wind whipped back her dark, shoulder-length hair, her scarf tied around her waist for safekeeping. With her feet securely anchored, she weathered the boat's movement well as she stared through the windscreen at the endless all-surrounding blue. There was no land in sight now. Even the island behind them had been swallowed up by the blue.

Stealing surreptitious glances at her, Paul once again found her unfathomable. There was no trace of alarm, which for one who had lived through a shipwreck and a night in shark-infested waters might have been expected. But the boat's speed appeared to have aroused in her no sense of exhilaration either: she was affected by nothing and simply gazing at nothing, or so it seemed. Everything about her was unreadable. Paul was worried. Has she gone away again? he wondered. Have I lost contact with her?

He pulled back on the revs, reducing the roar of the engines, slowing the boat so that it ploughed strongly through the waves rather than spanking along the top.

'Are you looking forward to your adventure?' he asked.

Jalila turned to him, her eyes meeting his directly. 'Yes,' she said. She still had no idea what an 'adventure' might be, but whatever it was, she was looking forward to it.

Paul wanted to cheer. Jalila's facial expression and body language might be unfathomable, but her eyes were not. The dead eyes that had once said nothing now said everything, and in their green depths he could see the light of excitement.

'That's good,' he said simply.

But Jalila was about to offer more. She wanted so much to please him. 'I prepare for adventure,' she said, picking up from the passenger seat the small cloth bundle she'd brought with her. It was actually a tea-towel knotted at the corners. She untied it and displayed the contents. 'See?'

Paul looked down at the items nestled in the tea-towel: a toothbrush and a comb, the tiniest sliver of soap and an all-but-devoured tube of toothpaste. Jalila had obviously taken only the dregs of the group's communal toiletries that would have been destined for the rubbish bag. Something about the pathetic little collection she'd packed for her adventure touched him deeply.

'We'll buy you these things in Geraldton,' he told her.

But Jalila wasn't listening. She'd put down the bundle, taken up her firm grip and was once again staring through the windscreen.

'We go fast now?' she asked.

They arrived at Geraldton marina shortly before one o'clock, by which time Bev was waiting patiently on the jetty. As arranged, he'd rung her on his mobile phone when they were half an hour out.

He didn't even bother tying up – the breeze was keeping them alongside anyway.

'G'day, Bev,' he said, 'climb aboard.'

She did, and very nimbly. Courtesy of her brother and grandfather, Bev knew a great deal about boats.

And then they were off. The whole procedure had taken less than thirty seconds. The marina was busy, it was a Saturday and no one had paid them any particular attention. Upon Paul's instruction Jalila had remained in the passenger seat, under cover of the half-cabin and out of sight to general passers-by. The episode had gone unnoticed and they were out to sea in a matter of minutes.

'Bev, this is Jalila,' Paul said, slowing the engines right down to a gentle cruise level so they wouldn't have to raise their voices to be heard. 'Jalila, this is my sister, Bev.'

Jalila rose from the passenger seat and turned to meet Paul's sister.

'Hello, Jalila,' Bev said. *He didn't tell me she was this bloody beautiful*, she thought.

'Hello,' Jalila said. *She does not look like his sister*, she thought.

Presuming that Jalila would retain her customary silence, Paul decided to speak on her behalf in order to break the ice.

'Jalila's very much looking forward to her adventure –' but to his surprise Jalila interrupted. She was quite prepared to play her part.

'Yes,' she said. 'Adventure is good.'

'Well I certainly hope it will be,' Bev said pleasantly, noting as she did that the girl wore a blouse that had once been hers, and that the shawl tied at her waist had once belonged to her mother. Bev recalled it had been one of Maria's favourites many years back. She grinned at Paul. 'I see Jalila has scored some of the gear intended for Thelma,' she said wryly. 'I must say it suits her well.'

'Yep,' he replied, 'Lou and I decided half to Thelma and half to the island.'

'Good thinking,' his sister agreed, 'very clever.'

Jalila was attempting to follow the conversation, but with no success. The fact in itself did not bother her, but she would like to have contributed, knowing if she did it would please Paul.

Aware she was trying to understand, Paul explained the situation. 'The blouse you're wearing was a gift from Bev,' he said slowly and clearly. 'She thinks you look very nice in it.'

'A gift?' Jalila peered down at the blouse. She gently stroked the braided neckline with her fingers. 'Is pretty,' she said. Then she looked back at Bev. 'Thank you.'

'My pleasure, Jalila,' Bev replied with a smile. 'We'll buy you some more pretty things in Geraldton.'

Paul gave the girls a leisurely run around in *Anni* for half an hour or so, he and Bev talking through the plans they'd discussed over the phone. Jalila was to stay at Bev's flat for the next few days, perhaps a whole week, and he was to drive down by car from Shoalhaven to show her around. Their cover would be that Jalila was a friend of Bev's up from Perth on a holiday visit.

'And when the visit's over, I presume you'll borrow the speedboat again to take her back to the island?' Bev asked.

'Probably,' he said; he hadn't really given this aspect much thought. 'Jukka and Hekki wouldn't mind. Or else I can come down in *Palermo Miss* – she's off the slip now. That'd be a whole day's trip of course, but . . .' He shrugged; either way he didn't much care. Giving Jalila her taste of freedom was all that mattered to Paul.

'I'll take you out each day and show you the country-side,' he said to her eagerly. 'We'll drive down the coast, and I'll show you the beaches. And I'll show you the Pinnacles, too,' he went on. 'They're ancient rock formations from the beginning of time . . .'

Jalila had little comprehension of what he was saying, but his excitement was communication enough. As he talked, her gaze did not once leave his face.

During their run back to the marina, the conversation again took a practical turn. Bev was to go shopping with Jalila that afternoon.

'You'll get her whatever you reckon she needs, won't you?' Paul said. 'Just let me know the cost and I'll transfer –'

'Yes, yes, I know,' Bev replied briskly, 'we discussed all that.'

Paul said, 'Now remember, Jalila, Bev will keep you safe. If you're not sure, just let her take the lead.'

'Yes, Paul,' she replied.

'I know everything will seem strange at first, but Bev knows what to do,' he assured her. 'You mustn't be frightened.'

'I am not frighten, Paul.' What could there possibly be that could frighten her? Jalila wondered.

They pulled up at the marina jetty, and this time the procedure was not rushed. This time he tied alongside and saw them properly ashore, climbing onto the jetty and assisting them from the boat as if returning them from a pleasant outing.

'Hope you enjoyed yourselves,' he said loudly for the benefit of any passer-by who might be interested, although no one appeared to be taking the slightest notice. Still, he told himself, best to be careful just in case word gets back. '*Anni*'s a speedy little number all right, good to have you aboard.'

'We had a great time, Paul, thanks,' Bev said, kissing her brother fondly on the cheek and linking her arm through Jalila's.

'I'll see you tomorrow then.' He hopped back on board, started up the engines and released the bow and stern lines. 'Bye,' he called, as he slowly headed the boat towards the bowser in order to fuel up.

His last glimpse was of the two young women walking arm in arm along the jetty, Bev chatting away as if she and Jalila were old friends. My sister's a bloody Godsend, he thought.

Bev was obeying her brother's every instruction to the letter, but even as she did so she was distracted. Bev was concerned. More than concerned, Bev was worried. He has no idea, she thought. He has no idea whatsoever. He doesn't realise he's in love with this girl.

CHAPTER THIRTEEN

Back on the island, Lou had fielded things with the others as he'd promised Paul he would. They'd both agreed it best not to let the group know in advance what was going on, but, uncertain of the reception his news might receive, Lou didn't relish being the bearer. He'd wanted at least to tell Hala and Rassen, but Paul had been insistent.

When, after a good hour's run, he'd returned the old Princess to the jetty, Karim and Azra had appeared disappointed the speedboat was still nowhere in sight. They'd obviously been hoping for a ride when Paul got back. But they hadn't hung about waiting, which would have seemed presumptuous, choosing instead to kick the soccer ball around with little Hamid.

Lou joined Rassen and Massoud on the verandah of the yellow hut where they were hunched over the chessboard. As the group's leader, and for translation purposes, Rassen must be the first to know.

Both men glanced up, acknowledging his presence with a smile and Rassen looked down to the jetty, which was clearly visible from the verandah.

'Paul and Jalila not back yet?' he asked.

'Ah . . . no . . .' Lou said hesitantly.

'Is something wrong?'

'No, no,' Lou assured him, 'nothing that can't wait until after you've finished your game.' He sat. 'Please do go on, I don't want to interrupt.'

But by now he also had Massoud's full attention.

'No point,' the young Iranian said, 'I'm going to win anyway. 'Now tell us what's going on, Lou – you look uncomfortable.'

'I do have some news, I'm afraid,' Lou admitted. 'Mightn't be a bad idea if Hala was here too, a woman's point of view and all that, you know.'

Massoud rose from his chair with a whimsical look to Rassen that said 'something important'. The Australian was all but squirming.

He left wordlessly to return only minutes later with Hala, and the four of them convened inside the hut where the seating was more comfortable.

Lou told them everything, including Jalila's background, as he and Paul had decided he should, and all three listened without saying a word.

'He'll bring her back to the island in a few days,' Lou concluded, 'perhaps a week. He's determined to give her "a taste of freedom" – those were his very words.'

Lou turned to Hala, keen to assure her that Jalila would be safely chaperoned by his granddaughter. 'She'll be staying with Paul's older sister, Beverley,' he said. 'Bev's a fine young woman, strong, capable – she'll look after Jalila, I promise you.'

But Hala, an unconventional woman at the best of times, was the last person he needed to convince.

'Well we've all seen the effect Paul's had on the girl,' she said. 'That young man's a miracle worker. In my opinion Jalila was completely beyond repair.'

Rassen didn't appear to embrace the situation with quite the same degree of fervour as his wife, but he was in agreement about Jalila. 'Yes, I would have considered her a lost cause too, I must say, and having now heard the reason for her condition, little wonder.'

He looked to Massoud. 'This is a bold idea of Paul's,' he said with a touch of uncertainty, 'but I believe it may be a good one, do you agree?'

'Yes,' Massoud said, 'without a doubt.' Then he added wistfully. 'A taste of freedom – lucky Jalila.' There was a moment's pause, both men reflective, both aware of what the future might have in store for them.

'We'll inform the others,' Rassen said, 'but not now. When we're gathered together for lunch in the blue hut. They'll want to know what's happened to the speedboat by then.'

It was close to four o'clock when Paul returned and they were all there to greet him at the end of the jetty. He hadn't known what to expect. An outcry perhaps? Mixed emotions at least, some jealousy, some bitterness, an element of why her, why not me? But there was no such reaction. They simply stood there respectfully while Rassen, as always, acted as their spokesperson.

'We all agree this is a fine thing you are doing for Jalila, Paul,' he said. 'You are helping to heal this girl.' He looked about at the group, 'This is good, yes?' Every single one of them nodded in agreement, even little Hamid who had simply been told Jalila had gone away to visit a friend. 'Is good,' they all said in English. 'Yes, this is good.'

Rassen himself had been surprised by the reception he'd received from the group as a whole. He hadn't told them of Jalila's past, but it hadn't been necessary. They'd all been through their own form of hell, and they recognised that the girl, too, had suffered immeasurably. Rassen had told them only that Paul was offering Jalila a taste of freedom in the hope it would help heal her. He'd needed to say no more. Every single one of them knew the damage war could wreak upon the human spirit, and they'd all witnessed the recent change in this girl who had appeared beyond saving. They were genuinely happy about anything that might advance her recovery.

Perhaps ignorance is bliss under circumstances like this, Rassen had thought. Perhaps they really do believe that ahead of them lies the freedom they seek.

Now as Paul stood on the jetty accepting handshakes all round, he too, like Rassen, was touched by the generosity of the group's reaction.

Then Sanaa stepped forwards, saying something in Arabic and offering him a parcel wrapped in brown paper.

'Sanaa is worried that after your long trip, you will be hungry,' Hala translated. 'She says you have probably not had lunch, and that this is a meal of rice and meat, which is still pleasant eaten cold.'

'Thank you, Sanaa.' Paul smiled appreciatively as he accepted the parcel. 'You are quite right. I have not had lunch, and I am very hungry. I shall eat this on the trip home.' He looked around at the group and pointed at *Anni*. 'Now who'd like a quick trip on the speedboat before I leave?'

Karim's, Hany's and little Hamid's hands all went up like a shot.

While Paul took them all out for a run, Lou left aboard the old Princess in order to get a head start. They'd already loaded the vessel up with the rubbish to be returned to the mainland.

Paul caught up with him a good half-hour out of Shoalhaven, and the two boats ambled into the marina side by side.

First thing the following morning, after refilling *Anni*'s fuel tanks, Paul returned the keys to the brothers who, like him, were early risers.

'Was your sister's friend impressed?' Jukka asked at the front door of their fisher's cottage, coffee mug in hand.

'Bloody oath she was,' Paul replied. '*Anni* went down a real treat, just like you said she would. In fact I wouldn't mind borrowing her for another spin,' he said, paving the way for Jalila's return. 'Say, maybe next week? If that'd be OK?'

'Sure, no worries. Want a coffee?' Jukka opened the door wide. 'Come on in.'

'No thanks, mate, I'm heading down to Gero. Going to take Bev's friend out for a drive, show her the sights.'

'Jeez, you really *are* keen, aren't you?'

As Paul set off down the path, Jukka, a confirmed bachelor like his brother, at least in this stage of their respective lives, called after him, and only half-jokingly. 'You want to watch your step, mate. Starting to sound a bit dangerous to me.'

Paul just smiled and gave a backwards wave over his shoulder.

An hour later he pulled his Land Rover up outside Bev's apartment in Fitzgerald Street at the western end of Geraldton's CBD. An attractive two-storey block of six units built in the art-deco style of the late 1930s, Fitzgerald Flats was very conveniently situated for Bev and in an area that suited her lifestyle. A ten-minute stroll to the library, several nearby coffee shops, a local wine bar, the Provincial, which was one of her favourite haunts, and a very short walk to the foreshore. There was even a gymnasium across the road, which several of her fitness-conscious friends frequented, although Bev preferred the ocean to a gym workout herself.

'Can't be bothered, too lazy,' she'd say on a hot Saturday afternoon, 'going for a swim, see you at the wine bar.'

As Paul expected, Bev had already left when he arrived. During their run on the boat the previous day when they'd discussed their plans, she'd offered to forego her early Sunday morning tennis, which was a regular commitment and which he knew she loved, but he'd insisted she stick to her schedule.

'I'm putting you out enough as it is, Bev,' he'd said, 'and I'll be at your place by nine anyway.'

They'd even discussed the regular Sunday family roast in Shoalhaven.

'Mum and Dad'll be disappointed if neither of us turn up,' he'd said, 'and I'd like to take Jalila out to dinner. Why don't you go along as usual and I'll stay with her until you get back to the flat.'

'Oh.' Bev had been a little stumped for an answer, which was quite unlike her. 'You think that's a good idea, do you?'

'Yeah, sure. Why not?'

Because you're getting too involved, she thought, that's bloody well why not.

'Right you are then,' she'd said.

Paul let himself into the unit with the spare key that was imaginatively hidden under the pot plant by the front door.

Jalila was sitting in a chair by the windows, which looked out over the street. To Paul she appeared mesmerised by a palm tree that grew on the grassy verge of the sidewalk, but in actuality she was not seeing the palm tree at all. She was reliving the experiences of the previous afternoon. In any event, lost as she was, she didn't hear the front door open.

Paul found the sight of her extraordinary. There was a serenity about her, a grace, even in her motionless state, the straightness of her back, her long slender neck, the tilt of her chin. But Jalila has always been graceful, he thought, what makes the sight of her now so extraordinary? Perhaps, he decided, it was the fact that her head was not covered by a shawl and that the sleeveless, floral dress she wore was so very Western. Was that all it was? No, Paul thought, it was something that emanated from the girl herself, something from deep within Jalila.

'That's a very nice dress,' he said.

She turned to him, neither startled nor surprised, but clearly pleased to see him.

'Hello, Paul,' she said and she looked down at her dress with its pattern of little pink flowers; she'd never owned such a dress before. 'Yes, is very pretty.' She stroked her bare upper arms, unaccustomed to the public exposure of so much skin, but enjoying the experience. She did not in the least mind, also, being bareheaded, as Bev had suggested. The wearing of a shawl or scarf had become merely a long-term habit she'd observed – it held no special significance for her.

'If you're comfortable without the shawl it'd call less attention to us,' Bev had said, having noted aboard the boat that the girl travelled happily with her head uncovered, 'otherwise, no worries. Your choice entirely, of course.'

Jalila had decided then and there she would obey every single instruction of Bev's. The demands of her early village upbringing belonged to a lifetime ago, that person had long ceased to exist. She had, however, baulked at a bathing costume.

'But you'll need bathers for the water park,' Bev had said.

In their initial walk along the foreshore from the marina to Bev's flat, Jalila had been fascinated by the huge water park, where families and children of all ages played on the sculptures of all shapes and sizes that served as fountains and jets and geysers, spraying and showering and propelling water in all directions. It had seemed to her a most magical place.

'Paul will certainly take you there if you ask him,' Bev had promised her.

But during their shopping expedition, the sight of the flimsy costume on offer had been a step too far for Jalila. She'd shaken her head. Modesty forbade she expose that amount of flesh.

'Right you are.' Hands in the air, Bev had surrendered. 'Get drenched, ruin your new clothes then, see if I care.' Already Bev, good-natured and bossy, had adopted the role of big sister.

Jalila hadn't understood what Bev was actually saying, but she knew no offence was intended and that Bev was not cross. Bev was very nice. Jalila liked Bev.

'Bev buy me many pretty things, Paul,' she now said. 'We go shops . . . We go lunch . . . We eat . . .' she paused '. . . sand-wich,' she said, enunciating the word perfectly and with pride, it was a new word, one she'd only just learnt. 'We drink coffee in street . . . I meet Bev friends . . .'

Paul said nothing, but pulled up a chair opposite her and sat. Jalila wanted to talk and he wanted to listen. He realised then that this was the extraordinary and indescribable change he'd sensed emanating from the girl. Already, after less than one day, Jalila was embracing her freedom, and with this came an assurance he'd never seen before.

Bev had intimated as much when he'd phoned the previous night.

'Is she all right?' he'd asked. He'd been worried, beginning to doubt the wisdom of his decision, sure that Jalila must be, if not frightened, at least confused. The whole experience was bound to be nerve-racking for her. 'Is she coping with everything? I mean, it must be . . .'

Instantly aware of the anxiety she could hear in her brother's voice, Bev had been quick to reassure him.

'Jalila's absolutely fine, Paul,' she said. 'Honestly, nothing fazes that girl. She doesn't say much, but she's soaking up every new experience, every sight and every sound, it's wonderful to see. You really have done the right thing, you know.'

Paul's sigh of relief was audible. 'Where is she now?'

'Having a shower. She likes hot showers; they're a real treat.'

Then Bev proceeded to tell him all about their afternoon excursion, the shopping, the wonderment of a sandwich for lunch, coffee at a sidewalk café.

'We were even joined by a couple of the gang from the library,' she said.

'Oh hell,' his reaction was nervous, 'and how did that go?'

'Easy,' she replied breezily. 'I introduced her as the little sister of a close friend of mine from uni days. "This is

Jalila, my friend's little sister," I said. "She's just arrived from overseas to join her family in Perth and her English isn't too good, so you have to be nice to her."'

She laughed, Paul involuntarily joining in, either with relief or admiration, he wasn't sure, but probably a mixture of both. Bev had always been a highly accomplished and supremely effective liar. She usually only used this power in order to string someone along with a tall story just for fun, but her talent had rescued them from many a sticky situation during their childhood.

'Anyway, my mates were awfully nice to her,' she said, 'and why the hell wouldn't they be? She's bloody gorgeous. Oh and before I forget, make sure you bring your bathers tomorrow,' she warned. 'Jalila's desperate to go to the water park. She won't wear bathers herself though, wouldn't let me buy her any – too revealing it seems. You'll just have to let her get soaked in her clothes.'

'Tell you what,' she added as an idea occurred, 'I'll leave a pair of my bathers out on the bed, together with a wrap-around. Take them along with you just in case she changes her mind. Don't forget to grab a couple of towels too. Linen cupboard in the hall.'

Bev had rattled on a little longer. Then, 'See you tomorrow, probably be gone when you arrive, key's under the pot plant,' and the conversation, to which he'd contributed virtually nothing, had been over.

'Bev friends is nice . . .'

And now Jalila was recounting her day in her own way. The shopping, the sandwich, the coffee, Bev's friends. Paul found it enchanting.

'I like Bev friends . . .'

'That's good, Jalila. I'm sure they liked you too.'

Then, as if on cue . . .

'We go water park, Paul? Bev say you will take me, yes?'

'Of course I'll take you to the water park. Are you ready to go now?'

'Yes.' She stood. 'Ready.'

'I'll just get us some towels, back in a tick.'

After fetching the towels, he ducked into Bev's bedroom, collected the bathers and wrap-around she'd left out for him and, rolling the whole lot up together, reappeared with the bundle tucked under his arm.

'Let's go,' he said, and they left the apartment to walk down to the foreshore barely five minutes away.

Geraldton's foreshore was without doubt the town's major attraction, and a feature of which its citizens were justifiably proud, for stretching along beside the broad oceanfront promenade was landscaped parkland designed specifically for the enjoyment of the people. There were grassy picnic areas, tables and benches, drinking fountains, playgrounds for all ages, and a huge indoor-outdoor café, beyond which lay a holiday-maker's paradise – an ocean of the most inviting blue and a beach of the whitest sand that was separated by two jetties forking out into the sea. To the north of the foreshore was the marina and to the south the main port of Geraldton, but in between was the preserve of the people, most particularly those with families, and the most popular attraction of all, apart from the oceanfront itself, was the water park.

The day was fine. There was little breeze, and although it was barely ten o'clock in the morning, a late-October sun bore warmly down. Paul sought out a bench on the grassy verge of the park and he and Jalila sat watching the revellers. It being a Sunday, there were many frolicking amongst the array of inventive sculptures. Infants skipped about with their parents beneath fountains and shower-like structures, youths battled each other with fierce water jets, and youngsters squealed as they ran through colour-ful arrays of hoops and giant metal circles that triggered unexpectedly, releasing huge deluges upon them.

Jalila gazed at the scene, her eyes flickering here and

there, enthralled by a sight she'd never before witnessed and had never expected to witness. This was more than a magical place. This was a joyful place. She'd never seen so many people so happy.

They sat as silent observers for quite some time, then, 'Would you like to join in?' Paul finally asked.

Without taking her eyes from the revellers, she nodded.

He stood, stripping off his T-shirt. The blue shorts he wore served also as bathers, made of a synthetic fabric that dried quickly.

'Come on, then.'

He offered her his hand, and she took it and stood. But she made no further move, appearing confused.

'You can't join in without getting wet,' he said.

Looking out at the park, where everyone was running around on the colourfully patterned, spongy-wet surface, all of them saturated, all of them semi-naked, Jalila realised what Bev had meant. 'Ruin your new clothes then, see if I care,' she had said. She glanced down at her pretty new dress with its pattern of pink flowers. She didn't want to ruin her new dress.

Paul picked up the bathers and wrap-around from the bundle that sat on the bench and offered them to her. 'The change rooms are over there,' he said, pointing to where they stood on the other side of the park.

She studied the bathing costume he held out to her: a pair of Speedos, modest by Australian standards, but to Jalila incredibly revealing. Did she dare?

Paul recognised her dilemma. 'Go and put them on, Jalila,' he said, 'but wear this too.' He draped the wrap-around over her shoulder. 'Wear it to cover the bathers,' he explained. 'It won't matter if this gets wet. Do you understand?'

She nodded. Then, the wrap-around still draped over her shoulder, she took the bathers from him and walked off towards the change rooms.

Paul sat on the bench awaiting her return and thinking of her past. After all she'd gone through, after all the sexual abuse, the humiliation, the degradation she'd suffered at the hands of the soldiers, the modesty of her childhood remained somehow ingrained. It seemed to him incredible.

She appeared several minutes later, the wrap-around tied at her chest, carrying her new dress folded neatly, and as she crossed the grassy area that led from the change rooms, he could see the eyes of many mark her passing. Not only men, he noted, but women also. It was more than the girl's beauty: it was the grace of her every movement.

When she arrived beside him, he took the dress from her and placed it with the towels in a neat pile on the grass, leaving the bench for others who might want to use it; the park was getting busier by the minute.

'Ready?' he asked.

She nodded, but remained motionless, staring at the water park and the sea of carefree, wet, bather-clad bodies prancing about, the infants, the parents, the children and youths. Then she did the most amazing thing. Lifting her hands to her chest, she untied the knot of the wrap-around and let it drop to the grass.

'Ready,' she said, standing there in a bathing costume obviously too large for her.

'Good,' Paul said. 'Let's go then.'

If Jalila's acceptance of the bathing costume was to be perceived as a breakthrough, the following half-hour, to Paul, was nothing short of a revelation.

Self-consciously hoisting up the straps of her bathers, Jalila approached a giant yellow circular sculpture that grew out of the spongy surface of the playground. She stepped tentatively beneath its arch and was instantly hit by a deluge of water that appeared from nowhere. But instead of being alarmed she laughed. Instinctively, she threw back her head and laughed, just as the others she'd been watching in the park had done. It was a sight and a sound Paul would never have thought possible.

From that moment on, the water park continued to work its magic. Paying no heed at all to her bathing costume, now saturated and hanging baggily from her slender frame, straps slipping off shoulders, Jalila ran from one piece of equipment to another. And each time she was unexpectedly showered or hit by a jet of water, she laughed in delight.

She's become just one of the young people playing in the water park, Paul thought, and as he did he wondered if it was at all conceivable that one day Jalila might be capable of leading a normal life. He would not have believed so. None on the island would have believed so, but none on the island had seen her like this.

He joined in the fun. They played together like children, following each other through the hoops of the water canyon, competing to see who could second-guess the overhead showers that sprang on without warning, duelling with the high-powered water jets, knocking each other over, slipping and sliding. And a good half an hour later, they were thoroughly exhausted.

'Time to call it a day,' he panted, 'what do you reckon?'

She didn't understand the turn of phrase, but knew what he meant, and nodded, equally breathless.

Returning to their towels, they dried themselves off, Jalila donned her wrap-around and they sat on the grass basking in the sun. Their bench was taken, but they preferred the grass anyway.

'That was fun, wasn't it?' Paul said.

'Yes. Fun,' she replied, unfamiliar with the word, but correctly presuming it meant something good. After which she lapsed into silence, her attention again focused on the park and the people's enjoyment. Jalila had no need to discuss the pleasure she had just experienced.

It was there in her mind to relive when she wished, which was remarkable for one who had so efficiently trained her mind to close out all memory.

Paul registered the fact that she didn't need to talk, and even felt a little stupid for having made the obvious comment he had. He was rapidly coming to the conclusion that language was not the barrier at all with Jalila. That she only talked when she felt the need – when she wished to communicate. He realised also, and for the very first time, that this was who she really was, and that he was finally coming to know her.

A little later, when Jalila had returned from the change rooms in her pretty new dress and when Paul's shorts were virtually dry, they strolled down to the Dome Cafeteria, where they sat on the verandah overlooking the ocean and had lunch. Jalila opted once again for a 'sand-wich', relishing the sound of the word as she made her request.

'Is good,' she said, tucking in heartily, 'thank you.'

'My pleasure,' he replied.

They didn't say much after that, there was no need, they were comfortable with silence, but Paul's mind ran rampant as he looked out to sea, remembering the news reports he'd read and the televised footage he'd seen of the boat that had come ashore in 2013. It had been around about this time of day, they'd said, people had been lunching at the Dome, just as they were now, when to the amazement of all, a boat carrying sixty-six Sri Lankan refugees had pulled up right here on the shore. They'd travelled over five thousand kilometres. The news had of course made headlines at the time.

What had happened to those poor souls? he wondered. They'd disappeared, of course, whisked off to some refugee camp, Nauru, Manus Island, who could tell, he couldn't remember that part. The people of Gero had been kind, or so he'd heard; many had come down to the beach with blankets. But they'd been unable to save the Sri Lankans from their fate. Is that what lies in store for Jalila? he wondered.

After lunch, he took her for a drive.

'We'll pretend we're tourists,' he said, 'which of course we are.'

They visited the historic settlement of Greenough twenty minutes to the south, where they wandered around the heritage buildings and the unique leaning trees that were a popular tourist attraction, and then on their return to Geraldton he took her to the HMAS *Sydney II* Memorial, which stood majestically on Mount Scott overlooking the township.

The memorial, he told her, was dedicated to the six hundred and forty-five men who had lost their lives in 1941 when the HMAS *Sydney II* sank in the Indian Ocean off the coast of Western Australia following action with the German raider *Kormoran*.

'The whole crew,' he said, 'every single one of them. And the ship went down without a trace – the wreck wasn't discovered until 2008. That's their grave,' he said, pointing seawards, 'they're still out there, all those sailors. And she's still waiting.'

Jalila found the 'Waiting Woman' profoundly moving.

'So sad,' she said. He'd told her the life-size, bronze statue of the motherly woman, arm raised holding her hat in place, leaning into the wind and gazing out to sea, represented every woman who had lost a husband or a son or a brother in the disaster.

The statue itself had spoken very clearly to Jalila.

'And do you know the most incredible thing of all?' he went on. 'When the statue was placed here in 2001, they had no idea where the *Sydney* was. But seven years later, when the ship was discovered,' he held his arm out straight, indicating the Waiting Woman's direct eyeline, 'they found that she's gazing along the exact bearing of the wreck's site.'

The gist of this, too, Jalila understood. She had no doubt the woman's gaze was fixed directly on the burial place.

The centrepiece of the memorial she found just as moving. The 'Dome of Souls' was an immense canopy, nine metres high and twelve metres in diameter, supported by seven pillars. The dome itself was an open-weave filigree of stainless steel, depicting a vast flock of seagulls.

The two of them stood in the very centre of the dome, looking up at the gulls.

'There're six hundred and forty-five of them in all,' Paul told her, 'one for every sailor who died.'

Looking up, Jalila slowly turned, watching the birds in flight, feeling their movement through the air.

'The sailors,' she said slowly and with care, another new word she'd learnt just that day, 'the sailors, they is free.'

'Yes,' he replied, aware she was way ahead of him, that he need offer no further explanation.

When they arrived back at the flat, it was five o'clock and Bev was preparing to leave for the family dinner in Shoalhaven.

'Did you have a nice day?' she asked. Bloody stupid question, she told herself, they're positively glowing.

'We sure did,' Paul said. 'Starting with the water park. But I'm afraid you'll have to buy a new pair of bathers for Jalila – yours were far too big.'

'Really?' Bev's eyes were a little saucer-like.

'Water park . . . fun,' Jalila said with enthusiasm, remembering that was the word Paul had used.

'And then we had lunch at the Dome –'

'Sand-wich,' Jalila interjected proudly. 'I eat sand-wich, Bev.'

'That's nice.' What's happened? Bev wondered. They're different. Both of them are different. Fresh cause for worry?

'And then we drove to Greenough for a look-around,' Paul went on, 'and then we came back to the *Sydney Memorial* . . .'

'So sad,' Jalila said.

'Yes, it's impressive all right,' Bev agreed. 'Well I'm off.' She picked up her car keys. 'What do I tell Mum and Dad by the way?' she asked pointedly.

'Nothing. I've already phoned them, said I can't come. Phoned Lou too.'

'Oh yes? And what did he say?'

'He said to be careful,' Paul gave a shrug, 'why the hell I don't know.' He'd found the comment annoying, he had to admit, but he'd let it go.

You don't know, Bev thought. 'So where are you having dinner?' she asked.

'Haven't decided yet. Might even get takeaway and watch TV, that'd be something different for Jalila.'

Dangerous, Bev thought, but she didn't say anything. 'There's a nice café around the corner that does good lasagne,' she said, hoping he might take the hint. Then she left.

Paul didn't take the hint – he didn't realise he'd been offered one. Instead, he asked Jalila what she'd like to do.

'I like here,' Jalila said. 'I like be here with you.'

So while Jalila indulged herself in another hot shower, he went out and bought takeaway pizzas, two large, not sure what flavour she might prefer, or how hungry she might be.

As it turned out they were both ravenous and tucked into the food the moment he got back, eating straight from the boxes, which he'd set out on the coffee table, Jalila curled up on the sofa in the bathrobe Bev had lent her.

By the time they'd finished there was just over half a pizza left, which he stored in the refrigerator for Bev, knowing how much she loved cold pizza. Then he sat back in his armchair and turned on the television.

'What sort of stuff do you want to watch?' he asked, flicking through the Foxtel channels on the remote, 'news, movies, documentaries?' He knew the question was probably pointless, that in all likelihood she was unfamiliar with television, but it seemed impolite not to enquire.

She just shrugged. The decision was obviously his. So he turned on the news, which was devoted entirely to the American presidential campaign. Even switching channels, there was no escape: everywhere he looked political analysts, current affairs journalists, chat-show hosts and panellists were discussing the latest Trump/Clinton debate and the reason America was in such a state of chaos.

He settled back in his armchair to watch, presuming that Jalila was doing the same thing where she remained curled up on the sofa. But it wasn't long before he became aware that Jalila was not watching the television at all. Jalila was watching him.

He pressed the mute button. Silence.

'What is it, Jalila?' he asked. 'You want to talk, is that it?'

She nodded. He waited.

'Why you is so good to me, Paul?'

The question was genuine and required a genuine answer.

'Because I like you,' he replied. 'I like you very much.'

She thought upon this for a moment or so. And then . . .

'I like you also. I like you also very much.'

'I'm glad you do, Jalila,' he said. 'We've become friends. This is good.'

'Yes,' she agreed, 'is good.'

She rose from the sofa and, to his utter horror, untied the belt of the bathrobe, about to slip it from her shoulders. He was sure she was naked beneath.

Dear God, he thought, not again.

He was up out of the armchair and by her side in a second.

'No, Jalila.' He grabbed the robe just as it slid on its way to the floor, 'no, don't do this.' Hauling it back up over her shoulders, he ensured she was fully covered before seating her back on the sofa and sitting beside her.

'You mustn't offer yourself in this way,' he insisted. 'I don't want payment for being your friend. Can't you understand that?' he begged. 'Please, *please* can't you understand, I do not want payment.'

'No, Paul,' she replied, '*you* not understand.' This time there was no confusion, Jalila knew exactly what she wished to say, and her voice although soft, was firm. 'Is not payment,' she said. 'Is gift. You give me much. I wish give back to you.' She glanced down at her body, then looked into his eyes, begging his understanding. 'Is all I have. Is gift.'

Nothing in the world could have stopped him from kissing her. Just as nothing in the world could have prevented the rush of emotion that shocked him to the core. He loved her. How could he not have recognised the fact? He loved her. He wouldn't tell her this though. Not yet.

He held her close. Then kissed her again.

She responded to the kiss, just as she responded to the embrace. Not with passion, for passion was foreign to Jalila, but she returned his tenderness. Tenderness was something she welcomed, something to which she was quite unaccustomed.

He wanted her certainly, but despite the gift she offered he did not make love to her.

'Not yet, Jalila,' he said, 'not yet.'

He got up and made them a cup of tea instead.

Bev arrived home to discover Paul watching the late night news with the sound turned off. He was seated on the sofa and curled up in his arms was Jalila, bathrobe-clad and fast asleep.

Good God, she thought, aghast, it's happened.

Paul eased himself from the sofa without waking Jalila and crossed to his sister, who remained frozen to the spot.

'There's cold pizza in the fridge,' he said.

She didn't answer and he knew she was waiting for the explanation, which he also knew she deserved.

'How was dinner?' he asked, buying time.

'Fine,' she replied a little icily, 'how was yours?'

'Well, pizza, you know . . .' He gave a shrug, knowing she was jumping to the obvious conclusion, but not sure how to tell her the truth.

'Cut to the chase, for God's sake, what the hell's going on?'

There was only one way to put it. 'I'm in love with Jalila,' he said.

'I know.' Her tone softened. Despite the boldness of his admission, he looked so young and so vulnerable: she could see the realisation had shocked him. 'I know you're in love with her, Paul, I could have told you that yesterday. So you've slept with her, I take it?'

'No.'

She breathed a sigh of relief. Things weren't quite as bad as she'd expected then.

'Not yet,' he added.

Oh shit, she thought. 'So what are you going to do?'

'I'm going to marry her.'

Bev was struck dumb. My brother's insane, she thought. He's gone quite mad.

'If she says yes, that is, I haven't asked her yet.' He looked at the girl asleep on the sofa. 'I'll sneak off now. Tell Jalila to wait for me, I'll be here around ten, got a couple of things to do in the morning.'

He crossed to the front door, then turned back.

'And, Bev, would you mind buying some new bathers for her, about two sizes smaller than yours I reckon. What say you get them at lunchtime and I'll pick them up from the library? All right by you?'

'Sure.' What other option did she have?

'Great. See you tomorrow then.' And he was gone.

CHAPTER FOURTEEN

Paul arrived in Geraldton on the dot of nine the following morning, but as planned he didn't go directly to Bev's flat. Instead, he booked into the Ocean Centre Hotel on the corner of Cathedral Avenue and Foreshore Drive, the end room on the second floor, with a balcony looking directly over the water park. He was told he could move in at midday. Then he visited Mazzucchelli's Jewellers in Northgate Shopping Centre.

Finally, carrying the small, empty suitcase he'd brought from the car, he let himself into the flat in Fitzgerald Street. It was shortly after ten and she was waiting for him, seated exactly as she had been the previous day by the window. As before she'd been gazing at the palm outside, but this time she heard him. This time she'd been listening for the slightest sound of his arrival. The key in the lock was enough, and as the door opened she rose to greet him.

'Hello, Paul,' she said, smiling at the sight of him.

Paul was overwhelmed. He remembered the day on the island when he'd given her the shawl, and how he'd so longed to see her smile. Smile for me, Jalila, smile for me, he remembered thinking. Had he been in denial all this time? Had he been moved by the depth of Jalila's unhappiness as he'd told himself he was, or had he been in love with her from the very beginning? Whatever the answer, it no longer mattered and he no longer cared. He loved her now, and she was smiling now. She was smiling just for him.

He put down the suitcase. 'Hello, Jalila.'

They met in the centre of the room, drawn like magnets into a world of their own.

After they'd kissed, he held her at arm's length.

'I brought that for you to put your things in,' he said, pointing to the suitcase. 'Your new clothes, the bathrobe Bev lent you, the toiletries, everything.'

Jalila looked bewildered. She understood the suitcase, which was fairly obvious, and she understood new clothes, but *toiletries* had lost her completely.

'Come on,' he said, 'I'll help you.'

They packed her several items of clothing, then collected her bits and pieces from the bathroom.

'Toil-et-ies,' she said as they gathered the toothbrush, toothpaste, hairbrush and other items.

'Toiletries,' he corrected her.

'Toil-et-ries.' Another new word; Jalila was very happy about that.

'No, you won't need those,' he said as she started folding up the towel and the flannel Bev had given her, 'they'll have them at the hotel.'

She obeyed him unquestioningly, but the mystery deepened. Where were they going?

After driving the several blocks to the Ocean Centre Hotel he parked the car in the hotel's car park, then they sat in the downstairs lounge overlooking the foreshore, drinking cappuccinos until their room was ready.

Jalila loved the view through the windows. 'Water park,' she said, staring out at the activity and presuming this was why he'd brought her there.

'You wait till you see the view from our place on the second floor,' he promised her. 'There's a balcony, looking right over the park.'

She was puzzled. *Our place* confused her.

'I've booked us in here for a few days,' he explained.

'Us,' she queried, 'you, me, here?'

'Yes, us.' Her surprise aroused in him a sudden doubt. What if she doesn't want to marry me? he thought. What if the prospect frightens her? 'You, me, here,' he said tentatively. 'Is that all right?'

Again the smile, so guileless, so infinitely trusting. 'Oh yes, you, me is good.' For Jalila, anywhere with Paul was good.

The very nice woman at reception informed them their room was ready, so they climbed the stairs to the second floor, Paul carrying the small suitcase, his own backpack slung over one shoulder, Jalila following wide-eyed, silently marvelling at the foyer and the staircase and everything that to her appeared so grand.

The 'room', as it was referred to, was really a fully equipped open-plan apartment, light, airy and comfortable. An island bench separated the kitchen area from the lounge and bedroom, beyond which sliding glass doors, flanked by huge windows that ran the full width of the room, led onto a large balcony overlooking the foreshore.

Jalila made straight for the balcony where the view over the water park and the ocean beyond was certainly impressive. There was a table and chairs, but she didn't sit, preferring instead to lean over the railings and gaze at the revellers; she could spend all day there.

They unpacked their things, 'setting up house' as Paul said jokingly, wondering as he did why he was talking too much. 'I'll duck out and do some shopping in a tick,' he went on. 'We'll need stuff for cooking and all that, and I have to call in at the library and collect your new bathers from Bev . . .'

He wondered if perhaps it was the prospect of Bev that was making him jumpy. He'd left his sister speechless the previous night, he knew, but Bev was never speechless for long. Bev was bound to have quite a bit to say. But Paul knew his nerves really had nothing at all to do with Bev.

Jalila didn't understand everything he was saying – he seemed to be speaking more quickly than usual. She realised no comment was required, however, so made no enquiry as she continued to explore the cupboards and drawers and nooks and crannies of the kitchen. Besides, she simply liked listening to the sound of his voice.

Paul knew time was running out, that Bev would be returning from lunch soon, expecting to see him, demanding what was going on. No more delay tactics, he told himself, get on with it. But how?

'Jalila, come and sit down,' he said, pulling out one of the several chairs that were tucked around the room's small dining table. 'There's something I want to talk about.'

He was speaking more slowly now and she understood every word. Paul had something serious to say. She sat, giving him her full attention.

He pulled out another chair and sat opposite her.

'You offered me a gift yesterday,' he said.

She nodded. So this was why he was serious, he wished now to take her. She was quite prepared to give herself.

'I cannot accept the gift you offer unless you accept my gift in return,' he said.

His reasoning made no sense at all to Jalila. 'But already you give gift. You give much. My gift is return.'

'Ah, but if that is so, then it would make your gift a *payment*, wouldn't it,' Paul replied emphatically, 'and you know I do not wish payment. You *do* know that, don't you?'

'Yes. No payment.'

Jalila was studying him intently. Even given the language barrier she recognised the impasse his argument presented, but what was his intention? She had no idea. She could not fathom where this might be leading.

'I want to marry you, Jalila. I want to be with you always and I want to look after you. Do you understand what I'm saying?'

She nodded, but did not reply. She understood the words and their meaning, yes, but she could not comprehend why he should say them.

Jalila was strong, her survival was proof of the fact, but she was also astute. She had recognised that, in the short time she had known him, this man had become her saviour. At this moment her whole world revolved around him. Paul had changed her, she knew this, but such a change could never last. She had revelled in her moments of freedom, of happiness even, but she expected them to be over, she expected to lose him. He was a good man with a life of his own. Why did he not just take the gift of her body for as long as he wished to enjoy her and then move on? She would be left with the greatest gift he could have offered: the memories he had given her, memories that might perhaps mask those she wished to obliterate forever. She continued to study him, bewildered.

Paul took the jeweller's box from the top pocket of his shirt. He opened it and placed it on the table before her, revealing the rings inside, two simple gold bands.

'I love you, Jalila,' he said. Why was she looking at him so strangely? he wondered. 'Please be my wife. Please marry me.' He felt a desperate need to beg. She must realise this was no empty gesture, that he was in deadly earnest. 'I love you and I want to look after you. Become my wife, Jalila, please. Become the mother of my children.'

She bowed her head. He presumed she was looking at the rings, admiring them, and the thought allayed his doubts. Until he saw the puzzling drops on the table. Reaching out his hand, he gently raised her head. She didn't resist; she was incapable.

Tears were flooding down her cheeks, but they were not the tears of joy he might have hoped for. Her eyes were the haunted eyes of one tormented.

Oh my God, Paul thought, what have I done? What's going on in her mind, what horrors have I brought back?

'Jalila . . .' He quickly closed the jeweller's box, pushing it aside in case the rings had been some sort of catalyst, and taking her hand was about to offer words of comfort, although he could think of none. Then suddenly the tears were no longer silent rivers of pain, suddenly the tears were racking sobs from deep within her being, something primal; she was in agony.

He stood, raising her to her feet and holding her fast, feeling the convulsions of her body.

'Shh . . . shh . . .' he whispered, stroking her hair, caressing her, wishing the pain away, guilty for being the unwitting cause, but thinking also that such a release might perhaps be a further sign of her healing. He could only hope so.

She clung to him briefly – without his support she would have fallen to the floor. Then as quickly as the emotional outburst had manifested itself, it was gone, faded to nothing.

'I sorry.' She stepped away from him, turning her face so that he shouldn't see her. 'I sorry, Paul,' she said, wiping away tears and mucous with the back of her hand.

'There's no need to be sorry, Jalila.' He disappeared briefly to the bathroom, returning with a box of tissues, ripping out a dozen or so and thrusting them into her hand. 'There's no need to be sorry at all. *I'm* sorry.'

She wiped her face and blew her nose, then turned to him, strong once again, resolute, as if nothing had happened.

'Are you all right?' he asked.

'Yes.'

'Will you marry me?'

'Yes.'

It should have been a joyful occasion. He had hoped that it would be. But he could see she was still haunted, and that perhaps she always would be. Perhaps there was no final healing for Jalila.

'We're going out shopping now,' he announced, deciding a return to normality was called for, 'and we're going to see Bev and collect your new bathers.'

'You go, Paul,' she said softly. 'I stay.'

'Will you be all right?' he asked, concerned.

'Yes.' She glanced over at the balcony. 'I look water park.'

'We'll go there this afternoon if you like.'

'Yes. I like very much.'

He left her sitting on the balcony staring out at the water park and the people at play, but he wondered if she was really seeing either the park or the people.

In fact she was, but the sight was bringing her no joy, not at the moment. She was simply using the image to blot out memory, a well-practised mind-control exercise that preserved her sanity. There were some places Jalila dared not revisit for any extended period of time, knowing that way lay madness.

'You do realise, don't you,' Bev said with deliberate brutality, 'that buying a couple of gold rings doesn't in any way whatsoever make it a marriage.'

They were seated in the library's deserted staffroom with cups of half-finished coffee. She'd been appalled when he'd bluntly announced he'd booked into the Ocean Centre Hotel, bought two wedding rings and that Jalila had accepted his proposal.

'It'll be a marriage to us, and that's all that matters,' he calmly replied, 'for now anyway. Perhaps further down the track we'll be able to legalise it.'

'Further down the track!' she exclaimed in disbelief. 'Where the hell do you think Jalila's going to *be* further down the track? Have you thought about that?'

'Yes.' Paul refused to be rattled, he'd known he'd cop a big serve from Bev and was quite prepared to weather the storm.

'She'll probably be sent to Nauru – what'll you do then?'

'If that happens I'll go to Nauru myself and set up camp right outside the refugee compound and I'll see her every day.'

'*If,*' Bev scoffed. 'Try *when*!'

He just shrugged.

'And what if she's sent back to Iraq?'

'Then I'll go there too. I'll go wherever she goes. I won't be separated from her, I can promise you that.'

Bev was starting to fume. She knew he'd have an answer however illogical and unrealistic to every obstacle she could throw in his path, and there were so very many obvious obstacles begging to be thrown. This was a side of her young brother she recognised only too well. The unruffled, immoveable Paul Miller, obstinate to the bitter end when he'd set his sights on a particular path. As a rule though, she thought, he's not so blind to reason.

Quelling a desire to scream, she tried a different tack. 'You're obviously not taking her back to the island.'

'Obviously.'

'So what are your plans? A brief honeymoon at the Ocean Centre Hotel, and then what?' Aware her attempt not to sound cynical hadn't worked, she opted for simple common-sense. 'I mean honestly, Paul, what are your plans, have you thought them through? How are you going to hide her? Where are you going to run away to?'

'I'm not going to hide her and I'm not going to run away. I'm going to bring my wife home. We're going to live in Shoalhaven.'

Bev was rarely dumbfounded, but right at that moment she couldn't come up with a response. Her expression clearly said, 'You're what?!' but she seemed unable to reply, or to make any form of comment. She was vaguely aware this was the second time he'd done that to her in two days.

Good, Paul thought, I've floored her. He'd been patiently waiting for his sister to calm down and shut up long enough for him to explain his plan.

'We're going to live a lie, Bev,' he said, 'well, for as long as we can. I do understand what you're saying, you know,' he added reasonably. 'I'm aware we may be on borrowed time, but the longer I can give Jalila her freedom, the more quickly she'll heal.'

In the short walk to the library, Paul had decided not to tell his sister about Jalila's harrowing outburst, for fear it might be interpreted as a sign of a permanently unstable mind. He had no idea himself how it should be interpreted, but he now firmly chose to believe the outpouring of emotion he'd witnessed was a step in the right direction.

'The difference in her is already amazing,' he continued enthusiastically. 'You've seen yourself how she responds to everything around her, every new experience. You said I was doing the right thing bringing her here, remember?'

Bev bit back the caustic retort that sprang instantly to mind. *I was hardly recommending you marry the bloody girl!*

'So what particular lie are you going to live?' she asked, trying not to sound arch.

'The one you've set up for us so perfectly,' he said. 'Jalila's the younger sister of a friend you went to uni with. I've met her several times here in Gero with you; we fell madly in love so we got married. Simple. Particularly with your help – you're the best liar I know.'

'Thank you,' she said drily.

'It's true,' he insisted, 'you're the most unlikely librarian I've ever met – not that I've met many – you should have been an actress.'

'I'm not sure even *my* acting skills are equal to convincing the town you've married a girl they've never heard of without your parents or any friends there to see it.'

Elbows on table, he leant forwards, an urgent plea. 'You will help us, won't you?'

'You really are serious about this?' She felt she might hit him.

'Bloody oath I am. We can pull it off, I know we can. Shoalhaven people don't pry. They'll accept the fact that

I'm in love and they'll accept Jalila – they won't ask questions, you know what they're like.'

His boyish enthusiasm, which under normal circumstances might have charmed her, was now enough to push her over the edge. Her brother was naive to the extreme – it was time he grew up, and Bev wasn't going to take any more of his nonsense. 'What the hell's wrong with you, Paul?' she barked angrily. 'You're behaving like a romantic idiot, can't you see that? This isn't Romeo and bloody Juliet, you know, this is *real life*! What you're proposing to do is downright *irresponsible*! Furthermore, it's a criminal act. You've smuggled an illegal immigrant into this country.'

'A refugee.' Paul remained implacable. He refused to be angered, this was the sort of reaction he'd expected from his volatile sister. He was only surprised she hadn't blown her stack earlier.

'An *illegal immigrant* . . .' Bev ignored him. 'You plan some sort of sham marriage that'll never be recognised! You intend to salt her away in a community where she'll have no legal status, where at any moment she can be discovered and kicked out of the country –'

'And as I told you, if that's the case, I'll go wherever she's sent,' he said. His sister's needling was beginning to take effect.

'She has no qualifications, her command of English is poor, if your relationship doesn't work out what the hell will happen to the girl!'

Paul's resolve was rapidly crumbling; he was about to lose his temper. 'Our relationship isn't a brief affair, I can assure you,' he replied icily. 'I intend to look after Jalila for as long as I live.'

Bev didn't heed the warning signs. 'What you're doing is far more than *irresponsible*, Paul,' she went on, 'it's downright cruel! You're giving the girl false hope, you're leading her on . . .'

He stood, slamming his fist on the table, making the coffee mugs jump. 'I don't give a fuck what you think, Bev.' She'd gone altogether too far. 'I don't need your help, forget I asked. I'll do this on my own.' He glared at her, they were both angry now. 'But I'll fucking well do it, I can promise you that. I'll marry Jalila and I'll bring her to Shoalhaven, and I don't give a shit what you or anyone else thinks!'

He was about to storm off, but just at that moment the door opened and Susan, the Library Manager, popped her head in, investigating the sound of raised voices.

Bev stood and the two women exchanged a look. Bev's was one of apology. Susan's, upon recognising this was an argument between siblings, was one of *I'll leave you to it*, after which she quickly closed the door.

The moment had been broken. 'That was Susan,' Bev said, 'she's my boss, I think you've met her.'

Paul didn't reply. His burning anger had faded, he was sullen now.

'You've probably cost me my job.' Bev knew she wasn't under threat, she and Susan were good mates, but she couldn't resist having a dig.

'I'm sorry,' he said stiffly. He rarely lost his temper, out loud anyway, as a rule he fumed inside, keeping his thoughts to himself. Deep down, he was still fuming.

Bev had no intention of apologising, but she did realise she'd hurt him. 'I know you're not deliberately leading Jalila on, Paul,' she said. Of course she knew this. Her brother might be naive but he was certainly not shallow. That was part of his problem – Paul felt things too deeply. Despite his youth there was no doubt at all that he loved this girl. 'And I know you love her. I knew before you did, remember?

No reply.

She was silent for a moment. Then . . . 'You do realise everything'll fall apart when the refugees are discovered on Gevaar Island. People will twig Jalila's one of them.'

'That's possible,' he said.

'More than possible. Probable, I'd say. Ah well,' she went on briskly, 'we'll face that when we come to it.'

She sat. Paul stared wordlessly at her.

'Come on, sit down,' she said. 'We've got another five minutes or I really will get the sack.'

He sat.

'If we're going to do this together,' she went on, 'we're going to do things my way.' Bev recognised her brother's love for this girl was unshakeable. Just as she recognised she would do all in her power to help him. And he'll need help, she thought, he'll need all the help he can get. 'My way,' she repeated. 'OK? You promise?'

Paul nodded. He'd stopped fuming now.

'Right, first thing, we'll have to let the family in on the story.'

'Lou, yes of course –' he said, and was about to go on.

'No, not just Lou,' she interrupted, 'we need Mum and Dad on side as well. We have to tell them everything, and I mean absolutely everything.'

'Dad?' Paul's turn to be taken aback.

'You didn't think that part through, did you?' Bev said with a touch of irony. 'Of course Mum and Dad have to know. Did you really believe they'd accept without question you turning up out of the blue with an exotic new wife?' She found his blank look in return irritating. 'Didn't it occur to you they might want a few details, like for instance, where you got married?'

'Registry office,' he said defensively.

'Oh come on, Paul,' she was downright scornful now, 'give me a break, you can't just palm them off like that.'

Bev realised she might be coming close to overstepping the mark once again, so she dropped the scorn, but pressed on relentlessly nevertheless.

'Mum and Dad have to embrace this whole mad idea as much as we do, can't you see that? They have to accept you and Jalila as a couple who love each other desperately enough to take this sort of action.'

'Mum maybe, but *Dad*,' Paul protested. 'If we tell Dad about the refugees on the island he'll report them to the authorities. He'll see it as his duty to do so,' he added scathingly. 'Christ alive, you know how he is.'

'Yes, I do,' she replied in all seriousness, 'but I don't think you do.'

'Eh?'

'You've always been critical of Dad, I know.' She could have added *and I know why*, but she didn't. 'He's a conventional man, I agree, he does things by the book, he doesn't have Lou's charisma and all that . . . But there's a part of Dad you've never recognised.'

'And that is?'

'He's a romantic. He tries not to let it show of course, probably thinks people would see it as a weakness, but I can promise you at heart Dad's an out and out romantic. You won't have any trouble at all convincing him how much you love Jalila. Believe me,' she said drily, 'it shows.'

Paul couldn't help feeling dubious. He'd never thought of his father in such a way. David Miller a romantic? David Miller was a man who never displayed his feelings.

'Besides,' Bev added the clincher, 'Dad'll do anything Mum says.'

'Yeah, that's true.'

Which is proof positive, you dumb bastard, Bev thought. Mum's the love of his life – he gave up a successful career and settled in a backwater just because of her. The man worships the very ground she walks on, always has. But he never dines out on the fact. Keeps everything to himself. God you two! You're so bloody alike! 'Leave things with me for the moment, Paul,' she said, rising from the table. 'I'll ring Lou and drop the news on him.' God only knows what reaction I'll cop there, she thought. 'Between the two of us we should be able pave the way with Mum and Dad, to a certain extent anyway. I'll leave it up to Lou as to how much we tell them at this stage, but at least we can prepare them for the fact that you're seriously in love.'

'Thanks, Bev.' He stood, hugging her impulsively.

She returned the hug. 'I don't know what the hell's going to come of this,' she said, 'but good luck to us all.'

He was about to leave.

'And don't forget the bathers.' She picked up the little boutique carry bag that sat on the table. 'That's what you came here for, remember?'

He grinned as he took the bag. 'Thanks for these too,' he said.

Jalila was still out on the balcony when he returned to the hotel, sitting there watching the water park. But she was enjoying the sight of the revellers now, and upon hearing him enter the room, when she turned, her face once again lit up with pleasure at the mere sight of him. It was as if her explosion of anguish had never happened.

She stepped inside, into his arms, and they kissed.

Holding her close, so aware of her body, the shape and the feel of her, the touch of her skin, Paul fought against his stirring of sexual arousal. Not now, he told himself, not yet, the time isn't right.

'Do you want to go to the water park?' he asked, gently disengaging himself from the embrace. She would have stayed there quite happily in his arms while he fought off a burgeoning erection.

'Yes, please.'

'Good, then that's what we'll do.' He picked up the carry bag from the table where he'd dumped it. 'Look,' he said, 'new bathers.'

Paul loaded up his backpack with towels and bathing costumes and Jalila's wrap-around, and they left the hotel, crossing Foreshore Drive to the parks and the oceanfront beyond.

They bought takeaway sandwiches at the Dome and ate them sitting on the grass, looking out at the beach and the ocean and the dozen or so early-season swimmers, whom Jalila very much admired.

'In the middle of summer,' he explained, 'when it's holiday time and the weather's really hot, there are many, many more people swimming. Australians love to swim.'

'You will teach me swim, Paul?' she asked.

'Sure, I'll teach you to swim.'

'*To* swim,' she corrected herself. 'You will teach me also English?'

'Yes, Jalila, if that's what you'd like. I'll also teach you English.'

'Also teach,' she said to herself.

When they'd finished their lunch, they changed into their bathing costumes in the respective change rooms and spent a good half-hour frolicking in the water park as they had the previous day. Then, back in dry clothes, they went shopping.

To Jalila, the supermarket was a wonder-world. She'd found the dress shops that she'd visited with Bev on the day of her arrival fascinating, but the supermarket was something else altogether. The endless shelves of packaged foods, the vast aisles of refrigerated goods, the huge, colourful displays of fresh produce, all this was of far greater interest than clothes.

They returned to the hotel laden with supplies, which they packed away together, Jalila delighting in the process. Stacking butter and eggs and cheese and vegetables and goodness knows what else into her very own refrigerator!

'Is like house, Paul,' she said, standing back to survey the well-stocked kitchen, the bowl of fruit on the island bench, the vase of flowers on the table. It wasn't actually a vase, they'd had to make do with a water jug, but she loved the flowers.

'You'll have your very own house soon, Jalila,' he said. 'When we go home to Shoalhaven you'll have your own pretty little house just a block from the beach.'

She smiled, putting her arms enticingly about his neck. He had told her he was taking her 'home', wherever that might be, but she hadn't really given the matter much thought. Jalila lived only in the moment, it was wiser that way. And each moment with him was precious, wherever they were.

Now, Paul thought. Now the moment is right.

She was expecting him to kiss her, she was inviting him to, but he didn't. Instead he unlaced her arms from around his neck and crossed to the table, where he picked up the jeweller's box that still sat there.

He returned to her, opening the box warily, wondering again whether it might possibly have been the sight of the rings that had acted as some sort of catalyst to her outburst.

It hadn't been, he had no cause for worry. She smiled as she looked down at the open box he held out to her.

'Will you marry me?' he asked.

'Yes,' she replied. Her eyes were not haunted this time.

He lifted out both rings, slipping the empty box back into his pocket, and took her left hand in his.

'I don't know the right words, Jalila,' he said, embarking a little stiffly upon his formal declaration. 'I don't know what a priest would say, but this ring is a symbol of my love and I must make a vow to you . . .'

He slipped the ring onto her finger and they looked up to meet each other's eyes. He was about to start on his vow when he realised she hadn't understood a word he'd said. He also realised that the gist was all that mattered anyway. And she had certainly understood the gist.

'It fit,' she said happily.

'Yes.' They looked down at the ring, which she now twirled on her finger, and he smiled, thankful both for the fit and the fact that he didn't need to make a formal declaration at all. 'I asked the girl in the jeweller's shop to try it on. She seemed to be about your size.'

'Is pretty.'

'Very pretty.' He offered her the other ring. 'You have to give me mine now,' he said, holding out his left hand, fingers splayed.

'Ah yes.' She took his hand and slipped the ring onto his finger.

'It fit. Is good.'

'Yes,' he agreed, 'it's very good.' He gathered her in his arms. 'I now declare us husband and wife,' he said and kissed her.

'We is married?' she asked.

'Yes, we are married.'

'*Are* married,' she corrected herself. Then she laughed. It all seemed something of a game to Jalila. A game she was very much enjoying.

Paul crossed to the wall of windows and the sliding glass door that led to the balcony. With careful deliberation, he pulled closed the heavy, ceiling-to-floor drapes, shutting away the outside world.

By the time he turned back to her, she was already naked, clearly visible in the half-light, standing by the bed, ready to offer herself as 'payment' or 'gift' or whatever they were going to call it, but obviously prepared to be taken.

This wasn't the way he would have wished. He would have preferred to kiss her, and while kissing her to slowly undress her, perhaps for them both to undress each other. But of course, he told himself, given her past, this would hardly be natural to Jalila.

He undressed himself hastily. It seemed wrong to be fully clothed while she stood there naked, and as he approached her he couldn't help but feel some trepidation. How would she receive him? What would be her reaction? The times she'd offered herself to him there had been no fear, despite the violence she'd known at the hands of men, and there appeared no fear in her now. But she was so detached. Was he to be nothing more than a business transaction?

It seemed he was. As he stood naked before her, still uncertain, his mind wondering which tack he should take, she surprised him by suddenly demanding instruction. Unnervingly like a servant seeking orders from a master: 'How you want, Paul? What you like?'

Jalila was keen to please him, but he seemed undecided so she took the initiative. She needed to know whether he wished to take her from the front or from the back, or perhaps he would like her on her knees before him – he might wish her to take him in her mouth.

Paul did not answer, nor did he make any overtly sexual advance, kissing her instead with infinite tenderness.

She returned the kiss with equal tenderness, and as he lowered her onto the bed he continued very gently to kiss and caress her. She responded in kind, kissing and caressing him too. Such displays of affection were unfamiliar to Jalila and she liked them very much.

When finally he entered her, their coupling, too, was something quite strange to her. How could a man take her like this, easing himself inside her with such care? Why would a man kiss and caress her as he possessed her body? Why would any man wish to do such a thing? Men when they pleasured themselves were always brutal.

Jalila was bewildered by Paul's tenderness. No man had ever made love to her. She had not known love in any form, apart from vague recollections of childhood and family, long-since repressed for sanity's sake.

Then as she felt his movement become more urgent and recognised his time was near, she was further bewildered by her own reaction. Instead of closing off her mind and waiting for it to be over she was gladdened by the thought that her body had given him pleasure. At that moment, bewilderment became realisation. She loved him.

Paul rolled away to lie on his back, breathing deeply and looking up at the ceiling.

'I'm sorry,' he said, aware there had been no enjoyment for her. How could he have expected there might be? He was just another who had invaded her body. He felt wretched and guilty and ashamed all at once. 'I'm sorry,' he said, still staring up at the ceiling, unable to look at her.

'Why sorry?' Jalila was confused. He seemed miserable and she couldn't understand why. The thought worried her. She propped on one elbow and gazed down at him. 'I do wrong?' she asked. 'Why you is sad? I not make you happy?'

Her concern was heartbreaking. 'Of course you make me happy, Jalila,' he said, stroking her cheek with his fingers. 'It's not your fault – it's mine. I can't make you happy. That's why I'm sad.'

'Oh,' she laced her fingers with his, kissing his hand, and smiled gloriously, 'I happy, Paul. I very happy.' She snuggled beside him, her head tucked in the crook of his shoulder, her body nestled against his. 'I love you.'

Jalila had never even known the meaning of the words. Hassan had said them to her often, but they had been empty words, they had meant nothing, she had not believed him. Paul had said those very same words to her just today, and they had certainly meant something, she had believed him. Now she was saying those words herself, words she had never thought she would say, and they meant everything.

Paul put his arms about her, holding her close, their naked bodies fitting together flawlessly like two halves creating a perfect whole.

'I love you too, Jalila,' he said

How could he possibly ask for more? She'd known only violence. She might never feel passion, she might never experience her own sexual gratification, only time would tell. But they would take joy in the love they shared.

PART THREE
THE JUDGEMENT

CHAPTER FIFTEEN

When Bev had phoned Lou to break the news, she hadn't been sure what sort of reaction she expected, but it certainly wasn't the one she received. She'd been deliberately blunt, having told herself that nothing was to be gained by pussy-footing around.

'He's not taking Jalila back to the island,' she'd said. 'He's madly in love with the girl, as she appears to be with him, and they're going to live together . . .' a telling pause '. . . in Shoalhaven.'

No reply. Well, the poor bloke'll be in a state of shock, she thought.

'He's even bought two gold wedding bands and intends to hold some sort of sham marriage,' she went on, wondering why she found a certain perverse pleasure in ramming the point home. I can be such a bitch, she thought. But she was aware that her purpose in being harsh was really because she couldn't stand the thought of fielding endless argument. She waited for the explosion.

Still no response.

'Are you there, Lou?'

Silence. Not that it mattered – the question had been rhetorical anyway. She knew the old man was still there, mobile phone to ear, no doubt aghast at what he was hearing.

'He's not going to change his mind, you know. We won't be able to talk him around.'

Then finally . . . 'Of course we won't. That's Paolo's way.'

'Oh.' Bev was taken aback. 'You're not mad then?'

'With Paolo? No. With myself? Yes, a bit.'

'Why?'

'Because I should have seen this coming. I sensed something right from the start, but I presumed it was just a young man's attraction to a beautiful girl.'

She heard quite distinctly his sigh of resignation. Or was it regret? Or disappointment? Difficult to tell.

'How dumb of me – I should have known better. Paolo's not the shallow youth I was at his age.'

She found the comment somehow touching, though she wasn't sure why. Perhaps it was the old man's criticism of his younger self, or perhaps it was simply because he knew his grandson so very well. Then Lou's voice changed; he was no longer reflective, but brisk, business-like.

'Ah well, I can't change things now and I probably couldn't have changed things back then anyway, so what are our plans?'

Bev breathed her own sigh, one of relief at having escaped the almighty row she might have expected. But the discussion that ensued was nonetheless lengthy. All they could do, they both finally agreed, was to help buy Paul and Jalila as much time as possible.

'He's convinced the longer she has her freedom, the more thoroughly she'll heal,' Bev said.

'And he's quite right, I'm sure.'

It was settled that between them they would pave the way with Paul's parents and prepare them for the fact that their son was seriously in love, after which Lou said he would also tell David and Maria about the refugees on the island.

'Already?' Bev queried. 'Before they've met Jalila?'

'Yep.' He was adamant. 'They'll have to know sometime – better to fire both barrels at them right from the start. Hell, they're the ones who're going to have to play out this whole bullshit that Jalila's the sister of your mate from university. They'll need a few days to prepare themselves for the performance.' Then he added with grim humour, 'I can see Maria pulling it off, but I have my doubts about David. Unlike you and your mother he's not a born actor.'

Oh dear, Bev thought, her misgivings rapidly multiplying.

Lou had further misgivings of his own.

'I'll make a trip out to the island and let the others know Jalila's not coming back,' he said. 'They'll worry about her otherwise; they're a very close group.' He didn't relish being the bearer of such news, for a number of reasons he chose not to discuss over the phone.

They'd said their goodbyes, Lou promising he'd come down to Geraldton before the end of the week. 'We'll leave the two of them alone for a few days, eh?' he'd suggested. 'Honeymoon time and all that.'

'Yes,' she'd agreed, thinking how warm he sounded, and how kind, and how if she'd said those very same words they would have come out decidedly brittle. Ah well, I can't help being a bitch, she thought. 'See you, Lou,' she'd said and she'd hung up.

The following few days were most certainly a honeymoon for Paul and Jalila, who revelled equally in their freedom. Not once did Paul contemplate what lay ahead. Nor did he concern himself with the troubles he might have laid at the doorsteps of others. If he had, he might have felt guilty about the problems Bev and Lou were facing. But he gave them no thought as he shared his world with Jalila, things familiar seeming strangely new to him viewed through her eyes.

They drove south to the coastal town of Cervantes, where they sat on the beach eating fish and chips, as he must have done any number of times, but the fish and chips tasted different now. Much better than he remembered. Jalila had never eaten fish and chips.

They visited Nambung National Park and he showed her, as he'd promised he would, the eerie landscape of the Pinnacles.

'It took millions of years to form those things,' he said as they stood on the lookout mound, gazing across the area of arid desert that sat so surprisingly in the midst of the surrounding heath. Here thousands of limestone pillars rose from the yellow sands like an army, in all shapes and sizes, some four metres high, smooth and elegant, others squat and ugly, ancient soldiers, petrified for all time.

'Pretty breathtaking, eh,' he said, watching her as she observed in silent wonderment. He'd always found the Pinnacles mysterious and impressive himself, but he sensed she was experiencing something deeper.

Jalila was indeed fascinated, not only by the sight, but by the spiritual aura of this strange place, where she felt surrounded by the souls of the dead. This must be a very old and sacred burial ground, she thought. These were surely the gravestones of a people who had passed on.

'Is peoples long time ago?' she whispered to Paul, feeling it disrespectful to speak out loud.

'No, no, they're not built by people,' he explained. 'Wind and water shaped them from seashells over many millions of years, or at least that's what the scientists say. Truth is, nobody really knows how they were made. The Pinnacles are one of this country's great mysteries.'

They stayed for some time, driving around the four-kilometre track that wound its way through the rock formations, alighting here and there to explore further, but the more they explored, the less the scientific explanation meant to Jalila. She could feel more strongly than ever the souls that inhabited this land. And by now, as if through some form of osmosis, so could Paul.

The following day, he showed her other sights, closer to

Geraldton and in and around the city, but he didn't head north. They wouldn't face the music until Saturday, he'd decided – that's when he'd take her home to his cottage.

And then on the Thursday night, Lou rang.

'I'm coming to Geraldton tomorrow, Paolo,' he said, 'we need to talk.'

Even the sound of his grandfather's voice didn't burst Paul's bubble.

'Sure, Lou,' he said. 'Bring your bathers though – we're going to the water park. I promised Jalila.'

'Lou . . .' it was Jalila who greeted him, throwing open the hotel room door, her hand extended in greeting '. . . how nice it is to see you,' she said, and they shook. Then, unable to resist, she hugged him impulsively. 'Is good, Lou, truly. Is so good!'

Lou looked wide-eyed at Paul, who stood a pace or so behind her.

'She wanted to show off her English,' Paul explained, 'she's been having some lessons. Well, not really, she's been teaching herself more than I have.'

'What I say is right, yes?' Jalila asked eagerly.

'Absolutely,' Lou replied, 'what you said is absolutely right.'

'Said,' she corrected herself. 'Yes, *said.*'

'See what I mean?' Stepping forwards, Paul embraced his grandfather. 'Come on in, Lou,' he said.

Lou entered the room, still in a state of amazement, although the couple didn't appear to notice, standing side by side as they now were, arms around each other's waists like any young newly married couple. But it wasn't Jalila's English that had so amazed Lou; it was her demeanour. It was everything about her. This wasn't the same girl he'd known on the island.

'Did you bring your bathers?' Paul asked.

He nodded obediently. 'Got them on under my shorts.'

'Good. We'll have a coffee and a chat and then head over to the water park; Jalila's raring to go, what do you say?'

'I say we go now,' Lou replied. 'We can have a coffee over there, can't we? I'm not really a water park person, Paolo, I'd prefer a dip in the ocean after we've had a chat.'

'Yeah, sure.' Paul felt somewhat chastened, aware he'd sounded if not selfish at least thoughtless; of course his grandfather wouldn't want to play in the bloody water park. 'Much better idea.'

Forty minutes later, they were seated on a park bench, takeaway coffees in hand, watching a bather-clad Jalila splash around in the water jets and fountains, and this time Paul was only too aware of the old man's amazement.

'Bloody miraculous, isn't it?' he said.

'Yes,' Lou agreed. 'In fact I would never have thought it possible.'

As they watched in silence, Paul was visited for the first time by a rush of guilt. His love for Jalila had so selfishly consumed him that until this moment the thought had not once occurred. Had he unknowingly abused his grandfather's trust? Did the old man feel betrayed?

'I'm sorry, Lou, he said.

'For what?'

'For putting you through all this,' he replied awkwardly, not sure exactly what it was he was trying to say. 'I never meant for this to happen, I swear I didn't. It wasn't my plan to steal Jalila away – I just wanted to give her a few days freedom. That was my only intention, honestly.' He was aware he was starting to sound a little desperate. 'I was trying to do the right thing. I didn't know I was going to fall in love with her.' He averted his gaze, staring down at the ground, uncertain how to interpret the look in his grandfather's eyes, but determined to be honest. 'I didn't know that I was probably already in love with her,' he admitted shamefacedly. Everything he was saying sounded so lame.

'I'm aware of all this, Paolo. You don't need to justify yourself.'

Paul looked up. There was no judgement in the old man's eyes.

'I'm on your side, mate, so you can give the guilt trip a rest, but thanks anyway.' Then Lou got straight to the point. 'Your mum and dad have been wised up and you're to bring Jalila to dinner on Sunday.'

'I'm to what?'

'You're to bring Jalila home for the family roast dinner the day after tomorrow,' Lou repeated, ignoring his grandson's stunned reaction, 'so be forewarned. Bev's told Maria and David the story we're going to put around town about Jalila being her friend's sister . . .' he paused meaningfully '. . . and I've told them the truth about the refugees.'

'You told Dad about the refugees!' Paul was horrified by the thought. 'And before he's even met Jalila?'

'Yep.'

'Jesus! What was his reaction?'

'He was appalled by our duplicity of course,' Lou said with more than a trace of irony. '"Absolutely appalled," as I'm sure you can imagine. And I'd better warn you he's not particularly keen on keeping them a secret.'

Which is putting it mildly, Lou thought as he recalled his son-in-law's instant outrage.

'You mean the two of you have been concealing the presence of . . . illegal immigrants?' David Miller had exclaimed, aghast. 'And for a whole *two months*!'

He'd simply nodded and waited for the man to continue, as he knew he would and as David did.

'But that's a *criminal act*!' David had looked to his wife for support, but Maria had remained silent, a sign he'd taken to mean she was equally shocked. 'How could you be so duplicitous, Lou! I'm *appalled*! I'm *absolutely appalled*! And for you to have involved Paul as well.

Although frankly I'd have thought my son might have displayed more common-sense.' Another glance to his wife. 'Of course we'll have to report the presence of these refugees, it's our duty as citizens.'

But Maria had had other ideas. 'Why don't we wait until we see Paul, dear? I agree our son is a very sensible young man,' she'd said, with just the slightest emphasis on the 'our'. 'I think we should hear his views on the subject. And we should most certainly meet the girl. After all, as Bev told us, he cares deeply enough about her to consider her his wife. The least we can do is meet this young woman before reporting her to the authorities. Which of course, my darling, as I'm quite sure you're aware,' she'd added, 'would alienate our son forever.'

David had been flummoxed. For the moment anyway.

'Let's ask Paul to bring her to dinner on Sunday,' Maria had suggested to Lou. 'That seems like a good idea to me.'

Lou had been grateful for the power Maria had over her husband and for the delicate way she'd wielded it. He'd known, too, that at that moment of confrontation Maria didn't care one bit about the refugees. Her only thought was of her son, who was prepared to devote himself to this woman he loved, and in doing so possibly ruin his life. Bev had been most explicit over the phone the previous night. Maria, beneath her feigned composure, might well have been fuming at the fact that her husband seemed to have forgotten all about this.

'I agree with you, Maria,' Lou had said, 'and I know Bev will too. We'll have a family get-together to meet Jalila.' He'd beamed in patriarchal fashion at his daughter and son-in-law, but his thoughts had been far from benign. You have no inkling of the ordeal you are about to put this unfortunate young woman through. Poor, poor Jalila.

Now, watching this same young woman at play amongst the water fountains, seemingly carefree, no longer the broken creature he'd known, Lou wondered whether perhaps he'd been wrong. He certainly prayed that he had been.

'So what exactly was it that Dad said?' Paul asked, already bristling at the thought of his father's blanket condemnation.

'You don't need to know,' Lou said, 'but I'm warning you, Paolo, don't antagonise the man: we need him on side.' He stood. 'I'll leave you two together for a while. I'm going for a dip – see you back at the hotel.' Draping his towel around his neck, he set off for the beach. 'Oh and by the way,' he called over his shoulder, 'we're meeting Bev at the library, one o'clock. We'll talk through our plans over lunch.'

An hour or so later, during a companionable lunch at a café near the library, Lou's worry for Jalila's impending ordeal was apparently not shared by Jalila herself.

'I meet your parents, Paul.' The prospect obviously excited Jalila. 'Is good, I like this. I is daughter to them now, yes? No, no,' she carefully corrected herself, 'I *am* daughter to them, yes? That make me sister to you, Bev,' she smiled happily, 'I *am* sister to you, yes?'

'Yes, Jalila,' Bev said firmly, not daring to look at the others, 'you are sister to me.'

The only person at the table who did not dread Sunday's confrontation was Jalila.

The following mid-morning, as planned, Paul booked out of the hotel and he and Jalila drove north to Shoalhaven. He didn't take her directly to his cottage, but gave her a tour of the town first, driving up Main Street, pointing out the principal shops and businesses along the way. To the right the Wong's Chinese restaurant and laundry, then Nina Adrejic's bakery, which always smelt so good, then the clothing and drapery store, which he told her was run by a very elderly couple called Geoff and Freda, who'd been there forever.

'Just as well they stick to the drapery side and their daughter Izzie orders in the clothes, otherwise we'd all look like we'd stepped out of the distant past.'

As they neared North Terrace he pointed out the imposing hardware store, three times the width of the other shop facades.

'Gordon and Sandra Shadforth,' he told her. 'They're pretty well-off. The store services the whole area, fishers and farmers alike, but they also have a sizable property just out of town, wheat mainly, managed by their son. Gordon's a nice enough bloke, but Sandra's a bit of a snob.'

Responding to Jalila's blank look, he went on to explain, 'Sandra thinks she's better than other people, which doesn't go down too well with some in Shoalhaven.' He grinned. 'She was furious when the locals started calling her Sandy in order to annoy her. "I'm not Sandy," she'd say, "I'm not a beach. If you must use a diminutive, I'm Sahndy." Now everyone calls her *Sahndy*,' he said with clownish over-emphasis. 'I don't think she realises that by doing it they're taking the mickey out of her even more.'

He laughed and Jalila laughed too, not understanding much of what he was saying, but loving the sound of his voice and committing all that she could to memory, particularly people's names. She considered this extremely important for she would be living in this town and meeting these people.

'And over there,' he said, pointing to the post office on the right, 'is my parents' business.'

'Ah,' Jalila was impressed, 'is big too, like Gordon and Sahndy shop.'

'Yes, it's the post office and general store and news-agency all wrapped up in one – my father's the town's postmaster.'

Paul didn't add that if there was any form of self-imposed pecking order in Shoalhaven, which in a way there was, David Miller was at the very top right along-side the Shadforths. It was a fact Paul found personally irksome. This was a classless town, or so it was considered to be by most, and so it should be in his opinion.

They rounded the corner into North Terrace.

'And that,' he said, indicating an attractive single-storey bungalow on the left with a leafy front garden, 'is my parents' house. That's where we'll be having dinner tomorrow night.' He tried to sound jovial.

'Ooh,' she breathed admiringly, 'is beautiful.'

As they neared the junction of North Terrace and Marine Parade, he pointed out the community hall and the picturesque church that sat beside it, on the very corner, stalwartly facing the sea. The old stone church, complete with spire and cross, remained the weathered and welcoming beacon it had been for generations.

'The church is the oldest building in town,' he explained. 'It was a mariners' chapel, built in the late nineteenth century when the fisher community first started up here. The spire and cross served as a marker for boats coming into harbour. It still does.'

'The hall was built about fifty years later,' he continued as the Land Rover rounded the corner into Marine Parade. 'It's used for all sorts of things, fetes, community meetings, the odd dance now and then. And that cottage there,' he said, 'next to the church, that's where the pastor, Sam Lyttleton, and his wife, Thelma, live.'

Jalila committed another two names to memory.

He kept up the guided tour as they headed down Marine Parade. 'And that's about it,' he said as they approached Cooper Street. 'The hotel's just down there on the next corner and, apart from that, nothing much else to see. She's a pretty small town all right.'

'Oh yes,' Jalila agreed heartily, 'she is *very* pretty town.'

He turned the Land Rover into Cooper Street and halfway down the block pulled up outside his cottage.

'Welcome to your new home, Jalila,' he said.

The cottage was not altogether unlike those Jalila had known on the island. A typical fisher's cottage, timber-framed with a corrugated iron roof and a small front verandah. But this cottage was much smarter in appearance than those on Gevaar Island, with its own little waist-high picket fence and its own little path leading up to the front steps. The cottage itself was painted a light aquamarine-blue, the colour of the sea on a mild day, and the picket fence, the gate, the front door and the window frames were all white. Paul had worked hard and was justifiably proud of his home, modest as it was.

They alighted from the car and he opened the front gate. 'Come on, I'll show you around.'

They walked together up the path and up the several steps to the verandah where he opened the front door for her, it was never locked, and together they stepped inside.

Since purchasing the cottage, Paul had modernised its interior, replacing a dividing wall with a square timber arch, creating an open-plan living and kitchen area. His was one of the older dwellings, and had previously consisted of poky little rooms. The two bedrooms at the rear remained small, but the previous owner had added a proper bathroom, complete with lavatory.

There was a decent-sized backyard too, in need of a bit of tidying up, he admitted, but with garden plots either side.

'You'll be able to grow vegetables and herbs and all that sort of stuff like you did on the island,' he said. 'I've been meaning to plant things for ages, but I just never got around to it.'

Jalila had said nothing at all throughout their general tour of the house and the yard.

'So what do you think?' he asked when they'd returned inside to the living area. 'It could do with a bit of a female touch, that's for sure,' he said as she continued to gaze about in utter silence, 'but it's got everything you need. What do you think?'

'I tell you what I think,' she said, very slowly and very carefully, weighing the words as if each was as precious as the meaning she intended to convey. 'I think this is most beautiful home in whole of world.'

He gathered her to him and they kissed.

'It's *your* home, Jalila,' he said. 'This is your home now. This is where you belong.'

They kissed again, and then . . .

'Damn it, you're my wife,' he said as if he'd suddenly remembered, 'I should've carried you over the threshold.'

She had no idea what he meant.

'Come on,' he urged, taking her by the hand, 'let's do this properly.'

He hauled her out onto the verandah, picked her up in his arms and carried her back through the front door.

'There,' he said, putting her down, 'consider yourself properly married, you've now been carried over the threshold,' and he laughed.

She still wasn't sure what he meant, but she laughed anyway because he was so happy. And she laughed because she was happy too, happier than she had ever imagined possible. But no, that was wrong. She had never imagined happiness. She had never imagined anything. Imagination had no place when the daily fight for survival relied upon the obliteration of thought.

'We'll buy you lots of new things,' he said a little later as he watched her unpack her meagre belongings from the small suitcase, stowing them lovingly where they belonged, in the drawers and the wardrobe of the bedroom, and on the shelves of the bathroom. He found the sight touching. This humble little cottage was as grand to Jalila as a palace might have been to others, for this was obviously unlike any home she'd ever had, even as a child in Sinjar town.

They cooked lunch together, a modest lunch of pasta with tinned tomatoes and garlic and parmesan cheese, but to both no lunch had ever tasted so good.

'We'll go shopping on Monday,' he promised her, 'and we'll stock up the shelves and the cupboards and the fridge with everything you can think of, every kind of food you could possibly imagine.'

Jalila smiled. Yes, imagination was now a luxury she could afford, but she would not take it for granted. She would treasure every single minute of her happiness, living each precious moment as if it were her last. Who knew when all this might come to an end?

After lunch they walked down to the foreshore, crossing Marine Parade and turning left, heading away from the township. Paul rather hoped he wouldn't bump into any of his mates: he wanted to keep this special day just for the two of them. As they passed the pub on the opposite side of the road, he half-expected someone to yell out, but no one did, for which he was thankful.

They sat on the beach and talked.

'Where is island?' Jalila asked, staring at the vastness of the ocean that stretched to the horizon with no land in sight.

'Out there,' he said, pointing directly ahead, 'forty kilometres off the coast. When I took you to Geraldton in the speedboat we went that way,' he pointed to the south, 'much, much further.'

Jalila paused thoughtfully, then said, 'We can go back to island, Paul? Just one time,' she added, turning to him, hope in her eyes. 'I can say goodbye to little Hamid and others?'

He hesitated. That's maybe not a good idea, he thought. Oh, no wait. There *was* a way he could make it work – it would actually help get the story around town.

'Yes, Jalila,' he said. 'Yes, I'll take you out to the island.'

She hugged him gratefully.

Half an hour later, as they walked hand in hand back towards town, someone did wave from the pub's verandah.

'Hey, Paul,' a voice called across the street, 'fancy a wee drink?' A beefy arm beckoned. 'Come on over.'

Mac was starting earlier than usual; Arch and Ian hadn't arrived as yet and he was in need of a drinking companion.

'G'day, Mac,' Paul waved back, 'no thanks, mate, heading home.'

When they got home, they talked some more. In fact they talked for quite a long time, sitting cosily at the small dining table drinking cups of tea. Jalila even told him a little about her family, not of their deaths, but of her early childhood days in Sinjar town, memories she had suppressed for years. She felt that, as she was about to meet his family the following day, he was owed some knowledge of hers, but most importantly, she felt safe enough now to remember her parents and her sister. She told him so.

'I not think family for long, long time, Paul,' she said. 'It make me sad. I think now and I not feel so sad. This good, yes?'

'Yes, Jalila,' he agreed, 'this is very good.' Another breakthrough, Paul thought, further evidence of her healing. He longed to know more, but he would never ask.

They ate sardines on toast for dinner. He made the toast from the sliced bread he kept in the freezer. 'Bachelor tucker,' he said. 'There's always plenty of tins and frozen food around here. But from now on we'll stock up on heaps of fresh stuff, I promise.'

And then later, in the half-light of dusk they made love. Tenderly, as they always did, she willingly offering herself, he as gentle as was humanly possible.

Afterwards, lying in his arms, Jalila felt that her happiness was complete with this man who loved her.

'I love you, Paul,' she whispered, 'you is my life.'

'You are my life too, Jalila,' he whispered in return, holding her close.

Then he smiled as in the gloom of the small bedroom he heard her scold herself.

'*Are*,' she said, 'yes. You *are* my life.'

The next day, filling in time before the ordeal that loomed that evening, and perhaps also to distract himself, Paul took Jalila on a drive north to Kalbarri National Park, where he showed her the sights. The magnificent gorge that extended as far as the eye could see on the lower reaches of the Murchison River; then near the town of Kalbarri itself, the spectacular coastal cliffs over a hundred metres high at the mouth of the mighty Murchison.

'The Yamatji people who've inhabited this area for many thousands of years have a Dreaming story about how the Murchison River was created by the Rainbow Serpent,' he told her.

'The Rainbow Serpent?'

'Yes. To Aboriginal people, the Rainbow Serpent is the creator of all things,' he explained. 'Their beliefs are very connected to the land and very spiritual. The Rainbow Serpent is central to all these beliefs.'

Looking up at the towering cliffs that had possibly been there from the beginning of time, Jalila found the explanation eminently believable. There was without doubt a spiritual presence in this place, just as she had felt at the Pinnacles. This was an ageless land. And the Rainbow Serpent sounded to her not unlike the Peacock Angel of her own peoples' ancient religion. To the Yazidi, God was the creator of the world, but of the seven Holy Beings to whom He had entrusted its care, Tawuse Melek, the Peacock Angel, reigned supreme. The Peacock Angel was as central to Yazidi creational beliefs as the Rainbow Serpent was to the Aboriginal people of this country. Or so it would appear.

Jalila found comfort in the thought. And as she did, she realised that here was yet another area, once so important in her life, to which she had long closed her mind. The faith of her people; the very reason they had been persecuted and massacred by the thousands. She had abandoned her religion in the belief that God had deserted her. Yet now, in this spiritual landscape and with this man she loved, her faith was creeping back.

They had a late lunch, just a sandwich and coffee at a café in the small township of Kalbarri, after which Paul decided he'd eked out the pleasure of the day as long as was possible, and it was now time to gird his loins for the evening ahead. They drove back to Shoalhaven and prepared themselves for the family dinner at his parents' house.

Jalila wore her pretty dress with the pink flowers, and insisted he teach her the proper formal response she should make upon her introduction.

'How do you do, Mr Miller,' she enunciated perfectly, and when Paul held out his hand she shook it with just the right degree of firmness.

'How do you do, Mrs Miller,' she repeated the process as they rehearsed the introduction to his mother.

'Honestly, Jalila,' he protested, 'I can't be sure how they'll receive you, honestly I can't. They'll be polite, I know that much. And my father's bound to be formal,' he added, 'he's a stitched-up bloke, always very proper, but apart from that . . .'

'Is no matter,' Jalila assured him, wondering why he seemed anxious. 'I want to get right is all.'

Paul knew he was being jumpy, which couldn't be helping her, but the attitude he was expecting from his father was already making him want to punch the man's lights out.

'Everything'll be fine,' he said, trying to calm himself. 'They'll like you, I know they will.'

'I hope this.' Jalila smiled, she was very much looking forward to meeting his parents. Lou and Bev would be there too. It would be a real family gathering.

They arrived on the dot of six-thirty, the allotted time, to discover Lou and Bev already there, seated in the lounge room, having arrived early as a sign of solidarity. Paul signalled his thanks as his mother ushered them inside.

'Hello, my darling,' Maria said, kissing him on the cheek and smiling brightly at Jalila. 'Come in, come in.'

Lou and Bev rose from their respective chairs. David was already on his feet; he'd stood the moment the doorbell had sounded, and was waiting, stiff-backed and solemn for the official introduction.

Paul bristled at the mere sight of him. Couldn't the bastard at least *pretend* a welcome? Couldn't he paint on the vestige of a smile? But no, of course, David Miller never pretended.

Stepping forward, Bev embraced Jalila affectionately.

'Hello, Jalila,' she said, 'you look lovely.'

'G'day, Jalila.' Lou remained where he was but grinned and gave a friendly wave. 'Good to see you.'

'Hello, Bev; hello, Lou.' Jalila smiled. 'Is good to see you also.'

'Mum, Dad.' Paul addressed his introduction to both parents, but his eyes remained solely upon his father. 'I'd like you to meet Jalila Domle.'

A distinct flicker of surprise from Lou and Bev, although they tried not to show it. So Jalila finally had a surname.

'Jalila is a Yazidi refugee from Northern Iraq.' Paul went on without drawing breath. 'She also happens to be my wife.'

Jesus Christ, Lou thought, does the boy have to come on so bloody strong!

Oh hell, Bev thought, he's just declared war.

In the brief but awkward pause that followed, Jalila smiled at Paul's parents, awaiting the offer of a handshake.

Instead, Maria stepped forwards and embraced the girl.

'Hello, my dear,' she said, 'welcome to our home.' Maria was cursing her son for deliberately annoying his father, but she was also cursing her husband for being as aloof as she'd anticipated he might be.

'You will try and be pleasant to the girl, won't you, dear?' she'd said tightly when they'd talked about the impending meeting.

'I will reserve my judgement,' he'd replied just as tightly. 'If this girl is attempting to use our son as a means of illegally entering this country, as she very well may be, she will receive no welcome from me, I can assure you.'

It had appeared to Maria that her husband had already passed judgement before even laying eyes on the girl. But Maria had not.

'I've looked forward very much to meeting you, Jalila,' she said, knowing the warmth of her reception would grate with David.

'How do you do, Mrs Miller.' How beautiful Paul's mother is, Jalila thought, just like Bev, only older.

'And this is my husband, David.'

David extended his hand. 'How do you do,' he said frostily; he would not refer to the girl by name.

Jalila performed her handshake to perfection. 'How do you do, Mr Miller,' she said, looking him directly and unflinchingly in the eyes as they shook.

David was taken aback. Not just by the girl's beauty, which was certainly extraordinary, but there was something startling in her gaze. Something confronting. He didn't know what it was, but where he had expected timidity, or at the very least uncertainty, he saw in the unwavering green eyes that met his something he could only define as fearlessness.

They sat in the lounge room with their customary tray of pickings, having their customary pre-dinner drinks, Bev and the men beer, Maria a glass of red wine, Jalila opting for orange juice, and the following half-hour was devoted solely to small talk, led in principal by Maria with occasional input from Bev. How had Jalila been enjoying the sights? Where had she and Paul visited? Which was her favourite?

Seated side by side on the sofa, Paul answered mono-syllabically now and then, but Jalila held her own in the conversation. She loved the Pinnacles and the big, big cliffs that she'd seen today. She loved the Waiting Woman, looking forever out to the sea, and she loved the Dome where seagulls of steel remained in perpetual flight.

'All birds is spirits of dead men,' she said. 'Is sad, but beautiful also.'

'Yes,' Maria agreed, 'the memorial is very beautiful indeed.'

The frostiness between father and son was palpable as the women kept up the conversation; even Lou failed to join in. When the hell is someone going to introduce the topic that's on everyone's mind? he was wondering.

'And Paul take me water park also.' Jalila turned to Paul and clasped his hand. 'Many times we go water park. I like water park very, very much. Yes, Paul?'

Her hand in his, the joy of her smile, Paul couldn't help but respond in kind. 'Yes, Jalila, you like the water park very much,' he said, 'we both do.'

The moment shared between the two was not lost on any of those present.

Maria couldn't help but warm to the love her son so obviously felt for this young woman, and to the love this young woman appeared to feel in return. Her husband's reaction, however, was something altogether different.

David Miller was on instant alert, alarm bells sounding. What if this girl was manipulating his son? What if this display of affection was an act on her part? David could think of nothing else. Is she using Paul? he wondered. Dare I accuse her? And if I were to do so, what would be her reaction? Would she give herself away?

His face must have betrayed his thoughts, because Maria suddenly jumped to her feet.

'Enough chat,' she announced, 'time to serve up. Darling, will you come and carve the lamb?'

David reluctantly stood.

Bev stood also. 'I'll help you, Mum,' she said, and all three disappeared to the kitchen.

'Somebody's going to have to bring up the subject, Paolo,' Lou suggested quietly. 'You and your father are on the verge of exploding.'

'I know,' Paul agreed. 'I was sort of hoping we could leave it until after we'd eaten. I didn't want to fuck up Mum's dinner party.'

'I don't think you're going to be able to wait that long, either of you,' Lou said. 'Leave it to me. I'll introduce the topic as gently as possible. Although,' he added wryly, 'I don't suppose there *is* a gentle way really, is there?'

Five minutes or so later, they were called into the dining room.

Lou waited until they were halfway through the meal, the women having successfully eked out small talk about the food, while David and Paul remained focused on their plates and conspicuously silent.

'Well, I suppose,' he said, during a lull, 'we should have a bit of a chat about the current situation.'

Silence reigned, apart from the scrape of cutlery on china while Bev and Maria continued bravely to eat as if there was no attendant drama to the suggestion.

But David and Paul were no longer eating. Both had put down their cutlery. Battle stations had been drawn.

'I presume we're all clear about the story we're going to put around,' Lou continued pleasantly, 'that Jalila is the younger sister of Bev's friend in Perth?'

Maria, Bev and Paul all nodded; David gave no such indication.

'One thing we've neglected to cover,' Lou went on, ignoring the ominous reaction, or lack thereof from his son-in-law, 'and that's the name of your mate, Bev. We should have a name for Jalila's fictitious sister, don't you reckon?'

'Yes, I suppose you're right,' Bev agreed and then hesitated, trying to come up with a suggestion. She didn't know any Yazidi names.

'Paraza,' it was Jalila who spoke, 'my sister name Paraza.'

'Are you sure you want to do that?' Paul asked, concerned. Paraza was her murdered sister, the sister about whom only he knew. Was Jalila prepared to have her sister's name bandied about?

'Yes,' she replied firmly to the table in general, 'I want do this.' Then leaning in to him she quietly whispered, 'Paraza alive, she live in Perth. I like this, Paul. I can remember her now. Is good I remember her.'

'Paraza it is then,' Bev declared. 'Jalila's sister is my friend, Paraza Domle.' She looked at Jalila, who nodded and the two young women shared a smile.

'Right,' Lou said, 'everyone happy with that?'

'No,' David loudly announced, 'everyone is most certainly not happy.'

All eyes turned to him. Oh shit, Lou thought, here we go.

'I will not lie,' David said. 'I have never lied in my life and I do not intend to start now.'

'So what particular story are you going to tell?' Paul's voice was deathly calm.

'The truth, of course.'

'You're going to report the refugees?'

'They're not refugees, as you're very well aware. Both of you,' David snapped, including Lou in his address.

'They're illegal immigrants, and you should have reported their presence. You should have notified the authorities the moment you discovered them.'

'What the hell would you know, Dad?' Paul countered, fighting back his anger and frustration. 'You haven't met these people. You don't know who they are. You don't know where they come from. You don't know what they've been through. You know nothing about them!'

'I know their status, Paul,' David replied.

'Oh for Christ's sake, you pompous prick, you know fuck all!' Paul exploded; he couldn't help himself. More than ever he longed to punch his father's lights out.

'Now, now, calm down, calm down.' Lou's was the voice of reason. 'Your father is only stating the obvious, Paolo: you forget that your reaction was very much the same when I first told you about the refugees. You accused me of aiding and abetting illegal immigrants, remember?'

Paul nodded, aware his grandfather was right and that a further outburst would serve no purpose other than to ruin the evening for his mother, and most particularly for Jalila who, having expected no form of confrontation, was looking from father to son, confused and concerned.

'I do believe though, David,' Lou went on, turning his attention to his son-in-law, 'that we should leave our friends on the island in peace. Paul is right. They're good people who have suffered enough, and they'll be discovered any time now. I don't think we should report them.'

All eyes were now on David, as if in judgement.

'I didn't say I was going to report them,' he replied stiffly.

'Oh no?' Lou queried.

'No, that's not what I said at all. I simply said I will not lie.'

'Then if you're asked, what story will you tell about Jalila?'

'I will say that she is the girl with whom my son is in love and that they live together. No more than that, which is the truth. Whatever conclusions others may draw from the lies the rest of you tell,' he said, 'is not my concern.'

He glanced at his wife, who nodded. It was the plan they had agreed upon when she had reminded him, and most forcefully, that to report the refugees would be to lose their son forever.

'The people on the island will be discovered,' Maria had said, carefully avoiding the word 'refugees', which he seemed to find annoying, 'and when they are, so will the girl.'

Maria had been wise in her choice of timing. She'd brought up the subject just after they'd made love. The passion they still shared remained the great leveller it always had been between two people who otherwise might have had little in common.

'Let Paul and Jalila have this time together, my darling,' she'd said. 'They're very much in love, I believe, and they'll be parted soon enough.'

David now looked around the table, his reluctance patently obvious. 'I will still be lying by omission of course,' he admitted, 'but I suppose I shall just have to live with that.'

He glanced once again at his wife, and this time she smiled. Maria knew how difficult it was for her husband to act against his very strict principles.

One thing was still of the greatest concern to David Miller, however. Did the girl love his son? He turned to her.

'Jalila,' he said, referring to her by name for the first time that evening, 'what are your feelings for my son?'

She met him with that same fearlessly direct gaze. 'Paul is my life.'

Jalila meant the words quite literally. If she were to be separated from Paul she would end her life. She had said nothing of this to Paul himself, of course: he might not understand and she would not wish to burden him.

But she would leave this world with no more blackness surrounding her, with only love and joy and the happiest of memories. Should they be separated, this was her plan.

'Your son is my life,' she said to the man who was scrutinising her so closely.

And David believed her.

CHAPTER SIXTEEN

Paul lost no time introducing Jalila to Shoalhaven, or rather, introducing Shoalhaven to his new wife. He started the following morning at the marina where he sought out the Laaksonen brothers, knowing they'd be working on their fishing vessel, which was now off the slip and back in the pen. He didn't take Jalila with him to the marina, but the plan was nonetheless an introduction, the idea having strangely enough come from Jalila herself, albeit unknowingly.

'G'day, Jukka, Hekki,' he called from the jetty on approach.

It was a bright spring day in early November and the brothers were seated in *Annikki*'s cockpit taking a coffee break.

'G'day, Paul,' Jukka called back, standing and raising his mug by way of salute, 'want a coffee?'

'No coffee thanks, mate,' he said as he reached the pen, 'but I'd love a bit of a chat if you've got the time.'

'All the time in the world,' Jukka gave a wave, 'come aboard.'

Paul climbed aboard and joined Hekki, who was seated on top of the cockpit's giant, gleaming freezer; everything about *Annikki* was impressively big and shiny. The brothers' work on the vessel was really more a labour of love than necessity.

Hekki, who had a bowl of sugar cubes cradled in his

lap, grinned a welcome and shuffled along a little as he swigged from his mug.

'You sure?' Jukka queried, holding up the thermos flask, 'plenty left, and we've got another flask anyway.'

'No thanks.' Paul always avoided coffee with the brothers who, although Australian to the core in all aspects of behaviour, had inherited the Finnish habit of their parents when it came to coffee, as had their younger sister. The whole of the Laaksonen family drank coffee incessantly, and they drank it black and very, very strong, sucking the lethal mix through cubes of sugar, which they placed on their tongues. It was a taste and a practice Paul had never acquired.

'What can we do you for?' Jukka asked. Jukka was invariably the spokesperson of the two, and besides, Hekki had just embarked on a fresh cup of coffee and was contentedly sucking through his sugar cube.

'Well actually I do have a favour to ask,' Paul admitted. Given the opener, he decided he might as well get straight to the point.

'Fire away.'

'I was wondering if I could borrow *Anni* again. No rush,' he added, 'whenever it's convenient, say, some time over the next few weeks.'

The brothers looked at each other and nodded in unison.

'Sure, mate,' Jukka said on their joint behalf. Then he smiled suggestively. 'Getting real serious, eh? Same girl – your sister's mate?'

'Yep. Same girl and real serious. She's my wife now.'

Hekki nearly choked on his coffee.

Jukka stared at Paul, jaw agape. 'She's *what*?' he exclaimed.

'My wife.'

'You gotta be joking, mate.' It was Hekki's turn now to voice his amazement.

'Nope,' Paul said calmly, 'we got married in Gero last week.' He splayed the fingers of his left hand, flaunting his wedding band.

The brothers shared a look of astonishment, which, if it contained an element of disbelief, did not in the least bother Paul, who didn't care whether people believed him or not. He had decided not to bring up the subject of a registry office marriage or to go into any form of detail, as he'd originally intended. Why should he? If some chose to believe he was pretending marriage for propriety's sake then their views were their prerogative. As far as he and Jalila were concerned they were married and that was all that mattered – let others think what they wish.

Paul was thankful to his father for leading the way in this regard. He remembered vividly David Miller's reply when asked what he would say about Jalila should he receive enquiry.

'I will say that she is the girl with whom my son is in love and that they live together. No more than that, which is the truth. Whatever conclusions others may draw from the lies the rest of you tell is not my concern.'

Paul had very much admired his father in that moment. He'd actually found himself liking the man.

'Well, you're a quick mover, mate – I've gotta give you that much,' Jukka said.

'Yep.' Paul grinned. 'Didn't want to lose her.'

Hekki offered his hand. 'Congratulations, Paul.'

'Too right,' Jukka agreed and they shook hands all round. 'As far as *Anni* goes, just give us a yell,' he went on, 'you can take her out any time.'

'Yeah,' Hekki said, 'consider it a wedding present.'

'That's great; thanks, guys.' Paul stood. 'Hey, are you going to the pub when you knock off?'

The brothers shrugged, they hadn't made plans.

'I'm taking Jalila along late this arvo, introduce her around a bit, have an early dinner maybe.'

'In which case we'll definitely be there,' Jukka said.

'Good. We won't be staying long – Jalila doesn't drink – but it'll be good for her to meet my mates.'

The brothers didn't look at each other, they didn't dare. They were both thinking along the same lines. Everyone in Shoalhaven drinks – well all the mates do, that's for sure – has Paul married a wowser?

'We'll look forward to meeting your wife, mate,' Jukka said as Paul climbed onto the jetty. 'See you at the pub.'

They watched as he walked back towards the marina.

'Do you reckon they're really married?' Hekki muttered.

'Nah, probably not,' Jukka said, 'they probably just want things to look proper because they're living together. But shit, why bother,' he shrugged nonchalantly, 'who the hell cares these days?'

'Some of the old fogies around town might,' Hekki warned. 'I reckon we should pretend to believe him, don't you?'

'Course we will. Goes without saying. Hope she's not a bloody wowser though.' Jukka popped another sugar cube into his mouth, picked up the coffee flask and poured another round.

Paul returned home and informed a delighted Jalila they would visit the island in the next week or so. Then together they walked into the centre of town to embark upon the shopping trip he'd planned, their first port of call being Marston's Clothing and Drapery Store.

'Morning, Freda, Geoff,' he said to the elderly couple, who looked up from their work as the tinkle of the shop's bell sounded.

'Good morning, Paul,' they replied more or less in unison.

'I'd like you to meet my wife,' he said, ushering Jalila forwards, his arm about her.

'Good heavens above,' from Freda and, 'Oh my Lord,' from Geoff.

They both bustled out from behind the counter; he from his ledger, she from the bolt of cloth she'd been measuring.

'This is Jalila,' he said. 'We were married in Geraldton just last week.'

'Oh my goodness, how wonderful,' Freda said. She kissed the young woman warmly on the cheek, thinking what an exceptionally pretty girl she was. 'Congratulations, my dear.'

'Indeed,' Geoff echoed, offering his hand first to Paul, then to Jalila.

'How do you do, Mrs Marston, how do you do, Mr Marston,' Jalila enunciated perfectly. Paul had told her all about the Marstons and how nice they were.

'Oh, Freda and Geoff, my dear, please,' Freda insisted. 'We've known Paul since he was a baby. Izzie,' she called towards the rear of the shop. 'Izzie darling, come and meet Paul's lovely new wife.'

A smart, well-dressed woman in her late forties materialised from one of the curtained-off changing cubicles, where she'd been looking after a customer.

'G'day, Izz,' Paul said as she approached them. 'This is my wife, Jalila. Jalila, this is Isobel Marston, otherwise known as Izzie.'

'Hello, Jalila.' Izzie, like her mother, gave the girl a warm and welcoming kiss on the cheek. 'Congratulations.'

'Thank you,' Jalila replied.

'Well, well, well, a married man, eh?' Izzie hugged Paul affectionately. 'You're a fast mover, sweetie.' She wondered why the Millers hadn't spread the word around and why it had happened so quickly, but what the hell, she thought, none of her business.

'Yep,' he agreed, 'love at first sight. For both of us, fortunately,' he added with a smile to Jalila.

Geoff and Freda beamed happily at one another. They saw no reason at all to doubt Paul's speedy marriage. Young people moved so quickly these days.

'We want to buy a few new outfits for Jalila, Izz.' Paul said.

'Of course, come with me.'

Izzie led the way and they followed her towards the rear of the shop.

'What sort of outfits, Jalila?' she asked as they went. 'And what size are you?'

Jalila looked blankly at Izzie and then at Paul, who answered for her.

'A couple of dresses,' he said, 'tops, skirts, that sort of thing, not sure about size, we leave it all in your hands.'

'Happy to oblige.' It would certainly be no hardship to dress a beautiful young creature like this, Izzie thought.

Having gathered from the girl's accent that her knowledge of English was limited, she wondered briefly where Jalila came from, but unless information was offered, she had no intention of asking. 'Have a look around, Jalila,' she said as they reached the racks of clothes, 'see if there's anything that takes your fancy and I'll find it in your size.' Then she added apologetically to Paul, 'Back in a moment, sweetie, I have another customer to tend to,' and she silently mouthed, '*Sahndy*.'

Ah, he thought, grateful for the warning, so we're about to cop Sandy. Oh well, better to get it over with sooner rather than later.

'Everything all right in there?' Izzie asked through one of the cubicle's curtains. 'Need any change of sizes?'

'No thank you, Izzie,' came a familiar voice. 'I'm all done, I'll be out shortly.'

Sandra Shadforth hadn't been even halfway through trying on the plethora of garments she'd selected, but having heard every word of the exchange between Paul and the Marstons she'd climbed rapidly back into her own clothes and was now freshening her makeup. She couldn't wait to lay eyes on young Paul Miller's new wife.

Barely seconds later, the curtains were swished aside and she stepped out from the cubicle, a tall, elegant woman in her mid-fifties. Regal of bearing, perfectly coiffed and impeccably dressed, she would have been handsome had it not been for the perennial air of dissatisfaction that marred her well-chiselled face. Many years back one of the town wags, probably Mac, had remarked 'Sandy always looks like somebody's farted,' and the comment had struck a chord with many.

'I'll take the dove-grey,' she said, handing a blouse to Izzie, 'hello, Paul, so this is your lovely new wife?' It all came out in the one breath.

'Hello, Sandy. Yes, this is Jalila. Jalila, this is Mrs Shadforth.'

'How do you do, Jalila.' Sandy offered her hand.

'How do you do, Mrs Shadforth.' They shook.

'My goodness, you are indeed lovely,' Sandy said, 'and how did you two meet?' It was a talent of Sandy's developed over the years, running two different thoughts together, usually involving a query, and all without drawing breath. Many people found it disconcerting, which was perhaps her intention.

Izzie, blouse in hand, started off towards the counter and in passing gave a brief eye-roll to Paul. The inquisition was about to begin.

'We met through my sister, Bev,' Paul said, 'in Geraldton. A number of times actually, but we only recently started going out together –'

'Surely Jalila can speak for herself, dear,' Sandy said, flashing one of her supposedly gracious smiles that somehow never quite managed to reach her eyes.

'Well no, she can't really, *Sahndy*.' This time Paul gave the name the comic over-emphasis that the woman never seemed to register as mockery. 'Jalila's English is not very fluent.'

'Ah, how interesting, so where does she come from, how long has she been here –'

Sandy might even have managed to string on another query had Paul not interrupted.

'Her family comes from Iraq,' he said, gabbling the answers out at the same rocket speed the questions had been fired, 'they've been in Australia for a long time now, living in Perth, Bev went to university with Jalila's older sister –'

'My sister Paraza live in Perth,' Jalila added loudly. 'Paraza and Bev, they is good friends.'

'Yes,' Paul said, loving her boldness, 'Paraza and Bev are very good friends. And now, Sandy, if you'll excuse us, we must get on with our shopping.' He gave the older woman the friendliest smile.

'Of course, dear,' Sandy returned her own tight smile, 'how nice.'

She left for the counter to settle her account; she'd really wanted to buy far more than the one dreary, dove-grey blouse, but having emerged she could hardly now go back into the cubicle where all those untested clothes remained hanging on their hooks.

As Sandra Shadforth ferreted out her reading glasses and focused on her credit card transaction, Izzie signalled congratulations to Paul.

'Be with you in a moment, Jalila,' she called.

They left the shop a good hour later with at least a dozen items of clothing, which seemed to Jalila amazingly extravagant.

'Is too much, Paul,' she argued. 'Who need so much clothes?'

'Rubbish,' he insisted, 'all girls buy this much stuff. Well,' he corrected himself, 'I know Bev does – she buys heaps more.'

They'd actually shopped economically: Izzie had seen to that.

'It's a case of mix and match,' she'd explained to Jalila, quickly realising the girl had no idea of how to go about shopping. 'This light jacket will go with that skirt, that dress and those trousers, and these shirts and blouses can be swapped around, you see. You end up with a whole new wardrobe.'

Jalila had cottoned on to the idea very quickly.

'I like mix and match,' she admitted as she and Paul walked next door to the coffee shop. Despite her protestations Jalila was secretly thrilled with her 'whole new wardrobe'.

Nina's Bakery assailed the senses the moment they stepped inside.

'Told you it always smells good,' Paul said as they were hit by the heady mix of freshly baked bread and muffins mingling with the richness of home-made pies and pasties.

'G'day, Paul,' the girl called from behind the counter, where she was serving several customers from the extraordinary array of goods on display.

'G'day, Alex,' he called back, 'your mum not about?'

'Nup, she's in the kitchen cooking up a storm, won't be out until the crowd turns up.'

Nina's bakery and café was another family business, run by Nina Adrejic and her seventeen-year-old daughter, Aleksandra.

'We'll go through, OK?' He gestured at the open doors that led into the coffee shop.

'Sure, I'll be with you in a tick.'

It was not yet lunchtime and they had the café to themselves, as he'd hoped they might – he'd looked forward to having a quiet chat with Nina. He chose a table in the far corner, and they dumped their parcels and sat.

Five minutes later, Alex was by their side, a rather heavy-browed and attractive girl of central-European appearance.

'What'll it be, folks? Name your poison,' she said, pen poised and order pad at the ready. Her voice belied her Serbian heritage – born in Shoalhaven, young Aleksandra Adrejic was an out-and-out Aussie. She gave them both a friendly smile while trying not to stare at the beautiful young woman. Paul's new girlfriend's a stunner, she was thinking, how come I haven't noticed her around town?

Aware young Alex was dying of curiosity and playing it cool, Paul made the introduction.

'Jalila, this is Alex,' he said, 'Alex, Jalila.'

'How do you do, Alex.' Jalila offered her hand.

'G'day, Jalila.'

'Jalila and I got married in Gero last week,' Paul said casually.

The girl dropped her 'cool act' altogether. Utterly gobsmacked, she made no attempt to hide her amazement. 'Crikey, are you for real?' she asked, gawking at the two of them, wide-eyed.

Paul nodded. 'Yep, we're for real,' he said with a smile. Much as Alex tried to be worldly she was really just an overgrown kid.

'Can I go and get Mum? She won't want to miss out on this, and she'll kill me if I don't tell her.'

'Of course.'

Young Alex belted off eagerly to fetch her mother, as Paul had hoped she would. He'd been disappointed not to discover Nina in her usual spot behind the counter – he'd wanted her to be one of the first to meet Jalila. Nina Adrejic could prove a valuable asset, he was sure. She was bound to spread the news of his marriage around, and in just the right way. Nina might well become a true ally for Jalila.

His reasoning proved sound.

'Oh my dear girl,' Nina said in her mangled accent when, the two of them having risen to greet her, Paul made the introduction. 'Oh my dear, dear girl,' she repeated, embracing Jalila as if she was a lifelong friend. 'You are *married*! This is *wonderful*!' She beamed from one to the other. 'I may join you?'

'Yes, yes, please do,' Paul urged, pulling up another chair.

'Coffee, Aleksandra,' Nina ordered peremptorily as she sat, the others joining her while Alex scuttled obediently off to the counter.

'Now you tell me, dear girl,' she went on, leaning forwards, elbows on the table, her full focus upon Jalila, 'where you from? How long you been here? How you meet our beautiful Paul?'

A short woman in her mid-fifties with an age-thickened body, Nina still had the striking features of her youth. The high cheekbones, the piercing grey-blue eyes and dramatic Slavic brow were an arresting mix, particularly combined with the forcefulness of her personality.

'You tell me all,' she said, smiling broadly, 'and I mean *all* of *everything*,' she added with a wave of her hand and in the butchered accent that had not changed during the thirty years she'd been in the country. An intelligent woman, Nina's vocabulary and command of the language had improved in leaps and bounds since she'd arrived as a twenty-two-year-old unable to speak a word of English, but as she'd greedily soaked up the cadences and oblique vowels of her fellow countrymen her accent had remained the ghastly, mangled mess it had been from the start.

She now sat back and waited to hear Jalila's story.

Jalila stared uncomprehendingly at the woman, who seemed so very nice. She knew she'd been asked a set of questions, but at such speed and in such a peculiar accent, she hadn't fully understood them.

'Ah,' Nina nodded knowingly, 'you don' speak English.' She turned to Paul for verification. 'That's it, eh? She don' speak English?'

'Yes, I do.' Jalila had understood that part perfectly. 'I *do* speak English,' she said firmly. 'Not good, but I do speak English.'

'Ah,' Nina beamed once again, 'this is excellent. It is essential you learn the language of your new country, quick, quick, quick, soon as possible. Communication of vital importance for immigrants. So where you from? How long you been here?'

Aware that Jalila was once again becoming confused by Nina's rapid-fire barrage, Paul intervened.

'I think you'd better ask your questions a bit more slowly, Nina,' he suggested.

'Ah yes,' she replied apologetically, 'I talk fast when I get excited, this is true. I am sorry, my dear girl,' she said to Jalila. Then with solemn deliberation and pausing between each word, she asked, 'Where . . . are . . . you . . . from?'

Paul smiled as Nina proceeded to interrogate Jalila in a voice like a faulty recording slowed to half-speed, enunciating each word with what she perceived to be great clarity, unaware she was highlighting the hideousness of her accent. Nina was often unwittingly funny.

He didn't interject as the interrogation continued, but sat watching, a contended bystander, feeling proud when Jalila fielded all the questions to perfection. Her family had come out from Iraq some years ago . . . she had recently joined them . . . she had met Paul through Bev, who had gone to university in Perth with her sister, Paraza . . . Jalila didn't put a foot wrong, and Nina tastefully did not push for any further detail, she was interested only in the basics.

Paul didn't find Nina Adrejic's forthright enquiry in the least offensive or overly intrusive as Sandy Shadforth's had been, even though she was asking the very same questions. It was quite clear Nina identified with Jalila and was genuinely interested in the girl. They were fellow immigrants and she wished to welcome Jalila to her new country and her new town and her new home, just as she herself had been welcomed all those years earlier. In fact Nina was behaving in exactly the way Paul had hoped she would. The woman would indeed be a valuable ally.

Young Alex delivered the coffee, longing to join them at the table, but ordered by her mother to return to her post at the counter.

'And you bring us fresh muffins,' Nina demanded, 'hot ones, mind, be sure of this, hot ones from the kitchen.'

Then Nina proceeded to tell Jalila her own story, a brief shorthand version, just in order to make the girl feel at home. And she told it slowly so that Jalila, whose knowledge of English was obviously limited, would understand. At least that was Nina's intention. As she warmed to her theme, however, the speed of her delivery grew exponentially.

'I am little older than you when I come here from Yugoslavia,' she started out. Nina never referred to herself as Serbian, always Yugoslavian, simply because her mother had always referred to herself as such. 'I am twenty-two when I arrive with my husband. He also is Yugoslav, but he is not a good man, he leave me thirteen years later. And I tell you what's more he leave me with *two children*!' She snarled the words, her lip curling contemptuously, already she was getting carried away. 'I think he don' like when Aleksandra arrive, he is nearly forty and don' want another baby. No matter, no matter . . .' with a wave of her hand, she dismissed her husband to the oblivion where he belonged '. . . he is bad man, I am better off without him.' She smiled at Jalila in the friendliest manner, as if they shared something deeply personal. 'I am happy in this beautiful country, with my beautiful daughter and my beautiful son.'

Nina then went on to boast of her son. 'Born in this country, same as Aleksandra,' she said with great pride. 'Both son and daughter true Australian.'

Twenty-five-year-old Boris Adrejic was currently up north working on the oil and gas fields, she told Jalila, but he would return for the lobster season.

'He is fisher, like your Paul here,' she said, referring to Paul for the first time since she'd embarked upon her story, 'and like your Paul, he live out on Gevaar Island during the fishing season. You will get to meet him when the season starts, Jalila, and you will like him very much. A fine young man. I hope one day,' she added warmly, 'my Boris will meet a lovely girl like you.'

Attentive and interested though she had been, Jalila had absorbed only half of Nina's story, due again to the speed of the delivery and the peculiarity of the accent, but the mention of the woman's son living on the island during the season instantly hit home. She wondered which hut was Boris Adrejic's. Could it be the one she herself had lived in? And if so, how would Nina feel about such an intrusion?

Jalila had been pleased that she'd answered correctly the questions asked of her and she'd basked in the knowledge that Paul was proud of her, but now, given the warmth of Nina's welcome, she regretted the need for deception.

'Ah, the muffins,' Nina said as Alex arrived at the table. 'Apple and cinnamon, baked fresh this morning.' Then to her daughter, 'You chose these from the latest batch still warm from the oven?'

'Course I did, Mum, just like you said.' Having placed the dish of muffins in the centre of the table, Alex doled out the side plates and serviettes. 'Hey, you better come and give me a hand though, the lunch mob's turning up.'

'Oh.' Swivelling in her chair to look behind her, Nina was surprised to discover several people now seated in the café, and beyond the door a number gathered at the counter. She'd been so carried away she hadn't heard or seen them arrive. A few of the customers gave her a wave, which she returned, but she didn't rise, remaining seated at the table, quite unfazed.

'Get back to work, Aleksandra,' she said. 'I will be with you shortly.'

'Right you are.'

As Alex scurried away, Nina took Jalila's hand in both of hers and offered the young woman her final heartfelt words.

'I welcome you to Shoalhaven, my dear girl. You will be happy here: we are good people in this town, and you have a good husband.' She flashed a smile at Paul then returned her attention to Jalila, patting the girl's hand briskly to emphasise the importance of her advice. 'But you make sure you work very hard on your English,' she instructed. Nina had sensed Jalila hadn't fully comprehended all she'd said. 'It is very important for immigrants they should learn to speak good English. Australians like that you do this, and it is right you should. This shows respect for your new country, you understand me?'

'Yes, Nina,' Jalila said obediently, 'I understand you.' She had – more or less.

'Good.' Nina sprang to her feet. 'Good, good, good, and now I must return to my work. You want I should bring you some lunch?'

Paul looked a query to Jalila, who shook her head – she was far too excited to think of lunch.

'No thanks, Nina,' he said, 'the muffins will do us fine.'

'I get Aleksandra to bring you fresh coffee,' she said. 'You don' pay her, this is my shout for Jalila.'

She beamed at them both then sailed off to the counter.

Jalila turned to Paul, puzzled by the remark.

'She means the coffee and muffins are a present for you,' he explained.

'She is very nice, Nina.'

'Yep, and she's a bloody good cook what's more,' he said, biting into a fresh, warm muffin that was truly delicious.

Well so far so good, he was thinking. Nina Adrejic had proved as accepting of their marriage as the Marstons had, and she would certainly spread the word around in the best of ways. Paul was pleased with their progress.

After leaving Nina's Bakery, they went shopping for food and general supplies, and the reception they met along the way continued to be favourable. As they walked up

Main Street, they passed several people who greeted Paul, and when he stopped to introduce his new wife they were surprised, but unreservedly warm in their congratulations.

The reaction was the same when they entered the general store and post office, where Paul introduced Jalila to Tillie, the girl who served as a shop assistant on the days his mother was teaching at the junior school. Today being a Monday, Maria was not in the shop and Tillie was stacking the shelves.

Having acknowledged his father, who was working behind the post office counter, Paul carefully avoided David Miller's gaze as he made the introduction.

'Jeez, married, eh?' Sixteen-year-old Tillie wondered why Mr Miller hadn't said anything to her, but she grinned as she shook hands with Jalila. She was a gangly, dusky-skinned girl of Aboriginal-Scottish descent, her grandmother being a Yamatji woman, her grandfather a Scot who had died some years previously. The current extended family of cousins and aunties and uncles lived on the outskirts of town and, although Tillie's older brother worked at Kelly's Garage, they were known to do it hard. David Miller's employment of young Tillie had possibly been one of the true links between father and son. Paul had been proud of his father for taking time out to train the girl and give her a future.

'That's right, Tillie,' Paul said, 'we tied the knot in Gero last week.' He continued to avoid looking at his father, but he could feel the baleful stare of disapproval.

'Gee, you sure know how to pick them, Paul.' Tillie's grin widened even further. 'You're very pretty, Jalila.'

The girl's grin was so incredibly infectious, Jalila had to smile back. 'Thank you.'

They spent the next half-hour shopping for groceries, Paul introducing his new wife to a number of other customers who arrived, all of whom were warm and congratulatory, just as everyone had been throughout the day.

Several of the customers had included David when offering their congratulations.

'You must be very proud, David,' they'd said jovially, 'a beautiful new daughter-in-law.'

David Miller had been extremely busy with his postal duties, or so it had seemed. 'Yes,' he'd said, looking up briefly from his reams of paperwork, 'Jalila is a fine young woman; they love each other very much.'

Paul had had to be content with no more than that. He was aware there were those who might suspect his marriage was merely a ploy for propriety's sake, but he was aware also that his father's detached attitude was not likely to be a giveaway to those who did not harbour suspicion. Everyone knew that David Miller, while being respected by all, was a stitched-up sort of bloke, remote at the best of times.

When they'd finished their shopping, Paul arranged for Tillie to store their bags including those from Marston's Clothing in the back room.

'I'll come and pick them up later in the car,' he said.

They were about to leave when the store's front door opened and a familiar figure stepped inside.

The little woman gave a respectful nod to David then did a double-take on his son. 'Oh hello there, Paul.' There was a look of surprise in her beady eyes as she took in Jalila.

Paul mentally groaned. Oh God no, he thought, where are you when you're needed, Bev?

'Hello, Thelma,' he said.

Thelma transferred her handbag and shopping bag to her left hand and stood waiting for the introduction.

'I'd like you to meet Jalila,' Paul started out. 'Jalila is my –'

'Wife.' Thelma got the word out even as he said it, her eyes trained on his mouth, lip-reading intensely, head nodding bird-like. 'Wife, dear me, what a surprise, wife, yes, yes, of course.'

'Jalila, this is Mrs Lyttleton.'

'How do you do, Mrs Lyttleton,' Jalila said.

Thelma extended her spidery hand. 'How do you do, dear, yes, yes, how do you do.' Then to Paul, 'And where were you two married?'

Paul sped up in the hope he might beat her to the punch, although he knew it was a lost cause. 'In Geraldton,' he said, 'just –'

But there she was again, that fractional beat behind him. 'Just last week, yes, yes . . . just last week. And what are your plans for the future?' Thelma was prepared now for a good old chinwag.

Paul turned to Jalila, avoiding the woman's fierce focus upon his mouth, which was so intensely irritating. Thelma rarely looked anyone in the eyes, and certainly never during conversation, when anticipation was of tantamount importance.

'Well we'll settle –'

'In the cottage, yes, yes, of course,' came the echo. Even with her subject in profile, Thelma's lip-reading talents were phenomenal.

'We don't plan to –'

'Leave Shoalhaven, no, no, well that's very good to hear, Paul. We wouldn't want to lose a fine upstanding citizen like you. Now tell me –'

Then out of the blue a voice came to the rescue. 'I've cleared the mail from your postal box, Thelma. Would you like to collect it now?' David called across the shop.

'Thank you, David, yes, in a little while,' Thelma replied, her gaze still firmly fixed upon Paul.

'I also have your postbox renewal form here, which needs to be filled out and sent off as soon as possible.'

'Yes, I'll do that shortly, too.'

'Better we address the matter now,' David said with a headmaster, no-nonsense edge. 'Your renewal will shortly be overdue and if I don't get the application through in time I'm afraid you'll have to reapply altogether.'

'Oh dear, well in that case, yes, yes of course.' Thelma bustled off to the post office counter.

Paul flashed a look of gratitude to his father, who returned a nod before focusing on the totally unnecessary form he'd dug out of a drawer.

During the twenty-minute walk home, they bumped into several more townsfolk, who were all most welcoming to Jalila upon introduction.

'I meet so many nice people,' she said when they finally arrived back at the cottage.

'Yes,' he replied, 'Nina was quite right, they're good people in this town. And tonight when we go to the hotel you'll meet others too, some of them fishers like me who live on the island during the season.'

His remark prompted Jalila to ask the question that had earlier played on her mind. 'Nina's son, Boris,' she said, 'what hut he live in, Paul?'

'He and Pete, the young bloke who crews for him, live in the smallest one, the lurid sort of pinkish hut at the end.'

Massoud's hut, Jalila thought.

A little while later, as they sat at the dining table having a cup of tea before Paul left to collect the bags they'd left at the store, Jalila plied him with more questions. She demanded to know who lived in which cottage and asked him to repeat the name, committing each to memory, just as she had the townspeople when he'd taken her on the guided tour of Shoalhaven.

Then that night, on the pub's verandah being introduced to Paul's friends, she was able to apply many of the new faces to where they belonged. There was Mac, he had the fishing store, Archie from the marina, Ian from the Tuckshop, but of far greater import to Jalila were those whose names she now associated with the island. Jukka and Hekki had spread the word about, and a number of fishers had turned up in order to meet Paul's new wife.

'This is Kath and Bill Buckley,' Paul said, 'but Bill's known as Buck.'

Yes, Jalila thought, the elderly couple who have lived on the island longer than anyone. Theirs is the yellow hut, Rassen's and Hala's.

'And Jukka and Hekki Laaksonen,' Paul said, 'who have very kindly agreed to once again lend us their speedboat, *Anni*,' he added with a smile.

Yes, the brothers, Jalila thought. Theirs is the blue hut, Hany's and Sanaa's, where we meet for our meals.

'And this is Manos Papadakis,' Paul said, 'but he's Manny to everyone.'

The grey hut, Jalila thought. Manny's is the grey hut with the white front door. Manny's is *my* hut.

Young Pete was there too, Boris Adrejic's crew mate.

The magenta hut, Jalila thought, recalling how Massoud had explained to her that in English the colour was called 'magenta'.

Lou had turned up also to lend support and to show his approval of his grandson's new wife.

Lou and Paul the green hut, of course, Jalila thought, completing her inventory, Karim's and Azra's hut, the workshop where Karim does all our repairs.

There was another of the island fishers present, a young Italian-Australian called Nat Franelli, but Jalila didn't know which of the huts was his.

Paul was aware of all that was going through Jalila's mind as she met these lobster fishers, the people who lived much of their lives out there on the barren island she and her fellow refugees had come to call home. He'd been aware of her interest the moment Nina had mentioned her son Boris, and he'd known exactly why, upon their return to the cottage, Jalila had wanted the names and details of these island hosts who had unwittingly saved her life and the lives of her companions.

The people she was meeting tonight accounted for six of the island's eight huts, he thought, and it was quite possible she might even be wondering about those who owned the other two.

But Paul was wondering about a great deal more. He was wondering what all these people, fishers and townsfolk alike, would do when they found out the truth.

CHAPTER SEVENTEEN

Paul's new wife was quite the talk of the town.

'She's exotic, you've got to give her that much.'

'Bloody oath she is. Where did he say she comes from?'

'Iraq, evidently. Family's been out here for quite some time.'

'Well she's a looker all right.'

The blokes at the pub were all in agreement. Jalila was not only bloody good-looking: she was a nice bird to boot. She certainly had the seal of approval from the Laaksonen brothers.

'You can see why he got hooked as quick as he did,' Jukka said. 'And who cares if she doesn't drink. She's not a wowser – she doesn't cramp his style.'

'Yeah, she's a really nice bird,' Hekki said. 'I like her a lot.'

The others agreed, however, any woman who was that good-looking would automatically have the Laaksonen brothers' seal of approval.

There was a little gossip in some quarters about whether or not Paul and Jalila were really married, but the general consensus was nobody cared. And nobody chose to raise the subject or challenge the point with the more conservative of the town's citizens. 'Live and let live' was Shoalhaven's motto; no one wished to disturb the peace.

But less than one week later, the subject of Paul Miller's exotic new wife was no longer the town's hot topic of conversation. On 9 November, the final result of the long-running American election campaign astonished the nation and the world at large. Donald Trump was now President Elect of the United States of America. Who cared about Paul Miller's new wife?

As promised, Paul took Jalila out to the island. It was several weeks later, the end of November, a hot day but breezy, the wind flicking the ocean's surface into white-tipped waves as they left the marina.

They set off in *Anni*, ostensibly for a couple of hours' run-around, but caught up with Lou, who was ostensibly out fishing on *Principessa*, the two vessels meeting in the deep swell of the ocean just several kilometres from the island.

They made their approach together, the sleek speedy *Anni* slowed down to a crawl and the sturdy old Princess chugging along at her customary pace, to be greeted by the familiar sight of the group gathered at the end of the jetty, waving their customary welcome.

The reunion was emotional on all sides.

The others could not believe the change they saw in Jalila. This could not be the same girl who had landed with them on this island just three months earlier, the mystery girl with no name, the girl who never spoke, the girl with the lifeless eyes.

Jalila was overjoyed to be reunited with those whom she had come to regard as true friends. She sensed them marvelling at the change in her, which she did not find surprising. She was only too aware herself that she had changed over the past month or so since she'd seen them. But she didn't know how much. She had no memory at all of the dinghy and of the group's arrival on the island. She did not remember the girl she had been then.

As they circled about her offering greetings, she hugged them one by one, speaking a mixture of Arabic and English, stumbling over her words. Then finally she knelt on the jetty to hug little Hamid, who had been waiting patiently for the special attention he knew he was about to receive. He was not disappointed.

'I have missed you, Hamid,' she said in Arabic.

'I have missed you also, Jalila,' he replied in English, determined to show off to her. He would be four soon and felt very grown-up. 'I have missed you very much.'

Jalila laughed. 'You speak English more good than me,' she said.

'Yes,' he agreed and they hugged each other fiercely.

The group unloaded the fresh provisions that Lou had brought out on the old Princess, Hany and Karim delivering the bag of ice and the items in need of refrigeration to the green hut and stacking them carefully into the icebox.

The others gathered as usual in the blue hut, and while Sanaa brewed tea Hala and Azra unpacked the supplies and stored them in the pantry.

The men sat huddled together in a corner, Rassen and Massoud eager as always for the delivery of news from the outside world. Their astonishment upon hearing that Donald Trump was to become the 45th President of the United States of America echoed the reaction of many around the globe.

'This is not a joke?' Rassen queried incredulously.

'Nope, no joke,' Lou assured them.

'You are really serious?' Massoud, who had laughed out loud at the news, was equally incredulous – he'd been sure the old man was playing a game with them.

Paul nodded. 'Yes, he's serious,' he said.

As the men talked and the women worked, Jalila was spending her precious time with Hamid, painfully aware she might never see him again. Paul and Lou had both told her this was to be her last visit to the island, until the group was discovered in any event. Who knew what would happen after that?

'If we're to somehow keep you in Shoalhaven,' Lou had said, 'we must avoid all suspicion. That goes for you too, Paul. You mustn't visit the island again until this is all over, not even aboard the old Princess with me. When the group is discovered no one must suspect there has been any connection with the mainland. But if by some chance they *do* find out, then that connection must be me, and me alone.'

Lou now brought up the subject of discovery with Rassen and Massoud, warning them that the likelihood of their detection grew ever more imminent.

'The lobster season doesn't really take off until a month or so into the New Year,' he said, 'but families sometimes come out to holiday in the huts over Christmas, or fishers might lend their huts to mates or relatives over the Christmas–New Year period. Your time could well be running out, my friends.'

Rassen looked across the room to Jalila, where she was seated on the floor in earnest conversation with the boy. She was telling Hamid a story and the child was spellbound.

'And when we are discovered,' Rassen said slowly, 'there will be eight of us, not nine. There were only ever eight of us who managed to make our way ashore after our dinghy sank.'

'That's right.'

Rassen and Massoud exchanged looks. 'We will inform the others of this,' Rassen said, 'and we will rehearse our story well, every single one of us.'

Hany and Karim had returned from the green hut, and the group sat around companionably drinking tea and eating biscuits from the cardboard box little Hamid passed around. Inside were the gingerbread men Jalila had bought from Nina's Bakery. She'd presented them to the boy as a personal gift, but Hamid would never have considered keeping them for himself. On the island everyone shared.

It was Jalila who kept the group entertained for the most part. She told them in Arabic all about her adventures, and they listened in amazement to this girl who had had no voice. She told them of Geraldton and of the water park's magical fountains; she told them of the memorial and of the beautiful dome where the sailors' souls flew; and she told them of the Pinnacles that were as old as time itself.

As she spoke of the Pinnacles, Hamid closed his small fingers around the stone she'd given him, just a pebble really, a rough, orange-hued nugget no bigger than a marble, but it held a special significance.

'This comes from an ancient place, Hamid,' she'd told him, 'a place where the spirits have lived since the beginning of time. The spirit that still lives in this stone will protect you.'

Jalila had believed this herself when she'd gathered up the stone. She'd said nothing to Paul as she'd slipped it into the pocket of her dress, thinking it was surely wrong to steal a memento from this sacred site. But the stone was far more than a memento to Jalila. The stone represented hope, a connection to the past should she and Paul be separated, a spiritual link that she could take to the next world when she departed this earthly one. In giving such a gift to Hamid she was sharing something very special.

'You must keep this stone close to your heart,' she'd instructed him, 'and the spirit that still lives in this stone will link us forever.'

Now, his eyes trained on Jalila as she spoke, Hamid carefully placed the stone into the breast pocket of his shirt, where it would sit close to his heart.

Sanaa was about to commence her ritual lunch preparation, but when she and the others implored them to stay, Lou was adamant.

'No, no,' he said to the group in general, 'Paul and Jalila must return to Shoalhaven. If they're out in the speedboat for too long people might suspect they've stopped off at the island and that would put them in danger when you're discovered.'

Rassen made the translation to the others, adding Lou's warning that their discovery would not be far off now, and the tone of the gathering became solemn.

'This will be the last visit Paul and Jalila will make to the island,' he announced.

Little Hamid was shocked upon hearing the words. So this was why Jalila had given him the stone – she was saying goodbye, he would never see her again. He couldn't help himself. The tears gathered and, very quietly, he started to cry. He didn't mean to. He didn't want to. He would be four soon.

His mother took him aside and they knelt together on the floor, the others unashamedly watching.

'It is all right, my son,' she said, 'you are allowed to cry.' Azra could see he was trying hard to hide his tears, wanting so much to be grown-up. But he was just a little boy. 'It is no sin to cry, Hamid,' she said, speaking in their Hazaragi tongue, taking him in her arms and rocking him gently.

'Why does Jalila have to go?' he sobbed into the comfort of his mother's shoulder.

'There, there,' she said, 'there, there. It is something that simply has to be. Hush now, there's a good boy, hush, hush.'

'But *why* must it be?'

Azra could tell by his insistence that he was over the worst of his shock, that he was becoming a little calmer now and seeking a genuine answer. He needed to be treated like the grown-up he wanted to be. So she obliged. Holding him at arm's length, she spoke to him like an adult.

'Jalila has found a true friend, Hamid, one with whom she would like to spend the rest of her life. She and Paul love each other the way your father and I love each other. They want to be together, and to do this Jalila must leave the island.'

'We cannot go with her?'

'No, my son, we cannot.' Azra wiped away the final trace of tears from his cheek with her thumb. 'You want Jalila to be happy, don't you?'

'Yes.'

'Then you must say goodbye and wish her well.'

The little boy nodded. He would not cry again.

Looking on, the others were touched by the scene between mother and son, even though only two had understood the actual exchange. Massoud glanced at the boy's father. He gave Karim a congratulatory nod that said, *You should be proud of such a son* and Karim returned a nod that said *I am*.

The group accompanied them to the jetty as usual, and while Paul loaded the rubbish bag aboard the old Princess, they made their final farewells to Jalila. At least it felt like their final farewells, though who could tell?

Massoud watched from the sidelines as again, one by one, they exchanged hugs. His manner was strangely aloof. No one noticed except Hala, but Hala had been observing the change in Massoud for some time now. The young man, whose spirit she had so admired, had become morose of late.

It was true: Massoud did feel detached from the emotionalism on display, cynical even.

They're acting as though Jalila's free, he thought. They actually seem to believe none of us will ever see her again. Rassen and Hala know better, of course, but the others? How foolishly naïve they are. Jalila will be discovered, and when she is she'll be incarcerated along with the rest of us. No refugee status for boat people, remember? We'll all rot away together in some ghastly detention centre no better than a prison.

Unlike the others, Massoud's stay on the island had not proved a healing experience. With ample time to reflect upon his actions, now more than ever he cursed his stupidity. How could he have allowed himself to be so duped by common people smugglers? Why hadn't he researched the politics of this country that was about to reject him? Too greedy for a quick solution, that was why. Massoud Ahmadi had become a bitter young man.

But when it came his turn to embrace Jalila, his well-wishes for her were genuine, despite the fact he didn't believe there would be any successful outcome.

'Good luck, Jalila,' he said, and the sentiment was heart-felt. Good luck to us all, he was thinking.

Then, watching her kneel and embrace the child, Massoud had to admit he envied Jalila. He envied this brief spate of freedom allowed her, no matter how fleeting it might be. He would have loved such a gift himself.

Lou promised the group he would return in a fortnight, he and Rassen having discussed the wisdom of cutting back on the frequency of his trips to the island, which had previously been on a weekly basis.

'I reckon I could make two more trips safely,' he'd said, 'before we run the risk of being caught out.'

'We can look after ourselves, Lou,' Rassen had insisted. 'The fish we are catching from the jetty are plentiful, and we are once again growing our vegetables. Do not concern yourself with us any further, my friend.'

'No,' Lou had insisted, 'two more trips should be fine. That'll take us to just before the Christmas break.'

But Lou proved wrong on both counts. He made only one more visit to the island. And they were not caught out by the Christmas break.

It was a week before Christmas when Gary Walton from the Department of Fisheries in Geraldton arrived in Shoal-haven to conduct his customary annual check on fishers' licences. Or this may perhaps have been an excuse, for he was conducting his licence check earlier than usual. In any event, he was asking questions.

'G'day, Lou, how've you been?'

'G'day, Gaz, fine thanks, mate.'

The two shook. They'd met up at the marina's fore-shore, Gary on his way from the coffee shop near the car park, takeaway in hand, Lou on his way to *Principessa*'s pen. He and Paul had already stacked the old Princess with supplies earlier that morning and he was about to take off for his final trip to the island.

'Got a moment?' Gary asked.

'Sure. You doing a licence check?'

'Yeah, yeah, no rush though, just had a query to run by you. Want me to grab you a coffee?' He held up the fresh takeaway.

'No thanks, mate, had one before I left home.'

They sat together on one of the wooden benches that faced out to the attractive view of the marina, boats bobbing cosily at rest, the metallic tinkle of stays on masted vessels.

'So what can I do for you?' Lou asked. He liked Gary Walton. A big man in his mid-forties, well built, freckle-faced from a life spent on the ocean, he had a practical, no-nonsense attitude. A man's man, you always knew where you stood with Gary.

'Just been having a chat to Archie Lang about the comings and goings to the island,' Gary said.

Lou froze. Oh hell, he thought, they know something.

'Arch is pretty sure none of the fishers have been staying out there,' he went on, 'reckons most of the boats have been in their pens or up on the slip or just out for a day's fishing.' He paused to take a swig of his coffee.

'Yep, that'd be right,' Lou replied, doing his best to sound casual. 'So what's the problem?'

'Well, we've had some odd government aerial surveil-lance reports come in. Thought I'd just check around with the fishers and see if there's a simple explanation before I make the official trip out there.' Another swig of his coffee. 'I'm sure there is,' he said, 'maybe a couple of the blokes taking some day trippers out and leaving them there while they do a day's fishing,' he gave a careless shrug, 'you know, whatever.'

'What exactly is it that's so odd about the aerial surveillance reports?' Lou asked, already knowing the answer.

'They show evidence of activity on the island,' Gary said, 'but there's no evidence of any vessels. A bit puzzling. Got any ideas?'

Lou hesitated, his mind racing. Gary had given him a plausible answer. He could say he'd taken a group of day-trippers out there and gone fishing, but was it worth it? How much time would that buy Rassen and the others? He could pretend ignorance, but Gary would only ask around and the other fishers would have no answers so an investigation would be carried out anyway, possibly a team of government officials landing on the island, scaring the hell out of everyone. The cold hard fact was, the refugees' presence had been discovered. In which case, what should he do? Remain silent, or tell Gary the truth?

With no knowledge of the turmoil churning in Lou's mind, Gary assumed the old man was giving the matter some thought.

'Arch says you've been out fishing most days,' he went on, 'but then when are you not, eh,' he added with a grin, 'retirement doesn't come easy to you, does it, Lou? Anyway, I just wondered whether you might have stopped off at the island, seen anything odd, you know, something that might offer an explanation.' Another shrug, another swig of coffee. 'Whatever.'

'I do have an explanation, Gaz,' Lou said, 'as a matter of fact I can tell you the whole story.'

Lou's decision to tell the truth, and to tell it in every detail, was born of a sudden clarity. Of all the people destined to discover the refugees, or at least to learn of their existence, Gary Walton was without doubt the ideal choice. The man was fair and honest and would listen to reason.

I'll be able to plead their case, Lou thought. It won't make any difference to the outcome, and it's bound to land me in a sea of trouble, but at least Gary'll treat them with the respect they deserve. If they're discovered by the fishers there could be an angry scene, and I wouldn't wish that on them.

So he proceeded to tell his story, leaving out only one element: Jalila.

Eight refugees, all from Middle Eastern countries, had landed on the island over three months ago, he told Gary, one of them a child barely four years old.

'Jesus,' Gary breathed incredulously, 'and they've been there for three whole months!'

'Closer to four really.'

'How come there's no evidence of a vessel?' Gary's shock was momentarily outweighed by his puzzlement.

'The Indonesian fishing boat they were on foundered in a storm,' Lou explained. 'All aboard perished, over thirty or so I believe, except for this eight who existed for days at sea in a dinghy, God only knows how. The dinghy had been storm-damaged though, and it finally sank not far from the island. They managed to swim ashore.'

Well most of that's the truth, he thought as he awaited the man's response.

'Christ alive, Lou,' Gary said with another incredulous shake of his head, 'you've known about this for a whole four months!'

'Not quite, they'd been there living in the huts for a couple of weeks before I found them.' He gave a sheepish smile, knowing he sounded pathetic.

'It didn't occur to you to report them, I take it?' The query was made with an uncharacteristically cynical edge.

'No, frankly it didn't. Not once I'd spoken to them anyway,' Lou admitted in all honesty. 'These are gentle people, Gaz, and they've been through the sorts of hell you and I couldn't possibly imagine. Several of them are highly qualified. There's a doctor and his wife who's a nurse – they worked as volunteers in *Aleppo* of all places . . .' everyone knew the hellhole Aleppo had been for years '. . . and there's another who was an activist in Iran, he's an academic, a specialist in languages, really clever young bloke.'

Lou remembered the endless discussions he'd had with Rassen and Massoud, both of whom he deeply admired.

'I've learnt so much from them, Gaz, and they've told me the stories of the other refugees, and I've learnt so much from them too. The doctor translates everything they say to me, the thanks they offer me personally, the apologies they make for intruding on the property of others. I've come to know them all so well.' Lou was aware he was getting carried away, but he didn't care in the least. 'There's a great dignity among them. It's humbling just to be in their presence, mate, honestly it is. You wait until you meet them, you'll see what I mean.'

'You do know I have to report them, don't you?' Gary said drily, interrupting the old man's enthusiastic flow.

'Yes.' Brought to a halt, Lou looked out beyond the marina as if he was seeing the island, which in his mind's eye he was. 'Yes, of course I know that.'

'It's not something I enjoy doing, Lou,' Gary said quietly. He didn't. He'd been involved with boat people before, most recently the Sri Lankans who'd arrived in Geraldton – desperate people, sad to see. Sadder still to know they'd risked their lives for nothing, that there was no hope of their settlement in this country.

'So you've been making regular trips to the island, presumably helping them.' There was no accusation in Gary's tone. He wasn't even asking a question, it was more a statement of facts that appeared to him obvious.

'Yep,' Lou admitted. 'I've been taking supplies out to them more or less on a weekly basis.'

'You could be in big trouble for not reporting illegal immigrants, Lou, and in even bigger trouble for assisting them.' Gary studied the old man intently. 'But you knew that right from the start, didn't you?' Of course you knew, Gary thought, you're nobody's fool. Why on earth had Lou told him about these people, he wondered – why hadn't the old man just kept his mouth shut?

Lou nodded. 'Yes, I knew that.'

'OK, I give up. Why have you told me all this?'

'I thought it'd be better for you to discover them rather than the fishers, who might get nasty and put on a turn. Or the authorities for that matter. If full government forces landed on them without warning the poor bastards would probably be scared shitless.'

'The government authorities will land on them anyway, Lou. Immigration, quarantine, police, border control – they'll all be involved. I'll have to take the officials out there in the fisheries vessel. There'll be up to a dozen or more, all wanting answers.'

'Yes, I'm aware of that. But if you were to personally discover them first up, Gaz . . .' an eager light was once again in Lou's eyes '. . . you know, you and your crew just doing a routine check and lo and behold there they are . . . Well, you'd be able to prepare them, wouldn't you? I mean that's what you'd automatically do, isn't it? Give them fair warning of what to expect?'

Gary said nothing, but waited for him to go on. You shrewd old bugger, he thought, you've got this all planned, haven't you?

Lou found Gary's attentiveness most encouraging.

'You must explain everything to the doctor,' he instructed. 'His name is Rassen, and he's the leader of the group. Rassen Khurdaji, a really well-spoken bloke, you'd swear he's English, he and his wife worked for years in London. Anyway, he'll translate for those who don't speak English and he'll keep everybody calm and prepare them for the onslaught. What do you say? Sound like a plan?'

'Is there any evidence out there that they've received help from the mainland?' Gary asked. 'Did you supply them with a generator or anything like that?'

'Crikey no,' Lou scoffed, 'I wasn't that much of a dill. I even brought back any rubbish that might seem incriminating. I took them some clothes, sure, but they wear mostly Western gear anyway. It looks like they've been living off the sea and the produce from the gardens and whatever's hanging around in the huts, exactly as they were doing when I first discovered them. And nobody on that island's going to say they've had help,' he added. 'They wouldn't want to get me into trouble. That's the sort of people they are, you see.'

'Yes, I see exactly,' Gary said with something that might have been a touch of begrudging admiration. 'You expect me to pretend I know nothing at all about your involvement, that's it, isn't it, you cunning old bastard.'

Lou was taken aback. No, that hadn't been it at all. He'd automatically presumed Gary would report his involvement. But hell, he thought, I'd be mad to knock back an offer like this.

'Well,' he said diplomatically, 'if that's the way you'd like to go about things, Gaz, I wouldn't say no.'

Gary stood, dumping his half-drunk coffee in the bin beside the bench; it was cold now anyway.

'I'll make a trip out to the island tomorrow to investigate the activity that's shown up on the aerial surveillance reports,' he said. 'And don't you dare go near the place today, Lou, don't you even take your boat out of the marina. There'll be no forewarnings, no priming these people on their story. If they say they've had help, I'll end up dobbing you in – I'll have to. But for now this is out of your hands, nothing to do with you, right?'

'Yes, mate, absolutely right, I promise.' Lou couldn't

believe his luck. 'Thanks, Gaz,' he said. 'Jeez, mate, thanks a lot.'

But Gaz was already walking off to the car park.

The following afternoon, a crowd of well over fifty was gathered at the marina jetty, fishers and townspeople alike. Quite a substantial crowd by Shoalhaven standards, certainly as many as could be called together at short notice. They were intrigued, every single one of them. Gary Walton of the Fisheries Department had radioed ahead to the marina requesting as many as possible gather to hear the announcement he would make upon his arrival by sea. What was going on?

There were several of them who knew. The Miller family was there. David and Maria, Paul with his arm around Jalila, and of course Lou. But they said nothing, gazing out to sea along with all the others, eyes fixed on the fisheries vessel as it approached.

MV Endurance entered the marina and pulled up alongside the jetty where they were all standing, a magnificent craft, twenty-two metres long with twin Cat V12 engines, built for speed, efficiency and stamina, with every form of modern navigational and tracking equipment to hand.

Two of the four-man crew secured the vessel, and Gary stepped up on to the upper deck, where he had a good view of the crowd in order to make his address. Legs astride in the manner of one accustomed to anchoring his weight on a vessel at sea, he was a figure of command, a man they all knew and respected, particularly the fishers.

'Thanks for turning up, everyone,' he said, his voice carrying loudly and clearly to all. 'I have an announcement to make, and also some orders to issue on behalf of the government. An incident has arisen and no one is to visit Gevaar Island until further notice is given. Two of my men have been posted there and will stay in charge overnight . . .'

There were mutterings amongst the crowd, but as Gary raised his voice, they quietened in order to hear more.

'. . . and tomorrow a party of officials will arrive from Perth,' he continued. 'They'll be flown to Geraldton by charter and driven up here to Shoalhaven.'

'What *sort* of officials?' a strident voice demanded.

Gary ignored Ian Tuckey, who was always a mouth, and continued to talk over the further mutterings that Ian's interjection had provoked from others.

'We'll be staying here for the night,' he said, indicating the vessel and his crew, 'and tomorrow we'll take the officials out to the island, which will then be placed under federal quarantine.'

Ian's voice wasn't the only one raised now. There were cries of protest, particularly from the fishers present.

'What's the hell's going on, Gaz?'

'Come on, mate, give us a break.'

'What's this all about? Tell us the truth.'

Gary held up his hands and they quieted down. 'I'm not at liberty to say much more, I'm afraid, apart from issuing the order I've received by radio. As of this moment Gevaar Island is strictly out of bounds. No one is to land there under any circumstances, and I must warn you there will be severe consequences for any who attempt to do so.'

A furore broke out – frustrated cries of 'Why?' and 'Tell us the truth for God's sake!'

Then cutting through the cacophony, the unmistakeable tinny tone of Ian Tuckey. 'Reffos, I'll bet! Bloody reffos have landed on the island! Illegals! Probably shacked up there! That's it, isn't it?'

Ian's vehemence aroused the fishers, who were none too happy at the thought of strangers shacked up in their huts. Voices became discordant.

'All right! All right!' Again Gary raised his hands calling for silence, and again the crowd obeyed him.

'I will admit to you there are people on the island . . .'

Jesus, Gary thought, they have a right to know, particularly those fishers with property there, we can't treat them like imbeciles '. . . and these people need to be investigated by the authorities. That's all I can tell you at this stage.'

Again the questions were fired at him.

'Who *are* these people?'

'Where are they *from*?'

'How many are there?'

He shook his head to every single query. 'I'm not at liberty to answer any of these questions.'

Then a female voice piped up, tough, belligerent. 'How long will this quarantine last?' Kath Buckley, scrawny arms folded across scrawny chest, husband Buck by her side. 'We was going to take our grandkids over for Christmas,' she said. 'Does this mean we can't now?'

'I don't know, Kath,' Gary admitted, 'I seriously don't know.

He concluded his address to the crowd in general. 'All of your questions will be answered in good time. When the authorities have conducted their investigations, announcements will be made, but until then I'm sorry, there's nothing further I can tell you.'

The crowd was restless now that the meeting appeared over, but he called for their attention once more.

'However,' he declared loudly, and waited for the obedient lull that followed, 'there is one more request I've been told to make of you all. While I'd ask you to inform the rest of the town's citizens that the island is strictly off-limits, the authorities are keen to keep this matter under wraps. They don't want any media involvement. So for the moment, until we receive further instructions, everything stays right here in Shoalhaven. No spreading the news. Have we all got that?'

There were mutters of agreement, although people still weren't happy; they were being kept in the dark and they wanted more news.

'Thanks, everyone.' Gary gave them a wave. 'That's it for now. We'll keep you posted.'

The crowd started to disperse, discussion rife, but there were those several who remained, trying to nag Gary further, most particularly Ian 'the Mouth' Tuckey.

Gary wouldn't have a bar of it, swatting them away with a pleasant enough, 'Sorry, no further comment,' and to the Mouth, 'Piss off, Ian,' which he knew would not offend. It was impossible to offend Ian Tuckey.

Then he started the engine, his crew cast off, and they took the *Endurance* over to the marina's fuelling station, where they filled her with diesel in preparation for the following day. Gary really wasn't looking forward to tomorrow.

Gary Walton's trip out to the island that morning had gone very much as planned. He'd taken a crew of six with him rather than his customary four. It was understandable he should do so, given they were investigating the surveillance reports and a possible presence on the island. But of course he'd known he'd have to leave two men there overnight.

He'd been as impressed by the refugees as Lou had told him he would be. He'd presumed the old man had been exaggerating, as Lou Panuzza was at times wont to do: he was a colourful man with a passionate nature. But Lou hadn't been exaggerating at all. Gary, too, had found these people dignified and gentle.

There'd been not a soul in sight as their vessel had approached the island, but the moment the *Endurance* had moored alongside the jetty and he and his team had stepped ashore to conduct their inspection, the group had appeared.

One by one, two by two, men, women, and a small child clutching his mother's hand had materialised from apparently nowhere as if offering themselves in surrender, which he'd quickly discovered was exactly their intention.

They'd assembled in quiet, orderly fashion before the yellow hut, which was the closest one to the jetty, taking their lead from the man whom Gary had presumed to be the doctor.

As he and his team had approached, they'd been greeted in English.

'Good morning, sir,' from the leader, followed by a chorus of 'good mornings' from the others, even the little boy.

When the leader, who had proved indeed to be Dr Rassen Khurdaji, had introduced himself, they had adjourned inside the yellow hut where Gary had conducted his interview with the group.

One of his crew, young Jason, had remained present while the other five crew members, tough experienced men, had searched each of the huts on the island for evidence of any further refugees. There had been none. As the doctor himself had stated, the eight present were the sole survivors of the tragic voyage they had all undertaken.

Throughout the interview, Gary had been touched by the respect afforded him by the refugees, including those who spoke virtually no English. He'd been touched also by their quiet resignation. But he had come across this quality before, and he'd been touched by it then too. Twenty years previously, as a young man, he'd worked out of Darwin, where he'd been involved in the apprehension of Indonesian fishing boats run by ruthless fleet owners who trafficked in human cargo, which yielded a far greater profit than fishing. Their boats transported poor despairing souls who had sold all they owned in a bid to find sanctuary in a country that was safe. Upon their apprehension, these people had had that same look of resignation.

Gary didn't like this sort of work.

He'd waited until the end of his interview before asking the question that, to him, was of the greatest importance.

'Have you had contact with anyone from the mainland, doctor? Have you received help from any Australians?'

'Oh yes, we have most certainly,' the doctor replied. 'Without the help we have received from our Australian friends we would undoubtedly be dead by now.'

'I see.' Gary exchanged a look with his crew member, young Jason raising an eyebrow in return. Sorry, Lou, he thought, can't save your hide now. 'And who would these Australians be?' he asked. 'Would you happen to know their names?'

'Every single person who owns these cottages,' the doctor said, 'we do not know their names, but we give thanks to them all.'

'We most certainly do,' the doctor's wife interjected, the woman who looked and sounded so extraordinarily English. 'We were on the verge of death when we arrived on this island. These people have saved our lives.'

The young man who also spoke perfect English then chimed in.

'We are deeply indebted to these people, and we apologise for having invaded their homes.'

The non-English speakers were trying desperately to follow the conversation, eager to have their say, so the doctor translated what the young man had just said, and there was a sudden outpouring of Arabic, which the doctor in turn translated for Gary's benefit.

'They say the same as Massoud,' he told Gary. 'They thank their benefactors from the very bottom of their hearts.' He placed his hand on his heart as he said this and the others all made the same gesture, nodding fervently, hands on hearts. 'And they apologise most sincerely if they have caused any offence to these people for living in their homes.'

'Right,' Gary said. OK, Lou, he thought, looks like you're off the hook. For now anyway. Oh hell, if anyone finds out you told me about this I'm gone for all money.

*

Gary Walton normally slept well aboard his vessel, like a
baby in fact. But not tonight. The gentle cradle-like rock
and the soft lick of the water against the side of the vessel
did not work their customary magic, his mind baulking at
what lay ahead.

Christ, he thought, talk about the tip of the iceberg. This
whole thing's going to cause a furore. Boat people living
undetected on Australian soil for a whole four months!
How do they reckon they'll keep that out of the media?

CHAPTER EIGHTEEN

By the end of that day the news had spread throughout the whole of Shoalhaven, and the following morning the town could talk of nothing else. Illegal immigrants had been discovered on Gevaar Island. There had as yet been no official verification, but everyone was nonetheless sure these intruders must be refugees from somewhere. Even at this early stage the term varied in its application, some referring to them as refugees and others as illegal immigrants, but the same questions abounded. Where were these people from? How many of them were there? How long had they been on the island?

Then as the morning wore on and the officials arrived, having been driven up from Geraldton airport, tempers started to become a little frayed, particularly among the fisher community who had property on the island. The official party, a whole coachload of them, well over a dozen investigators from various government departments along with police, were taken directly to the marina where they boarded the Fisheries vessel and were whisked off to Gevaar Island with not a word of explanation to the fishers who had gathered at the jetty.

'No comment,' was the brusque reply from the party's principal spokesperson, clearly a plain-clothes cop, and most likely a Fed, they all agreed. 'You'll be informed in due course. Announcements will be made late this afternoon, either here upon our return or at a meeting place you might wish to nominate.' And then they were gone, officers as it later turned out from the Immigration Department, the Australian Quarantine and Inspection Service, Customs/Border Protection and a number of police.

So the fishers, and by now the townsfolk too, were left to fume, the fishers frustrated, not knowing what was happening with their property, and the townsfolk downright annoyed by the dismissive attitude of the authorities. How dare they treat us like children!

The Shoalhaven Residents' Group called an extraordinary general meeting, and at a moment's notice. As a rule they met only four or five times a year, usually to discuss a community improvement or to raise funds for a charitable cause, and always they gave a good week's notice in advance. This time was altogether different.

The group had been formed many years previously by three prominent and well-respected citizens who worked on an honorary basis and who had the town's best interests at heart. Gordon Shadforth of Shadforth Hardware was president, his wife, Sandra, was secretary and David Miller, Shoalhaven's postmaster, was accountant and treasurer. At each meeting, Sandy Shadforth would record the minutes, her fingers whipping across the keyboard of her laptop with lightning speed, after which she would print out each report and pin a stapled copy of the pages up on the church hall's noticeboard, should anyone wish to inspect it, which no one ever did. Attendance numbers were always good, however. Signs would be posted in the windows of the hardware shop and the post office, and the organisers would send out word by email or text or simply via the grapevine that a meeting was to be held in the church hall to discuss a specific matter or matters that affected the citizens of Shoalhaven. As a rule fifty, sometimes even a hundred might turn up, dependent upon the matter to be discussed, and also of course the lobster season.

This time, despite the late notice, there were well over two hundred in attendance. The federal police spokesman had said 'late afternoon', whatever that might mean, so the meeting was called for three-thirty just to be on the safe side. And everyone sat waiting for well over an hour.

All the fishers were there, or rather all the fishers who had remained in Shoalhaven during the off-peak season. Most of the townspeople were there too, leaving their assistants to look after their shops and businesses. Gordon Shadforth of course had two very capable assistants who were accustomed to running his store, but David Miller had left young Tillie in charge of the post office, which was a definite first. His wife, Maria, who would normally have filled in for him, had insisted upon attending the meeting herself, and it had been Maria's firm opinion that Tillie was by now perfectly capable of taking over postal duties for the last two hours of the working day.

Nina Adrejic had left Aleksandra to run the bakery on her own; Henry Wong had left his wife, Florence, to look after the Chinese restaurant and hamburger bar; young Nessa was running the pharmacy for her parents, Alfred Tran having decided it was too bad if anyone needed a prescription urgently, they'd just have to wait until the morning; old Geoff and Freda Marston had left Izzie in charge of their shop; and so the list went on. Everyone's business was operating with the barest minimum of staff. Everyone's business that is, except Ian Tuckey's. Ian had closed the Tuckshop altogether.

Huddled in the church hall, which was virtually at capacity with many people standing up the back due to a shortage of chairs, for which there wouldn't have been room anyway, they waited. And they waited. The muttering of voices, the shuffling of feet – Sandra Shadforth up on the small platform of a stage, seated at her desk, impeccably poised, laptop at the ready – they waited.

Gordon Shadforth and David Miller were also waiting, but not at the church hall. Gordon and David were at the marina, seated on a foreshore bench, coincidentally the very one where Gary and Lou had sat just the previous morning. They were there to meet the official party and escort them, or their spokesperson, who would presumably be the federal police officer, to the church hall.

They sat in silence, an impressive-looking pair. They'd talked for a while as they'd stood gazing out to sea for the first sign of the fisheries vessel, but as time had passed they'd decided to sit and conversation had dwindled. They were now comfortably silent.

Gordon, a tall man in his sixties, around the same height as David, but with a fleshier body and a head of silver-white hair, was not a particularly talkative man at the best of times, possibly because of his garrulous wife. Gordon Shadforth was perfectly happy to talk about things of importance, but the social chitchat he always left to Sandy, for she was so very good at it.

David, who was also a man not given to small talk, was grateful for the silence. He was in a particularly introspective mood, his mind on Jalila, the girl he had come to accept as his daughter-in-law. He didn't care in the least that she and his son were not legally married: the girl was as much a wife as any woman could be. She loved his son deeply and with an unquestionable loyalty that was plain for all to see. David considered loyalty one of the greatest of all human virtues.

During the month he had come to know and admire Jalila's qualities, however, David had tried to distance himself from the subject of the refugees. He had no wish to become biased in any way; the law must take its course as it inevitably would. But he'd found it difficult to close his ears at the Sunday family dinners when Maria, to whom the subject was fascinating, asked endless questions. At first he'd been irritated.

'I hardly think it wise we pursue the subject, my dear,' he'd said a little stiffly. He rarely argued with his wife, preferring to avoid confrontation whenever possible, and most particularly with Maria who, when pushed, could become quite volatile.

'But why, my darling?' Maria had queried airily. 'Jalila doesn't mind, do you, Jalila?'

'No, no,' Jalila had assured her, 'I like talk of my friends. They is good . . . *are* . . . good peoples.'

'There you are, you see?' Maria had said with an air of triumph. 'Where's the harm?'

'We are speaking of those who have entered this country illegally, Maria,' he'd remarked, this time quite tightly, a distinct warning, 'people of whose existence we are supposedly unaware.'

'Yes, but we *are* aware of their existence, aren't we, my darling, there's no point in pretending we're not.' Recognising her husband was in one of his prickly moods, Maria had tried to sound as reasonable as possible. 'I mean it's not as if anyone can hear us.' She'd smiled pleasantly around the table at her family, at Lou and Paul and Bev. 'There's only us here and each of us knows the truth, so why should we pretend?' Then she'd looked directly at Jalila, adding in all sincerity, 'And I certainly would not ask any questions that might be intrusive or insensitive – God only knows what those poor people may have been through.' Another pleasant smile, this time to her husband. 'I'd just like to know a little about Jalila's friends, my darling, that's all.'

What option did he have? David had wondered. His wife could appear so infuriatingly 'sensible' when presenting an argument that, to him, was totally irrational – it was a great talent of Maria's. What action was he now supposed to take? He could forbid further conversation, which would spoil the gathering altogether and alienate him from his family, or he could leave the table. But either option would be to make a scene and he preferred to avoid scenes.

From that day on, David Miller had remained silent during the family dinners, trying to close his ears to the chatter about the group out there on the island. But as Lou and Paul and Jalila had openly talked, and as his wife and daughter had listened with avid interest, like it or not, he had come to know these people out there on the island. And that was not right.

I shouldn't know them, I mustn't know them, he now thought as he sat with Gordon Shadforth awaiting the arrival of the Fisheries vessel.

'There she is,' Gordon said, rising from the bench, 'and about bloody time too.' He cast a brief smile to David, who had risen to stand beside him. 'Better not say that to their faces though, eh? We are the town dignitaries after all.'

'Yes we are,' David agreed, politely returning the smile. Gordon could be amusing at times in a dry sort of way, not in the least pretentious like his wife. But David was not amused today. Today was not a day to be amused.

They strolled down to the jetty in leisurely fashion, the vessel was still some distance off, and as they did David's mind turned to the dangers his family would face should Jalila be associated with the refugees.

Lou's glib assurance that the doctor, the man whom they called Rassen, and the others also, would say nothing of the contact they'd had with the mainland had done little to settle David Miller's nerves as he'd listened to Gary Walton's address the preceding day.

'They'll make no mention of Jalila either,' Lou had assured him when he'd told the family of his meeting with Gary that very morning. 'Eight people made it ashore to the island after their dinghy sank.' Lou had stated the fact quite categorically as if it were the absolute truth. 'Rassen will have rehearsed them all in their story, you can be assured of that.'

David had been assured of nothing, however, as he'd watched Gary Walton, listening to the man's every word, expecting at any moment that Lou would be exposed as an accomplice to these people on the island. But there had been no accusatory statement, not even the merest indication of complicity. Gary had addressed the crowd in general, not once looking in Lou's direction. And Lou had not for one minute appeared threatened. David had found his complacency annoying.

The old man's a bloody rogue, he thought as he now stood on the jetty, watching the approach of the vessel with its official party aboard. Lou might have got away with things so far, but if anyone makes the link between Jalila and those on the island, our whole family will be exposed. It was Paul who brought Jalila ashore and Bev who was his accomplice, lying that the girl was her friend's sister. We're all involved, every single one of us. We can't pretend ignorance and I certainly don't intend to try.

How on earth had he become involved in this, he wondered, it was so unlike him; a man who throughout the whole of his life had obeyed every letter of the law.

But how could I have reported my own son, he asked himself, what father could do such a thing? And the only wrong Paul committed after all was to help a group of people desperately in need. He hadn't planned to fall in love. No man ever does.

David Miller had not succeeded in his attempt to remain unbiased. Despite himself, he had come to know those people out there on that island, and he couldn't help but feel sympathetic to their plight. He was powerless to help them, it was true, but he would do all he could to protect Jalila. While still condemning his 'rogue' of a father-in-law for involving his son in an illegal act, he was now prepared to weather the storm. We'll see this through as a family, he thought. We'll see this through together, come what may.

The official party was shepherded ashore and the necessary introductions made, after which Gordon and David led the federal police officer, Inspector Terence Henley, to the church hall. They were accompanied by local WA state police officer, Inspector Leslie Brock, who was stationed in Geraldton, and also Gary Walton of the Fisheries Department. Les and Gary, who knew each other well and who were known by the locals, would presumably be a calming influence if feathers became ruffled, which might well be the case.

As the five men set off by foot for the nearby church hall, only several minutes' walk away, the other members of the official party were offered tea, coffee and refreshments at the marina before boarding the coach that was waiting to transport them back to Geraldton, where accommodation had been arranged. Following the meeting, Les Brock would drive Terence Henley to Geraldton in his police vehicle, while Gary Walton would return to his vessel that remained berthed at Shoalhaven Marina.

It would be the end of a long day's work for them all, but only a taste of what lay ahead.

A hush fell over the gathering as the five men entered the rear of the hall and made their way through the crowd to the small stage at the far end where Sandy Shadforth remained at her desk, still poised, aware that her infinite patience served as a fine example to her fellow citizens.

The shuffling of feet stopped, dissatisfied mutterings died away, and all heads turned to follow the men's progress.

Upon reaching the stage, which was really no more than a platform, Gordon and David stepped up, Inspector Henley joining them, and Gordon made the opening announcement. Given the stage area was limited, Les and Gary stood respectfully to one side.

'I think we can dispense with the customary procedures,' Gordon said, glancing at his wife, who he knew would be disappointed. 'This is an extraordinary meeting after all, and everyone knows why we're here.'

Sandy's lips pursed just that little bit tighter than normal. In her opinion customary procedure should most certainly be observed. The meeting should be formally declared open, and, most importantly, the minutes of the preceding meeting, which she had painstakingly printed out and posted up on the noticeboard, should be approved.

'This is Inspector Henley of the Australian Federal Police Force,' Gordon said.

As he made the introduction, all eyes focused on the burly plain-clothes police officer who stood in typical cop stance, legs astride, hands linked behind back, eyes trained front. This was the same man who'd made the brusque 'no comment' address to those who had gathered at the marina that morning. The same man who had treated them like children. Already there was a feeling of hostility in the hall.

'Without further ado,' Gordon went on, 'I'll hand you over to Inspector Henley, who'll give you an account of the situation and tell you exactly what's going on.'

'As much as is within my power.' Henley's correction to Gordon appeared more of a reprimand. 'There will be information I am not at liberty to impart.'

In just a matter of seconds the feeling of hostility had filtered throughout the entire hall. The man had successfully alienated the citizens of Shoalhaven, who did not take kindly to his form of authoritarian superiority.

Gordon and David edged to one side in order to give Henley centre stage, and the police officer stepped forwards and commenced his address.

'Eight unauthorised maritime arrivals have been discovered on Gevaar Island,' he announced.

There was not the merest ripple of reaction to the fact that he'd mispronounced the island's name as 'jeevar' instead of 'hoofire'. All strangers did that, though there was the general thought that a federal police officer could perhaps have been better briefed. No one intended to correct him though, not even Gordon Shadforth or David Miller. Let the man continue to make a fool of himself.

'These people claim to be refugees and have been living there for some time,' Henley went on.

'How long's "some time"?' a strident female voice demanded from a seat at the very back of the hall. Kath Buckley could make herself heard anywhere.

Henley ignored the question altogether, turning instead to Gordon Shadforth with a look that quite clearly said, *You're supposed to be the president, you tell them the rules.*

Gordon stepped forwards, his hand held up.

'We'll get to questions after Inspector Henley has made his address,' he said, eyes raking the hall, seeing Kath up the back. 'I'd appreciate it if you'd all keep your questions until then. Thank you.' He gave a respectful nod to the gathering and stepped back.

'As I believe you've already been informed,' Henley continued, 'the island has been officially placed under federal quarantine. A further order is now issued that there will be a five-hundred-metre exclusion zone beyond which no vessel may approach the island.'

Mutterings followed this announcement. People appeared bewildered.

'There are a number of reasons why the government deems this necessary,' Henley went on to explain, 'but one of the principal concerns is the media. The media must be allowed nowhere near the island. In fact, I cannot express strongly enough to you all the need to avoid any form of media involvement in this incident.'

For the first time, Terence Henley appeared to be genuinely reaching out to them, keen to make direct, and urgent, contact. These had in fact been his orders with regard to the issue of media.

'In the days, and possibly the weeks to come,' he continued, 'there will be a great deal of activity here in . . . Shoalhaven.' There was a fractional pause while he reminded himself that this place was Shoalhaven, he'd come very close to saying Geraldton. He'd been briefed at the very last minute and he was tired: it had been a bloody long day.

'Given the current political climate worldwide, of which I'm sure you're well aware,' he went on, although he doubted they were aware of anything much, they were fishermen in an obscure town at the arse-end of the earth, 'the arrival of asylum seekers by boat is a delicate issue under any circumstances. The government has a strong policy in place, again as I'm sure you know,' he added, trying to sound as if he gave them credit, which he didn't, 'and the more speedily these boat-people are moved to a government detention centre for processing, the better it will be for all concerned.'

Henley then, mustering his patience, went on to explain the situation in the simplest terms possible, that those gathered before him might understand.

'The trouble in this case, however, is that the boat in which these particular people travelled was not turned back at sea, but foundered before it could be discovered by our border control. These eight who managed to survive have since been hiding out on the island undetected for some months.' He gazed about at the gathering, his face, stern at the best of times, seeming somehow to convey that this was all their fault.

'It is now essential that the island be placed under the strictest quarantine regulations for a substantial period, which would unfortunately allow the media, should they become aware of the situation, ample time to blow the story out of all proportion. The government wishes to avoid this unnecessary publicity. As I'm sure,' he added meaningfully, 'do you, the people of Shoalhaven. Being the centre of media attention, possibly even worldwide, would be most unpleasant for your community, I can assure you. In which case we ask you to avoid any form of communication that might spread this news, either electronically or by word of mouth.'

Henley glanced at Gordon Shadforth and gave a brisk nod, which Gordon rightly interpreted to mean it was time for him to once again play president.

'Well that's how the situation stands,' Gordon said, stepping forwards and addressing the crowd. 'So all those of you who might have any questions, if you could put up your hands, I'll call on you one by one and Inspector Henley will address each query in an orderly fashion.'

It was a none-too-subtle hint. Any questions, Gordon was thinking; he'd sensed the aura in the room right from the start. Hell, if I give them open slather they'll all be yelling out at the tops of their voices, he thought, and who could blame them?

But everyone got the hint; Gordon was held in high regard by his fellow citizens. Hands shot up all over the place, but no one yelled out.

'Yes, Kath.' Gordon pointed to Kath Buckley, who stood up from her chair at the rear of the hall.

'How long will the quarantine last?'

'I have no idea,' Henley answered, once again brusquely; fatigue, both genuine and born of boredom, was beginning to set in. 'That's not my department, that's up to AQIS,' he said, referring to the Australian Quarantine and Inspection Service. 'But I would estimate possibly several weeks.'

Kath nodded and sat. She had a dozen other questions she'd have liked to ask. But fair's fair, she thought, it's someone else's turn. Her questions were bound to crop up anyway – they were all thinking the same thing.

Gordon pointed to Aappo Laaksonen next, Jukka's and Hekki's father. The whole of the Laaksonen family was there, mother and daughter seated at the end of one row, father and sons standing against the wall nearby.

'Yes, Aappo,' he said. He considered it only right to favour the questions that were coming from the fishers who had property on the island.

'What does this quarantine entail?' Aappo asked in his heavy Finnish accent. 'What is done to the fishers' huts on the island?'

'Again that's up to AQIS,' Henley replied. 'They'll probably fumigate the whole place, I would think, but most certainly the huts, and of course they'll conduct full medical examinations of the people on the island. Their job is to protect Australia's environment and human health from the importation of pests and diseases.' Henley was becoming irritated now. 'Again not my department,' he said, which moved them hastily on to the next question.

'Yes, Paul.' Gordon pointed to Paul Miller next.

Paul had raised his hand along with everyone else, knowing that as an island fisher it would seem extremely odd if he didn't. He was standing up the back with the majority of the men, Lou beside him. Jalila and Maria were seated together in the centre of the hall along with the other wives and mothers and daughters, most of the chairs having been left for the women.

Paul boldly asked the most important question of all. The question he considered of most importance anyway, the question he would have asked had he not known the answer. 'These people on the island,' he said. 'Where do they come from?'

'Ah yes.' Henley was once more on the alert, hunger and weariness forgotten as he realised he'd neglected to mention the ethnicity of the immigrants, which was a particularly pertinent aspect. 'There are eight illegal immigrants and all predominately from Middle Eastern countries,' he said.

There was an immediate reaction, mutterings of surprise, most of those present having automatically presumed that the refugees would be of Asian ethnicity, from Indonesia or Malaysia, somewhere closer to Australia.

'Yes indeed,' Henley said, holding his hand up for silence. 'As some of you might realise, given the worldwide focus upon the ongoing conflict in the Middle East and the mass exodus of migrants causing chaos throughout Europe, the media would take particular delight in over-emphasising many aspects of this current situation, which is exactly what the government wishes to avoid.'

The hall started to become a bit unruly then, people forgetting Gordon's call for queries in 'orderly fashion'.

'So the government's scared because they're Middle Eastern Muslims!'

'Are these people militants then?'

'They could be bloody terrorists!'

Most of the comments weren't queries at all, but sounded more like accusations.

Terence Henley had had quite enough by now.

'There is no further information to hand,' he called above the crowd with a voice more than adequate to regain control, 'and if there were I would not be at liberty to impart it. Thank you for your attention.'

He stepped down from the platform and, with a brisk nod to Les Brock, a distinct order it was time he be driven back to Geraldton, he made for the rear of the hall. It had been a very, very long day, what with the interminable flight to Perth, the charter to Geraldton, the drive up there and the boat to the island. He was tired and hungry and thoroughly pissed off.

Les had no option but to hurry after the man, which he did with a muttered, 'Sorry, mate, it's all yours,' apology to Gary Walton, who was obviously going to be left with a crowd demanding more answers.

Upon the departure of the two police officers, the crowd did not, however, turn to Gary for answers. The idea didn't seem to occur; instead, they started shouting at each other, everyone wanting to voice an opinion about something of which they knew nothing, or at least very little.

The mention of the Middle East appeared to have had an unsettling effect on most.

Gordon called the meeting to order and it was he who suggested Gary might answer some further questions.

Reluctantly, Gary took to the stage.

'It's not my place to officially answer questions,' he said both to Gordon and to the crowd in general. 'And I certainly can't tell you any more than Inspector Henley has, for the simple reason that I don't know,' he added apologetically.

'Aye, but you've met these folk, haven't you, Gaz?' Mac called from the sidelines. No one was bothering with decorum now. There was no raising of hands; this had become a discussion among locals. 'You're the one who discovered them, when all's said and done.'

'Yes, that's true.'

'So what are they like, man?'

There was an expectant pause. Mac's question had hit home.

'They're people,' Gary said, 'people just like you and me. There's a child amongst them too, a little boy of four.'

'Yeah, but they're Muslims, aren't they?' a female voice piped up. It was Kath, of course.

'I suppose they are; I didn't ask them.'

'So how do you know they're not terrorists?' Kath demanded.

Ian Tuckey's tinny voice rang out from the back of the hall. 'Oh give us a break, Kath.' He was standing right behind her chair, and his remark was directly to her, but he made sure everyone else could hear, as Ian always did. 'That argument went out with ark. Terrorists don't travel in leaky boats, terrorists catch planes.'

Kath whirled about in her seat and glared at him. 'Oh and you'd know, wouldn't you, Ian!'

'Yep, common-sense.'

Ian's smug smile was infuriating and Kath was about to

go him, but Alfred Tran interrupted; he was a quiet man as a rule, but an intelligent one, who assiduously followed world affairs and who had his views.

'There are terrible things happening in the Middle East,' he said, 'and many are no longer able to escape through the normal routes available to them. For these people to have travelled this far and to have made the perilous journey by boat, must mean they have had to flee from great horror.'

There was a moment's respectful silence. Everyone knew Alfred Tran's background. He was a boat-person himself. He'd been a small boy when his parents had undertaken the sea journey from Vietnam in 1976, a journey that had resulted in the death of his mother.

Alfred's input appeared to have calmed the bickering.

Until another voice spoke up. It was Nina Adrejic, seated in the very front row, and she stood, turning her back to the stage in order to address the entire gathering.

'I don' care if these people be Muslim or maybe-perhaps terrorist, or maybe-perhaps real-life refugee or whatever you want to call them,' she said at the top of her voice and in her execrable accent, waving a hand about wildly to express her contempt. 'These people come here illegal. They jump the queue. If they want to come to Australia, they apply! Like me!' She stabbed a vehement forefinger into her chest. 'I . . . wait . . . my . . . turn!' she declared, each word accompanied by a vicious jab that looked as if it must have hurt. 'I am proud Australian and I don' like people who push in the queue. Is not fair. They wait their turn like me. And like Jalila's family too,' she said, pointing to where Jalila sat. 'These people should do things proper, the way we did.'

Nina's passionate outburst had taken them all by surprise and once again there was a moment's lull.

Up on stage, observing the crowd, David Miller couldn't help feeling a stab of anxiety upon the reference to Jalila, which had a lot of people automatically glancing in her direction.

Then old Geoff Marston rose from his chair in the centre of the hall where he and Freda were sitting together. He stood in order to draw attention to himself, for he knew his voice was not as strong as those who had been contributing to the proceedings.

'Perhaps these people did not have the time you had at your disposal, Nina,' he said mildly, and his voice, although weaker than the others, was heard by all. 'Perhaps, as Alfred said, these people were forced to flee. Perhaps if they had "waited their turn", as you say, it might have proved to their peril.'

Nina didn't push her argument any further; she'd said her piece. Besides, the elderly Geoff Marston was such a thorough gentleman and such a figure of respectability that had she done so she might have appeared vulgar. So she gave a loud 'harrumph' of disapproval instead, which clearly announced her views had not changed, and plonked herself back in her chair.

Voices started up again as people became quarrelsome, exchanging differing views and generally bickering. Up on stage Gordon and David shared a look. The meeting was getting out of hand. Nothing was being served by everyone's squabbling.

Gordon called the gathering to order. 'I think we might leave things here,' he said. 'It's rather late and I'm sure everyone's keen to get home for dinner; what do you say, David?' He didn't refer to his wife, who was seated behind him at her desk. He could literally feel the daggers of her disapproval.

Sandy was most certainly scowling. She'd looked up from her laptop where her fingers had been frantically scrambling, trying to keep abreast of the proceedings, these would surely be the strangest minutes. And now they were going to close the meeting informally? Just like that?

'Yes, good idea,' David agreed, and he stepped forwards to address the crowd with a final word. 'In the meantime,' he said, 'I'd like to offer a suggestion to everyone present, myself included. Let's make no judgements on these people whom we don't know. It seems to me a futile exercise.' It seemed a futile suggestion on his part, too, he thought, people would always talk, but he felt compelled to say something in the defence of those on the island, who were bound to be maligned.

'Hear, hear,' Gordon chimed in heartily, 'no point the whole town getting riled up.' But like David he was thinking, Just try stopping them. 'Well that's about it, so let's call it a day.'

Sandy Shadforth keyed in her husband's final words of this 'extraordinary' Shoalhaven Residents' Group meeting, pressed 'save' and closed the lid of her laptop. She was not happy.

People started filing out of the hall, talking nineteen to the dozen, but Paul remained where he was, watching as his father stepped from the stage. He was proud of David's closing words. Brief though they'd been, he was well aware of their intended purpose. He watched as his father joined Maria and Jalila, and he noted with pleasure the fond exchange between the three as they started towards the rear doors of the hall. Jalila was now undoubtedly part of the family.

There had been a distinct shift in the father and son relationship of David and Paul Miller, and it had all been due to Jalila.

'The bastard's making a statement,' Paul had said when his father had remained conspicuously silent throughout the family dinners. 'He's sulking because we're talking about the others.'

'No,' Jalila had said, 'this not true. He try not to hear is all. He think not right he take side.'

Her answer had astonished him. 'How do you know that?'

'He tell me. He say, "Jalila, is not that I no feel for your friends. But I must keep . . ."' She fumbled for the word, pushing the air away with her hands.

'Distance?'

'Yes, distance. He wish no involve, he think is not right.'

'He said all this to you?'

'Yes. One night when family in kitchen. He tell me I am good wife to you. Loyal, he say. Your father he like me. I like him also. Your father is good man, Paul.'

The shift in the Miller father–son relationship had happened that simply. At least from Paul's point of view. Jalila had altered his blinkered vision, opening his eyes to the man his father was. A conventional man, yes, a stitched-up man, yes, by most people's standards, but a man who did not judge others, and a man who valued loyalty above all else.

Paul had loved his father for the brief closing words he'd made at the meeting.

'We've decided we're doing dinner at our place,' David now said as he and Maria and Jalila joined Paul at the church doors. 'Don't know about you, but I could handle a beer myself.'

'Sure, Dad, you go on ahead with the girls. I'll give them a hand here clearing away the chairs.' A number of the young regular churchgoers were already stacking the fold-up seats. 'Liked what you said by the way.'

'Good.' David smiled. 'That's good.' He didn't know why or how, but lately the ice had somehow been broken.

As Inspector Terence Henley had warned, the following days saw a great deal of activity in the sleepy hollow of Shoalhaven.

Further vessels arrived in the marina. Equipment arrived by truck to be transported to the island in order that adequate accommodation could be set up there, together with an interview office and quarters for medical examinations. And of course officials arrived: medical officers, quarantine officers, police officers.

Among the equipment and supplies were military-style tents and furnishings, generators, huge boxes of general provisions to sustain the camp, a miscellany of quarantine and medical items and an endless array of other goods. The streets and the marina of Shoalhaven had never been busier.

And the busier the town grew, the busier became the talk among its citizens. In the shops and businesses, the marina and the pub, wherever people gathered, the talk was about the refugees. And in private homes too, around dinner tables, the topic was always the same, although points of view varied.

'I did find last week's Residents' Group meeting a little abrasive, I must say,' Sandy remarked. 'I tried to notate the proceedings to the best of my ability, and I've posted the minutes, if you can call them that, up on the noticeboard, but I did consider some of those present to be –'

'Quite rude.' Thelma's words were right on key, she was in top form tonight, but then Sandy was sitting directly opposite her, which made things a great deal easier. 'Yes, yes, quite rude, I agree,' Thelma said, head nodding bird-like as always.

It was just before Christmas and Sandy Shadforth was having one of her dinner parties, just six to a table, she and Gordon, Samuel and Thelma Lyttleton and Geoff and Freda Marston. She'd intended a table of eight, but David and Maria Miller had been unable to attend. They'd said they were dining with Paul and Jalila that night. Sandy was rather thankful now; it gave her a little extra licence.

'In printing out the minutes and reading through them,' she went on, 'I found David's advice to us all just a *little* bit ...' She put down her knife and fork, leaving her chicken momentarily aside and paused as if searching for the word, but actually in order to defeat Thelma. Like everyone else in town she found the woman's lip-reading compulsion intensely irritating. If Thelma hadn't been married to the pastor, Sandy Shadforth wouldn't have given her the time of day.

'. . . patronising,' she hastily concluded and with great success. Thelma had been left high and dry.

'Oh is that so?' Geoff Marston was surprised. 'I thought it was rather sensible advice myself. I really –'

'Really did, yes, yes,' Thelma parroted, 'so did I.'

'Yes, indeed.' Samuel was in complete agreement. 'Best not to make judgements on people we don't know.'

For some strange reason, which no one had been able to ascertain, Thelma never parroted her husband, Samuel. Perhaps they had had words earlier in their marriage; perhaps beneath his benign exterior Samuel Lyttleton was a bully and she feared him. No one knew.

'Most certainly best not to make judgements, of course,' Sandy said, giving her mouth a delicate dab with her crisply starched linen napkin. 'But I had the feeling he was advising people to stop *talking* about these illegal immigrants, and I'm afraid I beg to differ there. You'll never stop people from voicing an –'

'An opinion.' Once again Thelma was right on the money. 'No, no, of course you won't.'

'Thelma,' Sandy said in her sharpest razor-blade voice, 'you've hardly touched your meal. In fact you've barely even *looked* at it. Now will you *please* concentrate on your chicken breast?'

Thelma gazed instantly down at her plate. Sandy had spoken to her like this on many an occasion and she was frankly terrified of the woman. For the next ten minutes, much as she ached to join in the conversation, her focus remained steadily fixed upon her chicken breast, even though in her rattled state she was barely able to taste it.

Sandy picked up her knife and fork, once again the gracious hostess. 'Of course I realised upon reflection just *why* David wouldn't wish any derogatory discussion about these people from the Middle East.' She popped a sliver of chicken into her mouth. 'I mean, his daughter-in-law is from Iraq, isn't she?' Sandy was one of those who could chew and talk at the same time with the utmost delicacy; she considered it a sign of good breeding. 'So of course he would wish to speak well of these *supposed* refugees, despite the fact they're illegal immigrants.'

'I don't think he had any hidden agenda,' Gordon said in mild disagreement. 'I think he just wanted to stop people bickering.'

'Perhaps he did, dear, yes, but as I said, you'll never stop people talking. And for all her vulgarity, I must say I found a degree of common-sense in Nina's views.' She smiled graciously at Geoff Marston. 'I know you tend to side with Alfred, Geoff, which is a credit to your humanitarianism and also to Alfred's, but the fact is these people *have* jumped the queue, they *have* entered the country illegally.' Another sliver of chicken, another dab of the linen napkin. 'And then of course when it comes to Muslims there's always the problem there may be a terrorist element. We must bear that in mind.'

Geoff Marston and his wife exchanged looks of concern. Shoalhaven was becoming a town divided.

CHAPTER NINETEEN

Christmas came and went, unnoticed by many in the excitement that now engulfed Shoalhaven, and during the days leading up to New Year, nowhere was the town's division more evidenced than at the pub. Perhaps it was the grog that fuelled the flames, perhaps it was the fact that many who gathered there had interests on the island, namely those fishers with huts, but opinions differed, argument was rife and tempers occasionally flared.

'Christ knows what these shitkickers from the Middle East have done to our property,' Kath snarled. 'Jesus, that arsehole copper said the huts'd have to be fumigated! What the hell does that mean? They've spread some fucking disease all over the place? That's what it sounded like to me and Buck. Eh, love?' She dug a bony elbow into her husband's side; he was a tall man in his late sixties, scrawny and tough like his wife and as fit as many a man half his age.

'Yep, reckon you'd be right, Kath.' Buck just sipped his beer, implacable as always. Buck left the thinking to his wife; life was easier that way.

Most of the island fishers were present, with the exception of the several working up north and also Paul, who didn't go to the pub as regularly as he once had, preferring to stay at home with Jalila. The town's old die-hards were there too of course. Archie, Mac and Ian Tuckey never missed a night at the pub. The whole lot of them were gathered around the tables they'd pulled together on the verandah.

'The quarantine blokes might do a bloody sight more than *fumigate* the huts, Kath,' Manny said ominously. Now in his late forties, Manny Papadakis had inherited his fisher's business and hut from his father who had retired, but who still lived in Shoalhaven. Old Nic Papadakis ran the fishing co-op next to the marina.

'Me and Dad was talking about all this just last night,' Manny went on, 'and Dad says the authorities might burn the huts down.'

'*Whaat!*' Young Pete, Boris Adrejic's crew mate, voiced the horrified amazement of everyone present. Pete believed it only right he should represent Boris's interests while his boss was up north, and he was quite prepared to give voice when necessary. 'They can't do that!'

'Too right they can't,' Nat Franclli agreed, outraged. 'They bloody well can't and they bloody well won't! I'd like to see them bloody well try!' Young Nat could get quite fiery at times, particularly with a few beers under his belt. It was the second-generation Italian blood in him.

'Dad reckons it's happened before,' Manny insisted. 'About ten years back, on an island further north. A small fishers' camp, only a few huts, off-season, empty at the time, a boatload of Indonesians come ashore and set themselves up there. Dad says that after the authorities found 'em and shipped 'em out they burnt the huts to the ground. It was all kept quiet of course, they didn't let the news get around, but Dad says he heard it from a mate who was working up there.'

'I don't think they do that, not here,' Aappo Laaksonen said gravely, shaking his massive, white-haired head at his sons, who were in instant agreement, as they always were with their father. 'Not here I don't think they do that. Too many of us here, eh?' The snow-white eyebrows in the square-jawed face raised ever so slightly and the familiar, mischievous twinkle appeared in the ice-blue eyes. For a relatively old man by some people's standards, Aappo was still attractive, and in an extremely masculine way. 'I think too many of us here not keep quiet, eh? Like to see them do this to the fishers of Gevaar Island.' The mischievous twinkle broadened into a grin. 'No, no, I don't think so.'

The tension eased a little. Aappo could have that effect upon others, and most particularly upon men.

'Yeah, well, I suppose we just wait and see what they say,' Manny conceded. 'I mean they'd have to tell us before they torched the camp, wouldn't they?'

'Too right they would,' Nat said, 'and Aappo's spot on. If they want to keep this whole thing a secret, they better not try and burn our huts. If they do, we don't keep bloody quiet like they want us to, we let the media in on everything. That's a damn good idea.'

Aappo nodded. That hadn't actually been his idea at all, he'd been thinking more along the lines of the whole lot of them taking on any who dared threaten their huts – as he and his sons most certainly would – but this new idea sounded like a good one so he was happy to take the credit.

'Why do you reckon they've got this big thing about secrecy anyway?' Manny asked. 'Me and Dad was talking about that too, and we don't get what all the fuss is about. I mean, eight illegals landing on our island? It's not really that many is it, and boat-people aren't anything new, are they?'

'Don't you and your dad know what's going *on* in the bloody world?' Kath demanded. Manny's ignorance didn't surprise her, she found him a bit on the dim side herself, but she would have expected more of Nic Papadakis, whom she knew well and who in his time had been the island's longest term resident, a title that she and Buck now proudly shared. Old Nic was of Greek peasant stock, uneducated, certainly, but sharp as a tack. 'Don't you and your dad follow the bloody *news*, for Christ's sake?'

'Well, not much,' Manny admitted self-consciously. 'I mean, we don't read newspapers all that much.' His father couldn't read at all, he thought, she knew that! And he'd left school himself at twelve, he'd been a fisher for over thirty years, why would he read newspapers?

'You don't have to read bloody *newspapers*,' Kath scoffed. Fucking moron, she thought. Who reads newspapers these days anyway? Everyone gets their news online. Everyone except poor, thick-as-pig-shit Manny. 'You've got bloody *television*, haven't you?' She knew damn well he did. When she went for her evening walk, she'd see him plastered to his TV every night of the week; the Papadakis cottage was only a block or so from hers and Buck's.

'Yeah,' Manny nodded guiltily, 'but I don't watch the news much.' He never watched the news: he loved reality shows, all of them, even the cooking ones. Reality shows were his favourites. Jeez, he wished Kath'd lay off.

Surprisingly enough, it was Ian Tuckey who came to the rescue.

'Reffos have been in the news a helluva lot lately, Manny,' he said benignly, 'particularly Middle Eastern reffos like these ones out on the island.'

It wasn't fair of Kath to pick on Manny, he thought, the bloke wasn't the sharpest tool in the shed. For that matter neither was Nat Franelli. Kath should pick on a brain her own size.

If the truth be known, Ian wasn't so much coming to Manny's rescue; rather, he was picking the right time to enter the discussion. He loved a good verbal stoush, and Kath had just put herself right in line for one.

'You see thousands of these reffos who're escaping the conflict in the Middle East have flooded into Europe and they're causing all sorts of strife,' he explained very patiently to Manny. 'Mainly because they're Muslims and they've got different views about things, but a lot of people are scared because they reckon they might be terrorists. A misguided view in my opinion,' he added with a smug look to Kath.

Kath knew instantly he was referring to their run-in at the meeting and that she was being baited. Fuck you, Ian, she thought and was about to fire back, but Nat Franelli got in first.

'But these people on the island aren't thousands,' he said, puzzled. 'There's only eight of them. Hardly the same thing.'

'It's the *symbolism*, mate,' Ian said significantly. 'It's what they stand for that matters. Eight Middle Eastern reffos have landed in Australia and they've been living here for months? The government wouldn't want that to get out. It could open the gates for the hordes – they could come pouring in by the thousands.'

'I don't think they let this happen,' Aappo said with another shake of his leonine head, 'no I don't think so.'

'Course they bloody wouldn't,' Kath snapped, 'he's talking a load of bullshit!'

'It's not bullshit at all,' Ian countered. 'Righto, a touch of exaggeration about the hordes,' he said with a patronising smile, 'but the furore this could cause if it gets out! Crikey, no wonder the government wants to keep it under wraps. They're in enough trouble already with their turn-back-the-boats policy, the rest of the world thinks we're bastards not welcoming reffos with open arms. Australia needs this sort of publicity like a hole in the bloody head.'

Ian was thoroughly enjoying himself now, centre stage was where he belonged. 'I tell you what, if the media gets hold of this there'll be demonstrations all over the place, left-wing softies demanding these reffos be given asylum, hardcore right-wingers demanding they get kicked out because they reckon every Muslim's a potential terrorist. It'll be sheer bloody mayhem.'

'And you'll be on the side of the left-wing softies, won't you, Ian?' Kath sneered. 'These *reffos* as you call them, who are really *illegal immigrants . . .*' she stressed for the benefit of the others, '. . . couldn't possibly present a terrorist threat, could they? In your opinion these eight are as innocent as newborn bloody babes, aren't they?'

'No, that's not my opinion at all.'

'Bullshit,' Kath declared triumphantly. 'Terrorists don't travel in leaky boats, terrorists catch planes, that's what you said! Your very words, mate!' There, you bastard, she thought, got you now, good and proper.

'Actually, Kath, they don't even come by plane these days.' Ian's response dripped superiority. 'They're radicalised from within Australia itself. Haven't you been reading the *news* lately?' he goaded her mockingly.

You arrogant prick, Kath thought, Christ how she'd like to belt him.

'I agree,' he went on, 'it's quite possible these reffos on the island could pose a threat.' He was addressing them all now, and in full pontificating mode. 'The fact they follow Islam's a threat in itself – they believe their Sharia's above the law of the land. That's the whole bloody problem with these people. And I'll tell you something else for nothing,' he went on, intent upon winding up his audience and winding himself up in the process, 'Gary said, there's a small boy with them, didn't he? Well who's to say whether in ten years' time that kid mightn't be radicalised? An out-and-out Jihadist like these young blokes who make bombs and want to cut off coppers' heads in the street? You just don't know, do you?'

'Oh shut up, Ian!' Kath had had quite enough.

'Yeah, shut up, Ian.' Manny had had enough too. He was accustomed to Kath's belligerence, they all were, but he'd take her side any time rather than Ian bloody Tuckey's. Gevaar Island fishers stuck together.

'Too right!' Young Nat Franelli exploded. He'd had far more than enough; he was thoroughly pissed off. Why should they have to sit around and listen to big-mouth Tuckey sprouting his smart-arse knowledge when their properties were at stake?

He stood, slamming his glass down on the table with such force that it shattered.

'Shut the fuck up, for God's sake! You don't have a hut out there, do you? You've got bugger all to lose! No government bastards are going to burn your bloody house to the ground, are they? No one's out there right now wrecking your bloody property, are they?'

Nat was getting himself so worked up that Archie and Mac, who'd wisely kept out of the conversation, hoped he wasn't about to throw a punch. If he did they'd have to go to their mate Ian's assistance even though, in their joint opinion, Ian had asked for it, the way Ian so often did.

'I think no one wrecking our property. I think this not so.' Aappo's measured tones had an instantly calming effect. 'Gary say this group on Gevaar are just people,' a careless shrug of huge shoulders, 'people he say just like us. Why they would wreck our property? I think no.'

Aappo actually had no problem at all with these refugees or illegal immigrants or whatever he was supposed to call them, these people who were living in his hut. These people were obviously in need and had sought shelter there.

'I don't mind they stay in our hut,' he said, with a look to his sons, whose agreement was automatic. 'Why I should mind if they do no harm?'

It seemed to put paid to the argument, whether the other fishers agreed or not. In any event the situation had been successfully defused.

Nat Franelli resumed his seat and Archie and Mac breathed a joint sigh of relief as they went off to buy the next round.

*

To the fishers and the townspeople of Shoalhaven alike the endless arrival of equipment and goods and supplies and officials had seemed a great deal of time, trouble and expense to outlay on just eight illegal immigrants. They had steadily come to the conclusion that the situation was of even greater significance than they'd been led to believe.

The curiosity of all had been aroused and a number of vessels, both professional and leisure craft, had ventured out from Shoalhaven, the fishers in particular keen to see for themselves exactly what was going on. The exclusion zone had been meticulously observed, but from their boats they'd watched through binoculars, and they'd zoomed in with their iPhones and cameras, taking pictures of the distant activity on the island and the strange tent-town that had mushroomed out on that barren rocky place. And naturally they'd reported back to Shoalhaven, where the rest of the townspeople were eagerly waiting to hear.

But for all of the talk and conjecture and local reportage, everyone respected the firm instruction they'd received with regard to the media. Any news remained strictly within the community of Shoalhaven, which didn't prove difficult, for this was a community already close-knit. And besides, the town had no media. There was no newspaper, no radio station, and certainly no one made contact with the media in Geraldton or Perth.

So how did the word get out? No one knew for sure. But as the New Year of 2017 dawned and as the days crept on, it was clear someone had talked.

Enquiries were made around town. Had anyone sent a photo of the government camp to a close friend or relative? Yes, one or two honestly admitted, but they'd accompanied it with strict instructions that this was highly confidential. Had anyone phoned or texted the news to someone close? Again one or two said they had, but again with the strictest of instructions it was to go nowhere.

But somehow it had, from a relative to a relative's friend, to a friend of that friend and to that friend's friend, harmless to start with no doubt, but by then it had hit the digital highway. People were chatting on social media, people unknown to the citizens of Shoalhaven. On Facebook, Twitter, Instagram and other sites, the word was out there for all to see. It was rumoured the government was trying to cover up the arrival of boat-people on a remote island off the coast of Western Australia. Conspiracy theorists in particular were having a field day. This might have nothing to do with immigrants, some said, this might be an elite military training camp that the government's set up in the middle of nowhere and wants to keep secret from the Australian people. Which led others to go a step further. It could be a training camp set up by terrorists, they said, ISIS might have landed right here in Australia.

And so the media descended.

Inspector Terence Henley was quite prepared for the onslaught and even agreed to hold a press conference mid-morning in the deserted dining room of the Shoalhaven Hotel. Best to give the media the bones of the facts, he and his superiors had decided. Get it over and done with, put a stop to the speculation.

Henley wasn't in the least surprised all this had come to pass; in fact, he was amazed the news hadn't been leaked much earlier. Even as he'd made his request of the townspeople to avoid all communication, he'd known it was inevitable they'd spread the word. Human nature, pure and simple. He'd actually expected the media to be on the case the very next day. The people of Shoalhaven, however, had taken him by surprise – it seemed they were a breed apart.

They've kept this secret to themselves for a whole two weeks, he thought. Astounding! Pity we couldn't have dragged it out another week or so though; we'll be bringing this mob ashore by then and we could have done it on the quiet. Now we'll cop the full media circus. Pity about that.

Terence Henley might have been prepared for the onslaught, but the citizens of Shoalhaven were most certainly not. The influx of strangers wandering the streets of their town was not only unprecedented, it was invasive, not to mention the handheld cameras pointed in their direction and the microphones shoved in their faces.

The majority of townspeople avoided the impromptu interviews thrust upon them, ducking out of sight whenever they could – they did not in the least enjoy the experience. With the exception of Ian Tuckey. Ian was in his element.

Mawsie and Robbo, who ran the pub, were among the few who didn't mind the invasion. Why should they? Their business was normally bar trade and pub food, but their upstairs accommodation was suddenly all booked out. Limited in number as their rooms were, they would have taken in more guests if they could, but those from the media who'd missed out were forced to commute to accommodation in Geraldton.

Henry and Florence Wong, too, were not unhappy with the situation. All of these people needed to eat! If they stayed for any particular length of time, Florence said to her husband, they might need their laundry done too.

As for the rest of the town's businesses, they would have preferred to live without the added profit and see everyone leave.

But no one was going to leave. Not until the refugees had been brought ashore. And as the days passed, the assault on Shoalhaven continued to burgeon. A helicopter even flew over both the township and the island camp, filming aerial footage, which was shown on television news and current affair shows throughout the country and streamed online.

A large cruiser had also appeared, a charter from Geraldton, and berthed in the marina with several camera crew and a journalist living on board. During the day they ventured out to film the island through their high-powered zoom lenses in the hope of capturing footage of the refugees, but without success. The government obviously kept these people well out of sight, perhaps hoping that, unseen by the nation, the interest in their presence might fade.

It didn't. Everyone was waiting to see the refugees, who were currently the hottest news topic in the country. The subject was so keenly debated on talkback radio, commercial TV chat shows and the ABC's evening panel discussion it even threatened to oust in importance the forthcoming inauguration of Donald Trump as president of the United States of America.

Those of the media who'd been placed on the scene were ordered by their superiors to come up with further material, the live footage and still images received so far being very limited. So the journalists and their teams became increasingly demanding of the locals, which was intensely irritating.

One particular on-air TV journalist from a national morning chat show, determined to outdo his rival network, was even more persistent than the others.

'Come on, boys, don't you want to be on TV?'

Jarrod Keeling flashed his most winning smile. A handsome man in his forties, tending to fleshy, his was a face that featured daily onscreen and in the pages of women's magazines, setting hearts fluttering. He knew how to do charm.

'You'll be famous all over the country, you'd like that, wouldn't you?'

Jarrod had already tried to win over several of the older fishers he'd learnt had huts on the island. 'We'll make it really worth your while if you can get us in closer,' he'd promised when he'd asked them to take him and his crew out on their boats. But to a man – and to a woman –

they'd said no. Well, Aappo Laaksonen and Buck Buckley had said no; Kath Buckley had told him to fuck off.

He was trying a different approach now with the young Laaksonen brothers and Nat Franelli, whom he and his two-man crew had hunted down at the marina. The six of them were standing at the end of the jetty where the view was picturesque, but Jarrod had filmed picturesque views already a dozen or more times, he needed to get out to the island, and closer than the five-hundred-metre exclusion zone. For this he needed young bloods willing to break the rules. So he was appealing to the vanity of these boys instead, and to their sense of adventure. Young studs always liked to strut their stuff on TV.

'You've got boats, you boys, haven't you?' he queried. 'And you've got huts on the island?'

'Yep.' Jukka answered for both his brother and Nat, but with a touch of surliness. He looked about at the three-man team, the smarmy journo whose face he knew well from the telly, the burly cameraman and the reedy little sound guy, no more than a boy. Their equipment was not operating, but they were standing at the ready, set to go at any moment. Jukka thought the journo bloke had a hide fronting up to him and Hekki when their father had already said no.

'So where's the harm in showing us where you live?' Another flash of finely crowned teeth. 'Australia's very interested, you know.'

Jarrod had a feeling he wasn't making much headway. All three of the young men were simply staring back at him.

'Come on, boys, where's your sense of adventure?' he urged. 'The authorities aren't going to hang, draw and quarter you for breaking the exclusion zone. We'll just zoom in and zoom out, eh? One of you boys on the wheel and Danny here on the camera.' He gave a debonair laugh to match the smile.

But he still wasn't winning.

'The answer is no,' Jukka said and the other two shook their heads, still staring steadily at the journo.

Some might have found the situation a little unnerving, but it took more than three simple young hicks to frighten off the likes of Jarrod Keeling.

'Right you are, no it is. But you boys don't know the opportunity you're missing out on,' he said jovially. 'Getting your face on TV is the way to win women, I can promise you.'

At that, the three exchanged a look and a smile. As if they could be had that easily!

'Well we all like to win women, don't we,' Jukka said with a laugh, 'but we're not that desperate, mate.'

Breakthrough, Jarrod thought, misinterpreting the smile. If they wouldn't take him out to the island, which they obviously wouldn't, he could at least get an interview with three young studs who lived there. Better than nothing, he thought, giving a nod to Danny on camera and little Buzz on sound.

Within only seconds he and his team were fully operational.

'Here I am reporting direct from the tiny town of Shoal-haven in Western Australia . . .'

Jarrod beamed at the camera. He didn't need to avail himself of the microphone Buzz held; that was for his interviewees. He was already rigged for sound.

'And I'm about to chat to several young fishermen who live on Geevar Island . . .' He chose to use the term 'fish-ermen' as the local preference for 'fishers' would confuse his audience.

'No you're not, mate,' Jukka said firmly, his mouth normally humorous now set in a hard line. Both the refer-ence to 'Jeevar' and the term 'fishermen' had aroused in him instant and intense annoyance, as it had in the others.

Jarrod continued as if oblivious to the antagonism. He was accustomed to 'foot-in-the-door' style tactics when necessary, and any footage was better than none.

'So tell me, boys,' he went on while Danny, immediately reading the signal, homed in with his handheld on the young men, moving steadily from one face to another, a study of each, 'what's it like out there –'

The reaction from all three was instantaneous.

'Did you hear what my brother said!' from Hekki.

'We're not bloody *boys*!' from Jukka.

'Get that fucking thing out of my face!' from Nat Franelli.

Poor little Buzz, who was only eighteen, wavered around the periphery with his microphone, but Danny wasn't giving an inch and nor was Jarrod.

'Oh they're hard boys, these fishermen of Gevaar Island,' Jarrod went on – a little aggression was not a bad thing, livelier than all the picturesque stuff he'd been sending back anyway. 'They breed them tough over here in the West.'

At that, all three went berserk.

'Right, that's it! Fuck you!' Nat Franelli roared.

He charged the cameraman and would have hurled both him and his equipment off the jetty if Danny hadn't dropped his precious camera, which crashed to the jetty with the most ominous sound, Danny crashing beside it.

Perhaps inspired by Nat's example, or perhaps driven purely by their own joint fury, the Laaksonen brothers charged the journalist.

Jarrod Keeling wasn't as fortunate as his cameraman. He ended up spluttering about in the ocean, while Danny, ruthless opportunist that he was, picked up his camera and despite its damage successfully filmed his star journo as a conclusion to the interview. Great footage when all was said and done. Jarrod would have to agree with that.

'Can he swim?' Jukka muttered to the others.

'Do you fucking care?' Nat replied, and he meant it: he'd have been happy to let the bloke drown.

'Yep,' Hekki said, 'he can. More or less,' he added as they watched Jarrod clumsily swim for the shore.

The Laaksonen brothers and Nat were arrested by two of the police officers from Geraldton. Since the refugees' discovery there had been coppers on regular roster to Shoalhaven.

The three were taken to Geraldton, where they were charged with common assault and damage to property, after which they were released on bail.

Back in Shoalhaven early that evening, over a beer at the pub, they were in time to see themselves on television. Just a brief cutaway following a segment about the refugees, but the national news no less. The network had considered it worth sacrificing the dignity of its morning chat-show star for a glimpse of something just a little bit different.

The three of them fell about laughing.

'Do you reckon that'll win us any women?' Jukka asked, and they cracked up once again.

The refugee situation in Western Australia was by now receiving quite a degree of global interest, and after several more days with still no fresh footage to present, the media focused instead upon the reaction of the general public. On-the-spot interviews were conducted with people in the streets of Australia's major cities. How did they feel about these Middle Eastern refugees who'd been camping out illegally and for so long on Australian soil? Should these people be granted asylum or should they be sent packing? There were clashes between far-left and far-right wing demonstrators and these too were filmed, some pushing for the rights of refugees, others firmly against the immigration of any Muslims.

The government's fears had been realised. The group on Gevaar Island had become a symbol of Australia's deep-seated unrest, and this was now being called to the attention of the world.

As for the people of Shoalhaven, they'd had quite enough. Even the mispronunciation of Gevaar Island by the entire population of their country had ceased to amuse and was by now a source of irritation. In every one-on-one interview conducted, on every radio program, in every television news report and panel discussion, Gevaar had always been 'jeevar', never 'hoofire'. Not one Shoalhaven local had bothered to correct the journalists, surprisingly enough not even Ian Tuckey who, like everyone else, had found it amusing. There must surely be some Dutch people out there who were having a huge chuckle over this, they'd all thought. They were no longer thinking that. They just wanted everyone to go home.

The people of Shoalhaven had been too suddenly and too brutally hauled from their tiny protected enclave into the broader world.

This fact did have the inevitable effect, however, of prompting further conversation. Many were forming opinions on subjects they'd never before thought of, raising questions that had never before occurred. Many had known very little about Middle Eastern countries. Until now.

'Paul's wife, Jalila, she'd have to be a Muslim, wouldn't she?' Manny asked. He was having a beer at the pub with the three regular die hards, Archie, Mac and Ian. 'I mean, she's from Iraq, so that'd make her a Muslim, wouldn't it?' he went on. 'But she seems a normal sort of bird.' He gave a bit of a snort. 'Well, apart from being drop-dead gorgeous,' he added. 'I mean, she doesn't seem to be a terrorist or anything like that.' Everyone was talking about Muslims and terrorism these days, so Manny had been giving the matter some thought.

'Being a Muslim doesn't make her a terrorist, Manny,' Ian said with infinite patience. He didn't bother wasting his energies on Manny, scorn and derision were reserved for those with a brain.

'She's not a Muslim actually,' Mac directed his response to Ian. 'I asked Lou that same question a while back, pre-

suming she was Muslim, but secular because she doesn't
wear a hijab or anything, and he said, no, she's a Yazidi.
That's why her family came out here as refugees – the
Yazidis have been persecuted for a heck of a long time,
apparently.'

'Ah. Yazidi? Really?' Ian's ears pricked up at the introduction of a fresh conversational topic. 'That's interesting.'

'Who are the Yazidis?' Archie Lang asked.

'Well, basically they're Christians,' Mac said, though
he really wasn't sure. 'I take it they'd have to be anyway,
that's why they've been persecuted.'

'They're Kurds from the north,' Ian said, having read a
little about the Yazidis. 'It's a very old religion they follow,
a sort of mix of Hinduism, Judaism, Christianity and
Islam, or so I believe. ISIS has been trying to wipe them
out for years . . .'

Ian Tuckey was off again.

Lou had worried about the extra attention being paid to
Jalila since the discovery of the refugees and the endless
discourse inspired by the media. The girl had been warmly
embraced as Paul's wife and had become part of the community, but Mac's was not the only query he'd fielded
lately. The other queries had been along the same lines as
the Scotsman's, simply questions of interest, like where
she was from or what religion she might be, nothing particularly threatening, nothing that seemed to indicate suspicion. But Lou worried that at any moment people might
link her with the refugees on the island. Was the fact that
she'd been in Shoalhaven two months prior to their discovery enough to avert suspicion, or would people wonder
whether she might have been brought ashore? Everyone
knew the refugees had been out there for some months
before their detection by the Fisheries Department.

Lou held himself solely responsible for this fact. Why,
oh why, he agonised, hadn't he lied to Gary Walton when

he'd blurted out the truth that morning? Why hadn't he said he'd discovered the group living there just the previous week? He'd actually told the man they'd been there close to four months – he could hear himself saying the words. Why?

He knew exactly why of course. He'd been so desperate to convince Gary that he had come to know these people, that he'd learnt so much from them, that they were good people, gentle people. He'd been so keen for Gary to discover their presence on the island, rather than the fishers or Border Control, that he just hadn't been thinking straight. Of course he should have lied. Too late now.

David Miller worried also. David hadn't stopped worrying since the meeting in the church hall when Nina Adrejic had referred to Jalila and he'd watched from the stage as all heads had turned to the girl. Now, with this intense media attention and the whole town talking, was it only a matter of time before people put two and two together?

The one person who, strangely enough, was not worried was Paul. Paul's attitude was fatalistic. What will be will be, he thought. Resigning himself completely to whatever the outcome, he was sure of only one thing. Come what may, he and Jalila would never be parted.

Besides, he had something else on his mind. Something that had consumed him for the past two days, ever since he'd discovered Jalila on her knees in the bathroom, head in her hands and apparently in anguish.

'What is it?' He'd dropped to the floor beside her, terrified. 'Oh hell, Jalila, what is it, are you all right? Are you hurt?'

She'd lifted her head, allowing him to take her hands in his, and he'd seen the tears flooding down her cheeks and that same haunted look in her eyes. It was the look he'd seen on the day he'd proposed to her. She was being revisited by the same ghosts of the past that had tormented her that day.

He raised her to her feet and held her fast, feeling the convulsions, expecting this silent expression of pain to break into the same fearful, racking sobs that had overtaken her then. But the sobs didn't come.

Within a very short time, her body had ceased to shudder and her breathing had returned to normal.

She eased herself away from him and crossed to the washbasin, pulling several tissues from the box that sat on the vanity, blowing her nose, wiping her eyes.

'I am sorry, Paul,' she said, looking at him in the mirror. 'I am most sorry, I am not wish for cause you worry.'

'I know that, Jalila, I know.'

He crossed to stand behind her, circling his arms around her waist, nestling her to him, and she tucked her own arms comfortably about his.

They stood entwined, gazing at each other in the mirror.

'Is there anything I can do?' he asked. 'Would it help to talk? Would you like to tell me?'

She nodded. 'I tell you one day,' she said. 'Not now. But I tell you one day. One day soon. I promise.'

He'd had to settle for that. Nothing was to be gained by pushing her further. But he couldn't help wondering how soon 'one day soon' would be. And he couldn't help wondering what it was she would tell him. And he couldn't help wondering if in the telling she would finally be exorcised of the demons that haunted her. All of these thoughts consumed Paul.

Jalila hadn't been certain until that morning. She'd missed two of her menstrual cycles, but that had meant nothing, her cycles were rarely regular – she'd missed many throughout her life. During the latter days of her captivity, she'd not menstruated at all. But that morning she'd been ill, and she knew this particular sort of illness. She'd had it before.

The child, which Jalila had conceived at the age of sixteen, had saved her life. During the early days of her capture, given the opportunity, she would have suicided, but now with the baby growing inside her, she could not bring herself to take two lives. And as the months had passed the child had given her a reason to live.

She'd said nothing to the soldier who owned her and at first she'd said nothing to the *malik yamiin* with whom she was housed, those other young women and girls who served as sex slaves. But as her belly had started to swell, she had taken one of them into her confidence, an older woman of around thirty, who was kind to the young ones. The woman did not speak Kurmanji and Jalila spoke no Arabic, but language was no barrier, their communication was perfectly clear. The woman had given Jalila a kaftan that disguised her growing belly and, through mime, she'd advised the girl to offer her backside for sex and to take the man in her mouth. There were many ways to service the soldiers.

Jalila's pregnancy had remained undetected until she was nearly full term, but when the soldier who owned her had finally discovered her condition he'd been angry. He'd beaten her. And he'd beaten the baby too, punching her in the belly. But Jalila was strong, and so was her baby; both had survived.

The soldier had left her alone, choosing one of the other girls to service him, and two weeks later, assisted by the woman who had befriended her, Jalila had given birth to a baby girl on the dirt floor in the corner of the crumbling stone building that housed the *malik yamiin*.

But the soldier had wanted her back. He'd paid good money for her; she was his property, and the most beautiful of the *malik yamiin*.

A week after the birth, one sultry late afternoon, he'd come into the women's compound seeking her out. She'd been nestled on her matting in the corner that had become her own special world, leaning against the stone wall, the little mouth sucking greedily at her breast.

He'd snarled, clearly irritated by the sight of her suckling her child, and the other women present had shrunk away, frightened.

She'd stood, accepting the fact that she must return to her sexual duties, and disengaging the baby from her breast, she'd been about to place it on the matting. But the infant, abruptly deprived of its food source, had started to cry, which further annoyed the soldier.

The woman who had befriended Jalila was brave. She had stepped forwards, her arms outstretched – she would mind the child while Jalila went with the soldier.

But the soldier had drawn his weapon and shot her dead. Then he'd ripped the baby from Jalila's arms and, holding it by its feet he'd swung his arm in a wide arc before slamming it head-first into the stone wall, the baby's unformed skull exploding upon impact.

That was the day Jalila had died.

The soldier had soon tired of her. He'd sold her to another soldier, who had also tired of being serviced by a dead woman, so he'd sold her in the marketplace, knowing her beauty would fetch a good price.

Jalila would happily have welcomed her physical death should it present itself, but the thought of suicide had not occurred, perhaps because one could not kill something that was already dead.

She had, however, preserved her sanity. Over time, she had learnt to blot out memory. The soldiers had been easy – in fact, the soldiers no longer existed, relegated to a past that had never happened. But the sight and the sound of her baby's death was more difficult, the moment always there on the peripheries of her mind, threatening to return. And she needed to practise great care: the slightest thing could call it back. Like the day Paul had asked her to marry him. She'd been totally unprepared.

'Become my wife, Jalila, please,' he'd said, 'become the mother of my children.' That's all it had taken.

And now, discovering she was pregnant, a fact that should have filled her with the greatest joy and which deep in her heart did, still she had been forced to relive that terrible moment.

She must regain control, and she would. She was a past master at mind control. Furthermore, she would tell Paul her story. She would tell him everything, as she had promised she would. But not until she felt secure in her pregnancy. She didn't dare.

She would tell him when her pregnancy started to show, she decided. Then they could both rejoice in the news, and perhaps the awful image, which she knew could never be forgotten, could at least be relegated to a place that no longer threatened. She would tell him when she knew that the child inside her was safe.

CHAPTER TWENTY

At long last the refugees were to be brought ashore. Inspector Terence Henley, in a rare gesture of courtesy, informed the town's citizens, via Gordon Shadforth and David Miller, before announcing the news to the media.

Gordon and David didn't arrange an extraordinary meeting of the Shoalhaven Residents' Group, choosing instead to spread the news via email, phone, text and the ever-reliable personal grapevine, while Terence Henley made his official announcement to the media at a mid-morning press conference he'd called for that very purpose in the dining room of the Shoalhaven Hotel.

The refugees would be brought ashore the following afternoon, he told the gathering, although as a federal police officer and representing the Australian government, he knew to avoid the term 'refugees'. These people may be seeking refugee status, but they'd entered the country without authority so the term did not apply.

'The unauthorised arrivals on Gevaar Island –' not unsurprisingly still 'Jeevar' '– are to be transported by sea directly to the port of Geraldton tomorrow afternoon,' he announced. 'There they will be assembled for transport to the airport and immediate flight to a transit camp in Darwin.'

He looked gravely around at the gathering. 'It would be very much appreciated if this exercise could be conducted smoothly and with minimal interference from the press and the media in general. I recognise the interest this situation has aroused, which is understandable, but I would ask all those present to keep a respectful distance and let the authorities get on with their job. Thank you.'

He had not invited questions, but a barrage hit him nonetheless.

'How long will they be in Darwin?'

'Where will they be taken after that?'

'Will they go to Nauru?'

Terence Henley held up his hand, not even attempting to talk over the babble, and eventually it died down. 'I can answer none of your questions,' he said calmly. 'This is not my area.'

And he walked away.

It had been, without doubt, the shortest press conference any of those present had ever attended, but its effect was instantaneous.

Within less than an hour Shoalhaven had returned to normal, the journalists, the crews, the reporters and photographers having disappeared in a general exodus south.

Even the chartered cruiser that had been berthed at the marina had headed south. The journalist aboard had considered staying in order to accompany the boat that would transport the refugees to Geraldton the following day, but both the skipper and his own cameraman had convinced him otherwise.

'I won't be allowed anywhere near the vessel,' the skipper had said.

'The other blokes'll be all lined up on the dock in choice positions to film the boat's arrival and the refugees disembarking,' the cameraman had said, 'and we'll be stuck out on the water. Bloody stupid idea.'

The journalist had all too quickly realised the wisdom of this argument. His cameraman was the one who usually ran the show anyway.

The citizens of Shoalhaven were deeply relieved to have their town back. And they most certainly did have it back – not a vestige remained of the past several weeks' media frenzy. The madness might all have been a dream. Shoalhaven was once again the sleepy enclave of old where everybody minded their own business and knew their own place.

So who could it possibly have been who leaked the news barely two hours later? Certainly no member of the press, otherwise they'd all have been swarming back into town. Inspector Terence Henley? But if so, why? The leak had obviously come from someone in the know. Perhaps some official on the island. But again, why?

No one knew who rang Gordon Shadforth. No caller ID appeared on his phone and he didn't recognise the voice. But then there was a lot of static, so much so that he could only just hear what the caller said. Did the background static perhaps mean it had been made from the island where mobile-phone reception was notoriously poor?

'The refugees will be coming ashore at Shoalhaven mid-afternoon today. They'll be taken by coach directly to Geraldton airport in order to avoid the media.'

That was all the caller said.

It was around lunchtime and Gordon immediately contacted David Miller, following which the Shoalhaven Residents' Group's grapevine sprang into action, Sandy Shadforth emailing and texting and phoning, the locals spreading the news like wildfire.

'So the whole thing was a ruse,' Lou said. 'The media pisses off to Gero and they bring the refugees ashore here a day earlier: pretty smart.'

'Yes,' David agreed, 'the press will be all lined up at the Geraldton foreshore tomorrow and the refugees will already be in Darwin.'

The two men were having a quiet chat in the back room of the post office, David having rung Lou and asked him to call in.

'But who on earth do you think leaked the news?' David went on, 'And if it was an official from the island, as Gordon seems to think it was, why would they risk word getting out to the media?'

'I'd say it's someone who knows the people of Shoalhaven,' Lou said, 'someone who knows we can be trusted.'

David nodded. 'And someone who wants the word spread around town.'

'Exactly.

'Well it's spread all right – I can assure you of that. I think half the town will turn up when they're brought ashore.' David voiced his principal worry, which was why he'd asked his father-in-law to call in. 'You and Paul mustn't be there, Lou,' he urged, 'promise me you won't.'

But Lou was very laid-back about the whole situation, alarmingly so from David's perspective.

'Oh, I don't think there's any cause for worry,' he said. 'No one in the group will point the finger at us. If they were going to give us away they'd have done so already.'

David found the old man's cavalier attitude extremely annoying, particularly under the circumstances.

'If you don't care about yourself,' he replied, 'you might at least care about Paul. When I phoned him he said he was going to be there, and what's more he said Jalila was insisting upon going with him.'

'Oh.' Lou was jolted from his complacency. 'Oh hell, that's a different matter altogether.'

'Yes, it most certainly is,' David agreed stiffly. 'I'd appreciate it if you'd have a word with him. Your advice always carries more sway than mine.'

'Of course I will, mate.' He'd have a word with Paolo all right, Lou thought. And with Jalila too. Her presence might well court disaster if any of the locals were to make the connection. 'Of course I will – don't you worry about that.'

'Good. Thank you.'

David regretted having been so snappy with the old man; he'd allowed his nerves to get the better of him. But for all the calm displayed by both his son and his father-in-law, the normally unruffled David Miller was having trouble disguising his deep concern. Was his entire family about to be exposed as frauds? Was the girl he'd come to love as a daughter-in-law about to be discovered and the lie they'd all been living made public? His whole world felt on the verge of collapse.

'So who on earth do you think made that call to Gordon?' he asked, feigning normality, trying to sound casual.

'No idea,' Lou said, although he did have an inkling. Could the caller possibly have been Gary Walton? And could the purpose of the call have been a warning to him? Was Gary telling him to stay away from the refugees when they came ashore for fear of exposure?

Lou's reasoning was correct for the most part. It had been Gary Walton who had made the call, from a mobile phone belonging to one of the medical staff on the island, a very pleasant and capable middle-aged nurse called Brenda.

'Mind if I borrow your phone?' he'd asked. 'Just a quick local call.'

'Sure, be my guest,' Brenda had said cheerfully, handing it over, 'but good luck, I doubt you'll get through.'

He'd taken the phone up to the benches not far from the huts, the one area where he knew reception was possible.

Gary's purpose in making the call had been twofold, however. A warning to Lou Panuzza to steer clear when the refugees were brought ashore, yes, perhaps, but something else, something that he considered of far greater importance. Gary knew that Rassen Khurdaji wished to deliver a message to the local people on behalf of the group, whether it be simply to one person or to several, whoever might happen to be present when they came ashore. Gary intended there should be a good crowd there to hear the doctor's message.

A compassionate man at the best of times, Gary Walton considered this a fine opportunity for the citizens of Shoalhaven to see these refugees for who they really were, just as he'd described them in his brief answer at the church hall meeting.

'They're people,' he'd said upon being asked what they were like, 'they're people just like you and me.'

Time to redress the demonising of genuine refugees such as these, Gary thought. His one regret? He only wished the media could be there to capture the moment for the rest of the country to see. A true Catch-22 situation if there ever was one, he told himself with a sense of irony. The banishing of the media had been the only way this could happen.

The whole of the town was abuzz with expectation. After all the hype of the past several weeks they were finally going to see these people in the flesh. Despite the endless talk and even the occasional hostility that had accompanied it, the general feeling now was one of interest. There was no animosity. There'd been no reports of damage to property on the island and, although some remained critical of the boat-people, there were others who felt a strong degree of sympathy. Not only for what these people had been through in order to reach these shores, but also for what was about to happen to them.

Once again, the townsfolk arranged for their shops and businesses to be run by skeleton staff, and as early as two in the afternoon on this baking-hot, breathlessly still, mid-January day people were gathering at the marina's foreshore, well before any approaching vessel was in sight.

Then Archie Lang, from his mechanics workshop up near the car park, rang around with the news. Four words only.

'The coach is here,' he said.

And fifteen minutes later, the crowd had doubled.

By the time the Fisheries vessel appeared, a distant
speck on the still waters of the horizon where sky and sea
blended, close to two hundred people were gathered on
the parkland slopes of the marina's foreshore. Everyone
was facing the jetty, waiting for the show to commence,
chattering and watching expectantly as the distant speck
drew ever nearer.

Forty metres away, standing at the end of the jetty,
also watching, were two local state police officers, there
specifically in order to oversee the arrival of the refugees.
Inspector Terence Henley was not in attendance, having
departed for Geraldton, his presence there necessary as
part of the media evasion tactic.

The senior officer awaiting the vessel's arrival was
Geraldton Inspector Leslie Brock who, like his junior
partner, was wondering how come so many people had
turned up.

Someone must have tipped them off, Les thought.
I wonder who. Not that it makes any difference, he told
himself, they're not here to cause trouble, and we've successfully pissed off the media. That's all that matters.

As the *MV Endurance* entered the marina, the chattering slowly died away. And by the time the vessel, with
Gary Walton at the helm, his crew and eleven passengers
on board, had drawn alongside the jetty the crowd of two
hundred had lapsed into virtual silence.

The crew secured the vessel and Gary stepped ashore
along with the party of three who were to accompany the
refugees to Darwin: a state police officer, an immigration
officer and a nurse from the official medical team.

Like Inspector Les Brock, the party of three was surprised by the crowd that was awaiting their arrival.
Someone must have leaked the news to the locals.

I wonder if that's why Gary Walton borrowed my
phone, Brenda was thinking.

Then finally, with the police standing by, the refugees

alighted onto the jetty one by one, assisted where necessary by Gary and his crew.

To the onlookers gathered forty metres away, the spectacle unfolded like a pageant, the jetty a stage, the gentle
slopes of the marina's foreshore an amphitheatre, their
view perfect.

First was a dignified-looking man in his sixties. He
was followed by a woman who seemed to the onlookers
extraordinarily English in appearance. The two were obviously a couple, joining each other to stand side by side and
watch as the others alighted.

A middle-aged couple followed, handsome the pair of
them, the man refusing assistance and offering his hand to
his wife, who stepped very tentatively from the boat. He
shepherded her to one side with infinite care, an arm about
her, whispering words of comfort no doubt, for she was
obviously frightened.

Then a young couple with a child. The father came
first, the little boy in his arms, and the wife followed.
Once safely on the jetty, the father put the boy down and
the mother took his small hand in hers. A bold little boy,
he did not hide behind her skirts, but stood looking out
at the crowd with great interest. The young father was
bearded and the young mother, petite and pretty, wore a
hijab. It was more or less the appearance those watching
had expected.

The last to alight was a young man who literally leapt
ashore, ignoring any offer of assistance. Like the little boy,
he too looked fearlessly out at the crowd, but with something akin to defiance.

The group joined ranks, clearly supportive of each
other, and stood awaiting orders.

Gary Walton said something to the local police inspector, whom all those watching knew to be Les Brock. Les,
like Gary, was well thought of by the townspeople and
fishers of Shoalhaven. Les nodded in obvious agreement,

and Gary gave a signal to the older man, who appeared to be the leader of the group.

Then the refugees, accompanied by Gary, began to walk slowly down the jetty towards the crowd, the several police and officials following behind, the crew staying with the vessel.

From the crowd, Lou watched the procession. Beside him was Paul. And beside Paul was Jalila. They'd been unable to prevent her from joining them.

'If you not let me go with you, I go alone,' she'd said. 'You cannot lock me up, Paul. I do nothing, I say nothing, I promise,' she'd implored. 'I just look. Just look, no more, I promise. I see my friends one last time. Please, Paul, this I beg you. It mean so much to me. Please.'

Paul had finally agreed with one proviso. She must remain out of sight in the crowd, tucked close in beside him. There would be glimpses only of her friends, he warned. Under no circumstances must she be seen. If attention was drawn to her in any way people might make the connection. And what if little Hamid were to catch sight of her and cry out? So many things could happen.

To Lou now watching, the procession on the jetty appeared to be taking place in slow motion as memories tumbled through his mind.

The day he'd discovered the group on the island . . . how they'd adopted the homes as their own . . . the warmth of their welcome . . . the tadig they'd shared.

His gaze came to rest upon Rassen. The conversations they'd had . . . the hours spent together . . . the things that he'd learnt . . . how much he admired the man . . .

I'll miss you, mate, he thought with regret. I'll miss every single one of you, he thought as before his eyes the image of the approaching group seemed to hover haze-like in the mid-afternoon sun.

The procession halted barely ten metres from the crowd, and Gary Walton stepped forwards.

'This is Dr Rassen Khurdaji,' he announced, gesturing for Rassen to step forwards also, which he did. 'Dr Khurdaji has something he would like to say to the people of Shoalhaven, and most particularly to the fishers of Gevaar Island.'

So I was right, Brenda thought, that's why Gary Walton borrowed my phone.

Well we sure as hell know who leaked the news, don't we? Les thought. He'd realised the moment Gary had told him out there on the jetty that the doctor wanted to address the locals.

'I'd like to let him go ahead, if that's OK,' Gary had said.

'Sure,' he'd agreed, 'I don't see why not.' He'd realised then that Gary was the culprit. Strangely enough, knowing Gary as he did, the discovery hadn't surprised Les all that much. And no harm done. No need to make a fuss about it.

Rassen stood for a moment, surveying the crowd. He hadn't expected for one minute there would be so many. He'd hoped perhaps for a few who might carry his message to the others.

'Good afternoon,' he said.

As his voice sounded out strongly, there were surprised murmurs – his English was virtually accent-less.

'First of all I would like to introduce you to everyone,' Rassen went on. 'This is my wife, Hala.'

Hala stepped forwards. 'Good afternoon,' she said pleasantly, her voice also strong.

Further murmurs of surprise – she had to be English, they all thought.

Rassen then went on to introduce the group in pairs, each couple stepping forwards as their names were announced.

'This is Hany and Sanaa Awad.'

'Good afternoon,' Hany and Sanaa said one after the other, enunciating very carefully as Rassen had instructed they should.

'This is Karim and Azra Samar, and their little boy, Hamid.'

'Good afternoon,' Karim and Azra said, followed by Hamid, whose voice was the loudest of all three.

'Hello,' he called boldly to the crowd.

Hamid had been thoroughly schooled in preparation for some time now, well before the arrival of the authorities on the island. He was to say only the English that Rassen and Massoud had taught him. Under no circumstances was he to use any word or phrase he'd picked up from Paul and Lou. 'G'day, mate' and 'beaut' were strictly forbidden. Hamid had obeyed the letter of the law set down for him to perfection. Having grown up fast, he was a very adult little boy. He'd had to be. The group was his entire world. He was a part of them and they were a part of him. He would not let them down.

'And this is Massoud Ahmadi,' Rassen concluded.

'Hello.' Massoud's greeting to the crowd was curt. He could have sounded more pleasant if he'd wished, but he couldn't be bothered. He wanted this farce to be over with.

Hala glanced at him, concerned.

Throughout the physical examinations and the interviews conducted on the island during their quarantine period, the others had behaved impeccably. They'd been polite to the authorities, practising their limited English whenever possible and with care. Rassen had insisted these factors would make a favourable impression upon the immigration authorities when they were taken to the place where their refugee status would be processed.

Massoud's behaviour had been altogether different. He, who could have made the most favourable impression of all, had been indifferent, sullen, and at times even bordering on rude. Hala had tried to reason with him.

'Please, Massoud, make some sort of effort, don't alienate them, it won't do you any good.'

'Why?' he'd demanded. 'What difference will it make

to the eventual outcome? We'll still be sent to rot in some prison of a place. '

'You don't know that.'

'Oh yes I do, Hala. This country will not accept us.'

Hala had found his manner most disheartening. What had happened to the vibrant young man who had lightened the load for them all, whose ready wit had made her laugh? Their sojourn on the island had strengthened the others, but not Massoud. How sad, she thought.

'Wherever we are sent, Massoud,' she'd urged, 'we can serve a purpose. Rassen and I intend to offer our services. We believe our medical qualifications and experience can be put to good use, if not in general society then in aiding our fellow refugees.'

She and Rassen had discussed the matter in some depth. Aware that it was highly unlikely they would be granted asylum in Australia and that by now it may well be safe to return to England, they had nonetheless decided to remain with their friends.

'They have become our family,' Rassen had said. 'We must see them through their ordeal.'

'And others like them,' Hala had fervently agreed. 'We are needed, Rassen. Perhaps this was meant to be, my darling. We must stay where we are most needed, you and I.'

Massoud had continued to appear thoroughly disinterested as she'd told him of their plans, but Hala did not give up easily. Throughout the whole of her life, Hala had never been one to give up easily.

'Don't forget you're a linguist, my dear,' she'd said with the maternal tone she so often adopted when trying to reach out to the younger members of the group. 'And what's more you specialise in Middle Eastern languages. Just imagine how invaluable your skills would be to all those who need a voice.' She'd sensed a glimmer of interest, or rather she'd sensed he was no longer closed off to reason. 'You were an activist, Massoud,' she'd said, now with some urgency, 'an activist for human rights. That is why you were forced to flee your country. Never forget, my dear, young friend, that whatever happens your life serves a purpose!'

He'd hugged her then. Hugged her like the mother figure she'd become to him, as she had to them all. Hala's strength had perhaps been of even greater value to the group than Rassen's leadership, for at all times she'd continued to give them hope.

Hala had known that her words had made an impact, but now, as Rassen embarked upon his speech to the crowd, she could see Massoud was simply wishing it was all over. She tried to catch his eye and signal a message to him, but he was gazing vacantly into nowhere. Ah well, she thought, there's little more I can do.

Rassen's introductions of the group had had a strange effect upon Massoud. They'd seemed somehow to epitomise the despair he felt. Everyone had been introduced as couples, and now they stood together as couples, life partners sharing the good and the bad that was handed them. That was all Massoud wanted, a partner, someone to love and be loved by. It was what he'd sought in coming to Australia, a land of freedom where homosexuality was not a death sentence.

Hardly likely to find my true love at a refugee camp, am I? he thought cynically, and if they send me back to Iran I'm dead. Not a great deal to feel hopeful about. God I wish this exhibition for the locals was over and they'd just put us on the bus.

Rassen's speech was brief.

'When we came ashore to your island,' he said, and he extended his arms wide to include the others, conveying to the crowd that he was speaking on behalf of those whom he had just introduced, 'we were more dead than alive. We would most certainly have perished had it not been for the shelter and the food and the water we found there. We owe our existence to those of you whose houses gave us refuge and whose possessions and supplies we took advantage of. We thank you with all our heart for saving our lives.'

As he said this, he placed his hand on his heart, a signal to the others, who did the same, although Hala noticed Massoud did not. His mind was very clearly elsewhere.

'And we apologise, also with all our heart, for invading your homes as we did,' Rassen continued. 'We regret any offence we may have caused in doing so. We meant no harm. We simply wanted to survive.'

He looked around at the others who, again with the exception of Massoud, nodded, the non-English speakers knowing exactly what had been conveyed on their behalf even though they did not understand every word.

'That is all I have to say,' Rassen concluded, 'thank you for listening to me.'

He turned to Gary. They were ready to go now.

But someone stepped from out of the crowd. It was Aappo.

'I have something to say,' he announced, ignoring the crowd and addressing the refugees directly, Rassen in particular as the group's spokesperson.

'My name is Aappo Laaksonen,' he said. 'This is my wife, these are my sons and this is my daughter.' He gestured about at his family; they were all there the whole lot of them, white hair standing out like beacons, his wife and his daughter also being startlingly fair. 'We are Gevaar Island fishers and we are happy you use our home. You are welcome.'

He glanced briefly about at the other island fishers. He couldn't speak on their behalf of course, but his ice-blue eyes dared them to voice any disagreement out loud.

Then, turning back to the refugees, 'We have gifts for you.' He gave a brisk nod to his sons, and Jukka and

Hekki walked forwards and bent to place the bundles they held in their arms on the jetty at the refugees' feet.

'Blankets,' Aappo went on, as his sons came back to stand by his side. 'These are good blankets. They are new. I bought them for the season soon to begin. We wish for you to have them.' His smile, as always, was irresistible. 'Everyone need a good blanket, I think.'

'How very kind,' Rassen said. 'Our sincerest thanks to you and your family. We are most grateful.'

He picked up the bundles of blankets, there were six in all, and distributed them, explaining in Arabic the exchange that had just taken place.

'How fine it is that they bear us no ill will, Sanaa,' Hany said to his wife. The sight of her holding the blanket to her cheek, feeling the softness of its texture against her skin, pleased him immeasurably. She no longer appeared frightened.

'They are good, these people,' she replied. It was true: her fear had, for the moment anyway, receded. Sanaa felt welcomed to this country.

Massoud was at long last paying attention. Aappo's speech had taken him completely by surprise.

He accepted his blanket from Rassen. 'Thank you,' he said, directing his thanks out to the crowd, to the fisher and his family. Massoud had not expected this sort of reception. But he couldn't help himself nonetheless. Upon hearing the exchange between Hany and Sanaa, his cynicism returned. The gift of a blanket does not spell freedom, Sanaa, he thought.

Noting the pleasure with which his gifts had been received, Aappo felt proud. Once again he looked about at his fellow island fishers, and his expression was victorious. None of you thought to bring a present, did you?

But as it turned out, someone had.

Whether it was the doctor's speech, which had affected her, or whether it was Aappo's annoying look of one-upmanship, Kath Buckley was prompted to nudge her grandson.

'Go on, Benjy,' she muttered. The boy had wanted to bring along a present for the refugee kid, but she hadn't been at all sure herself. Shit, how would you know? she'd thought. This mob might be a right pack of bastards.

'We'll wait and see, love,' she'd said. 'Maybe, if the time's right.'

Well the time's right, she thought. 'Go on, love, don't be shy.' She gave him another nudge.

Seven-year-old Benjamin was anything but shy. He was a Buckley after all.

He strode up to the refugees, planted himself in front of the little boy and held out the soccer ball with both hands.

'That's for you,' he said very loudly; he had the Buckley voice to boot. 'It's a present from me.'

Hamid released the hold on his mother's hand and took the ball from the older boy. He was genuinely thrilled. He'd been ordered to leave his toys behind in the green hut, the one that belonged to Paul. They'd taken everything they'd been given by Lou and Paul to the green hut before the authorities had arrived. They'd left everything behind. The clothes, the playing cards, the chess set, the draughts, and of course, the soccer ball and the tennis ball.

'Thank you,' he said, his face alight with pleasure.

'It's not a new ball,' Benjy admitted in all honesty, 'but it's a beauty.'

'Thank you,' Hamid said once again, giving full voice and in his very best English. 'Thank you very much.'

'That's orright.'

Benjy turned and marched back to his grandmother.

Kath was so proud.

Jalila's view of the proceedings had been severely thwarted. Paul had kept her towards the very back of the crowd, tucked close in beside him where she'd caught

barely a glimpse of her friends, and certainly no view of
little Hamid at all.

Now, at the sound of his voice, she longed for the sight
of him, if only for a brief second or so.

She wriggled away from Paul and, before he could stop
her, she'd circled behind the crowd to stand at one side
where she had a clear vision of those on the jetty. But of
course those on the jetty now had a clear eyeline to her.

Horrified, Paul quickly joined her. If there was going to
be any risk of exposure then they would face it together.

He made no attempt to pull her back into the crowd,
which would only draw the attention of the townspeople,
a situation that in his opinion was equally dangerous.

This particular fear, however, appeared groundless. The
crowd's attention was focused solely upon the refugees.
No one took any notice of Jalila.

Little Hamid was the first to see her, which was not
surprising – his eyes had been searching the crowd for her
right from the start.

'Will I see Jalila?' he'd asked his mother when they knew
they were to be taken ashore.

'I do not think so,' she'd replied, 'but if you do see her,
you must not know her, Hamid. You understand this,
don't you? You must not know Jalila or Paul or Lou. They
are all strangers to you.'

'Yes, I understand this.'

He did. And now as he saw her, he displayed not a
hint of recognition. He was simply a little boy looking at
a crowd of strangers. But as their eyes met, his left hand,
the hand that had been holding his mother's, crept up to
the breast pocket of his shirt, where through the fabric
he could feel the shape of the stone that rested against
his heart.

The message was all Jalila needed. She could have melted
back into the crowd and no one would have known, but
her eyes looked up from the boy's and directly met those

of his mother, the woman with whom she had bonded so closely.

Azra had sensed from her child's very stillness that he was no longer searching the crowd – that he had found what he was looking for: Jalila.

The language of hands continued, a silent line of communication that no one else could read.

Azra gently rested her fingers on Hamid's shoulder, indicating she also had seen Jalila and that she was congratulating him on his self-control.

Jalila in turn raised a hand to her stomach in a clear message that Azra immediately understood.

Azra touched her husband's arm, a simple gesture of affection.

'She is here, Karim,' she said very softly and in their own language, feeling quite safe as she did so. No one else spoke Hazaragi, not even Rassen. 'And she is with child.'

But Azra had forgotten the talents possessed by the young man standing right beside her, the linguist who had understood her every word.

Massoud's eyes sought out Jalila where she stood a little to one side of the crowd, Paul protectively beside her.

You may be lucky after all, Jalila, he thought. You're safe for now in this close community in this isolated place, and one day when you are discovered, as I have no doubt you will be, your child may save you. A child fathered by an Australian and born on Australian soil. I hope for your sake this proves so.

It was time to leave. Flanked by the accompanying officials and police, the refugees set off along the front towards the marina car park where the coach awaited them.

Massoud drank in one last look at Jalila before he turned to go.

He found the sight of her uplifting. Jalila symbolised more than hope. Jalila was the face of freedom.

ACKNOWLEDGEMENTS

As always, my love and thanks to my husband, Bruce Venables, who remains a constant source of encouragement and inspiration, not to mention the fun and laughter we manage to squeeze out of life.

My thanks also to those invaluable friends who offer both encouragement and assistance of the most practical kind in their various areas of expertise: Michael Roberts, Colin Julin, James Laurie, Sue Greaves, Vanessa Downing and Susan Mackie-Hookway. To family members too for their highly practical help, particularly given the fact they live in Geraldton and have a great knowledge of the area: Rob and Dee Nunn, Cory Kentish and also Dee's mates, Kel and Matt Pirrottina.

Thanks again to my publisher, Beverley Cousins; my editors, Brandon VanOver and Kate O'Donnell; my publicist, Jessica Malpass, and the entire hard-working team at Penguin Random House Australia.

A very big thank you to my invaluable 'Geraldton connection', most particularly to Greg Finlay of the Department of Fisheries and to Susan Smith, Manager of the Geraldton Regional Library. Thanks also to Glenda Blyth at Gero's Visitor Centre.

I owe a huge debt of gratitude to my good friend and well-known human rights activist Dr Meredith Burgmann, and also to Phil Glendenning, Chair of the Refugee Council of Australia. Both were tremendously helpful with my research, but above all it was these two who introduced me to Mohammad and Shayesteh Sadeghpour, whose stories, shocking though they were, proved inspirational. Mohammad and Shayesteh, thank you so much for sharing your past with me, for introducing me to your friends and family, and for being the brave souls you are.

Among my research sources I would like to recognise:

Abrolhos Islands – Conversations, Victor France, Larry Mitchell, Alison Wright; Fremantle Arts Centre Press, 1998.

The Morning They Came for Us: Dispatches from Syria, Janine de Giovanni, Bloomsbury Publishing, 2016.

And in particular, the incredible collection of material lent to me by Mohammad Sadeghpour.